I0551925

lovetrust

a novel
by
t/james reagan

A *RiverVerse* Novel. First Edition: October 5th 2015
ISBN-13: 978-0692467572 / ISBN-10: 0692467572

Contact the author:
https://www.facebook.com/tjamesreagan
tjamesreagan@outlook.com
http://tjamesreagan.com
@t_jamesreagan

Also Available by T/James Reagan:
Famous For Nothing
Empire Waste
Leeds House
Southland Tales: The Complete Saga
Hot Blonde Girls With Heavy Eye Makeup
MISS JULIE 2020
Neon Blacktop

And the sequel to *lovetrust*:
beach house burning

dedication:

*This book is dedicated to my mom and dad—
the only two people who have never disappointed
me.
I love you both.*

"Beauty: (Placidly) It all sounds so vulgar.

The Voice: Not half as vulgar as it is."

~F. Scott Fitzgerald
The Beautiful And Damned

table of contents.

lovetrust

seven.

I counted down the days until her life would come to an end and mine would truly begin. My junior year of college was spent waiting for my mother to die. It's a period exclusively isolated from any other portion of my existence and defines the man I am today. It was then that I rode a carousel of seconds. In the process of waiting for her days to be numbered, mine lost their sequence. Emotions, deadlines, penetrations; they all floated on a timeline with only two milestones- the beginning and the end. I find myself reliving choice moments with photographic accuracy, while others have been completely erased. Some things may be out of order, but this, I'm positive, was the beginning of me praying for her end.

~

I'm darting through my apartment- a one bedroom, one bathroom slum with an adequate size living room.

My "American Dream" starter kit.

As I slide by Noni, I glance at the light switch. To my relief, the little finger is pointing to the sky. I always make sure the light switch's capital letters read ON. The switch was ON when I moved in, and I haven't figured out what it turns ON, so it's remained ON. There are no nearby outlets or overhead lights- no reason for the light switch to exist, but everything has worked when the light switch is ON, and I'm afraid of what it shuts off, so I guard it carefully.

I keep Noni in my peripheral vision, as her slim dancer's body does flying ballet pirouettes with no music to guide her. Her razor cut black bob bounces as she flings herself back and forth, back and forth, each time passing the switch. I'm not sure why I care if she turns the switch off, and I can't think of a reason why she would, but I rush over to my coffee table to get the magazine she wants to borrow so I can get her out of my apartment.

I grab the *Rolling Stone*, then walk over and place it in Noni's right hand at the precise moment she turns to me in mid-spin.

"Thank you," she says, then flashes me a busy smile, packed with teeth just a little too big for her face. Noni's voice sounds like she's always bored. Noni is never bored. Noni always has a task, and when she doesn't, she shatters the stillness with repetitive, drifting, semi-possessed movements.

Just before Noni crosses the door frame, satisfied that she's clutching the reason she came to see me, she asks, "Kurt, are you cheating on me?"

"We aren't dating," I say.

"But, you know, if we were and I asked that question, what would the answer be?"

I don't say anything.

She doesn't say anything.

Someone needs to do something, so I move my head in a no-ish manner.

She winks at me, then whispers, "Good."

Noni turns around, then waves as she pirouettes out of my apartment.

She might be insane.

I might be too.

I immediately go back and fix the stack of magazines on my glass coffee table. I had disrupted the proper magazine order while I was rushing to get Noni away from the switch, and now order must be restored.

Esquire/ Harper's Bazaar/ People/ Rolling Stone/ The New Yorker.

That is the only acceptable order.

I don't leave a gap for the missing *Rolling Stone*.

Esquire sits atop the shiny stack purely for alphabetic reasons, with the rest of the magazines visible only by an inch. I agree with *Esquire*'s cover selections about 30% of the time and this causes me a lot of unnecessary stress the other 70% of the time. The rules stipulate that I can't revoke *Esquire*'s position no matter how many times I have to have George Clooney staring up at me. The fact that *Harper's Bazaar* is the magazine alphabetically under *Esquire* further begs for the system to be violated. *Harper's* will throw Kate Moss on a cover at least once a year, and I just have to hope her face is within one inch of the edge of the magazine. When I get *the money*, either I'll subscribe to *Elle*, or I'll leave this pathetic apartment and the magazines will become someone else's problem. *Esquire* isn't the only guilty party in the stack; I've made a weekly chore of trying to cancel my subscription to *Rolling Stone* because its size seems vulgar when placed in line with the smaller magazines. Like the table they lie on, all of these subscriptions were purchased by the person who lived in my apartment before me, so I have no way of really stopping their delivery. The name on the little white postal labels is "Akkuta Afar," and I can never guess any of his security questions because the only information I have about him is that he has an American Express card. I know this because they send me updates regarding their terms and conditions, but they don't send any information with the card number on it.

When the new magazines arrive, I move the outdated issues off the coffee table and place them on a shelf in my coat closet. If Akkuta comes back for his magazines, they'll be here for him. I never rule out his return. Maybe he had to move out in a rush- that shot in the dark job application was accepted- that screenplay he toiled over for six years was finally bought- that girl that he was pining for finally said, "Come back to me, I'm sorry."

If I was to throw out Akkuta Afar's magazines, every plucky bing of my doorbell would send my heart into my throat, and I'd immediately *know* that it's Akkuta arriving as a weary traveler who will be disappointed with the man who inherited his home. The lingering inconvenience of keeping magazines that I don't read is preferable to the option of throwing them out every month, then dealing with the nagging knowledge that I've done something I can't reverse.

I must keep the magazines, as a rule. I've always followed very specific rules. These aren't the, "No running in the hall," or the, "No smoking on the airplane," or the, "Don't touch the dancers," admonishment-type rules. These are the rules on the back of the floor cleaner that direct you to, "Consult a physician immediately," if you break them.

Rule~ Everything I own must be placed at a perfect ninety degree angle. My magazines sit meticulously in-line with the edge of the glass on the coffee table. Everything on my wall is hung at a pleasant, perfect, ninety degrees- A painting of some old brownstone buildings in New York City/ A street sign bearing the name of "Harrington St" that I keep in memory of Nancy Harrington, a girl I dated in grade school/ A collage of pictures from various fashion magazines of models wearing outfits that I refuse to let my girlfriend, Joan, purchase.

Joan was, is, and perpetually will forever be, annoyed by my rearranging and need for organization. She's always bitterly reminding me, "There's medication for people like you." Joan's voice sounds like a cat that learned how to meow in English.

I refuse to take the medication that would help me ease up on these rules. I don't feel like I have OCD, I just have standards, I have healthy obsessions, I like collecting. Comic books, baseball cards, old cassette tapes; all various obsessions that have taken hold of me for a period of time.

My mother once told me, "Watching you obsess over collecting is like watching someone pour a cup of coffee in a dark room." My mother's voice sounds like a song.

There's something about the act of collecting that brings me peace. Few things in life are final, so when I can locate a definitive end, I feel a sense of accomplishment. If there are four different reissues of an album and I get all four, my collection is complete. Having three of the four will keep me up at night. My days will be consumed with searching the internet for the final piece to achieve absolute ownership. Since the age of 16, I haven't been able to walk by a thrift shop without stopping in, hoping and wishing for some rare albums mixed in with the normal bubble-gum fodder. I don't like the search; I like the end, the resolution, the comfort of completeness.

~

I mentally assemble a playlist that I'll leave on Joan's laptop, in hopes of transforming her into someone that I share common interests with. She doesn't care that I'm physically indexing music right now because she's busy sifting through the wall of rectangular cardboard boxes that the Macy's girl has brought out.

"These shoes make my feet look fucking disgusting," Joan informs the entire left side of the shoe department. She rips the blue pump off of her foot, then lobs it a couple of feet away, almost striking a display of riding boots.

For a moment, I relate to the blue pump. I walk over, and pick up the shoe, then I wrap it carefully in its crinkly paper bed and put the lid back on the box.

Joan rants, "All these shoes are made in China! Don't girls in China scrunch their feet up all small in their shoes? It's like, 'Hello, I'm living in America, I don't have four inch long feet.'"

I stare at Joan. When she's not foaming at the mouth, she's beautiful. She has sandy blonde hair that she keeps in a slick ponytail which brushes her back when she makes quick head movements to yell at me for something I found funny. She has perfect posture, and when I ignore her, she puts her hands on her hips like Wonder Woman. She has thin, peach pink lips, and usually doesn't wear lipstick, which I like because it makes it harder to tell when she's frowning at me. She has intense eyes, so brown that they're almost black, like a shark's eyes when they're honed in on their prey. Joan would be taller than me if she was wearing the blue pumps, but I don't have to worry about that now.

Those lucky blue pumps. A girl nicer and prettier than Joan will come along and take them home someday. I would harbor the same wish for myself but I'm aware that I'll never escape Joan. Blame mutual necessity.

Eventually, Joan decides on a pair of shoes without asking my opinion, and it's a relief for both of us.

Escaping Macy's, I leave a trail of apologies in my wake. People look at me with an understanding glint in their eyes, like I was a dog dressed up by Joan to look like another animal, like a bear or an Ewok.

All the "Back to School" sales have ended, and in a week our junior year at Kirtland University begins. The sales don't matter to me; I've reached a point in my life where I understand that a new shirt isn't going to change the lunch table I sit at.

Joan leads me into a clothing store decorated with huge black and white pictures of shirtless guys and near-shirtless girls that confront the tween shoppers as they enter the overly perfumed space.

I immediately realize that I'm alone, and the house music in the store is too loud for me to hear Joan's complaints so echo-locating her is nearly impossible.

No stranger to this situation, I use a compass of grimaces, and follow the trail of annoyed sales associates to my girlfriend.

In the back of the store, I find Joan standing in front of a mirror that's tilted on an angle so whoever stands in front of it looks thinner in their reflection. Joan turns to me, then asks, "Would I look cute in this?" while pinning a thin shirt to her shoulders with the tips of her fingers.

She wants me to say, "Yes," and I know this, but for some reason I say, "There's a hole in it." Maybe I say this because there's a massive hole in the shirt; maybe I opt for the observation to keep the word, "No," from escaping my mouth. Joan is sucking her teeth, and I remain perfectly still, hoping that I'm far enough in the shadows that she'll just text me her complaints. It becomes clear that she can see me wincing, and she says, "Ugh," as she throws the shirt down, then stomps away.

As I grab a hanger and begin cleaning up after Joan again, I notice something. My eyes are drawn to the careful sewing along the perimeter of the two inch hole- clearly a precautionary measure to keep the intended defect from becoming an unintended defect. I can imagine my grandfather looking at some skinny blonde model wearing a holey shirt, her head almost touching the massive *Teen Vogue* logo on top of the magazine, and saying to my grandmother, "These kids are so troubled that they want their outsides to match their damaged insides."

If Akkuta was a subscriber, *Teen Vogue* would go under *Rolling Stone*, and whatever ad was on the back of the magazine would press against *The New Yorker*, the content of the two magazines snarling at one another- *Teen Vogue* practically asking *The New Yorker* for a fifty so it can go to the mall with its friends.

Once I finish repairing the damage Joan has done to the purposely abused looking clothing, I enter the men's side of the store. Or at least it appears to be the men's side, but may actually just be the "college is about trying new things and learning about the type of woman you are" side. Beyond the flannel, Joan is looking at a pair of skinny jeans, pretending that she's interested in them, but in actuality she's waiting for me to catch up because I wasn't following close enough behind her. Still staring at the skinny jeans, she says, "It's really nice shopping with you, how you hate every article of clothing I show interest in."

"I'm providing an opinion on a request-only basis. If you like something, then buy it," I stupidly answer. If I had been thinking, I would've just put my head down and paid for the holey shirt to end the conflict, but I'm still coursing with life as a result of ordering a rare version of *Blonde on Blonde* online this morning. Simultaneously, I'm also coursing with hate, because Joan, after hearing the album title, asked, "What's that, some kind of porno?"

I passively listen, as Joan restates her shopping rules, "I can't buy something that could possibly look dumb; I need to know if it looks cute first. I'm not gonna pay fifty bucks for a shirt that makes me look like shit. I don't have the benefit of anorexia to make any and all of my clothing whims look valid, so I need to put a little work into this and I hate that you seem oblivious."

I say nothing, which, in the end, seems like the right response. We immediately make our way out of the mall, and I'm glad that Joan is driving because it will allow me to select what we listen to.

The moment I lean toward the radio, Joan snips, "Don't put on your music, I like to choose... it's my car."

It's brutally obvious that Joan doesn't like her own selections either, and during the twenty-six minutes it takes us to get from the mall to my apartment, we don't stay on a radio station for longer than twenty-two seconds. I count. She changes the station nineteen seconds into "In the Air Tonight" and for the thousandth time in a single day, I realize that Joan will never be happy.

~

I throw my mail, piece by piece, onto the glass coffee table.

Credit card offer/ Request for my blood/ Credit card offer/ A book of coupons/ A letter from Edie.

A letter from Edie!

I fix the mail so that it sits at a ninety degree angle on the table, then I open the letter from Edie. It starts out, as all of her letters do, with the word, "Remember."

"Remember that one day, you were walking to get apple pie, bread, cheese, corn flakes, cotton candy flavored bubblegum, eggs, milk, pasta, Ragu, Ramen, and a watermelon, and I was in my front yard, and you gave me that head nod type thing so as to acknowledge my existence, but since we had never talked you didn't say anything to me because that would be weird, and I ran and caught up with you so I could ask what you're doing, and you said that you were going to the store, and I asked what for, and you read the list, and I said that you could never carry all of that shit, and the watermelon alone would limit your capabilities of hauling everything, and you thought about it, then asked if I could help you, and I said yes because that's what I wanted you to ask me, and when we got to the store I broke that jar of pickles in aisle seven, and there was no one else in the aisle so you picked up another jar and heaved it over the aisle, into aisle eight, so if someone came they would be so confused that we wouldn't get in trouble, and no one noticed anyway so there were just two broken jars of pickles sitting there, and we ended up getting everything besides the watermelon because they didn't have any in stock, so it turned out you could have carried all the bags home, but you let me carry a bag anyway so I wouldn't feel like I was worthless, and when we got back you told me that I had purpose, and I said thank you?

Well, I work at that grocery store now and we just got watermelons.
xx Edie"

I fold the letter up and place it in the envelope it arrived in, then I walk to the desk in my bedroom and open the top drawer. Inside, wrapped in twine, is every letter Edie has ever sent me. I add this letter to the top of the stack, then make sure the twine is tied tight.

I do remember the day Edie detailed in her letter, but the list she rattled off is a reminder of the particulars of the trip. I appreciate that small things remain important to Edie, even after all this time. The day at the grocery store was the beginning of my friendship with a girl that I should not have been friends with. After the trip, Edie started to come by my grandparents' house, and she'd stand behind the screen at the front door and ask my grandmother if I was around. Every time Edie came over, my grandmother would start off with, "Now Edith, I'm worried about you."

Edie said she didn't like worrying my grandmother, and she also didn't like speaking with my grandmother, so she decided, instead of visiting, she would write me letters. We were neighbors, but Edie would still mail the letters because, as she put it, "I feel bad for those poor fuck mailmen now that everyone e-mails and texts each other."

It seems like Edie has always been 25. When I met her, she was only a kid, but I instantly recognized her as a sponge that sucked up other people's bitterness, which she then cataloged in her mind. This is exactly how she got so jaded in such a short amount of time- she studies everyone around her.

I sit down at my desk to write Edie back because responding is the only way to get another letter from her. I always write to her about a recent conversation I've had with a stranger. Edie likes hearing about the conversations I have because she says she's fascinated by the way my mind works, but finds my life boring. She prefers when I relay someone else's life, as if I can pick up on some sort of subtext. Maybe Edie needs these letters because I can tune out the bitterness that a story is being painted with, and I flatly report exactly what I'm told, without a description of *how* the information is presented to me.

I always write each letter twice. The first draft is scrawled in a spiral notebook, and it merely serves to get the information down. I have to write fast, oftentimes on the bus, so the u's look like a's, and words blend together so tightly that it appears that they have half the letters they're supposed to. The second draft goes to Edie with perfect spelling, no cross-outs, and carefully formed letters. When available, I like to use a black gel pen because I feel the texture of the ink is richer. I want my writing to look like a font, but I'd never use my laptop. Writing letters to Edie feels like holding hands.

I can't think of any good conversations for today's letter because usually, when someone says something interesting, I immediately hurry back to my apartment and write Edie about it. Twice.

When my phone vibrates next to me, I know that Joan is texting me, so I leave the cell on the desk, grab my wallet, then rush out to the bus stop in front of my building.

The moment I leave the courtyard, I spot an idling city bus at the curb- the last person in line climbing its stairs- and this impending departure turns me into a man who boards the bus in a sweaty panic. There was a time when this hurried arrival occurred so regularly that no one on the bus would even notice, but after that guy detonated himself on a Boston-bound bus last month, a frantic boarding yields complete attention. Buses have become the new airliner. Earbuds stay tangled in pockets. Cell phones are kept on video mode, waiting to pan at the first sudden movement. Sweaty lunatics stopping the bus, like *this* bus was the *only bus* in the entire world, are now instant suspects in the eyes of the rest of the passengers.

Commanding everyone's attention, I pay the $1.50 fare, then make my way down the aisle.

I notice I'm being videoed by a fat girl with a backpack on her lap, so I head for the first open seat.

I sit next to a man in a gray suit that has black speckles on the shoulder.

I start a conversation.

I share a granola bar.

I shake hands with Abe Carrol, then he gets off at his stop.

After a half hour and two different buses, I arrive back at my apartment, ready to write Edie a letter.

I write, "*Remember...*

...when you bought all that black house paint and those four Calvin Klein undershirts, and on each shirt, you painted a single letter? You would wear the 'F' shirt on Monday, then the 'U' shirt on Tuesday, and the 'C' shirt on Wednesday, then the 'K' shirt on Thursday, and the 'U' shirt, a different shirt than Tuesday's shirt, on Friday? Did anyone at school ever say anything? I wonder if they noticed. I wonder if they still made lead-based paint back then. I thought about you and your t-shirts today while I was on a bus ride to nowhere in particular. My seatmate, Abe Carrol, told me about how he lives in a big development in a suburb close to Kirtland. The development forms an L shape and Abe Carrol's house is right at the vertex of the L. He said I should imagine that the vertical part of the L was the positive part of the Y-axis, and the horizontal part of the L was the positive part of the X-axis. Abe Carrol lives at (0,0). All the houses in the development were built under the same specifications, and each one has; a one car garage, no front porch, three bedrooms, two bathrooms, a basement, a crawl space, a back deck, and red shutters. These houses, once built, were painted muted colors like eggshell white, sea-foam green, and sky blue. Abe Carrol's wife specifically chose the development because it's in a good school district, while also being three minutes away from Abe Carrol's job and ten minutes away from her own job. They could walk to work if they wanted to. The whole thing is so quaint that the neighbors throw 'development parties,' to watch the Oscars, or to bet on the Super Bowl. Abe Carrol admitted that his neighbors are great, and the town never gave him any trouble, but he despised how the development looked, and one day, he accepted that something had to be done. Last

winter, Abe Carrol got a Christmas bonus, but he had already finished his Christmas shopping, so he spent the money on himself. Abe Carrol said the only purpose for wealth is to create happiness. To create his own happiness, Abe Carrol went to a home improvement store and bought as many cans of black paint as his bonus would permit. He also bought a tall, tall, tall ladder. Supplies in tow, Abe Carrol went home, and in the dead of winter, he began to paint his house. He painted all weekend, but never once missed a family meal. He was always ready to say grace, then listen to stories about what his family did while he was on the ladder. During the next week, Abe Carrol would come home from work and resume his painting. He was so excited about this project, that sometimes he would even go out on the tall, tall, tall ladder in his suit because he didn't want to waste time changing after work. His wife asked him not to paint the house, 'Not black,' she begged, and Abe Carrol would make the tall, tall, tall ladder even taller so he couldn't hear her. He painted, and painted, and painted, until the entire house was black except for an 18' x 25' rectangle. Abe Carrol, content to leave the rectangle as it was, headed inside and happily sat at (0,0). A new peace blanketed everything after this tiny modification Abe Carrol had made in his life. Post-project, Abe Carrol slept like a baby. For twelve days straight, he would get into his bed, close his eyes, and instantly fall asleep. There was no tossing. There was no turning. Abe Carrol's wife noticed he stopped snoring. Thirteen days after Abe Carrol had completed his masterpiece, he awoke to a rocking jolt. The entire house shook, then immediately afterward, a portion of it collapsed. There had been an accident. Abe Carrol said it was particularly snowy that night, and Steve Brentman either lost control of his car or didn't see the black house in the dark of the night, and just kept going. Steve Brentman had forcibly parked in Abe Carrol's living room, and as the weight bearing beams cracked, a piece of the house sealed Steve Brentman tightly inside his car. Abe Carrol got his family out of the house, then went back in for Steve Brentman. Everyone survived, and Abe Carrol received a windfall settlement from his insurance company that allowed him to rebuild his house so that it stuck out like a sore thumb in the neighborhood. Abe Carrol doesn't mind the development anymore. His house now has a one car garage, no front porch, three bedrooms, two bathrooms, a basement, a crawl space, a back deck, red shutters, a fresh coat of olive paint that Mrs. Carrol picked out, and a bay window that no one else in the neighborhood has.

Love, Kurt."

I put the letter in a pre-addressed, pre-stamped envelope, then leave it on the coffee table, perfectly lined up with the other envelopes.

With Edie on my mind, and Abe Carrol in my notebook, I get ready for bed.

For the third night in a row, as I lie in bed waiting for sleep to come, I hear a weird thumping in the apartment above me. It's always the same noise, traveling from one side of the apartment to the other. The noise comes and goes, back and forth. The thuds sound like someone's dropping a bag full of potatoes. It goes on for at least a half hour, and I anticipate this happening, every night of this semester, until the man upstairs is arrested. A news crew will catch me coming out of the elevator the next morning, and a racially ambiguous woman speaking with a regionless accent will ask me, "Did you have any indication that your upstairs neighbor was the Kirtland County Strangler?" and I'll look her in the eyes, and say, "No. I didn't, because *I* am the Kirtland County Strangler."

~

It's the first day of my junior year at Kirtland University.

I run my hand along the rods of the black gate designed to keep the rest of the community off the campus. This gate reminds me that there is now a delineation between myself and my peers. I'm unsure about my feelings regarding this new distance.

The moment I swipe my ID and open the gate, I'm greeted by the familiar sights; lost freshmen, hippies hacking, blacks rapping, white girls protesting, nerds studying, jocks wiffleballing, and professors rolling their little airport style luggage filled with syllabi. It's always the same; this is the sitcom intro for the new season of Kirtland University.

I light a cigarette because I don't have any caffeine in my bloodstream yet.

The monotony of the day's predictability is broken as someone materializes on my back. They're mounting my backpack and both of their arms are around my neck. I bite down on the end of my cigarette, and my eyes start drying up from the smoke, while my nose is telling my brain, *It's Noni.*

Noni asks, "Did you see the white girls are already protesting? The semester started only eleven minutes ago."

"What now?" I strain to say, as Noni's arms constrict around me like a beautiful, but too-tight necklace.

"Laura says they're protesting the lack of racial diversity in the Kirtland University Hall of Fame."

"Isn't that accomplishment based?" I wheeze out.

"Yeah, the university was like, 'If you give us some diverse alumni candidates who have done great things that you feel we've overlooked, we'll be happy to correct this issue.'"

"Then, why are they protesting?"

"Because putting together that list would actually require them to look into the issue they're protesting about."

"But they've probably been waiting all summer, planning this."

Noni laughs, gets off my back, then looks to the white girls and says, "Let's protest the lack of diversity in this protest."

This moment encapsulates Kirtland University perfectly. Everyone mashed together, no one mixing.

Kirtland looks a lot different in the brochures they give out to tour groups. This brochure, thanks to a protest by the same people currently on the Green, now features Asian kids eating with the white kids. In the brochure, the hippies are studying textbooks. In the brochure, the professors are making eye contact with the students. All of these events, casually laid out in a tri-fold piece of propaganda, rarely happen at Kirtland, but I didn't come here because of the brochure. The only reason I picked this sad little place to continue my education is because the name sounded like "Kurt-Land." My own personal amusement park.

The brochure says that Kirtland is supposed to mean "the church land" or something. I have a feeling Kirtland is a Catholic University for two reasons.

One- The name.

Two- The fact that sometimes they let us out of class to go to mass.

I doubt they'd be able to do this if Kirtland was just a normal college. The white girls would surely protest.

The brochure also says that five thousand undergrads go to Kirtland, but I don't believe this figure. If there are five thousand people here, at least two thousand of them must be buried under the athletic center. They probably just want to make us feel like we aren't the only rubes whose parents are paying what amounts to the average American's yearly salary for ten classes, a shared broom closet for a dorm, some slices of pizza, and a library that's open fewer hours a week than any of the local banks.

Since everyone here is on their parents' tab, we're all business majors. The undergrad student body at Kirtland has no idea what they want to do with their lives, except the most sociopathic of us who want to become CEOs and entrepreneurs. We're painfully aware that there's a countdown, which, at max, allows for five years' worth of sand sifting through a towering hourglass before our fathers all have to answer the question, "So, what do your children do?" That question is the launching pad for all of us, and all we need to do is provide an acceptable answer. Kirtland University's motto should be a Latin sentence that translates to: "Don't make Dad feel embarrassed at his business lunch."

Avoiding the protest on the Green, Noni and I walk together along the brick paver sidewalk. Engraved in the bricks are names of alumni that once looked like Noni and I, and once walked this same path. In a desperate attempt to preserve their existence in a home they can never again inhabit, these alumni paid to leave a legacy more permanent than their hazy days and drunken nights.

Noni leaves me at Kozinski Hall, and I climb the stone stairs, glancing down at my schedule, while wondering who signed me up for this class that's named a series of vague buzzwords. I read and re-read the name, but fail to derive concrete meaning from it. The name itself provides so much information that I get distracted just by reading it.

What I've apparently volunteered for is essentially Introduction to Eco-Socio-International-required class.

Despite a nagging need to flee, I can't turn and run back to Noni because she's on her way to class as well, and I need my attendance record to be perfect so I can barely pass this semester, then take Advanced Eco-Socio-International-required class in the spring to complete my requirement of at least six credits of a multi-hyphenated course populated with unverifiable suggestions on how to succeed in the business world.

I eventually find the white, windowless classroom that I'm looking for. It's indistinguishable from the rest of the rooms in Kozinski; the seating is separated into two U shapes- the smaller of the two U's residing within the larger. The larger U is also about three feet higher than the smaller U, which creates the inconvenience of having a full view of an NCAA basketball player's screen as he watches double penetration pornography on his laptop a tier below. The professor's desk is located perfectly in the center of both of the U's, but set back, so he or she can write on the dry erase board that's mounted to the front wall. All the chairs are bolted to the floor, but can be pulled out and swiveled on a steel arm. Everyone is evenly spaced, and this is my favorite design feature of the room. Each student sits at a comfortable one and a half feet from their next closest peer, with no option to crowd closer or slide farther away.

I take my place in the upper left corner of the bigger U. I always sit in the big U that encases the small U because the altitude and angle make it prime cheating territory. This is my observation deck, with no one for a foot and a half to distract me. The professor can't tell if I'm looking down at my paper or at the kid's paper below me. It's likely that no one considered this design flaw because the people who constructed this building surely did not attend business school. They likely worked a series of jobs where they couldn't cheat to succeed- they just had to do the work.

Since it's the first day of class, I need to call someone over who I know is on the Dean's List, then I need to convince them to sit in front of me in the lower U. Most Dean's List students are small in stature and their bodies won't block my view from the observation deck.

This game of musical chairs is an investment. I'll have to talk to the nerd before class, but it will all pay off when the test comes and I can kick my feet up in the observation deck. This is, of course, figurative, as the chairs don't allow the mobility for one to kick their feet up.

I call over Ted Calvert, then quickly begin the plan to make small talk with him until class starts. I listen to Ted talk about a trip to Hawaii he just got back from, and I compliment him, "Nice tan," then give him a thumbs up.

When the professor rolls his briefcase on wheels into the classroom, Ted, being the gracious student that he is, quickly sits down so as to give the already exhausted, thankfully not foreign, professor his complete attention. Ted doesn't sit in the open seat in front of me- he instead sits one seat to the left, and it's a bad angle for me.

"Ted, I think someone's sitting there," I tell him- just a friend looking out for a friend.

Ted moves and takes a seat directly below me.

Class is quickly and predictably dismissed after the professor gives a monotone review of the course requirements, then answers, "Yes," to two questions, both of them essentially asking if the $120 textbook listed on the pink syllabus is "really necessary."

The kids with serious majors do work on the first day, we don't. We are the business major slush pool.

When we're dismissed, I quickly make my way out of the classroom so Ted doesn't try to continue our conversation.

Outside Kozinski, I hang a left, making my way to the cafeteria. The pamphlet calls it the café because I guess it doesn't seem as shitty if we call it a word that has its own accent. The non-buffet portion of the café is where the commuters hang out. I, as a newly christened commuter, find myself gravitating there. Despite my proximity to them, I still feel entirely opposed to- and outside of- this crowd of nerds, God freaks, momma's boys, epileptics, cutters, druggies, and fatsos. The café is the single largest melting pot of undesirables, while the rest have been given their own tiny reservations. The anorexics hang out at the library or the gym because food isn't allowed there. The theater kids have been given an auditorium to hang out in so we don't have to hear someone break into song in the middle of the day. The frat guys have been given a place called "The Greek Room," but it contains more Play-Doh than Plato. All of the commuters have something wrong with them, some reason why the university won't give them housing, some reason why Mommy won't let them move out.

This group of freaks can spend anywhere between two to six hours a day in this holding pen.

With a fear that's peppered with pity, I look across the mass of different groups in the café.

I can't find an empty table so I cruise the perimeter nonchalantly like I'm trying to figure out what I want to eat. After I return to where I started, I accept that there's nowhere I can sit and be by myself.

I'm going to have to dive in headfirst and assimilate.

I pick a table peppered with a bunch of average looking commuters who have a lot of food that they might share with me.

The kids must presume I'm a commuter because they instantly greet me as one of their own. I find this to be supremely offensive, but I really need a place to sit, so I smile warmly when a commuter with curly red hair asks me, "What's up, dude?"

I feel so bad for him- he has red hair *and* it's curly. "Another year," I say, then ask, "Don't any of these people have class?"

A fat commuter who's trying to grow a goatee enters our conversation by saying, "I'm beginning to question if some of these people even go to Kirtland. Maybe they just like the food here? Maybe they're plotting something? You don't need to scan your ID at the door on this side- the café's the perfect place to blend in."

Perfect unless you have red curly hair.

The fat commuter points to a trash can, and says, "You see those Asian kids over there?"

I don't see Asian kids, I see a trash can, and I wonder what's going on, again. The commuter next to me, this one's already balding- a real defective model- tells me in a muffled voice, "When he points somewhere, he wants you to look in the opposite direction. Follow his pointer finger backward instead of forward."

This seems to be some sort of commuter code they've created so as not to seem obvious that they're making fun of someone. Or stalking someone.

I follow the fat commuter's sausage finger backward, to two long tables pushed together. Both tables are claimed by Asians on laptops.

"Yeah, I see them," I confirm.

The fat commuter gets a little excited, "I've been watching them since last semester, and I think they're up to something. You know, with all the shit that is going on with the buses and trains... what if they want a piece of the action?"

The fat commuter refers to domestic terrorism as "the action."

"Every time I walk by, they're all just watching manga," I assure everyone at the table so the Asians can sit in the unassimilated peace they intensely desire.

A Mexican commuter wearing a black baseball cap leans in, and says, "No, dude. Manga is the comics, anime is what the cartoons are called. You meant to say they're all watching anime."

The black baseball capped commuter doesn't seem Asian. He's definitely Mexican, so how the fuck does he know the difference between manga and anime?

The fat commuter continues his rant, "Their laptops are always open. They type all sorts of shit and speak in code."

"I think that's Japanese that they're speaking," I offer.

"How do you know?"

"Well, I'm assuming."

"Exactly. What if they're talking to each other under the *guise of Japanese*?" the fat commuter asks. "They know their plans are safe because we don't understand what they're saying, and even if we were to get one of the black kids to steal their laptops, we don't know how to change the language settings on those fucking things. I can't even figure out how to take StickyKeys off of my laptop."

"Even if you did figure out the situation it wouldn't be long before the keys were sticky again," the redhead says, laughing.

"Ew," the bald commuter says.

"I meant from syrup and candy. Not cum."

"Oh. Right on," the bald commuter accepts this.

The anime scholar leans in again, and says, "Something big is gonna go down, something bigger than a protest."

"Bigger than a protest? What, like a bake sale?" I ask them, then look at the time on my phone. I don't have class for another fifteen minutes so, with faux concern, I ask, "How do we thwart their plan?"

All the commuters at the table look at the fat one as he leans back in his chair, folds his arms across his chest, then says, "We need our own Asian kid."

The rest of the table scoffs at this because they know we don't live in a brochure, and the fat commuter's suggestion is implausible.

A commuter with bad acne says, "But, how would we know that the Asian kid we get isn't just a double-agent for the other Asians? We could get fed a bunch of disinformation."

The commuters all nod their heads at this notion, and a commuter with a stubby Mohawk who was silent up until this point, says, "Dude, we're gonna have to meet one at the mall, or the dry cleaner, or something. Ya know, find one outside of the Kirtlandsphere."

Everyone at this table of commuters calls each other "dude" because, once the semester is over, they'll probably never see each other again. The commuters aren't wasting any time. Why learn someone's name if they'll just be a dim memory in a couple of months?

Maybe it's better this way. It's hard to talk behind someone's back when you don't know their name. If you try, most of the conversation is just you describing who you're trying to gossip about. Even if the other person thinks they know who you're referring to and are like, "Do you mean Kathy Montvale?" you just have to go, "Yeah, I think so," because you have no idea who it is that you have this hilarious and hurtful observation about.

No one needs a name when you can just reverse-point at them and everyone will know who you're talking about.

Sensing my window for an exit, I stand up, and everyone says things like, "Nice to meet you, dude," and, "See ya around, man."

I leave the commuters, allowing them to continue to exist in their paranoid bubble.

As I walk to my next class, British Literature, I think about what the fat commuter said, and I begin secretly wishing that the Asians really are planning something.

Keeping my head down, I avoid eye contact as I traverse the campus, and successfully make it to class without being stopped by a lost freshman or an old friend.

My British Literature class is in a building at the edge of campus that looks like a public high school. I've only entered this building once and that was to print a paper in the computer lab located in the basement. The classrooms in this building are all set up in the typical structure- individual desks with swooping tablet surfaces on the right, and all of the desks face a dry-erase board stained with years of notes scrawled with such a heavy hand that even the janitor's limited cleaning supplies are unable to completely erase these lessons. I imagine that many of the Kirtland alumni have retained the same amount of information as the board.

I traverse the first two floors of this building looking for the Brit-Lit room, then settle for a classroom on the third floor. I believe this is the Brit-Lit room for two reasons:

One- The class is filled with dozens of pairs of pale kids in chunky black framed glasses.

Two- The writing on the dry-erase board reads, "British Literature."

Thankfully, the professor isn't British- he's just old. He has a white beard, and his dress shirt was once white, but is now more of an eggshell color. He begins the class with some tirade about the administration not ordering the right books, so we have to read the "retard room abridged version." He slams the book on the desk for emphasis, "Now, if this was the real version, it would've perked up all the kids sleeping next door."

This professor is from a different era, and I imagine that no one protests what he says because he so thoroughly does not give a shit, that nothing would come of their outrage.

The old professor hands out a single-page syllabus that reads, in full, "Welcome to British Literature. In this class, we'll do required reading at night, then during the next class, we'll review the two 'Takeaways' you assembled regarding the reading." That's the entire syllabus. Considering that I entered the classroom based on two Takeaways, this system seems perfect.

"The administration makes me hand out a syllabus, and I'm not going to fabricate some sort of ten page outline of quotes and codes of ethics. If you're all going to masquerade as grownups, then you know better than to cheat. I'm interested in your asses being in the chair for class, and I'm interested in hearing your Takeaways. You don't have to like what we read, you just have to read it, then use your brainbox to spit out two coherent thoughts. If your Takeaways contain even the slightest hint of intelligent observation, you will do very well in this class. If you half-ass your Takeaways, then the next takeaway you'll encounter is Daddy cutting off your allowance. Any questions?"

Kids are packing up because the syllabus has been distributed, so the class is obviously coming to an end. "Since all we've read so far is the syllabus, let's do our Takeaways for the day, then you can go," the old professor says. He stands in front of the class and looks us over, "Well, are you going to answer the question or do we need to review the syllabus again?"

Since no question was posed, the class seems unsure about where to begin with an answer.

One of the members of the army of sexually ambiguous humans wearing chunky black frame glasses speaks up, "A Takeaway I got from the syllabus is that it's a rejection of the bureaucracy this university so often operates under, and it makes the statement that we shouldn't waste time *talking about* what we're going to learn, and instead, we should immediately begin the learning process." This answer confirms that this sexless being was at the protest this morning. Her voice sounds like the opposite of a British accent.

The old professor sits down in his chair and lets out a big breath. I think it was a discouraged sigh, but I can't be sure.

The next kid in the row says, "Uhh," because he thinks we're answering in seating order, "Well, my Takeaway is that we will be reading."

The old professor's eyes light up and his posture improves upon hearing this.

A girl wearing chunky framed purple glasses catches on, and says, "Then we'll be doing Takeaways." Her voice sounds like she's falling down a well, and when she says Takeaways, it sounds like, "Takeawayyysss."

The professor points at the last two students who provided an answer.

Time freezes for a moment, then people just start leaving, and the old professor puts his hands down.

It appears that this will be a supremely satisfying class, but I doubt I'll do the reading, so eventually I'll learn to hate British Literature- the class and the genre.

With two classes attended and adjourned, my day is over.

Instead of going back to a dorm, I have to leave campus now.

The walk back to my apartment is fourteen minutes of time that I spend with my left hand in my pocket, my head down, and my right hand holding a cigarette. That is my commute home. It's not as easy as just returning to a double in Corini Hall, but it's the next best thing. The university, in an effort to retain students on the weekend, purchased a large, section 8 style apartment building behind the baseball field and deemed it an "off campus dormitory" which, for a premium price, we could live in without a roommate. The moment I found out there was an option to escape the oppression that is a shared room, I signed the lease.

I swipe my card to get out of the gate, then I walk along the perimeter of the campus to my building. To pass the time, I sing ~the song~ as another ritual to distance myself from the moment. Walking alone, I sing:

> *"...you laugh a subtle laugh*
> *and your face opens the door*
> *then the ceiling slowly slides*
> *and your ear cups the floor..."*

Sometimes I only get short pieces of ~the song~ out, other times I cycle through ~the song~ over and over, but I sing ~the song~ and no other songs. There's no playlist, just a single track that I've been unable to locate except in my own faded memories. ~The song~ plays in my head when I'm between thoughts, and thus I'm haunted, not by a ghost of my dead relatives or some paranormal bullshit, but instead by a melody that remains nameless, as does the artist who recorded it.

I must have heard ~the song~ a thousand times as a kid. My mother would play it from an old labelless Memorex tape, and she would harmonize along with the man singing on the tape as if they were performing a duet. As the tape's quality diminished, my mother would just sing louder. When the man's voice became more cracked and distant, hers would become stronger and closer. The deterioration couldn't be stopped, and we didn't have a second deck to make a copy of the tape, so we accepted the gradual fade. I would sit with my mother in the living room, and we'd listen to this single sonic masterpiece over and over. At almost eight minutes long it's as transfixing a sound as I've ever heard, and I would do anything to hear it again, but the fact is that, like my mother, the tape is gone.

~

Starving, I barely have the strength to open my cabinets. My bony arms manage to get the cabinet above the stove open, and the pleasure I receive from visually scanning my well-ordered boxes is at odds with my disappointment regarding what they contain.

Rule~ All boxes must be arranged in size order from tallest (pancake mix), to shortest (a box of hot chocolate packets).

Most of the food in the line of boxes requires milk to prepare, and I'm positive that the milk in my fridge, if opened, would release a bizarre organism that would, at worst- contaminate my living space, and at best- kill the roaches.

I make my way to the freezer to check my options.

TV dinners/ Waffles/ Ravioli/ Frozen veggies.

I pick out a TV dinner, a Valu-cuisine turkey meal. I've had this exact meal at least once a week for the past two years. I never try different brands, or spend a little extra for a bigger portion. The items I buy always have labels that look like they haven't been updated since the mid 90's, and red bursting stars on the packaging always urge me to compare whatever their product is to a product from a brand I actually recognize and trust. Almost all of the labels also contain the braggadocious statement, "20% More Free." I've been eating these discount brands since I began college and the percentage never changes- I'm always getting "20% More Free." I haven't finished my math credits, but if I'm forever getting "20% More Free" it begins to beg the question, what exactly am I getting 20% more *of* for free? Most meals I eat have the classifications of real food like "white meat," or "smoked turkey," but always also come with a prefix that makes me a little worried. Sometimes it's "mostly," most times it's "contains," and in that case, it's followed by another percentage, "Contains 66% Real Smoked Turkey."

Who am I to complain? 66% is passing at Kirtland.

Once I get *the money*, I'll be dining on 100% quality, every night. I won't care about what I'm getting for free, because I'll have the money to pay for the 20% more.

~

The second day of the semester is identical to the first day, except people have already reunited with their friends, and the hangovers are worse.

I still haven't seen Gerard, and it becomes my objective to make sure that he's still attending classes at Kirtland.

This past summer, Gerard was convinced that it was in everyone's best interest for him to drop out and start a band.

This past summer, Gerard was convinced that it was in everyone's best interest for him to drop out and become a music video director.

This past summer, I habitually reminded Gerard that everyone has a band now, and people are recording music videos in their backyard.

This past summer, I took Gerard's dreams and made them as distant as my own.

I stand in my room on this warm morning, and begin a process that will eventually, hopefully, lead to me arriving on campus with enough free time to hunt down Gerard before class.

Rule~ I must shower at the start of each day. This shower has to happen during the first twenty minutes of mobile living. The snooze button slapping moments consisting of lying in bed and pulling the sheets over my head don't begin the countdown- the clock starts when I finally bring myself to get up. Not that go-for-a-pee get up, but when I *get up*-get up. The shower must end with a clean shave. I can hide behind my hygiene.

I walk into the bathroom to look at the wrinkled white T-shirt and dark blue jeans I tiredly picked out last night. I back up about a foot and see if they look as bad from a distance as they do up close.

They do.

The only hope I have is that the steam from the shower will leave them somewhat presentable.

I lift the handle of the shower and turn it up and to the left. If the shower handle was a clock, it would be pointing to about 11 o'clock. High powered streams of water shoot from the shower head, and when I step into their path, my body jolts, then adjusts to the temperature. I run my fingers through my hair, hitting snarls that yank at my scalp. I remember that Joan used the last of my shampoo on Tuesday, and it's been a few days since I've washed my hair so I use a bar of soap, running it from my scalp to the golden brown split ends resting just above my shoulders. The bar soap seems to do the job, and my hair feels clean again.

I step out of the shower, and while reaching for a towel, I catch my reflection in the mirror on the medicine cabinet and see these odd looking blue gobs speckling the top of my head. I squeeze a clump of blue, then slowly pull it out of my hair. I smell it. It's refreshing. I know this smell.

My Takeaways:

One- The blue gobs are bar soap.

Two- The blue gobs are why shampoo is a liquid.

I duck my head down in the sink and wash my hair under the tap until the blue streaks are gone.

After I blow dry my hair on a low setting, I apply a supposedly organic hair product to create a base that shines, then add on a distinctly chemical product to prevent curling.

I stare in the mirror, and decide I can go another day without shaving. This is not a direct rule violation because, recently, I've noticed that when I have a five o'clock shadow, my heart shaped face appears to have more defined cheekbones. I no longer fear looking like a man; I practically demand it.

My phone vibrates on the toilet lid, and when I see Joan's name, I briefly consider knocking the phone into the toilet, just so I have an excuse for why I haven't been answering her texts. In the end, I'm too much of a slave to my digital compulsions, so I choose the greater evil and indulge Joan with a response. I tell myself that a real man doesn't avoid open communication, then I proceed to be emasculated by my girlfriend in a series of texts about my distance.

~

I walk in two minutes late on the first day of some sort of Great American Novel class that I registered for, if for no other reason, than to counteract the Brit-Lit class I'm taking. I wanted something to compare the British stuff to, and due to the common language, the American novel class seemed logical. Plus, one of the math classes I needed was already full, so I registered for the first class that would take me. The Great American novel class is in the same building as Brit-Lit, which is okay because it's hard to cheat in lit classes, so the row-style seating won't impact my grade.

The professor- a short haired woman in her early 40's who's dressed like an art teacher- passes out the syllabus. I instantly know that this woman will not be like my Brit-Lit professor. I don't have a second Takeaway regarding this class, so far.

We go over the syllabus, then the professor starts asking each one of us what we like to read. I zone out during everyone's answers until one of the Asians from the table that's being watched by the ad hoc NSA of commuters, says, "I read anything besides Transcendentalist or feminist tripe." Immediately, the Asian boy has my interest, and I become jealous that I don't have the prerequisites to sit at his table.

Not everyone is as taken with the Asian boy as I am. The girl in front of me makes slimy noises that have no vowels in response to his answer.

The professor has set her gaze on the snarking girl, and there's a three or four second silence, but most people aren't even paying attention, and it's the first day of this class, so I can only imagine how comatose these kids will be three weeks in.

Finally, the Asian boy asks, "Was that the wrong answer?" and I want to hug him.

"Well, no," the professor says. Her voice sounds like a young boy trying to imitate his father.

I quickly make the decision that when it's my turn to answer the reading question, I'll say, "Anime blogs," so that the Asian boy will invite me to his table. At worst- I become part of a transit terrorism conspiracy, and at best- I get to be friends with this guy, and I can write to Edie about him.

The Asian boy isn't finished, and he rants, "This is a class about books right? And this is an exercise where we go around the room and when everyone is asked what they like to read, they have to say that they either read *Catcher In The Rye,* or nostalgia lists like 'Thirty Hate Crimes Only 90's Kids Committed.' Is that what I should have said? I haven't read *Catcher in the Rye* since eighth grade, and I don't count looking at 40 pictures of subtitled *Gilmore Girls* screencaps as reading."

I'm really jazzed by this prolonged answer, and I don't know why we all aren't appointing this Asian boy as our young king.

The girl in front of me seems to be getting progressively angrier, until she blurts out, "*Catcher in the Rye* is a classic, by the way."

The Asian boy quips back, "Name any fiction title, besides something on a high school required reading list or a Behringer book."

The girl in front of me sits, staring straight ahead, running her hand back and forth on her neck.

Flustered, the professor finally says, "Enough," and I want to respond, "No. Never enough. This is how we will usurp British Literature."

The Great American Novel class is everything I hoped for and more.

Viva American novels.

~

While I'm walking to the café, I try to figure out why I was so excited by the Asian boy speaking out. Normally I view any outbursts in class as way too "goth kid." I would always cringe at the goths in high school who were so pessimistic about everything that they wouldn't even stand up for the pledge of allegiance. They'd go on little tirades about how bullshit it is that we're all saying, "One nation under God," when church and state are supposed to be separate. They never noticed the fact that no one gives a shit what the words to the pledge are, they just stand up and say them because they appreciate that it delays the start of first period math class.

I suppose what appeals to me about the Asian boy's rant is that he wasn't making a mockery of the teacher, or American novels, or the class- he was merely satisfying a request after being disappointed by the answer every one of his peers had provided in a domino collapse of bland, uninspired, required-reading recommendations.

I get to the café, and mercifully, I see an empty spot- a little two person table next to a weight bearing column. I do a semi-sprint to get to the table before some paranoid commuter can snatch it up and turn it into a surveillance outpost.

I sit at my own personal table, and sing to myself, under my breath;

> *"...the words don't translate*
> *you lose your tongue*
> *play your vocal cords*
> *and the melody's off..."*

A girl sits down across from me, and I immediately stop singing and straighten my posture. I recognize this girl, but she isn't wearing glasses so I'm able to eliminate the possibility that she's in my Brit-Lit class, and I'm positive that the Socio-Economic-Whateverthehell class doesn't have any girls in it, not good-looking girls at least. The girl sitting across from me is unquestionably good-looking. My inability to place her immediately mutates into an interest in her.

"Hi, sorry about just sitting down- I don't usually do that, but there are so many people here," she says, all in one breath. Her voice sounds like wind chimes.

"Yeah... it's a perfect place to blend in."

"Huh? Did you not want to be bothered? I'm so sorry," The girl says, hiking her purse up on her shoulder.

I reach across the table and briefly touch her hand, then say, "Don't worry about it- stay- we can blend together."

"Okay," she says, smiling, then points out, "Now that I'm occupying this chair, you don't have to worry about any of the other commuter weirdos sitting with you."

I spin the plastic pepper shaker that sits between us, as the familiar girl asks, "So, Asians really hate American novels, huh?"

The novel class I just got out of. That's where I've seen this girl.

"Oh, that was nothing. Don't worry about him. He's my friend. He's a good guy," I say, hoping to will this into a truth.

"What's his name?" the familiar girl asks, and suddenly I'm totally fucked.

"What?" I ask, with a scowl that will hopefully redirect the conversation.

"I asked... what's your name?" she amends her question, and when she sees the smile slide across my face, her posture relaxes.

"My name is Kurt," I say.

"My name is Brittany," she responds back.

"How do you spell it?"

"Two T's, no E's. Think stripper, not Spears," she says.

This makes me laugh, and my laugh makes Brittany laugh.

"Do you live on campus?" I ask, realizing that there might be a letter for Edie in this conversation.

"Nope," Brittany says, then her smile disappears as she reveals herself to be the very same person she claimed to be saving me from.

"That was a dumb question, I mean we're sitting in the café," I say, exposing myself as a commuter as well. "Last year I lived on campus, but now I have one of the apartments behind the baseball field."

Brittany looks around at the mess of undesirables, then asks, "Can we go there, to your place, until my next class? I don't really feel comfortable here. The people are weird, and I try not to eat three meals a day, but smelling all this food makes it really hard."

Brittany and I are not commuters by nature, and we can't let ourselves slip into their patterns, so I accept her plan, and ask, "What time is your next class?"

"Not for like two hours," Brittany says, looking down at her phone to confirm.

My next class is in an hour, but I say, "Mine's in two and a half, so we can go to my place, then walk back to campus together."

This trip is predicated on the fact that I lack enough material for a letter, but I'm positive that I'll receive something from Brittany that Edie will devour.

Brittany and I leave the café, and during the walk, I don't sing because I'm talking with my new friend. We discuss how Brittany wants to get a tattoo, but doesn't know what she should get, and I do my best to talk her out of it without sounding like a parent. I try to explain that a tattoo should be something that she gets because she can't live without having it permanently placed on her skin. A tattoo isn't something that should be decided on like it's a fast food meal- that's how girls end up with a seashell tattoo. I'm careful in the way I explain this to her because she saved me from sitting alone, and even though she might be a temporary friend, I'm glad I met her and that we learned each other's names.

After a silent elevator ride, and a short walk down the hall, we reach my apartment, and I feel that swirling fear that always follows a girl into my apartment when she visits for the first time.

I walk inside, and the moment I pass the light switch, I make sure to confirm it's still ON. It is.

Brittany puts her purse on the floor next to the fridge, then she looks around my living room- at the wall of DVDs on the left, at the wall of CDs on the far right, at the massive flat screen mounted on the wall next to the coat closet. She drifts past the movie library, then flops down on the black futon.

Her posture tells me that we aren't going to fuck and that doesn't bother me because I haven't gotten a letter out of Brittany yet. Usually, I notice every little detail about a girl, but with Brittany, I don't really notice anything. Are there details to notice? I wouldn't be surprised if there are frames waiting to be purchased in some Midwestern department store with pictures of Brittany in them. She seems a little airbrushed, but her makeup is conservative- lipstick, mascara, and a dusting of eyeshadow.

I ask Brittany if she wants a soda or a glass of wine, and she says, "Whatever you're having." I pop open what's left of the Merlot I was working on last night while getting "20% More Free," and I over-pour us two glasses, then join her on the futon.

Brittany takes her glass, sips the wine, then scrunches her nose.

I ask her if she wants to listen to music, or watch TV, and she says, "Either one, I'm pretty neutral."

Brittany *is* neutral. She doesn't ever object to what I suggest, what I do, what I say. I should ask for a blow job.

I don't ask for a blow job. Instead, I say, "I envy you."

"And why would that be?" Brittany asks, then takes a big gulp of wine.

"Because of how you answer my questions- letting someone else make the decisions, then not complaining about what they choose. I don't afford myself the luxury of being neutral. It must be the greatest thing in the world to just feel content, no matter what. It's okay if your burger has onions, it's okay if it has mayo. It's okay if you see the romantic comedy, it's okay if you see the war movie."

It's okay if she wants to fuck you, it's okay if he wants to fuck you.

Brittany nods her head, then confirms, "I do it because being neutral eliminates the need to expend energy on choosing. No matter who or what I end up with, I'm satisfied. I have zero expectations for you, which means you can't fail. I think you probably sensed this, and that's why we aren't sitting in the café right now."

While I'm grouping, classifying, critiquing, excluding, begging, and refusing based on preference, the neutral Brittany is relaxing. The neutral Brittany probably reads more books, sees more movies, and makes more love. She has all this time to take things in, while I'm using all this time to rule things out.

"Aren't you ever disappointed with your decisions, though? You want to be neutral so you accept the red wine, but then you get a glass that's too bitter."

She takes a sip from her glass, then says, "I don't think it's bitter, but to answer your question, I just feel like if you don't put all that work into making the decision, you don't have such high expectations about the outcome. You enjoy whatever you get."

As I continue to speak with Brittany, searching for my letter, she agrees, she laughs, she doesn't ask for anything, she doesn't glance at the clock to see what time it is. Her phone beeps and she doesn't even check it.

Brittany tells me a bunch of stories, and I'm listening intently because I want to figure out why she's a commuter.

She's not gay- she talked about her ex, Brian. She's not a daddy's girl- she said she always fights with her parents over her outfits. She's not poor- judging from her black Saint Laurent boots with the cutout heel/ The black tights/ The off trend (possibly pre-trend) jean skirt/ The boat neck creme colored T-shirt with the giant red heart on it.

Her biggest defect seems to be that she's agreeable to a fault.

The third time Brittany's cell beeps, I pretend like I think it's mine, and I check the time. It's 12:58 pm, and my first Business Management class starts in two minutes. My absence shouldn't carry any repercussions because business classes always have a long syllabus, so I'm essentially saving myself from a 20 minute grading rubric conversation.

Why am I even signed up for a Business Management class? I'm not capable of managing a business; I can't even manage my fucking life.

The other essential question- the whole, *Why is Brittany a commuter?* thing- is killing me, so I wait for a lull in the conversation, then straight out ask her.

"It's cheaper to live at home so I decided to make the sacrifice. I'm saving money so I can record my demo," she reveals, nodding her head kind of like how a chicken moves its head when it walks.

"What type of music do you want to make? Can't you just buy a laptop and get to work?" I ask, not understanding why she doesn't use the tools that now reside in everyone's lap.

"I wanna be, like, a teen idol," Brittany admits.

I realize that, most likely, she didn't make up the "stripper, not Spears" joke herself- she probably read it in the comments on a picture or song she posted online.

"What type of music do you sing?" I ask.

"Bubblegum pop," she responds, then smiles shamelessly.

It's rare that bubblegum pop is someone's artistic inspiration. Bubblegum pop is more of a product than an art. It takes at least fifty different people to make a successful bubblegum pop record. Brittany knows this, and this is why she has to save up for a demo. The artist who records on a laptop is truly independent in their music. A small number of people will recognize this genuine reflection, and they'll feel it mirrors the complicated emotions that they are bursting with. Laptop artists create the sound that they hear in their heart- it's a direct uplink. This is a very different creative process than the way the pop star works. The bubblegum pop teen idol needs people around her. A lot of people. She needs people to write the song, and people to produce the song, and people to engineer the song, and people to remix the song, and people to vet the song, and people to book the appearances to promote the song. This costs money, so the neutral Brittany saves up to pay a bunch of people to fight about who she should be.

The problem with Brittany's plan is, if the committee creates an identity for her, but people don't connect with that identity, she has to either form a new committee, or she has to open that laptop and face who she really is and how she really feels.

six.

Someone bursts out from behind a carefully trimmed shrub, and yells, "Hey, don't walk away from me!"

The possibility that I'm about to be violently assaulted is preferable to the other potential reality- that Joan has finally located me.

I turn around, and face the aggressor... my girlfriend. I so very desperately wanted her to be a threatening looking man with a weapon pointed at me. Briefly, I consider giving Joan my wallet in hopes it will prevent the inevitable assault on my day that's about to occur.

"Hey, fuck. Remember me? Your girlfriend?" Joan says, getting very close to me. She was probably hiding in that bush all day, smoking cigarettes, waiting for me to walk by.

"I'm sorry, Joan. I've been busy with classes," I say, then start walking faster.

"It's okay, Kurt. I know that you're just sitting in your apartment, jacking off because you live alone now and don't have to worry about your roommate walking in on you."

"You act like I have to live alone to jack off. Your room is always packed and I still find a way to do it," I say, as Joan hands me her half-smoked cigarette.

"Yeah, by the way, Lena uses that little towel on her face, just so you know."

I wince at this information, then admit, "I didn't know it was a face towel. I wouldn't have used it if I had known."

"You're lucky that her face stuff has an odd consistency," Joan says, then we both shiver.

"Where are you off to?" I ask, determined to get her there as fast as possible.

"I'm following you," she says, and I feel my posture sink.

"In that case, you're off to British Literature."

"Fucking Brits, how do they get their own class?"

"Hey, lay off Brit-Lit," I warn.

"Whatever, Kurt. Are you an English major now, or something?" Joan hisses, like this is an insult.

"No, I'm still a business major. Remind me again what your major is?" I snark back.

"My major is watching you, and I'm going to be studying hard this semester," she threatens me, and I begin to wonder if someone told her that they saw me leaving my apartment with neutral Brittany.

We make it to the Brit-Lit classroom, and I immediately realize that I don't have class here until later in the day. Before I can slide inside the room and sit there alone for ten minutes, Joan notices that there's no one in the room, then she stares at me, and says, "It's a miracle you find your way home at night."

I check the schedule on my phone, then show Joan the screen to prove I do actually have a class right now. She accepts this information, then kisses me on the cheek, and tells me, "You're hanging out with me tonight. Think of something that will entertain me."

I anxiously make my way to Eco-International-Sociopath required class, grateful for its existence for the first, and what I presume to be the last time.

From my elevated seat in the classroom, I copy down about a half a page of notes, while thinking about having sex with neutral Brittany. The fantasy ends after I imagine asking her, "Did you enjoy it?" then receiving the response, "Sure, if you did."

Between classes, I sit on a bench at the center of the Green and search for Gerard's lanky frame.

As his predictable absence continues, I get bored with trying to locate him, so I send him a text mentioning that I'm out on the Green.

To remain visible, but busy, I do the reading for Brit-Lit. The story doesn't seem very British- in fact, it seems a little American, but I chalk this up to the old professor wanting to ease us into Brit-Lit. He doesn't want to start a war with the American Novels class. The Americans always top the Brits.

The much anticipated Brit-lit class lives up to my preemptive excitement from the moment I arrive, then strikes the greatest in-class moment of my tenure at Kirtland, when the professor admits, "I really am an old bastard, and before one of you points out my mistake, I'll come clean. The story I assigned isn't British at all. I misread the name of *The New England Magazine*, where the story was originally published, and I said to myself, 'What the hey, let's throw something new on here so I don't fall asleep during the first week.' Well, when I was going over the story last night, giving myself a refresher, I discovered that I am not very good at my job. This is a discovery that I have been habitually making for decades, and I'm still here, and you're still here, and we all read this story, so let's just make our first Takeaway of the day to be that I can't be trusted, then let's go over the short story that we were supposed to read last night about some chick who's locked in the house because she's a big whore, or so we're led to believe."

At least two girls sigh at this, as the old professor's apology becomes a new offense.

The old professor doesn't go back on his assessment, and he can't remember the main character's name, which further complicates matters. To move the discussion along, he just refers to her as the "Skank Wife."

"So, he locks his Skank Wife up," the old professor explains. "He assumes that his Skank Wife is a skank, but what he doesn't realize is that she's nutso, too," he tells us. "So, the lonely Skank Wife sits and ponders how she'll find a way to get out of the house. After all, it's hard to be a skank from a twenty foot window," he booms across the room.

This casual and blunt recapping continues for a while.

When one of the many girls in black framed glasses provides a Takeaway and uses the character's real name, the old professor asks, "Who?"

The girl says, "Um..." and her voice sounds like brakes on a school bus. She thinks that the old professor can't hear her so she says the character's name again, only this time she's almost yelling, and the professor shouts, "Who?" back at her, mocking the fact she raised her voice. Quietly, the girl says, "The Skank Wife."

I leave the class fulfilled.

My Takeaways:

One- Sometimes, when you have a skank wife, the best move is to leave her- don't lock her up physically like she's locked you up mentally. Leave, depart, exit. You aren't ruled by that queen like the British, you're an American, you're free.

Two- If you make a mistake, if you're totally off base, and you've passed the point of no return, keep going. Start gnashing your teeth and elbowing skeptics, because eventually you'll reach the other side, and you might be a little battered, but you'll survive.

As I make my way toward the café for dinner, I see Gerard across the Green. His gangly frame is taking wide steps forward, and his sliced up black Levis barely remain stitched together in the chaos. His brown hair is pointing in five different directions, and when he's ten feet away from me, he zigzags his fingers across his scalp as though he's fixing his hair, but even after this styling attempt, he looks like a man who was roused by a fire alarm only moments ago.

"I owe you ten dollars," is the first thing I say to Gerard. I'm palming the bill in my hand. It's been sitting in my wallet since the day after I borrowed the cash from him when we were drinking at The Brink, in town. Gerard didn't remind me about the money, so I kept forgetting to give it to him, but I knew that there was a possibility he was just being polite by not mentioning it, and I imagined him going home at night and dwelling on the fact that I've embezzled cash from him, all the while knowing that, at any moment, I could become a rich man.

Gerard smiles, then says, "Oh. Right. Cuz, um, for, the time, I lent, money, to you." He seems very lost. It turns out, he just forgot.

"Yes, *that* time," I say, then hand him the cash. He seems happy and almost surprised that this moment occurred.

"Alright, cool man. Ten bucks," Gerard says, rubbing the sides of the folded bill together.

I'm about to find my way out of this conversation because I'm afraid he expects me to ask him about classes or worse, he's going to ask me what I'm taking this semester, but before I can make an exit, Gerard says, "I have ten bucks, and I borrowed Ben's car. Do you want to go buy a bottle of vodka?"

I do want vodka, so we immediately leave the Green and walk to the parking garage.

Ben's car has parking passes all over the dash around a statue of Jesus that bounces on a spring, and the interior smells like weed and an electrical problem.

On the ride to the liquor store, Gerard talks to the car, encouraging it to remain in a single piece for the duration of the trip.

The bottle of vodka we end up buying isn't that big and it's a brand I've never heard of, but it's not in a plastic bottle and Gerard is paying for it, so I don't complain. To judge the vodka's quality, I check the label to see if it mentions that we're getting "20% more free."

~

I sit down on a sofa covered in a throw blanket that features a knit picture of a shirtless Jim Morrison, and I sip some vodka mixed in a glass of OJ that I got from whoever inhabits the apartment we're in.

Looking across the room, I see a girl that I had a class with freshman year. She always wears her hair up, but still lets her curls hang down on the side of her head, sort of like those girls on the covers of Jane Austen novels.

The girl catches me staring at her neck, and she seems to recognize me.

I make it clear that I have no intention of approaching her, so she walks over to me, then says, "I know you." Her voice sounds like the lady who used to call people to the main office in school over the intercom system.

"I know you, too," I say.

"But from where?" she asks.

"Your bushes. It's probably hard to recognize me in this direct lighting, plus I don't have my binoculars with me," I say flatly.

The Jane Austen girl laughs. She looks at her cup, then flips to page eight of the small-college-party conversation handbook, and asks, "So, what's your major?"

"Mine? My major?" I let out one of those laughs that aren't really a laugh.

"Yeah."

"It's..."

"Oh, you must be undecided."

"No, no I'm very decided."

"On what?"

I look her in the eyes, pause, smile, then say, "On wasting time here until I get rich."

"What do you want to be when you grow up, though? What's the point of being here if you aren't moving toward something?" she asks, still standing.

"I feel like as long as I'm moving, I'm moving toward something," I say, still sitting.

"You need to pick a field to go into. I don't know how you expect to be rich if you don't have a job."

"Someday a big sack of money is going to fall into my lap. I just have to wait until that happens."

"Righttt. Okayyy. I mean..." the Jane Austen girl sighs. She looks over at a black girl who's making two boys laugh, then she looks back at me and says, "Fine. What do you want to do with your life?"

"Nothing," I say.

"It's sad when your desire to do nothing is stronger than your desire to do *something*," the Jane Austen girl says.

"I want nothing more than I've ever wanted anything in my life," I admit.

"Now I know how my parents feel when they talk to me," the Jane Austen girl mumbles, then waits for me to ask about her major. When I don't, she says, "I don't believe you. Where's this magical money coming from?" as her curiosity outweighs her better judgment.

"My father," I say, then I take a sip of my drink and look up coyly. The rest of the conversation is pretty mapped out. I'll make her feel bad soon.

She says, as they always do, "Oh, he's one of *those* type of dads? He won't let you spend his money until you finish college because he's terrified of telling his other businessman friends that his son didn't go anywhere after high school?"

"No, actually he died young and left a bunch of money," I say, and the Jane Austen girl instantly wears a mask of horror and embarrassment on her face. I've gotten used to staring into this mask.

"I'm so sorry," she tells me- as though she was cheering him on when he did it- like she had a part in him taking the dive. She continues on the subject of her need for forgiveness, awkwardly dancing around the question she really wants to ask. Eventually, her patience wears thin and she blurts out, as they always do, "If you don't mind me asking, how'd he die?"

I lean to one side on Jim Morrison, and I take out my wallet. I open it, and remove a small well-worn piece of paper with a poem on it, then hand it to her. I didn't always have this poem. Things evolved. The first few times people asked the ugly question, I told them everything. Times twelve through forty, I summarized. Around the fiftieth time, I wrote the poem.

The Jane Austen girl stares at the paper, as I read along in my head;

What Happened
They all said my father was a strange bird
One day he tried to fly the coop
But his heart was hollow
Not his bones

They scraped him off the concrete like bird shit

The Jane Austen girl hands me back the piece of paper, then looks at me with concern.

After downing my cup of OJ and vodka, I look to Gerard, who's singing into an empty bottle on the other side of the apartment. Normally this wouldn't strike me as odd, but in this case, there's no music on.

I excuse myself from the broken conversation with the Jane Austen girl, then wander over close enough to hear what Gerard is singing. It's a big epic number about being out of vodka and needing more, but he's already spent his ten bucks. What the song lacks in structure, it makes up for in lyrics.

> *"Let's refuel my vodka powered spaceship*
> *And take it to the moon*
> *We'll have a case of vodka in the trunk*
> *And some green olives in the ashtray*
> *We'll make life on other planets*
> *But everyone will have fetal alcohol syndrome."*

Maybe this is the start of Gerard's new band. The fact that he was listening to me over the summer is both a comfort and a concern.

~

The register boy with the huge forehead never makes eye contact with me when I buy a cup of coffee from him in the morning. It's like he's ashamed to be charging for the black water, and the look in his averted eyes warns, "I hope you need this caffeine, *bad*."

Some days the coffee is very watery, and looks like tea. The next day, I'll fill up my cup, take a sip, and the coffee will be bitter.

As I pass the kid with the huge forehead, I ask, "How's the coffee today?" and he looks up at me. When our eyes meet, his forehead appears even bigger viewed straight on. He mumbles, "It's like, the same, as usual, you know, it's alright, worth the dollar seventy-five."

I walk over to the machine, and stand under the "Freshly Brewed" sign that was made with so much more attention than the coffee it's advertising. I take my cup out of my bag, then place it on the tray at the base of the machine. I always bring my own coffee cup because when I sit down in class I want to look like the host of a late night talk show. Sometimes, I'll designate the quirkiest kid in the room to be my bandleader. He's almost always oblivious to the job he's won.

With low expectations, and a heightened chemical need, I pull down the little black lever, then inhale the aroma of the brown water as it spits out of the machine's spout.

I don't wait for the coffee to cool before I take a sip. Today, the coffee is bitter.

Mug in hand, I walk over to the register, then ask, with a genuine look of concern on my face, "What's with the coffee fluctuations here?"

"Listen, man... they pay me seven bucks-" he starts out tiredly.

"-oh, this isn't a personal attack. It's more of a curiosity," I say, in an attempt to repair my unspoken friendship with the guy responsible for my profoundly necessary caffeine fix.

The boy swings his massive forehead from side to side, looking back and forth, then he makes a decision to tell me a secret. "Yeah, well, okay-" He leans in close to me, "We leave that thing on all day long. The guys who work at the water company come over here and fill up their thermoses in the morning when the coffee is freshly brewed, hence the sign above the coffee machine, but then later in the day, like when you come in, the coffee has been sitting there for a while, and instead of throwing out a perfectly good half gallon of coffee, I realized it's just the water that's evaporating out of the machine, because it's on the heat all morning, so I use that jug of water next to the coffee machine to balance out the brew. Some days you come a little early, and I haven't gotten time away from the register to fix it yet."

I hand the huge foreheaded coffee chemist my ID, and he swipes it.

As I'm leaving, I give him a pointer, "Use less water," and the register boy nods his huge forehead to show that he'll consider it.

I walk across campus with my coffee, and I'm careful not to spill it, even when I have to stop and lightly hug girls that I haven't seen since last May. I'm feeling confident going to my talk show, the Great American Novel class. My ideal bandleader, the Asian boy, better be ready to replicate the same passion for chaos that he embraced during the first class.

By the time I reach my desk, I'm down to half a cup of coffee, and the professor immediately takes charge by distributing a handout.

I stare down at a reading list that contains so many books, by so many different authors, mostly ones I've never heard of before. All these movies waiting to be optioned.

Someone asks what order the list is in. They want to know if the best books are at the top. The professor says that we'll just have to read and find out. The few books that I do recognize are last on the list, so it's obvious this list is in chronological order. Obvious to me; I wonder if the professor knows. I wonder if any of these authors are British.

~

Joan is sitting alone in a booth in the café, and she's wearing a hoodie. When I see her, I think, *Try harder*, but I don't say it.

"We need to go see *The Blessed Nothing*, like, today, Kurt," Joan tells me, as I sit down across from her.

The Blessed Nothing is on my reading list.

"Did you just roll your eyes? We're going, tonight, to the 6 PM showing, the first showing. You don't have a choice," Joan instructs me, anticipating my moves before they arrive.

Since I've already been accused of disinterest, I ride with the notion that I don't want to see the movie, and say, "I want to see something I'll actually enjoy if I'm paying for tickets."

"I never like the movies you pick. They have no structure; they're just, like, one long act. All your favorite directors seem unable to grasp the concept that they need to provide the audience with constant action or we'll lose interest."

I can't argue her point because her point is popular opinion

"Okay, order the tickets on your phone," I tell her, sliding my credit card across the table.

Once the tickets are purchased, I fully accept my fate. I eat some chicken fingers off Joan's plate/ I skip Business Management/ I sit in the window of Joan's dorm and smoke a pack of Pall Malls/ I masturbate with Lena's face towel in the bathroom/ I eat vending machine chips/ I take a piss, and hear the face towel calling my name for a second time, but Joan yells my name louder so she wins.

"Hurry, Kurt!" Joan mewls through the bathroom door.

I throw the door open, then shrug at Joan, whose expression is, as expected, a tight-lipped scowl of anger.

When she sees that I'm not more apologetic, she says, "Come on. Move your ass. We don't have time for your smoking and lolling."

People rush to a movie because they don't want it to be sold out. Even with all the screens and all the seats for each showing, they're still paranoid that the good seats will be gone when they get there. There's this mentality that Joan has- *We have to see this movie. We have to see this movie at the 6 PM showing, before the people on dates arrive. We have to be in the middle of the line in the theater so that we're standing long enough that the people in back see us ahead of them, but we need to be close enough to the ticket taker that we get a good seat when they let us in the theater. The line has to be held for at least five minutes so we can get a picture of us waiting, then we can agree on what to caption it with, whether it be an overly excited comment or a non sequitur that will make people question if they're reading an inside joke.*

All of this is part of the experience that keeps us returning to the cinema instead of just downloading a bad quality leak. All of this is Joan's ritual and I cannot deviate from it, like it was one of my rules.

After we see a movie, Joan will ask people the next day what they thought of the film, and when they tell her that they didn't get there in time for the early showing, she'll gloat and coo about how magical it is seeing a movie on opening night. She'll say that a movie never has the same impact as it does when it unfolds for that first Friday night audience. Usually, her speech goes something like, "It's an enthralling experience to be present when an artist unveils his work to the world." She'll say stuff like that regardless of the movie's quality.

"Every movie has this built up inertia. The first time the audience sees it, that energy explodes out into the crowd," Joan once told me, and I agreed with her. Verbally, not mentally. I never mention the midnight Thursday showings to her because it would only make the situation more of a burden.

After a ten minute drive, we arrive early at the Waldorf, the only theater that's screening *The Blessed Nothing* within thirty miles. I avoid going to the Waldorf at all costs because it's in a suburb that seems to consist of only real-estate offices and restaurants. The cinema is awkwardly squeezed into the middle of this town that, in twenty years, will be paved with the tombstones of its current residents. Soon, the population here will be a blessed nothing.

As we walk into the cinema, Joan says, "When your mother dies, I hope we move to a town like this."

We could, I wouldn't.

"Do you have the tickets?" I ask, suddenly fearing that I didn't print them out, and I'll be reprimanded for not presuming that this was my responsibility.

Joan reaches into her purse, then takes out two folded pieces of computer paper, and hands them to me. I read the details in the uneven ink, and find that not only am I being subjected to seeing "The Blessed Nothing," but I also have to watch it on screen three.

Everyone who's been to the Waldorf knows about screen three, but very few care about it as much as I do. The restaurant next to the Waldorf wraps around the left side of the theater, and screen three is right next to the restaurant, so it had to be placed at a slight angle because of the way the restaurant expands out in the back. Instead of watching the film projected on a flat wall like it does at every other theater, it projects onto a slanted wall. The left side of the screen is probably two feet closer to the seats than the right. The farther away you sit, the more obvious it becomes.

I never bring up this imperfection to Joan, because she'll agree with me about it, then I'll have to deal with the fact that I agree with Joan, which means that I must be out of touch and overly sensitive to microaggressions.

We stand in the line. We take a picture, then Joan posts it with the caption, "Date Night!" which is so bland that people will "Like" it as some sort of digital penny thrown in a relationship-based wishing well. I have to wonder if she's posting this so she'll receive enough online support in her enthusiasm pledge drive to keep our bond from completely dissolving.

Once everyone gets their pictures, the ticket taker checks my printout, then Joan and I walk silently to screen three.

Entering the semi-darkness, Joan walks about a quarter of the way down the aisle, then arbitrarily picks a place to sit. We arrive in time to catch the commercials that play before the movie. Everyone watches intently. They've paid their hard earned money to see these commercials so they aren't going to look away, not even for a moment. The delivery system is so big and loud that they could project anything onto that screen and command our attention.

All through the commercials and the trailers, I stare at the screen- the flicker of film absent because of the digital display- the excitement of the cinema only existing in nostalgia.

If nothing else, I appreciate the moment for its calm, even as the sound blasts in deafening rumbles. Joan sits silently, her usual commentary track of bewildered complaints mysteriously absent. I check twice to see if she's asleep- she isn't.

After the first twenty minutes of the film, I have to look away because of the distortion created by the slanted wall. With nowhere else to focus, I admire Joan, first out of the corner of my eye, then later I reposition myself fully, and I watch as she intently stares at the screen, while the light plays off her face.

Joan is beautiful. Her eyes follow the actors, while her thin lips stay buttoned and cover her perfect teeth. For the first time in a long time, I'm reminded of how stunning she is.

Seeing Joan at peace is worth the $24 I paid to see this terrible movie.

~

I stare across the tiny square table in Noni's kitchen, and I accept her ridicule. "You went to the Waldorf last night!" Noni half states and half laughs.

"For portions of the time that I was there, I was treated as an actual human being, not just a mobile nuisance," I say, trying to make it sound like a vaguely positive night out.

"I couldn't do it. Every time I accidentally end up seeing a movie at the Waldorf, I get the feeling that my existence is being viewed as a challenge to the residents there- like there's a very real chance that I'll be arrested for having no cellulite and an open mind about immigration."

"I get where you're coming from," I admit, "I was afraid Joan's car would be towed because it's last year's model."

Noni giggles at me, then checks the time on her phone and sighs.

I get up from the table, moving slowly, reluctantly, toward the inevitable return to campus.

"Wait, I have your Rolling Stone," Noni says, then scampers toward the bathroom.

While I wait for Noni to return, I wander aimlessly through her apartment, and begin looking through the junk sitting on the shelves. I pick up an older looking book with a white cover, then leaf through the pages.

Noni pops back out with the *Rolling Stone* cradled in her right arm, and asks, "Ditching me to go see your wonderful girlfriend again tonight?"

I read a sentence from the old book, "And waillynge al the nyght, makynge his mone."

Noni continues, "Why are you still with her anyway? You're not fooling anyone. You hate her guts. You hate Joan more than Joan hates everything she's presented with."

It takes me a second to respond because I want to figure out what the sentence in the book means, but eventually, I say, "Joan is beautiful. I like her just fine."

"No, no you don't. Your relationship with her, it's... illogical. Why don't you find someone that you love as much as they love you?"

I'm still looking in the book, but I manage to say, "I never liked this Middle English shit; it's like reading a speech impediment."

Noni laughs. She's laughing a little bit at my statement, but mostly at my dodging. "Ya know, Kurt, sometimes I'm convinced the blood in your veins runs backward."

I put the book back on the shelf, and ask, "You don't really read this shit do you?"

"No. Well, I read it, but it's for a class, so I don't *read it*, read it."

I take the *Rolling Stone* from Noni, then leave with none of the flourish she departed with when she first borrowed it from me.

Before I shut the door, I hear Noni say, "You never answered my question."

~

Joan gets out of bed, then starts searching for her pants in the covers.

I grab my laptop, pleasure rushing over me because I'll be alone in mere moments. I plan on throwing this day away, watching clips of old TV shows on YouTube and refreshing various social network feeds populated with people I admire, but I'll never meet, and people I've met, but don't care about.

Pausing her search, Joan puts her hand on her hip then cocks her head in the opposite way, pissed that I'm not walking her to class.

Since I'm being punished for taking out my laptop, I focus on the screen, clicking random vaguely interesting looking links until Joan whines, "I don't want to go to this class. It's so boring."

"Then don't go," I suggest, sabotaging both myself and Joan in a single sentence.

"It's Calc, I have to."

Joan has the same professor I had for Calc last year. Since there's so much material, the professor obsesses about attendance. This is the one Kirtland class that no one should ever skip.

"Skip it," I say.

"Ugh, I wish I could."

"You can, no one's stopping you."

"Professor Perry is. She'll totally freak if I don't show."

I nonchalantly say, "I'm sure she'll never notice."

Joan gives up on the search for her pants, telling me, "Well, I haven't missed a class yet so I'm sure it will be fine. I mean, fuck, I'm 20 years old, these are my best years. I shouldn't be wasting my precious time learning about numbers."

"Sure," is all I can offer.

"Plus now we can spend the whole day together! What do you want to do?"

Having to spend the day with Joan is a small price to pay for the repercussions she'll suffer by missing this class. She's going to be completely lost since the class builds on itself, and she'll be forever banished to Perry's shit list. Joan won't pull better than a 2.0 in Calc now. I had to cheat pretty hard for a 3.0 and I never missed a class. Physically, I never missed a class.

"I found this site that has VHS rips of all these old *Unsolved Mysteries* episodes," I say, typing in the URL.

"No. No way. No. One- those are creepy, and two- they're full of 90's fashion," Joan says, over the audio of the episode that begins streaming.

Without looking away from the laptop, I'm immediately glued to the dramatic reenactment playing out in front of me.

Where the fuck did the baby go? is the theme of the reenactment, and they look for the baby like a pair of misplaced car keys.

Joan falls onto the bed, not wanting to go to class, not wanting to watch the show I'm using to get her to leave.

"So, you're skipping?" I ask.

Joan nods at me, then she slides up on the bed so she can see the laptop screen.

This moment is the answer to Noni's question; this is why I don't find someone who makes me sick with love. With Joan, I'm pushing the limits of my influence. I'm seeing where the edge is, then I'm looking down from the precipice. I'm testing how much of an effect I can have on someone else's life, then I watch what happens when they follow my lead. Can you back someone to the edge of a cliff without them noticing?

I met Joan at Kirtland- my amusement park. Amusement parks are filled with games. I play a game with Joan in which I convince her to modify her life. Not ruin, but certainly rip, tear, dirty, chip, fracture, crack, scratch, or small scale fuck up things. To put it in a more positive light, I subscribe to the school of 'that which doesn't kill you makes you stronger.'

Joan may very well be our generation's Joan of Arc. Sometimes it feels like it's my job to figure out if she is or not. I'm invested and interested in

my influence, and the outcome- no matter how it ends up- will thrill me.
Even if Joan's life becomes a big, beautiful disaster, I'll be catching the acid
rain on my tongue and dancing in the gasoline puddles.

Proving her strength, Joan represses her very powerful need to bitch
about me being lazy, and she watches the *Unsolved Mysteries* marathon I
curate. I allow this to happen and it doesn't ruin my day because, when
Joan is peering into another world, I can watch her like a movie on a
perfectly flat screen.

Video after video feeds us events that, if occurring now, would be solved
thanks to the constantly connected, geotagged world we're existing in. I
find myself feeling angry that these people from the past were able to just
disappear. The invisibility cloak they sought out and put on- or were
wrapped up in against their will- feels so foreign, yet so desirable to me.
Being able to disappear without a trace is a dream and a nightmare of
mine. The fact remains, there are people who have answers to the
questions that are posed in these grainy episodes. There are people taking
secrets about graves to the grave.

Conspiracy and concealment. Escape and abandonment.

I close my laptop when I realize it's getting dark outside.

After hours of dramatized tragedy soaked in gritty voice overs, it's not
easy to walk home alone, so I escort Joan back to her dorm, even though
it's only dusk and there are no real threats of any mysteries occurring. At
this hour, in this neighborhood, any mystery that Joan would encounter
could be easily solved.

Once we're back on campus, Joan tells me, "Thank you for walking me
home. I didn't want to get in a situation where they'd find my bones in a
concrete block ten years from now."

I'm not totally sure how to respond to this, but thankfully Joan isn't
making me stay with her in her dorm, so I just kiss her, then leave.

On the walk back to my apartment, I experience a feeling that's
dangerously close to missing Joan. The interference of her complaining is a
steady static that prevents me from having the thoughts that are currently
invading my being. After a day shrouded in mystery, I can't help but think
about my mother.

I'm blasted back by the memory of when she disappeared- then
returned, bruised and fragile. I don't really remember the year, but I recall
what went on, and how I felt. She had taken me to my grandparents, then
she left without telling me where she was going or when she would be back.
I had a suitcase, so this wasn't a visit with my grandparents, it was a

vacation with them. As a full day passed by without mention of where my mother was, I realized that something was happening behind my back.

When my mother returned, she did so in bandages.

At first, because of the bruises, I thought she had been in a car accident, but when I looked closer, I noticed that, under the hurt, there was healing.

When she got better, she healed into a different person. This wasn't as jarring as it sounds. It was more like the effect of someone waxing their eyebrows. They still look like the same person, just... fresher. After my mother healed, she looked younger, and she smiled more.

Maybe she knew back then that she was sick, maybe she left me with my grandparents as a trial escape to see if I'd be alright. Even as a kid, I understood that she didn't want me to see her at her ugliest, but surely at some point she had to check and make sure I was still okay.

Why hasn't she checked to see if I'm okay?

The next time she sees me, it will be like I had a reverse facelift. My skin- a little less tight, my forehead- a little more creased.

My personality will also be different.

I've become colder.

~

I sit down at an open computer in the lab. I'm surrounded by people who are desperately printing out essays that they'll have to slide under a professor's door tonight because the digital submission window is now closed.

I log into my profile on the computer, then I google the lyrics from ~the song~ to see if I can find out who sings it, what its name is, if it exists to anyone else outside of my family. I do this at one of the lab computers because I've googled the lyrics so many times on my phone and laptop that I can't trust the results I'm being given. The browser has learned my habits, and adapted. I need a fresh start for this unsolved mystery about who sings ~the song~ and precisely what the lyrics are. This has been a ritual for years, and the internet has expanded at exponential rates, but never with the information that I need from it.

Starting at the beginning, I search one sentence at a time.

"you laugh a subtle laugh,"– no relevant matches.

"and your face opens the door,"– no relevant matches.

"then the ceiling slowly slides,"– no relevant matches.

"now your ear cups the floor,"– I don't even hit enter.

The futility of my mission once again feels insulting. I have access to an incredibly powerful tool that in no way opens the locked music box that I'm forced to drag everywhere with me. I give up again, and a string of aborted attempts becomes the chains that clatter when I type.

As I'm waiting for the lab computer to finish signing out of my account, I glance at the screen next to me, and real life presents me with a search result. Life begins to feel like Google, but with fewer pictures of people fucking.

On the screen is one of my search terms, "*now your ear cups the floor.*"

I sink my teeth into my bottom lip, then look around to see if anyone is headed back to this computer. When no one returns to the computer, I change seats.

On the screen is a website: 4353638332936382.com

It's a single page of prehistorically basic HTML. There are no colors on the site besides the white background and the black lettering. None of the words are capitalized and every sentence ends with a period whether appropriate or not.

The first entry on the site reads:

"*now your ear cups the floor.*

i'm not happy. in fact, i might be depressed. they that say a clear sign of depression is that a person will lose interest in the things they once loved. last week, i cleaned my room. now i have a desk, a bed, a mattress, a sheet set, two pillows, a standing light, a dozen polaroids on my wall, a pair of scissors, six blue pens, one black pen, a pencil, a sketchpad, a photo album, six notebooks, seven juice boxes, two boxes of cassette tapes, a stereo, twenty packages of ramen, a laptop, my clothes, a cup, a bowl, a basket filled with toiletries, and a pair of sunglasses. everything else was thrown out. roommate's things are already gone. i don't feel better, but i do feel different. i'm torn between the compulsion to rebuild and the compulsion to leave. i could re-buy the things i loved- my favorite albums, my favorite films, my favorite novels- effectively creating the perfect collection, free from impulse buys, bad suggestions, and crappy gifts. or i could disappear. i have almost nothing left pinning me down, yet i'm still down.

i hope you understand."

Imagine reading a transcript of your thoughts.
Imagine looking in the mirror.
Imagine running.

Imagine chasing.
I have to read more, and I do;

"ten facts about me.
~one~ i'm the only one out of all of my friends whose parents aren't
divorced.

~two~ when i see people writing about how a celebrity death affected
them, all I can see is their misplaced pleasure regarding the event.

~three~ sometimes at night when i come home late and the boy i like
that week didn't talk to me, i lock the doors to the bathroom in my suite
and quietly cry, while i tear out my blonde hair until a pile of the
brittle dyed straw sits on the floor in a ball.

~four~ i think too much so i don't sleep a whole lot, but i spend so
much time in my bed.

~five~ i didn't get drunk until my freshman year of college.

~six~ i'm the most jealous person on the planet. if i see an interesting
looking boy for the first time at the train station or on the way to class,
i'll be jealous if another girl approaches him or if he flirts with
someone. when he does this, i'll feel like he's cheating on me even
though we've never met.

~seven~ i love the snow. i relate to it. for three to five months of the
year, snow shows up and says, 'if you can't handle this shit- move,
because i'll be back next year, so take note of everything you hate
about me now, then be prepared for the ugliest deja vu.'

~eight~ when i was younger i used to wake up screaming from a
single night terror that re-appeared on and off in my childhood. even
now when i think about it, i still get chills. in the nightmare, there was
soft music playing, and something slowly falling- like a feather or a
snowflake. all of the sudden, the music would spike and the feather-like
object would be crushed violently by a tree ripping up from its roots.
the sound of the crashing tree was like bones being broken.

~nine~ if i could find one dependable person to genuinely listen when i
speak, i'd stop updating this site.

~ten~ i feel like there are only six interesting facts about myself.

i hope you understand."

I stop reading. I lean back in the computer chair.

I think about how I'm the only one of my friends whose parents didn't get divorced. They didn't get the chance to call it off.

I think about standing at my father's funeral and studying the look in people's eyes, behind the sheen of tears.

I think about the time I've spent on the cold tile floor in the bathroom in my apartment.

I think about how much I've wanted to install blinds to squelch every ray of sunlight.

I think about how the alcohol has turned off the record button in my mind so many times.

I think about my between bus stop crushes.

I think about how last winter seems both far and close.

I think about first seeing the cover of *Nightclubbing* by Grace Jones when I was younger, maybe around eight years old, and how that freaky mannequin from the future was in my nightmares for years.

I think about how I will listen to this girl when she returns to her computer.

I think about how I'm so interested in the person who wrote this list. I'm so floored by their words that I feel scared. Maybe I wrote this last night? Maybe I was typing in my sleep? Maybe I was making this page behind my own back. Maybe my words were being taken from me and mass marketed to a micro-faction of sad people on the internet.

I would kill to be the cause of a single dyed blonde hair torn from this girl's head. I want to matter to her. I want her to know me, and see that, yes, I do understand.

I'm not sure why she posted her journals, but based on the size of the scroll bar, she's been doing it for a very long time. Her site is clearly only to showcase these journals. There are no hyperlinks to sub-pages, just the single homepage. There are no pictures, no ads, no dates, no times, no details on the author of these journals, and no indication of how I can find her.

The question becomes, did she quote the song in the title of her most recent entry, or was it a coincidence? I buzzed with hope when I read about her tapes, and felt true excitement that she would not only possess the box of tapes, but that she would keep them during a scorched earth session of fall cleaning.

I want to Ctrl+F the entire page for more lyrics, but I don't. I stop at the second entry because I want to savor these tiny pieces of internal monologue made public. I need to spread them out little by little, reading only one a day. I can spend some time digesting what these first two said. I feel like I know the girl who typed out the lyrics to ~the song~. I think it's a girl's words. I hope it's a girl. Is this the journal of a gay man with dyed blonde hair?

I've never felt this type of faceless infatuation before.

Of all the ways to end up on this page, I found it in this lab, by my side. There's a very good chance that whoever wrote this goes to Kirtland- she might be in this room. I look at every girl here, but most of them are sort of gross so I just decide that whoever wrote the post isn't in the computer lab.

I copy down the URL, and once I'm sure I'll be able to find the site again, I shut down the computer I'm sitting at. I don't want anyone else to read these words because they could find this girl before I do.

I'm unable to pull myself away, and I wait for the mystery girl to return.

Eventually, the other people in the lab print their work and leave, and the work-study kid assigned to the room tells me to, "Print and get out," so he can leave too. I consider printing the journal, but this would give her writing a finite end. It would be even more telling than a scroll bar. At the end of a webpage there could be a link, continuing the narrative. At the end of a stack of papers, I would have to just go on with my life.

As I walk back to my apartment, I don't sing, I think about the journal entries, and about the girl who authored them. My mind searches for the fault, and creates a scenario in which the girl's nervous boyfriend is checking in on her by reading her journal on a lab computer so that the URL doesn't appear in his search history. To wash this image away, I focus on the idea that this girl arrives at the computer lab and writes these journals amongst everyone else, screaming in silence, and this reality excites me. If she wrote the latest entry in the computer lab, the question becomes, *Did she stay signed in, with her page up, so that her words would remain like an echo?*

No. I don't see that as the likely reality.

She would've logged out of this computer under normal circumstances. Something must have caused her to leave- a message on her phone, a call that she had been dreading the arrival of, a person she had been avoiding, a friend she needed to chase after; there's a reason why this site remained up on the computer in the lab.

When I arrive back at my apartment, I don't bring up her journal on my laptop.

I love the way her words make me feel, and I want to keep them for when I need them.

I think about my mysterious blonde girl, and it makes me wish it would snow in September.

~

It's eleven at night, and we're at The Brink. The club is a dive, outfitted with the occasional interesting feature provided by a vodka rep. Behind the bar, the liquor bottles are kept in a plastic mold fashioned to look like jagged blocks of ice. This fake coolness permeates everything, and instead of fighting it, I adopt it. Gerard forces me to go talk to some girls he likes, and I don't protest, I simply glide forward, cold drink in hand, cool.

As soon as he's close enough to the girls that the music won't drown him out, Gerard starts talking, "My dad owns this place, ya know."

Based on Gerard's body language and how the girls look, it's obvious which girl he likes and which one I'll have to entertain.

The girl on the right, the cute one with the nose ring, says, "I thought the guy who owned this place was black?" Her voice sounds like she has a Cher accent.

Gerard never quits- the girl's revelation doesn't even cause him to blink- and he counters, "Yeah. He is. He adopted me, which makes me his son. It's like this- Dad knew that he wasn't going to be young forever, and he needed someone who could appeal to a younger generation to keep the club alive. Being a businessman, he devised a plan of how to stay in touch with the kids. It was simple, he realized he needed to adopt a member of this new, confusing generation. He went through the paperwork, and the rigmarole- and trust me, a few palms were greased in the process- but finally he made it to the orphanage. He walked in the door and-" Gerard snaps his fingers so loud that it's audible over the music, "-he found the hippest kid there, who- don't mean to brag- was me. That's the quick story of how he adopted me, and I've grown up convincing the local youth to frequent his club to pay him back. It was a totally wise business decision on his part."

The girl with the nose ring blushes, then says, "I know lots of young people. We should probably hang out with them so you can network."

"Yes," Gerard says, "Good! That's good. If I don't get some new kids coming here, I won't be fed dinner this week."

The girl with the nose ring laughs, then says, "You can meet some of my friends, they know even more young people than I do."

The nose ring girl and Gerard disappear into the crowd- young people looking for more young people. This traps me with the girl on the left. She *was* the girl on the left. Now she's just *the girl*. Her hair is transfixing, in a mushroom cloud way. The sheer height and careful poof she arrived at this club sporting is almost inspiring. It's defiant in its ugliness. It challenges everyone in this club to resist pointing and snarking, "Someone brought their Twisted Sister."

I'm not mad about ending up with the Twisted Sister. I think she's nice. I assume she's nice. We haven't said anything to each other, so to find out if she's nice, I say, "My dad's black too, but he doesn't own a club. He does know how to steal a car equipped with The Club, though."

The Twisted Sister looks me dead in the eyes, and informs me, "That's not funny." Her voice sounds nothing like a hair metal frontman's would, which is a positive for her.

This moment begins to remind me of that scene in every buddy cop movie ever made where the tough cop punches out a henchman, then the sidekick tries it and breaks his hand on the guy's face.

Before I can even recover, the Twisted Sister is gone.

This is why I have the poem in my wallet. Every time I discuss my father, the conversation comes to a grinding halt, and I end up alone.

~

I stand in line for cigarettes at a Rite Aid down the street from The Brink. Everyone in this line, whether in front of me or behind me, lets out a series of audible sighs every time someone asks the register girl a question or raises a circular as evidence of a special on an item. I've never been able to fully key into the palpable frustration that a line buzzes with because I don't really mind waiting. Unless I have somewhere to be, lines are a calming moment of peace in an otherwise anxious and demanding world. If I'm waiting in a line, with exactly what I came for, it's one of the few moments that I know, with a degree of certainty, that I'm in the right place, at the right time, and I don't need to be anywhere else except exactly where I am. I don't even sing to myself in the line because there's always a conversation at the register or between employees, or sometimes people in the line step out of their comfort zones and exchange words beyond flabbergasted staffing complaints.

The two teenage girls behind me become my focus, and I listen to a conversation that must have been started as a result of the nervous headlines on the magazines to our right.

"Who did we catch? Like which terrorists do we have?" a redheaded girl with pigtails asks. I can see her in the mirror that's stuck to the top of the sunglasses display that I'm next to. Her brunette friend, who's holding a huge bottle of water, responds, "We have tons, I betcha. I don't know their names, but I bet we've caught a lot."

This begins a back and forth that, even if I was trying to ignore, is just so fucking ignorant that I have no choice but to listen along with.

"Did we ever get Bin Laden?" the redhead inquires.

"Maybe," the brunette responds.

"I don't know. There'd be a movie about it, if we got him. It would be like, 'Go America!' then we'd explode his fucking head."

"Gross. Men are disgusting animals."

"Yeah, but just get a woman to direct it, and problem solved."

"They shouldn't make movies about that stuff."

"But, like, how will we know if we caught him then?"

"I don't know, a mass-text maybe?"

"Refuse. I'm not gonna become text buddies with the president."

"Welp, then enjoy your forever-search for those terrorizing your life then, bitch."

After I buy my cigarettes, I walk home, and I don't text Gerard, and I write a letter to Edie updating her on US foreign policy, as told to me, indirectly, by the Rite Aid sisters.

~

A tiny sliver of light peaks through the blinds and rests on my face. I guess it's morning. I tell myself that today is the day I will break the habit of talking to myself, of singing to myself, of mumbling to myself under my breath. I want to become present, in the moment.

The self-talk originally started because my mind is in revolt; the thoughts just stopped staying in. Little sentences/ Verses/ Mantras/ began coming out every now and then.

I figure I can stop the habit by walking down to Starbucks in total silence.

The moment I leave the building, I have an internal monologue that betrays my goal.

Fight the song. Keep everything inside. Keep everything where it belongs.

As I walk, I silence the voices inside me, and I think about the questions that I want to ask the girl who wrote those journals.

I want to ask her what her name is.

I want to ask her where her favorite place is.

I want to ask her what her favorite photograph is.

I want to ask her what her phone number is.

These are needs. I begin to wrestle with my needs, and they begin to double as inconveniences.

Located in my psyche there's a desire to feel like my true, unchanged, unaffected personality is someone's dream. I want the feeling that I am, in this person's estimation, a perfect mixture of classy and asshole, obsessive and calm, smart and stupid. I want someone to read my letters to Edie, and even without seeing my face, regard me as beautiful. I want someone to sit up at night, thinking of me.

I'm still waiting for this experience. I've met girls who fulfill a portion of the dream- A girl who would be a great mother yet is unfaithful/ A girl who's unreliable yet tidy/ A girl who's ugly, but a great cook. They had pieces, but this made their shortcomings all the more frustrating. If I settle for less than the dream, then I'll always be thinking about the perfect girl. If I'm too picky, I will die sad and alone.

I will wait for her, still.

I make it to Starbucks and celebrate a small personal victory of forcible silence with a venti coffee that costs five times what one on campus does. I say to myself, "Good job, Kurt," and in doing so, I realize I no longer deserve praise.

I walk to campus, and I make it without a single verse recited.

In front of Kozinski, I balance what's left of my Starbucks on a handicapped ramp railing, then I take out my ceramic cup and transfer the coffee into it.

Host-mug in hand, I arrive at the Great American Novels class with the intention of using the day as an episode of my talk show, but the audience will not cooperate. They're yelling out answers, sometimes to rhetorical questions. People are wrong with an alarming frequency. Things disintegrate into chaos, and a chorus of names is offered:

"Truman Capote."

"Millard Fillmore."

"J.D. Salinger."

"James Stewart."

I tap my pencil on the rim of my coffee cup, and think to myself, *What the fuck are these kids trying to guess?*

None of those names are the answer that the professor is looking for, and as is always the case, I lose interest too quickly to find out what the question is.

~

I actually go to Business Management for the first time this semester and while scoping the room for an open seat, I see Gerard.

Apparently, Gerard has made the decision to not only register for, but also attend Business Management this fall. He even has a pen in his hand. I take a seat next to him in the small U, then fall victim to the waking nightmare that there could be a quiz today, and in a moment of total desperation, I'd have to cheat off Gerard.

"Why are you here?" I ask Gerard, as the professor tries to hook his laptop up to the projector.

"Why haven't you been here, dude?" he rightfully counters.

"Joan... had to... she had, a, uh," I stumble over my words, as my usual excuse generator is unable to come up with a reason why Joan has complicated my life and directly caused my personal failures. Normally this generator works instantaneously, with exceptional detail and reliable variation.

I'm bailed out by the professor, who has figured out his laptop issue, and the class begins.

As everyone starts taking notes, I type out a text to Noni that I'll never send, "I haven't seen you in a week, and that worries me."

Why do I worry about Noni? It makes no sense. At one point, yes, I did have a crush on her. The crush never became an obsession, so it faded. When I see Noni now, I feel none of the hormone-flaring feelings she initially stirred in me. We can go to lunch, to the movies, we can spend the entire day together, but I'm never struck by her sexuality like I was once before. The only time I care- really care, care- is when she's gone. It's when she isn't texting me or pirouetting into my apartment, *then* I wonder what she's doing; who she's talking to. I wonder if someone else is gaining her attention at the exact same time that I'm losing it. It's selfish, and it's jealousy in the worst fashion, but it continues to resurface, dragging down my quiet moments. I don't want anyone to experience what I've shared with her. I want to feel that what she and I have shared is something unique and intentional. No one wants to be filler paper, factory made, uniformly lined, indistinguishable from the sheet that comes before it and the one that follows after.

I watch as half the class flips their notebooks to a new page. It's creepy how robotic things have become.

~

Revere has a really nice apartment because he has lots of money. Lots of *our* money.

Gerard and I follow the sounds of gunshots as we make our way through Revere's living room, then his kitchen, then a second living room, and finally to his bedroom. The stainless steel appliances/ The signed sports memorabilia/ The pictures of Revere and his father with their arms locked around various sports stars- I pay attention to every detail of this apartment because it's a visual representation of the DNA of a rich person. It makes me look at money as a disease which slowly infects the carrier until any ounce of interesting charisma is zapped away and replaced by a Stepford Wife-like homogenized existence. After I get my inheritance, I won't be showing and telling people that I have money.

When we enter his room, we find Revere- blonde, pale, twitchy-lounging in a severely reclined chair, playing a video game. A smaller flat screen to the right of the larger flat screen shows a preview of the door from which we just entered. Revere pays equal attention to both screens, as two games play out in front of him.

"Sup," Gerard says, but Revere doesn't respond because he's been watching us on the cameras for so long that our presence doesn't need to be welcomed further. He's already reckoned with, and accepted, that we're here. I'm not sure I have, though. Revere is a stupid, rich, boring, douche bag, but he has pot. He comes from somewhere on the west coast, but no one cares where he comes from or if he goes to Kirtland- people really just want to know where he lives so they can score an eighth.

Revere finally pauses the game, then he hands us a pre-packed blue bong that he immediately tries to sell to Gerard.

Gerard hits the bong, coughs, then says, "I mean, yeah it hits really smooth, but I'm morally against giving rich people more money. When I walked in here, all I could think about was how I wanted to ransack your kitchen and flush your tea down the toilet like I was you, and the tea was drugs, and that security camera showed two sharply dressed, well-armed men."

Revere looks at Gerard, blatantly confused, then asks, "Is that where my tea went?"

"No. I was just telling you a fantasy I had."

"That's not a very sexy fantasy, dude. You should work on that. Fantasies should be hot."

Gerard accepts this constructive criticism with a nod.

I hit the bong a couple times- only when it reaches me in the rotation- and once it's kicked, the room falls into total silence except for the sounds of ammo being blasted- twelve shots, reload, twelve shots, reload.

I sit in a big white leather chair, and I think about ~her~. That mysterious blonde girl with her mysterious internet journal.

When Gerard and Revere switch out the first game for a nearly identical second game, I stand up, then simply walk out of the apartment.

I silently leave my friends, singing as I walk home.

Suddenly, I find myself in a mental duet of ceaseless interest.

It becomes about ~the song~ and ~her~.

~She~ continues to gain in importance, despite our distance being well established.

~She~ has pulled me away from everything, and I return with a magnetism to that glowing screen.

I key inside my apartment, shaking with lust for ~her~ words.

I glance at the light switch, and it remains ON, but I realize that I have to make this check because the switch being OFF exists as a possibility in the universe. This scares me because it also means that, in mere moments, I could arrive at my laptop, refresh the page, and a 404 error could appear.

I'm immediately able to resume my review because I don't shut my laptop off anymore- I leave it on, with the toolbar filled with a string of numbers that have now become etched on my brain. These numbers have gained the significance of my cell phone number, my age, my number of sexual conquests.

I turn on some music, then hit F5 on the page.

4353638332936382.com.

"roommate divorce.

roommate moved out today. roommate told me i'm not 'endurable to live with.' roommate thinks that listening to the same tape for an entire month is creepy. roommate had recently been returning from her

*psychology classes, then diagnosing me with whatever mental disorder
she learned about that day. she'd call up her friends and tell them she was
living with a crazy person, then she'd specify the type of crazy. after i was
informed of my defect, i'd google the diagnosis and usually it was wrong,
but sometimes she got lucky, and when she nailed it, i'd take out an index
card, write down the name of the disease or disability that seemed to fit
me, then i'd add it to the stack on my desk. when roommate would ask me
a mindless, or insulting, or hopeless question, i'd look through the pile,
find one of my defects, then i'd just hold up the card to remind roommate
of the caliber of wack job she was dealing with. roommate said that i'm
the most insulting conversationalist she has ever met. i responded by
telling her that her boyfriend fucked kati hertz. the odds were in my favor.
roommate packed up and left. this only leads me to believe my
impromptu lie was the truth.*

i hope you understand."

A roommate. My mysterious blonde girl has a roommate. *Had* a
roommate. The key here is that ~she~ lived with a student, maybe in a
dorm, or maybe in an off-campus apartment. ~Her~ site was up on the
computer in the Kirtland University lab.

My mysterious, blonde, college girl.

My mind gets stuck in this track, obsessing over the idea that ~she's~
on campus, as the John Frusciante album that was screeching out from my
laptop speakers starts skipping at the end of the fourth track. I have the
first four tracks of this album memorized because tracks five through
eleven, when I ripped them, were deeply scratched on the CD I borrowed
from Gerard.

My mind swirls with my missing girls.

My mysterious blonde college girl is all alone now.

Noni is focused on someone who isn't me, or maybe she's alone too.

Edie isn't responding to my letters, and things aren't severe enough that
she'd answer a call from me. In these moments, I go to the archive. This is
why I keep every letter. I go into my bedroom, open my desk drawer, then
pick up the twine-bound stack of loose-leaf.

Randomly selecting a letter, I start reading:

*"Remember Mr. McGrady, the dude we both had for art in 7th grade,
who was a pretty good art teacher because he loved art, unlike other
middle school art teachers who just love children or love jobs where their
performance cannot be objectively judged, and due to his genuine*

passion, Mr. McGrady would get really excited about the good pieces, and every time someone did a shitty watercolor or charcoal sketch he would say, 'You approached that in a very interesting way,' so as to portray all of our failing art as misunderstood, instead of pathetic, and he made himself look like the lesser man, saying in not so many words, that the art we made was above him, which is a good teaching technique, or at least it was until Mr. McGrady's excitement cost him his job when Willard Dillon, a fat kid who was consistently found sitting alone at lunch, asked Mr. McGrady, 'What's the point of making all this stuff,' then followed up this statement by declaring, definitively, 'I want to be a plumber, not a painter,' at which point Mr. McGrady walked over to Willard Dillon, put his hand on Willard's shoulder, and said, 'Creation is Godly, and your ability to create is the closest you can come to feel what it's like to be God, I mean, think about it, Jesus was a carpenter because, like his Father, he wanted to create,' and that was the part Mr. McGrady really got in trouble for, when he said, 'With that paintbrush in your hand Milton, it's like you are God,' and as I'm sure you recall Mr. McGrady was good with the students, but not so good with their names, but regardless, it's sad because we never saw Mr. McGrady after that day, due to the fact that he was immediately replaced by some old hippie who was appointed by the school board to take over the class, and I'm reminding you of all this because that hippie just got caught with a pound of weed, and I think the firing fucked me up because the school ousted someone who believed in the power of a single student, and when we asked where he went, we were told he was let go because he was teaching us his inappropriate personal beliefs.

xx Edie."

Edie speaks to me, even when she's silent, and I realize that the story she wrote me is also what happened with ~her~ roommate. At least, this time, Willard Dillon left and Mr. McGrady stayed. The right choice was made, and the right person left.

My cell buzzes, keeping me from further obsessing over the essential women in my life. It's a text from Joan, that reads, "What ru doing?"

I text back, "Homework."

She texts, "Right."

I text, "I'm tired."

She texts, "Then go to sleep."

I text, "Okay. I'll sleep"

She texts, "Gnight."
I text "Gnight."
I lean back in my chair and stare at the ceiling. I'm not tired. I'm lonely. I'm confused. I'm intrigued. I need to read more of ~her~ words. I'll hate myself later for it, because I'm consuming entries back to back, but I need them, so I get my laptop, then page down to the next entry:

"the snowball rolling down the hill.

during my perpetual plummet, instead of collecting snow i collect insecurities. i picked up a new one last week and it's been consuming my life as of late. misspellings. i got my african history test back last wednesday and my essays for it had to be done in those little blue books during the class. when my blue book was returned to me, i opened it and saw i got a middling grade. the comment next to the grade, in scribbled professor handwriting, said, "-content was fine- the spelling makes it nearly unreadable." ever since that moment i've obsessed over spelling. i'll be sitting, watching a movie, and all of the sudden i find myself focusing on the words they're using, quizzing myself to see how many i can spell. the ones i can't spell, i write on a little index card i keep in my purse.

here's my list so far:

righteous.
omelet.
surprise.
tedium.
intricate.
connotation.
february.

making mistakes with these simple words feels like a symptom of something more severe. for an entire month, it's february, and i am always discussing this month, but when i sit down to write it, i create a version of february that doesn't work. my version of february makes me look stupid. instantly, when someone sees my version of february, they will realize that i'm messed up and unintelligent. maybe that's why this is here. maybe that's what this sad little online journal exists for. it's a public service announcement- an easy way to spread the word and inform people that i don't know what i'm doing, even when i think i do.

i hope you understand."

My mysterious, blonde, insecure, college girl.

This entry not only provides additional information about ~her~ but it also provides a fence post in the chronology of the journal. The school entry, then the roommate entry shakes the foundation of the narrative I had constructed in my head. The gaps in time between these entries, as well as the fact that I'm reading them in reverse, may have bastardized the intended point of the events she's documenting. This is when it becomes scary, this is when I realize that I've become obsessed with a fraction of a person- a sliver of their being. Did the roommate move out because ~she~ was too much to live with, or because it was the end of the semester? Was the entry about cleaning everything from ~her~ dorm last year, or from wherever ~she~ spent the summer, or was it from ~her~ new dorm? This problem reveals that dates and times gain supreme importance when withheld. The past *can* change, all it takes is one confused observer. This is why touch is valuable, it would be a confirmation, ~*she's*~ *here*.

~

The morning sun feels electric on my back, and to sustain this feeling, I stand near the church, just beyond the shadow of the clock tower. This leaves me intermixed with my fellow peers, all of them staring down at their cell phones, probably checking what time it is. People are crowded around the clock tower now because they can't congregate here at the end of the semester since at least one Asian kid always cracks under the finals pressure and jumps off the goliath structure.

When the sun goes behind the clouds, I make my way to the library. This semester has started with me studying the women in my life, and avoiding the books in my bag. I need to apply myself to my coursework so I can stay enrolled at Kirtland. I need to focus on what's most important, merely to keep the university from contacting my grandparents to inform them that I'm not meeting the academic requirements demanded by the university.

Inside the library, instead of seeking seclusion in one of the swastika shaped desks that pepper the center aisles of the second floor, I choose to go up to the fourth floor where there are sofas and a glass lined observation wall that provides a view of the town beyond the campus. Of all the places in the library, this is where I imagine my mysterious, blonde, insecure, college girl would be, if she does attend Kirtland.

I'm the only person on the entire floor besides a Japanese girl who's painting the orange and red treescape on a wide canvas.

I sit down on a crescent shaped sofa, then open my backpack and take out the textbook for the business class with the multi-hyphenated name. The fact that I haven't even read the full name of the class, much less the first sentence of this book, is an unpleasant reality that I must confront. I check my phone to find out how far I should be in the textbook, and see that I'm over a hundred pages behind already. My careful system of buying time at Kirtland, which has worked so well in the past, hits a block. Suddenly, I become unwilling to devote myself to the repetitive, sometimes contradictory, often subjective business texts. I'm a man of ritual, yet I shun the forced requirement of consuming reworded stale paragraphs about the global marketplace, and this leaves me at odds with the business school at Kirtland. I sit in the library, surrounded by books, then I pack up and go to the computer lab to read.

~

I knock on Joan's door once. No answer.

I knock a second time. No answer.

I call out Joan's name. No answer.

I call out Lena's name. No answer.

I use my student ID to jimmy open the door, and as I walk into Joan's room, I glance at her Monday/Wednesday schedule on the wall, written in purple marker. According to the timetables, she won't be back until two at the earliest. The Tuesday/Thursday schedule is written in pink, and I take note of these times as well.

Lena doesn't have her schedule on the wall, so I work fast and I don't even have time to romance her face towel.

After less than three minutes in Joan's dorm, I'm gone- my mission accomplished.

I walk to the café, convinced that the bad energy in the library was harshing my ability to concentrate, and a new environment will fix things. I need the stimulation of people passing by me with some sort of sense of optimism that all hope is not lost because pizza will be in their near future.

I sit near the mail room, then take out my textbook, and start from the beginning, "*Chapter 1. With the state of the business world constantly changing in the early twenty first centu-*" my eyes close. "*With the shape of the business world constantly changing in-*" my eyes close. "*With the shape of the business world const-*" my eyes close.

I skip ahead- the intro is always filler.

I get to, "*Let's review,*" then stop reading mid-sentence.

Taking another break, I watch a girl slurp a questionable looking soup while she reads an oversized magazine. On the cover of the magazine is a wide-eyed brunette, staring intensely out at the world, a tinge of sadness in her eyes.

When the girl sets the magazine down completely, I can see that it's filled with ultra close-up pictures of celebrities and large blocks of varying sized text.

It occurs to me that this magazine has the same dimensions as a *Rolling Stone,* and I desperately want to approach the girl to offer her Akkuta's *Rolling Stone* subscription because it would look perfect lined up on her coffee table with the magazine she has in her hands, but before I can put this plan into motion, the girl gets up and leaves the magazine behind.

I wait five full minutes for the girl to return- the time going by fast because my brain is thanking me with endorphins for not being forced to read my textbook. I remained focused on the now-empty table because it's not lost on me that abandoning a magazine is similar to the act of leaving a webpage open. This is the lo-fi version of what my mysterious, blonde, insecure, college girl did in the computer lab.

Without drawing attention to myself, I pick up my book and move to the table where the magazine sits. I search for an address label on the cover, but it's been torn off and only two stripes of glue remain. My eyes scan up to the beautiful woman's forehead, then across the title, *Interview.* Akkuta Afar does not subscribe to *Interview.* With the dedication that I should be devoting to my textbook, I page through the magazine. The content is appropriately ridiculous- celebrities interviewing other celebrities for pages upon pages. I imagine that in the near future, famous people will band together and buy a massive "celebrity-only" island, filled with plush theaters that exclusively screen movies that didn't connect with an audience. The celebrities will attend the screenings and later agree that the public are assholes who can't recognize genius. Those without a major tentpole franchise or indie darling cred will only be allowed to step foot on the island if they're willing to do the shitty jobs like dishwasher and trashman. Minor celebrities would take these jobs to try to get in good with the major celebrities. The perpetually straight-to-DVD actor would learn to do hospital corners. This is the future; magazines are over, wealth-segregated islands are in.

Reading paragraph upon paragraph of celebrities congratulating each other while mutually validating their dislike of "haters" proves so unappealing that I close the magazine like it's a textbook. Desperate for a mindless diversion, I begin to concentrate on two café workers yelling across the commuter crowd to each other. An old café worker who's holding what appears to be a bag of shredded cheese, yells, "This is the cheap stuff, whatever happened to the normal stuff?"

The young black worker he's yelling to shrugs.

"Cheap is expensive," the old worker says to no one in particular, a lesson for the entire campus.

My focus is immediately redirected when I notice Gerard making his way through a maze of tables, seemingly picking his path based on how weird the commuters at each particular table seem. He implements a zigzagging multi-point route that takes longer than it should, but he eventually reaches me.

"Did you see the article on Winona Ryder in there?" he asks, his finger tapping the magazine as he sits down.

I shake my head no.

"She's back," Gerard declares.

"Back from where?"

"From *it*, dude."

"From it," I repeat slowly, then open the magazine to try and find out where she *was*, but I stop flipping pages when I hear a girl say, "Hey, boys," because I realize that this could be ~her~. The girl's voice sounds like a phone tree prompt.

I quickly close the magazine then push it to the center of the table.

Gerard and I both look up at the girl who interrupted us, and surprisingly, she's cute, but she's not blonde.

The girl asks, "You guys are, like, seniors, right?"

We both nod yes because we want to portray ourselves as men with answers, men who will say yes, men who are older than her and can buy her alcohol as long as she agrees to drink it with us.

"Do you still have your journals and shit from 1201, English 1201?" the girl asks, without shame.

"What plans do you have for our journals?" I ask, mainly so Gerard doesn't blurt out that we delete or burn our schoolwork in a bonfire at the end of every year.

"Well, we have to do twelve by tomorrow, twelve journals, and we need some inspiration. Basically, we have less than twenty four hours to do twelve journals," the brunette girl says.

"We?" Gerard asks.

The brunette nods. Gerard and I search for someone else who could qualify the moment as a "we" issue.

"The journals are on books..." the brunette says, then attempts to clarify another vague statement, but only causes further confusion by saying, "...but not full books, it's on... like, reading thingies, shit in a book. It's not a book though, it's like reading thingies."

"You mean like poems, short stories, plays?" Gerard lists.

The brunette nods her head.

Gerard pauses, like he's considering helping her, but the fact remains that he can't. "Come by my room later. I can help you out," Gerard promises. He writes down his address on a skin colored portion of the magazine cover, then carefully tears it off and gives it to the brunette.

She studies Gerard's writing, then asks, "Do you want to put your number?"

Knowing she's going to text with him until he relents and e-mails his journal- a journal that doesn't exist- Gerard says, "Nope," then he stands up, and we abandon the brunette, but I take the magazine.

Kirtland's population is drowning in the frustration of laziness blocking purpose.

As we step outside, Gerard tells me, "I want to fuck that girl."

"How are you going to do it?"

"I'll read a bunch of poetry, then write her journals."

"Are you even doing your own homework?" I ask.

"Don't be stupid, dude," Gerard says, "No one will fuck me if I do *my* homework. It's a waste of time."

My eyes must reflect my mild boredom, because Gerard segues into a new topic via a tenuous connection, "Speaking of poetry, let's go to The Crisper tonight. I heard they're having some poet who writes poems about natural disasters. The poet says that the most dangerous domestic terrorist there is... is Mother Nature. Crazy to think about, right?"

I put on my Wayfarers and hope this will suffice as a response.

"Or don't answer me, I'll just go to the poetry thing alone, and I hope he reads a poem about you being sucked up into a tornado," Gerard vents, pulling at his hair, and it stays stuck in the direction he yanks it, even after he lets it go.

"I'm not going. Every time I go to The Crisper, it's a bunch of depressed college kids reading shitty short stories that are vaguely masked accounts of how their girlfriend fucked a guy she met on the internet."

"Suit yourself," Gerard says, then shrugs.

"I'm going to go see Noni tonight," I say.

"Noni still goes here?" Gerard asks, either surprised or impressed.

It strikes me as odd that I have two people so important in my life, so close to each other, but they barely ever overlap. It's a hopeless feeling. If Gerard is this close to Noni- if there is only one degree of separation between them, yet they remain apart- how can I ever find my poor, mysterious, insecure, blonde, college girl?

"Noni still goes here," I say, confident in this fact, "Obviously, I mean, she's too smart to drop out, too dumb to transfer."

"All I remember about Noni is that she created a photo album filled entirely with pictures that she took of herself with her parents' gardener, unbeknownst to him."

"Oh, her George Hernandez survey?" I respond nonchalantly, so as to normalize Noni's troubling behavior by establishing it as art.

"Whatever it was. I mean, where do you meet these people? It's almost like you attract medicated, awkward, disenfranchised 18 to 24 year-olds," Gerard says, as we leave campus.

"Noni? Where did I meet Noni?" I think about it, then smile, "I met Noni freshman year. I liked the fact that she looked like she was on real high-powered pharmaceuticals that she stole from her dad after he had back surgery or something. I saw her at the bus stop when I was walking down to Starbucks one day, and I had to talk to her."

"You approached a girl? Kurt Jones approached a girl?"

"Well, yeah, she was magnetic, I had to. I knew that if I didn't talk to this girl, my life's trajectory would be significantly altered. I walked up to Noni, then sat next to her on the bench at the bus stop. I told her that I liked the way she did the makeup around her eyes, and that I'd never seen anyone use a red like that to complement their green eyes. She looked at me in her glassy-eyed way for a second, then said, 'I'm not wearing makeup. I just haven't slept in three days.'"

~

Noni is wearing a camo tank top with a yellow bra under it, and a little olive colored skirt. Camouflage in such an amount feels self-defeating.

"Kurtis, come in," Noni says, and as I enter I notice that papers are strewn across her floor haphazardly. Next to her futon is a stack of old phone books. Noni's laptop sits on the floor, and a long cord reaches over to her printer which rhythmically pumps out pages.

"What is... all of this?" I ask.

"I've found my purpose, Kurt. I found out why I'm here, why I'm at Kirtland. Have you seen the new Winona Ryder article in-"

Out of my back pocket, I pull out the copy of *Interview*.

"Yes! That's it!" Noni says, then rips the magazine out of my hand, and sits on the floor.

"She's back," I say, repeating the buzz.

"She lived through *it*," Noni confirms, as she flips through the pages while the printer stutters, then her finger hammers down on a picture of a guy with the sides of his head shaved and the top of his hair grown out about 5 inches. The guy stands in front of a painting in a warehouse. Easels, and various colored tapes, and bottles of wine pepper the background.

"This guy, Gene Manny, he's a famous artist, or an up-and-coming artist, or a trust fund kid with lots of paint," Noni cycles through the possibilities quickly, "And his studio is like 5 miles away from here, and okay... read this."

Noni hands me the magazine, but keeps her finger pointed to a specific paragraph.

I start reading aloud, "The monochromatic schemes I use are stol-"

"-no under that," Noni says, and I realize that her finger was being used as a page break, not a pointer.

"Oh, alright, it says, 'I just finished a collaboration with (sculptor) Nathan Butler, which will show at Capria, if things work out.'"

I silently re-read the quote, trying to determine its importance related to Noni. The best reaction I can come up with is, "I hate those douchebags at Capria."

"The article mentions Nathan Butler, Kurt," Noni says.

"And you're Noni Butler, so he's... like your brother or something?"

Noni shakes her head yes and makes a punk rock face, but in this context it means the opposite of punk's rejection of careful order.

"So you found your brother?"

"Not yet. I was wondering why I was here, what I was doing at this shitty college when I had emotionally transferred two semesters ago. It turns out, this whole time, this is why. It's so I can finally see my brother again."

"You're sure it's him?" I ask.

"How many Nathan Butlers do you know?"

"None, I suppose."

"Exactly. It's him. I know it is."

"Did you tell your Mom?"

"No, she wouldn't want to know. We never discuss Nathan."

I shrug, providing nothing.

"I think she likes that he's missing. At this point, she's probably telling people he's dead. She likes sympathy, regardless of how it's gained."

My mysterious, blonde, insecure, college girl's journal scrolls in my mind for a moment, then the printer stops printing and the silence cuts off my thoughts.

"So this is where you've been lately?" I ask, my worry changing shape.

"Yup," she says as her eyes dart over to read the expression on my face, "Aw, did you take my absence personally?"

"No, nah, no, I was just curious," I mumble.

Noni springs to her feet, then begins her dance, "You know, you aren't as layered as you think you are."

"Maybe I'm just excellent at hiding my layers."

"Or hiding the fact that they're a facade," Noni says, then she freezes and keeps her mouth open in a cartoonish reaction to her own words.

Noni found her brother in an abandoned magazine with her namesake on the cover. This campus is connecting people through discarded words. I don't look at the paper on the floor to see what the printer is printing.

~

Instead of going to the poetry reading at The Crisper, or returning Joan's texts, or doing homework, I walk and I sing and I miss someone I've never met or spoken to. The question of what I would say to ~her~ becomes important and it hums inside of me. I decide that I have to plan what to say, so when the time comes, I'll be prepared. ~Her~ presence, I imagine, is like a house fire. I can't rely on myself to act in the moment. I need to have everything figured out for the unlikely, soul changing occurrence when ~she~ bursts into my life and consumes everything.

It's obvious that I can't say something that could be confused as a pickup line.

I swipe my ID to get out of the gate, and I try to think of a compliment that isn't creepy coming from a wide-eyed stranger.

I'm unable to come up with anything.

I can't begin a conversation with a casual observation because ~she~ could just agree with me, and it would end there. The weather/ The condition of the school/ The people around us- all of these variables could be commented on, but it's not a conversation starter. Those are things that can be responded to with a tight-lipped smile or a head nod.

I want to hear ~her~ voice.

As the guard buzzes me into the courtyard of my building, I arrive at the most ridiculous of sentences as the answer; *I love you.*

The fear those three words provoked could unite us and would require some serious reckoning. She couldn't brush me off, and she'd have, at minimum, a curiosity about how these insane feelings developed in a total stranger. It would be in that quick allowance that I would have to explain that I found her words, and they were exactly what I was searching for.

The moment I get inside my apartment, before I even turn on a light, I open my laptop and refresh the page.

4353638332936382.com.

"the city that always sleeps.

there's nowhere to get coffee after midnight in this town. how is it possible that not a single person here can have things to do past twelve a.m.? maybe it's that not everyone is under the tyrannical hand of the university, or maybe they can make coffee in the privacy of their residence, unlike me. after the fire, the university began fiercely prohibiting on-campus students from even thinking about what a coffee maker may look like on the desk in their dorm. the school's website might as well read, 'we're very proud of our current students, but we don't trust them to operate a coffee maker without turning their dorm into a pile of ashes.' then again, as i look around at my fellow peers, i find a certain safety in the fact that we can't own coffee makers.

i hope you understand."

I feel the way I felt with the sun on my back this morning.

I regarded her as a fire, then a fire appeared.

She goes to a university. Never mind the fact that people outside of the US call all colleges "university." Never mind the fact that there are thousands of universities across America.

She mentioned a fire.

Kirtland's history rushes toward me- The plaque in memoriam/ The blue yardsticks being passed out to make sure every dorm has a clear fire lane/ The TV show where a survivor of the fire looks into the camera and states that they were saved by an angel/ The very public prosecution of the students who started the blaze.

Kirtland still struggles with the repercussions of what the fire claimed. A year later, from the same dorm, the smoke from another building could be seen. A year after that, a cross fashioned from the steel of that building would be placed in the front of the dorm. This is how a building ages now-it becomes a crypt.

I leave my apartment, and I try to find a place to get a cup of coffee, but everywhere is closed, and I'm ecstatic.

~

I'm finally able to get Joan back to her dorm so I won't be seen with her in town. I don't want to misdirect my poor, mysterious, insecure, blonde, Kirtland University girl so I eliminate any chance of her observing me holding Joan's hand in public.

I sit straddling the windowsill, with one leg inside Joan's dorm room and one leg hanging out of the window. I'm smoking a cigarette and eating jello out of one of those little cups, not the plastic cups they sell jello in, but a Dixie cup.

"Something very creepy is happening here," Joan says.

"Stop being so paranoid," I sigh.

"How can you say that? I'm telling you, someone is breaking in here and moving things around to fuck with me."

"Maybe it's Lena. She has keys to the room. It sounds like something psycho enough to be a Lena-ism," I offer.

Lena stops typing on her laptop, turns to face the window, then says, "Fuck you, Kurt. I have better things to do than further derail Joan's life. She doesn't need any help with that," Lena's voice sounds like she's always chewing.

"Oh, sorry, I saw you had your earbuds in, and..." I mumble to Lena, avoiding eye contact.

"Kurt, I'm serious," Joan shrieks, "I came in today and someone had taken all my panties out of the top drawer and replaced them with all my jeans, then put all my panties in the bottom drawer where my jeans were."

"Maybe it's a ghost?" I offer casually.

"The only ghost in my life is you, Kurt," Joan says, then she opens her mouth to say something else, but Lena's phone rings and interrupts her.

Lena answers the call, and instead of communicating like a human, she only responds with, "What?" five times, each response progressively louder, then she hangs up, and resumes typing on her laptop. Once she calms down, she notes casually, "Food's here."

The girls leave to go collect the Chinese food and pay the delivery guy. While they're gone, I reverse my work from earlier in the day and put Joan's panties back in the top drawer, and her jeans in the bottom drawer. Yes, Joan was right, even when she was wrong. I am the ghost in her life.

~

Socio-Eco-Necronomicon-required class begins and ends with a multiple choice test that I'm ambushed by. I utilize the observation deck, and the panic melts away when the pilot reaches cruising altitude. The test goes fine- the kid in front of me was well studied.

In a pleasant turn, what started as a potentially troubling situation ended up bearing fruit. I now have a better idea of what the class is about, based on the test questions, and the fact that I showed up on the exact day that there was a test is a dual victory. The Russian roulette risk of class skipping is that, if you don't check the syllabus, sometimes you miss a test worth 25% of your grade.

Time stretches and contracts at Kirtland, and today I have time to kill, which means it will move slowly, until I start singing ~the song~ or reading ~her~ words. I want to save those moments for when I truly need them so I search for a mediocre distraction as filler.

Cutting across the Green, I find myself returning to the café.

The midday rush is full-on, and I can't get a table near the mail room. Instead of watching other students open various gifts they've been sent, I scan the café to see if I will receive a gift today. Every blonde girl becomes my focus. Without any visual cues to rely on- beyond hair color- I have to hope that, in the same way ~her~ words immediately mainlined to my heart, the author's image will as well. I have a possibly misguided confidence that ~she~ will wordlessly announce herself.

Before any announcements can be made, the worst case scenario takes form as I lock eyes with the fat commuter I sat with at the start of the semester. He points at a trash can I'm standing parallel to, and the commuters all look at me. The fat commuter glances at the Asians, then points at a weight bearing beam. I follow the straight line from the beam to an empty seat at the Asians' table. I close my eyes and cock my head back, and when the words to ~the song~ begin to fight their way out of my throat, I walk over to the commuter's table.

I find an open chair, just like the seat at Asians' table, but this parallel is ignored, and as soon as I sit down, someone slides me their phone, and an article about a terrorist plot being cracked is on the screen.

"Read the name," the fat commuter demands.

I lift my hand and rub my eyebrows. "So they caught some random wack job," I say, without reading the name, because the name doesn't matter. These commuters are obsessed with the idea that their sanctuary could be snatched away by their fellow peers. For the commuters, Kirtland is temporary. The students on campus will always have a piece of their life tied to the time they slept, and fucked, and passed out on campus. The ethereal quality of this campus for these commuters has them obsessed with the idea that if something causes classes to be canceled, they have no reason to be here. This is an amusement park for the commuters in a different way than it's an amusement park for me. They are merely visitors, paying an admission price for the day, then leaving.

"Things are gonna be okay, guys," I assure them, then I stand up and immediately abandon the table.

I briefly consider sitting in the open seat at the Asians' table, just to fuck with the commuters- to expose myself as the spy- but seats are at such a premium in the café, that I need the commuters to regard me as one of their own.

I pace the Green, looking for ~her~ but it begins to rain so I run to Brit-Lit, and I'm the first one in the classroom. I don't reach for my laptop, I simply sit and listen to the rain. I challenge myself to be present in the moment. I make an effort to relax by relinquishing my leapfrogging obsessions. It's not lost on me that I'm always reaching for further stimulus to distract me from whatever unpleasant situation I'm in. Too often, I feel new addictions forming, and focused reliances being established. These mechanisms don't enhance my life, they pillage it.

Eventually, the rest of the class arrives, soaked from the rain, as does my favorite professor.

Surprisingly, there's also a test in Brit-Lit. I recall the syllabus, and there were no tests listed.

"If you did the reading, this will be simple. If you didn't do the reading, you better fill this page with compliments directed toward me," the old professor tells us as he passes out a single sheet of paper.

When I look at the paper, it shows a lone demand; "Write two single page essays based on your Takeaways."

This is a test I can't cheat on. Two tests in a single day is bad, but two tests, one of which I can't cheat on, is the worst. Somehow, this testing duplication continually happens at Kirtland. Weeks and weeks of no tests allows the student body to drift into this hazy part-time world of academia, then out of the blue, everyone is cramming for four tests in two days. The students say it's intentional and the professors are doing it to fuck with us, but we're perpetually assured that there's no secret deep web being used by the faculty to coordinate their test dates. They claim that it's not their goal to provide the maximum amount of sadness to the highest number of students- it just sort of happens. I stopped complaining about this phenomenon after Joan told me, "I swear my professors get some sick pleasure out of making my life miserable."

I do my best to bullshit the Brit-Lit essays, and after the test, I go back to my apartment to do the reading that the test was on to see how well I did. I was familiar with the stories from Noni telling me about them, but I never actually read them until now. As I sit on my futon and read the work, I receive the confirmation that- yes- I was right. Most of the stories were about love. Losing love, chasing love. I'm familiar with the latter and I'm horrible at hiding my familiarity so I'm sure I'll pass.

The need to find ~her~ becomes too all encompassing, and instead of making dinner, scrounging through the cabinets, I go into my bedroom and type "4353638332936382.com" into my browser, then tap "Enter." There are no new entries, so I scroll down to where I left off.

"a table for none.

the following is an explanation of easy mac, for those of you who aren't college kids and can afford real food.

easy mac claims to be a 'mac and cheese' that anyone can make, presuming they have access to water and a microwave. while i can verify that macaroni is included, i'm not 100% sure that the powder in the box is, in fact, cheese. when pondering the title, one does notice that the word 'cheese' isn't mentioned.

easy.

mac.

no 'easy cheesy mac,' no 'mac and easy cheese.' the appearance of 'cheese' can be found under the huge yellow block letters displaying 'easy mac.'

this brings me to my second point. The word 'easy' was chosen by the manufacturer to compliment the no-brainer 'mac' portion. it was a good choice. 'easy mac' is, well, 'easy.' this, i hope, is the only reason why people eat it. you take the 'mac' out of the plastic package, put it in a bowl, add some water, microwave it, then add the 'cheese' powder. pretty easy. they had to make it easy because there's nothing else positive they could

*have added to the name. maybe 'cheap mac,' would be the only other
viable alternative. if i was the marketing guru assigned to sell this stuff i
would've named it 'lonely mac.' this is the best way to describe the
product, and it hits the key demographic. college kids will walk down the
aisle of the supermarket and see 'lonely mac' and think 'hey, i'm lonely, i
better buy two boxes. if i buy a single box, it will seem even lonelier.
maybe i'll find someone to share my mac with this week. maybe this will
be the week i have mac for two.'*

 *all i can afford to do is to keep eating this shit, and convincing myself
that this will be the week, but it never is.*

 i hope you understand."

My poor, mysterious, insecure, Kirtland University girl.

I close my laptop, and make a solitary meal that might as well be named
Lonely Mac.

My phone vibrates with a call from Joan and I press the button on the
side of it to silence the call.

~

I'm cheating on the Great American Novel test, and after the third
question, I have to pause, even if it causes me to lose pace with the boy in
front of me. I sit in one of those moments when life becomes so illogical my
soul almost separates from my body.

The question that short circuits everything;

 "The main character's hat is:
   (a) Green
   (b) Blue
   (c) Red
   (d) He doesn't wear a hat."

This is what we are being tested on. Colors. Not the meaning of the
book, but, instead... hats. This question provides me the confidence to
continue to disregard actually trying this semester because I've learned that
my failures will be forgotten, but the significance of a red hat I once wore
will endure.

~

We don't take a test in Business Management.

We go over the test we took earlier in the week. The kid in front of me got an 85. Not bad. I think he could have done better though.

I'm sure that the professor's intentions were that, by going over the test, we could learn from our mistakes, but instead it turns into an elaborate bartering session. Everyone who's wrong thinks they're right, and everyone who's right assumes the kids who are wrong must have been wait-listed students, the college equivalent of a second class citizen.

Going over the test should only take twenty minutes. It takes the entire class. Nothing is accomplished. No additional points are given out. No partial credit is assigned.

Finally, the professor says, "According to my watch, it's 1:45 so our time is up."

Gerard raises his hand, and the professor calls on him.

Completely straight-faced, studying his wrist, Gerard says, "According to my watch it's only 1:43."

~

On the way home I see ~her~ seven different times. This beats the previous record by one and a half. The half is because of the time I thought I saw ~her~, but it turned out to be a fit guy with really nice, long, blonde hair.

When I get back to my building, I check the mail, expecting nothing, yet finding a letter from Edie. My brain buzzes and I have to blink away the emotion this pulls out of me.

I begin reading the letter immediately, deciding to take the stairs for privacy. I slowly climb to the fourth floor, as I read Edie's words.

"Remember Mrs. Brentwood's dog, that little poodle-looking thing that she would drive around with in the front seat of her boat/car hybrid, well I'm sure you remember it because it's like the dumbest looking animal ever, and I really hate it, and that hate had been filling my mind lately so I called up Paz because Paz works as a vet's assistant now, which is totally weird, I mean, it seems pretty obvious he'll end up stealing all the K, but that hasn't happened yet, and when I spoke with him, I asked him to do me a favor and neuter my dog, and he said he'd tell the vet that it was his dog, and the vet would do it for free, so that night, after all the Vet's appointments were over, Paz came to my house, and we got the poodle out of the cage in Mrs. Brentwood's yard and into his car, and Paz was all like, 'Why do we have to steal your dog from your neighbor's

house,' and I said that we have to leave the dog at the neighbors because he keeps trying to fuck people at my house, and Paz did his usual giddy laugh, and the whole procedure went off without a hitch, so when we were bringing the dog back, Paz started asking why we were returning the dog to the neighbors if it's neutered and won't try to fuck my dad anymore, but his voice was super loud, and a light came on in Mrs. Brentwood's house, and Paz knew to run, and we got back into his car, and at this point I was bellowing like a mad scientist while thinking about how hilarious it will be when Mrs. Brentwood sees that stupid dog's little privates shaved- all Paz had left was a skinny landing strip, but don't worry, when I show up at your college and kidnap you, I won't castrate you or shave your pubes, I promise.

xx Edie."

The cookie cutter predictability of my days makes it so that I can't imagine what spending a day with Edie would be like now. I almost yearn to be kidnapped because I know that I won't visit my grandparents until ~it~ happens.

~

While she eats my french fries, Joan tells me that she's going to switch her major to "something arty" because she wants to start painting again. I didn't know she stopped painting, and I've always assumed she was an art major so I have nothing to add to the conversation. It seems like just last week she showed me this boring painting of a country porch. It was the type of painting that's only exhibited on paper towel packages.

"I have this sensation that a big part of me goes missing when I stop painting, plus I don't feel like I've really made something I'm proud enough to show yet. This will give me a goal," Joan tells me.

"So what are you going to paint?" I ask, wondering which porch has caught her eye.

"You," Joan says, almost bashful.

"Me?"

"Yeah."

"Why?"

"Cuz."

"You want to paint me?"

"Yeah."

"Okayyy."

"You don't want me to paint you?" Joan asks, her confidence at zero.
"I'm not sure."
"Ugh. I was trying to be nice."
"You were going to paint me... to be nice?"
"Well, yeah. I thought it would be romantic."

I tell Joan I have to get to class, and I realize that I'm becoming a good student, not because I yearn for knowledge, but because my classes have become an excuse to exit conversations that I don't want to be in.

I leave for Brit-Lit, and I think about the painting she proposed- about how it can never happen. Soon after I began dating Joan, I developed this sick feeling that she was draining my life force, and following this logic, I instantly develop a paranoia that this painting is just another way for Joan to take something from me. I mess with her life to try and take back whatever she sucks out of me. I'm fighting to keep her from getting too powerful.

A take and take relationship.

~

The more I think about ~her~, the more I need to hear from ~her~.
4353638332936382.com.

"i'm refusing to dwell on this week so i'm writing again. i don't know why i wrote this, or what the purpose of it is, but i didn't stop typing until it was finished. i even used question marks for this one, it just seemed right.
    XX
    'garrett says he's coming with us on saturday,' beth tells sarah, then adds, 'but i doubt it.'
    sarah doesn't say anything as she exhales a puff of cigarette smoke, then the wind carries it to her left, and beth inhales the thin cloud.
    sarah hates that beth always has to be right.
    'i was so right when i said he'd have to check with tim before he accepted the invitation. i just had a feeling...' beth pauses, then when she doesn't get a response, she shivers, and says, 'it's fucking freezing out here.'
    sarah isn't cold, and she decides she might as well enter the conversation to fill up time before the bus arrives. it's fall and the dead leaves skip across the sidewalk. sarah picks a leaf up and twirls it, then offers her opinion, 'it's cute.'

'cute?' beth asks, 'you think it's cute that tim has garrett wrapped around his finger? i mean shit, garrett's only been gay for, like, two weeks.'

sarah is somehow offended by this even though she doesn't like garrett very much. 'he's been gay for a while, it's just tim is his first boyfriend so he's... excited.'

'every time i turn around they're stamping their feet and crying,' beth says, and sarah becomes unsure if this might be a veiled attack against her. this parallel is disregarded and the topic isn't broached. sarah is almost intimidated by beth, even though she realizes beth is likely using this rant just to fill dead air.

sarah's stomach gets tight and before she can stop herself, she says quickly, 'give them a break... you know some people just fall fast.'

'falling fast? let me tell you, only weak people fall fast, it's a habit of the inferior,' beth declares, with certainty and power.

sarah doesn't want to have this conversation anymore. she'll do anything to escape the incoming onslaught of words. she doesn't want to hear what beth will say because beth might say the same things sarah has been trying to bury in the back of her mind.

a guy in a business suit walks by and checks beth out, but she doesn't even acknowledge his existence.

feebly, sarah says, 'i can't believe october is already over.'

beth flies by sarah's comment, remaining fixated on the whole falling fast topic of moments ago. 'falling fast for someone is a sign of pure stupidity. think about it, you know virtually nothing about a person until you've been around them for at least a month. anyone i've fallen fast for... it was always just me overlooking all their shit qualities.'

sarah wants to walk away. she doesn't want to take the bus. she doesn't want to talk to beth anymore. beth doesn't understand.

it was different in the summer. sarah could still remember passing out with him and what it felt like. unfortunately, she also can't forget how the aftermath of these moments made her feel like a fool- an all too common feeling. to justify her thoughts, sarah thinks of something, anything, and says it, 'i guess you could be right, but i also think it depends on how much time you spend with the person. you could know someone for a month but have been with them for like ten hours total, or it's possible that you've spent two weeks together, never separated.'

it really was only two weeks wasn't it? sarah doesn't like the thought that a two week relationship still weighs so heavy this many months later.

it was summer, it was warm then.

it was summer, it was different then.

beth is gripping her knees, shivering in the fall weather, but this doesn't stop her from jumping on sarah's statement, 'when you first meet someone there's a grace period. you keep letting things slide, hoping they won't reappear again. everything bad is chalked up to a fluke. you have to do that so you can keep thinking they're great, but the fact is, they just haven't had the chance to disappoint you yet.'

stop talking beth. stop talking beth- this statement repeats in sarah's head. beth is wrong and she never knew him like sarah knew him.

is he thinking about her? he isn't, she's pretty sure of that now. sarah can still feel that temporary warmth. his arms around her. she's tried finding other boys to get that feeling, but if they hold her, it's just a body, there's no electricity. that addictive feeling now seems unachievable.

beth sees the bus approaching and gets up, ending the conversation, 'so for someone to get all wrapped up in the beginning, it's so easy, but so dumb.'

the wind whips, and sarah pulls her scarf tighter."

i hope you understand."

My poor, mysterious, fragile, insecure, blonde, Kirtland University girl. I write Edie a letter about Sarah and Beth.

I copy the words from the screen exactly as they appear, and this process brings me closer to ~her~. I feel the electricity pass through my pen. I mail the letter as soon as I'm finished- I don't copy over a second draft, because my letter *is* the second draft. ~She~ wrote the first draft.

As I walk back from the mailbox, I get a call from Joan. *Joan is your girlfriend*, I remind myself. She wants to see another movie at The Waldorf. I can tell her interest is genuine because the movie has been out for over a week and she still wants to go.

"Please, Kurt? Please," she begs.

"Fine."

"I'll make it fun, I promise, okay?"

"I said fine, Joan. I'll go."

"I know, but I want you to want to go. I don't want you to be miserable," pause, "I'll sneak a six pack in my big purse. We can drink them in the theater."

"I'm not drinking in a movie theater."

"Why?" Joan whines, "Sneaking alcohol into the movie theater doesn't mean we're alcoholics, it just means we'll both enjoy the movie."

I realize that I'm being more negative than Joan, and this makes me want to follow her plan.

~

I wake up in Joan's room, and I masturbate in the shower because Gerard told me that Lena has something, he thinks possibly HPV, but neither of us are sure if it can be transferred via a face towel, and I can't rely on his information that it's only HPV. In a world of acronyms, a one letter difference is important. Beating off in the shower isn't as good, because the face cloth kinda felt like a tongue. I still cum, if not for pleasure, than to satisfy my incessant need to finish what I've started.

I walk back into the room, and I look at the color-coded schedule. Today is purple, and right now Joan has class, so I sneak over to her laptop.

Sopping wet, I sit in her chair and bring up a private tab. 4353638332936382.com.

"i don't know you, and you're my best friend.

being single, i'm repeatedly told by girls with questionable judgment that i shouldn't date college guys. 'college guys are incapable of monogamy,' or 'they will hurt you,' or 'date rich guys,' they say. i've thought about it and i disagree. i don't see it the same way because guys have something girls don't, consistency. there's some type of comfort in the predictability of men. the fact that i can stereotype them further proves the point. some days i don't want to talk about anything important and those days i hang out with my male friends. my female friends are forever changing, not only their opinions, but also their physical appearance. most guys find a look and stick with it. they get a haircut in eighth grade and treat it as a lifelong commitment to the style. or it's just due to sheer laziness, i'm not exactly sure. my female friends at college change their appearance constantly. i say hi to every single girl on campus because there's a chance that maybe i don't know them... but there's also the chance one of my best friends has dyed her hair. i'm sure kirtland u's lack of a football team helps my opinion of the male species.

i hope you understand."

I have confirmation now.

My poor, mysterious, fragile, insecure, blonde, Kirtland University girl.

I've located ~her~; now I have to find ~her~.

I get dressed in my clothes from yesterday, and I make sure my hair looks good, then I begin to wander around Joan's building. I slowly traverse all seven floors. I don't find ~her~. I don't even pass a blonde haired girl, much less *my* blonde haired girl. Once I make it to the top floor, I reverse my route and re-check each floor until I'm confident that my poor, mysterious, fragile, blonde, Kirtland University girl is either locked in her room, doesn't live in Joan's building, or is outside.

I'm hoping for outside.

I walk around the campus, singing:

> "*...Right to brag about bragging rights*
> *Feeling glassy in the fog*
> *These times they are neurons*
> *Drink up until they're gone...*"

The song is a dirge and a song of celebration- it's played through the best and worst moments of my life.

I'm pacing around on the Green. I'm sizing everyone up.

You aren't ~her~ and you aren't ~her~, and you aren't ~her~, and I need ~her~.

I don't go to class because it would be a waste of my time. I don't go to the café because ~she's~ not a commuter.

I go into buildings on campus I've never been in.

Passing through the halls of the Science building, I find a couple of nurses, but I don't allow myself to get distracted.

In the art studio annex, no one has a normal hair color like blonde or brunette; everyone has pink or fire engine red hair springing from dark roots.

I don't go into the segregated theater kid building because ~she~ has an adult personality so ~she~ definitely wouldn't be in there.

I go into the building where all the history classes are, and I look at these cool fossils in a display case in the atrium. I wonder if they're real. The case is locked so I bet they are.

I go into the admissions office and use their bathroom, then pick up a course catalog for next semester.

I walk by the church, then go into the gym. ~She~ isn't using the elliptical, or the treadmill, or the bike, or the rowing machine, or the free weights. I check the pool. The swimmers are wearing swim caps which further complicates my hair color-based search. The girls who are standing outside the pool have weird bodies and broad shoulders.

I'm constantly updating a list of features that ~she~ can't have, and if someone was ever searching for me, sight unseen, I have to imagine that my skinny frame would be one of the items they would exclude with a, *Please don't be him*, silent hope.

Walking out of the gym, I stare down everyone who passes, half hoping to find ~her~, half scared shitless that I'll succeed in my search because if I do, then action is required.

I can't sleep until I find ~her~. I won't sleep tonight. I won't sleep this week.

~

Day turns to night, and night nears morning. I sit on a bench in the courtyard of my building and a girl wearing bright white sneakers, sheer black tights, and a black cocktail dress walks over and sits down at the other end of the bench. Her hair is yanked back on her scalp and a dirty blonde ponytail bursts from the crown of her head.

When I sense that she's looking away, I glance at her.

She looks over to me, and I look away.

I try to steal another glimpse, but when I do, I'm caught, and we make direct eye contact.

I have to say something, so I tell her, "I like your dress."

"This?" she asks, "This is nothing, it's just really breathable and I don't care what happens to it." When she says this, I watch her lips, and I notice a black and blue bruise on her chin.

"Ah, good for dancing," I say, then after a pause, I ask, "Is that what the sneakers are for, dancing?"

"No, I'm not going dancing. I'm actually waiting for someone," she says, and I focus on her eyes so I don't make her self-conscious about the bruise.

The Sneaker Girl looks at me, then beyond me. Her eyes widen and her posture straightens, which causes me to look where she's looking. I watch as a short, semi-bald guy makes his way through the courtyard, toward us.

The Sneaker Girl senses my fear, and quietly says, "It's fine, don't worry."

This man isn't a kid, and he's not a Kirtland student, but the girl might be. It's possible that he's one of those guys who decides to go back to school after a divorce, but why he's living in a building that's primarily student housing doesn't make sense. Maybe he's a previous resident that refused to move? I briefly consider that this quickly approaching man might be my Super. I try to think back to when I blew a fuse over the summer, but I can't recall the face of the man who arrived with the replacement fuses.

The semi-bald guy, when he gets about two feet away from the Sneaker Girl, snorts a loud, "Hemf."

"This is my friend. He lives in the building too," the Sneaker Girl says, then gestures to me.

I don't know what to say, so I just give more specifics, "I'm 4E, apartment 4E."

The semi-bald guy's face lights up, "Apartment 4E? No shit. I've wanted to thank you. I'm 5E- I live above you and the last guy who lived in 4E was a real bastard, always calling the cops and getting me noise violations."

"Because of the thuds?" I ask, comfortable enough to bring it up outright.

The semi-bald guy nods his head in confirmation.

"I don't mind it really... but I must admit I'm a little curious though," I edge to the question I want answered.

The semi-bald guy begins mulling something over, it's written all over his face. He looks at me, then looks at the Sneaker Girl, then scans the courtyard.

"Okay, follow me," the semi-bald guy says.

We take the elevator up to the 5th floor, then walk down the hall- the Sneaker Girl's shoes squeaking on the laminate tiles.

The semi-bald guy unlocks the door to 5E, and the three of us enter a sparsely decorated, dimly lit space with nothing on the walls. The floor plan is exactly the same as my apartment, but I don't feel at home here because of the way the space is used. Other than the sofas, which are pressed up against the walls, there's no furniture in the living room. I step onto the carpet that completely covers the hardwoods, and it's spongy. The semi-bald man offers me a seat, and I sit down on the sofa, but he doesn't join me and neither does the Sneaker Girl.

She and the semi-bald guy walk to the far side of the room together. I watch this reluctantly, giving in to my curiosity.

Suddenly, the Sneaker Girl starts running. I'm trying to figure out why. What's she running from? Is she coming for me? Should I be running?

The semi-bald man gives chase, and right before the Sneaker Girl makes it to the door, the semi-bald man lunges and catches her, taking her down hard. Her chin smacks the carpet along with a symphony of knees and elbows.

The Sneaker Girl snakes out of the semi-bald man's grip and they both get up. She darts away, back toward where she first started, and he again takes chase.

She makes it back to the other side of the living room, then down they go again. The Sneaker Girl wraps her legs around the man's neck, but before she can fully constrict on him, he maneuvers out of the lock.

Now back on their feet, they're heading in my direction, then the semi-bald guy dives, catching the Sneaker Girl by the tights, and she goes down with a thud.

The Sneaker girl pins the semi-bald guy with her forearm, but he barrel rolls out of it.

Back and forth.

Back and forth.

My eyes dart away from this bizarre, brutal ballet, and I begin to search the wall next to the door. Despite being directly above me, with the exact same apartment layout, the semi-bald man doesn't have a light switch in the same place that I do. This unsettling fact makes me turn my focus back to the sweaty chaos for the comfort of confusion.

I watch, numb, for ten minutes, until the Sneaker Girl's tights are ripped off, her dress is torn off, and her sports bra is heading toward the same fate. Her body is perfectly toned. She's unquestionably stronger than I am, but not stronger than the semi-bald guy.

After they both fall near my feet, I see that some places I originally viewed as muscle tone on the girl are actually bruises.

The semi-bald man slithers out of his pants while the Sneaker Girl tries to squeeze out of his grasp. He stands up and his legs look like they were chiseled from marble.

As though a switch was flipped, my exit becomes a personal demand.

I wait for the grappling duo to pass, then I make my way to the door.

I don't look back as I flip the bolt lock, then open the door and walk out into the hallway.

My legs feel too weak to take the stairs, so I get in the elevator and hit "4."

The Sneaker Girl and the semi-bald man are people that I won't write to Edie about. Somehow, in a way, I feel like I'm protecting Edie by not telling her this story.

~

Last night, I didn't stay in that room to the sweaty conclusion, and I'm proud of this, even if the edges of my time in 5E are hazed with regret. That haze is heavy with temptation, and I have to deny my body the easy release of masturbating to the thought of the Sneaker Girl. I lie in bed, and stare at the ceiling, wondering if she's directly above me at this very moment.

To distract myself, to better myself, I open my laptop.

4353638332936382.com

"show us your hits.

i can pick up anyone's greatest hits album and i'll usually like at least one song on it. at the thrift shop, i found some 99 cent greatest hits tapes of artists i had never heard of. for a week, i listened to one tape a day, fully taking in each lo-fi echo of the best an act had to offer. every tape i bought showed a flash of brilliance, a moment of grace, a fraction of time when everything worked as we all hoped it would. in my tape box, i now have:

XX

> *juice newton's greatest hits*
> *style - country/rock, breakup music.*
> *best song - it's a heartache.*
> *cover - what appears to be juice newton, head tilted in an off-center glamshot, with some very 80's teal and hot pink writing scrawled above the headshot.*

XX

> *squeeze's greatest hits*
> *style - repetitive new wave.*
> *best song - take me i'm yours.*
> *cover - cheese grader, eye chart, cartoon boxers. i bought the tape to figure out the meaning of the cover, but when i noticed the 'est' on the eye chart, I didn't need the music to decipher the meaning. grate-est-hits.*

XX

> *mott the hopple's greatest hits*
> *style - cheesy rock.*

best song - all the young dudes (written by bowie).
cover - 11 small covers, surrounding a big cover. it was like the band,
after selecting what is most certainly the worst band name in the
history of popular music, felt totally unwilling to make any other
decisions, at all. if they were to ask me, i'd tell them... the top left cover,
something about it, that's the one.
XX
 the brothers four's greatest hits.
style - white guys harmonizing songs that were hip in the early 60's.
best song - greenfields.
cover - four bad motherfuckers in some bad motherfucking sweaters.
XX
 if you have some greatest hits tapes i might like, think about them real
hard, then through your mental vibes i'll be drawn to them at the thrift
shop the next time i get money.
 i hope you understand."

My poor, mysterious, fragile, hip, insecure, blonde, Kirtland University girl.

I think about The Association's *Greatest Hits* really hard, ignoring that the act is pointless.

The cover to The Association's Greatest Hits is the six members of The Association sitting on the bank of a lake, all smiling. I imagine they're watching their seventh band member drown, happy because the royalties no longer have to be split seven ways.

~

I'm ready in record time. Showered, hair perfect, clothes wrinkle free, teeth brushed, clean shaven.

I grab a bagel from the café and head downtown.

I sing, "*...the kitchen is shining bare...*" on the bus

I sing, "*...except for that everlasting pair...*" on the street

I sing, "*...but you have all you need...*" while getting sidetracked down an alley because I see a blonde girl.

I sing until I'm standing in front of the thrift store. The mental prepping I'm doing before entering the store probably makes it look like I'm going to rob the place. It would be a victimless crime- people's past consumption being consumed by me for the same payment that the previous owner received when they turned the items over to the thrift store.

I walk into the store with tension contorting my frame.

In the book section, there's a young black girl in pink capris with teal barrettes in her hair, and she's holding seven novels. Her father stands close by, looking at covers of books written by political pundits who are dead serious about the minor mistakes of men who are now dead.

I make my way down the aisles of abandoned clothes, and I do not pass my poor, mysterious, fragile, hip, insecure, blonde, Kirtland University girl.

In the back of the store, I find an old particle board shelving unit lined with cassette tapes. I scan the names on the plastic spines, looking for any greatest hits tapes. There are none. I become sure that I'm standing in a place that ~she~ was once standing in, feeling excited, looking for something new.

I'm about to turn and go, but I notice that one of the labels on the tapes is *The Best of The Box*- a greatest hits collection that was compiled from a wide-ranging and quality-varying Nirvana box set.

~She~ took everything, besides Kurt.

~

I call Joan and she meets me in town. We both get tall beers and fries. Joan's legs are jackhammering on the floor, and I'm not sure if it's because she has to pee or if it's because I've not only initiated this meeting, but also bought her alcohol. I once read that if someone has restless legs, it means they're either in the sample set of a new medication with heavy side effects, or they don't want to be doing whatever they're doing. Joan refuses to get on medication, and I can't convince her to, because I have made the same refusal, so I know the jitters aren't side effects- Joan does not want to be here.

My legs now jackhammer in perfect synchronicity with hers.

"What's going on?" I ask, making eye contact with Joan. I want to put my hand on her leg to stop it from moving, but I don't because it could be misinterpreted as a tender gesture.

"It's nothing," Joan says, then takes a sip of her beer.

"It's obviously something."

Joan's legs finally come to rest and she looks me in the eyes, "I think someone is following me, like, you know, stalking me. I think they're breaking into my room to send a message," she says.

I actively try to frown so I don't smile, then I say "I'm sure you're overreacting," in an assuring tone.

"No, there's no other way to explain what's going on in my life, Kurt."

I realize why this moment needs to happen. I have been setting up the dominoes even before I knew that I'd be interested in initiating a chain reaction. I thought that I was playing these small pranks on Joan because it made Kirtland a more entertaining amusement park, but now I can study this crisis to find the threshold of what's menacing to a girl, what's insignificant to a girl, and what strikes terror in the hearts of the young, lost, and beautiful.

I tread lightly, knowing that this entire conversation is a thin piece of ice that I'm capable of traversing with careful steps, cautious pauses, constant progression, and a little bit of luck. "What's so bad about a person stalking you? You should appreciate the fact that someone thinks you're special enough to follow," I offer delicately.

"Ugh. You're ridiculous. You know, for how jealous of a person you are, I assumed you would take this a little more seriously."

"You're right," I say.

Joan looks at me with an increased level of concern.

"How can I help?" I ask.

Joan almost gags in response, then lifts both hands toward me and splays out her fingers. She whispers out a desperate request, "Make them stop."

"Alright. I can do that. I'll need some more information though, okay? I need to ask you a couple questions- are you comfortable speaking about what you've been facing lately? I think you're very brave to be handling this yourself, but I want to handle this with you. I want us to handle this together."

Joan nods in agreement, and I want to hug her, not because she's terrified, but because she's helping me improve my life. She's guiding me to my destiny.

"What scares you the most about this stalker?" I ask.

Joan sighs, then says, "Everything! He's... like... stalking around."

"Have you seen him?"

"No."

"Are you sure it's a man?"

"Yes."

"How?"

"He touched my underwear."

"That's a very narrow perspective to have on college campus sexuality."

"Fuck off, you dick," Joan says.

"You're right," I say, resetting, not finding what I want. "I'm ignoring your feelings and focusing on the surface. How does this stalker make you feel?"

"Shitty."

"Shitty, how?"

"Like, shitty as in no matter where I am, he could be there. He could be the guy who shows up to unclog the shower, or he could be the guy who serves me food- which means he's probably cumming in it."

"If you knew who he was, at least you'd know who to look out for," I say.

"I could contact the police about him then."

"Have you... contacted the police?"

"No, I'm not going to join that club of fake-rape girls in those internet think pieces."

"This is different than that."

"Without a face or a name, it isn't. What do I say, 'Keep an eye out for a shy human being on campus that finds me interesting?' I mean, come on."

"What if he's doing this out of quiet admiration without any malicious intent?" I ask.

"Of course he has maleficent intent, Kurt. If he didn't, he could just walk up and speak to me."

I wince at Joan's response, but force myself to move past it, "This isn't me turning him into an innocent, because what he's doing to you makes me sick to my stomach, but what if- however small the chance- this guy is just trying to become friends with you after seeing and liking your paintings, but he isn't sure how to approach you?"

"He crossed the line when he broke into my room. Of course it would be fantastic to find someone who embraces my art, but they should use their brain and find me in public, then gently provide a compliment. That's all it would take. That's almost something I would like. This is much different."

My body buzzes as I receive help with my heavy problems, and I want to do anything I can to repay the favor.

Joan begins to lightly sob, and I immediately slide forward, then reach out to comfort her, while whispering, "Hey, look at me. Look at me, Joan." I hold her face in my hands, and I say, "I love you, and I assure you that as long as that is true, you are completely and totally safe."

~

In Brit-Lit, we do Takeaways on *A Clockwork Orange*, and I come to the conclusion that, behind the tears, Joan loves the fact that she's being stalked. It's like how Noni's parents seem to love the fact that their son is so distant that they can create a narrative that works for them. It can be comforting to brag about something that instantly garners genuine sympathy and concern.

It's entirely possible that Joan's tears are a result of her inability to control the situation.

There are the dangerous stalking cases- usually the obsessed ex-boyfriends, jilted ex-girlfriends, or the cashier whose regular customer becomes their reason to go to work. Then, there are the malignant stalking situations- everyone with a Facebook account.

With the first situation, physical harm is pretty much assured. These situations end in black eyes, and hard cries, and changed lives.

With the second situation, people don't like their stalker getting too close for one single solitary reason- if the stalker reaches the intimate closeness they strive for, they could be disappointed, then they may lose interest. If the mystique dissipates, the peerless love could simply fade away.

People fear their stalker will find out they aren't worth stalking.

I'm not my poor, mysterious, fragile, hip, blonde, Kirtland University girl's stalker- I'm an admirer. I'm not a writing groupie- I'm a kindred spirit. I'm her soulmate, and soulmates usually need some extra time to find each other.

The whole situation with my mother has taught me to get used to waiting patiently for a woman who is worth it.

~

Joan comes over to my apartment unannounced. She brings a care package that her parents sent to her. It contains candy bars, and popcorn, and fruit snacks. Everything in the box is arranged to be aesthetically pleasing and because of this, I don't touch any of it. I don't want to disturb the balance.

We watch some movie that's been remade twice- something based on a Stephen King book. I sit through all of Joan's comments about how every movie based on a Stephen King book sucks, and she finally shuts up when I mention *The Shining*/ And *The Dead Zone*/ And *Carrie*/ And *The Green Mile*/ And *The Shawshank Redemption*.

After five minutes of silence, Joan says, "It's not like I read horror books. No one reads horror novels. How was I supposed to know that King wrote *Carrie*?"

I look at Joan, and think, *Plug it up.*

~

By the time I'm able to accept the morning and begin my day, Joan has already left for some meeting she had with her advisor.

I pull my laptop over and decide I'll google more lyrics to ~the song~. I hope for a new result, a complete listing of every word, or maybe a song clip. If I find another scrap of the song, I won't have to keep hunting for ~her~ with such a desperate focus. I need to meet ~her~ so I can ask who sings ~the song~. I need to meet ~her~ because she seems to be my other half. There's even a small chance that ~she~ may have ~the song~ on tape. I may be able to hear the music outside of my head once again.

The google results yield nothing. Only the one line connects and it connects with the exact person I need it to.

This shifts my focus. I try to figure out how I can seamlessly meet a girl who views me as a complete stranger. I need to go about it in a way that won't result in her showing up at a bar, leg jackhammering, as she says to a friend, "I think someone is stalking me, and I'm afraid."

I've already discovered ~her~ so now I need ~her~ to discover me. I've found that words travel farther and connect easier when they're sitting, waiting to be discovered. I need my own online journal. I'll title my first post with the next lyrics in line, then trust that the universe will send my message, reunite the couplet, and achieve perfection.

I want to cultivate a mutual obsession.

I can't figure out how to create a website with a specific URL, so I have to accept a blogging template and branded URL. This platform has pre-made layouts and little smiley and sad faces that you can add under the title of each entry. Apparently, your average blogger's writing is so worthless that a happy face has to be utilized to basically sum up, "This is an entry about me being content." Everything involved in this system seems to have a template, and I'm surprised that when I click on the happy face, the blog doesn't just write itself.

My derisive attitude is quickly muted when I face a block of white screen and a blinking cursor.

I search my desk for inspiration and my eyes settle on a Polaroid picture from this past summer when I went with Joan to a flea market. Some guy took our picture, then Joan made me give him a dollar for it. I remember the fat guy behind me saying, "Why the fuck would anyone want a picture of themselves here?" and I was so afraid that he could read my mind, I rushed Joan back to the car.

In the picture, I'm looking directly at the camera, squinting at the setting sun, and Joan has an arm around me, but her eyes are leading to the left.

For my first entry, I type:

"I tolerated your singing (which stopped when I sang along).
/And your poetry (which wasn't pursued long enough to fill a single chapbook).
/And your rancid coffee breath (mirroring the palatability of your opinions).
/And your snoring (that allowed you to intrude on even my silent moments).
/And your favorite movies (that you always seem annoyed by when we rewatch them).
/And your daddy issues (I'm not your father, FYI).
/And your slutty past (I wish you didn't cheat on him with me so you'd still be with him).
/And your boring paintings (if you paint me, I know that it'll come out exactly the way I see myself, ugly, because you can't paint faces well).
/And your bad playlists (you never go Britney to Christina. It's just not proper mix-etiquette. It's unfair to Christina).
/And your need to speak to dogs in baby talk (they're dogs. Your existence is enough to fill them with Christmas morning joy every second of your visit).
/And your constant text messages (never posed as questions, never ending with question marks, yet always requiring answers).
/And your unwavering optimism (that only appears when I'm acknowledging a situation is beyond my ability to fix).
/And your lack of social skills (if you can only offer, 'That's not funny,' you're worse than the guy who told the inappropriate joke).
/And your weight obsession (yes, you did gain ten pounds this year).
/And your delusion that I actually found you interesting (I just found you comfortable).
I was tolerant and no, our relationship is not genuine, but at least I give you the illusion that it is. It doesn't matter what type of inconvenience you've brought to the table, I've always eaten it, and I don't feel guilty for a second that I've led you on. This isn't goodbye, it's just... why?"

I spin around in my office chair and after one full rotation, I find myself facing the horrible entry I just wrote. This is why Edie asks me to write about other people. No one on earth could look at what I just wrote and feel an interest in me. No one will read my hateful rant and connect with it. Maybe that's why I wrote it? Stalker syndrome- I'm afraid to write something I know ~she~ could love, only to meet ~her~ in person and have ~her~ instantly feel a profound and sinking disappointment. The awful man reflected in this journal entry is me at my ugliest- it's the painting that I will never let Joan start. I hit, "Publish," and reveal how unhappy and bitter I am.

~

I walk out of Micro-Socio-Economical required class, confident that I did well on the multiple choice test. I've cheated on 8 tests so far this semester. I've taken 12 tests. I'd calculate the percentage of tests that I've cheated on, but I'd rather have someone else do it for me.

I bounce around the Green with a warm feeling because the test is behind me, and I have the rest of the day to search for ~her~.

This freedom is quickly rescinded by a text that I receive from someone whose number isn't even programmed into my phone.

"plz com2 gerards," reads the text.

I wonder if they mean that I should come to Gerard's place now, or if Gerard has a party this weekend that I should attend, or if Gerard has finally formed a band because it would most certainly be called, "The Gerards."

I don't want to miss something amazing, so I start walking toward Gerard's apartment.

Since the number that texted me isn't programmed into my phone, I convince myself that this is the universe texting me, then I silently hope that the universe was driving while typing the text because the spelling and grammar are a mess.

The moment I step inside Gerard's apartment, I instantly realize that a national tragedy has just occurred. Every face in the room wears the same expression, so it's obvious... we're now at war.

I've seen this posture before; I've seen these uneasy glances before.

Next comes the bright green news footage; next comes the color-coded warnings.

Laura Mellin runs to me and gives me a big hug, then says, "I'm so sorry, Kurt."

Her statement is delivered directly to me.

It's personalized with my name.

It's finally happened.

My mother is dead.

How did they know before I did?

A rush overcomes me, a desert heat.

I'm rich. My mother is dead.

The second before my heart explodes, someone in the room says, "I know how much Joan meant to you."

Joan.

Joan?

Joan.

Meant.

Past tense.

No.

Joan cannot be the tragedy; I wasn't done yet.

"What? Happened?" I eke out.

More people in the room start crying, and I'm told, "Joan was killed."

"Wh-who fucking killed her?" I ask, my heart racing. I look around the room to see if the cops are already here, holding a printout of my journal entry.

"Moving guys," Gerard says.

Noni peeks her head out from the kitchen, and she says, "Did it with a couch. They smooshed her with a fucking sofa. In-saneee."

People in the room sneer at Noni. She notices the glances, and says, "No joke," then she licks peanut butter off the dull knife in her hands.

I keep backing up until I hit the closed door, then I slide down and sit on the ground. "How did it happen?" I ask.

Gerard approaches me, then crouches down on the frayed knees of his jeans. He carefully walks me through it, "I guess they were lowering a sofa out of a third floor window over on Bard Place. They couldn't get it down those skinny ass stairs and so lowering it was the only option. Joan happened to be walking by on the sidewalk, when the security rope broke, and... the guys lost their grip."

A sofa fell from the sky, onto Joan.

The queen crushed by her throne.

"Can I have some time to... uh..." I mumble, and Gerard nods at me.

I stand up, and in a small voice, I tell everyone, "Thank you. I'll be okay," then I leave.

As I walk to my apartment, I sing the full song, twice. The first time I sing it, it's with sorrow. The second time I sing it, I regain my voice. I sing with what feels like relief.

When I get back to my apartment, I sit at my desk and look at the picture of myself and Joan at the flea market. I think about the first entry in my journal, and I wonder if I cursed her.

Bringing up the blog on my laptop, I realize that this is how I would've eulogized her when she was alive, and I focus on not letting my perspective change because she's gone. I could easily fall into the trap of securing attention for this situation, then constructing a vision of Joan based purely on nostalgia. I imagine making up T-shirts for Joan like the black kids at Kirtland do when one of their friends is shot- "The Good Smoosh Young" scripted over the picture of Joan at the flea market printed on 30 white T-shirts.

Joan is gone.

This is the moment that I worked so hard for and feared so terminally at the same time. Good or bad, Joan was there, always. She was there when I felt shitty, or horny, or social enough to actually leave my apartment. She would introduce me to people. She would tell me that I'm good-looking. She'd cut my hair for me and make me not only look, but also feel presentable. She kept the other side of the bed warm. She made me toast. She had a car. A couple of times she made alright jokes. She came quickly so I didn't have to work too hard. Her mom would send her care packages that she always shared with me. She once stabbed a girl. She owned a couple of really good novels in hardcover that I'll have to buy now unless she has some sort of will that leaves the copies to me.

Sometimes, it made sense that I stayed with Joan.

Now I'm more alone. I miss my mother. I need my poor, mysterious, fragile, hip, blonde, Kirtland University girl.

I'm quarantined from the ones I love like I have a disease.

I try to step closer because it's impossible for ~them~ to back away further.

I leave my blog.

4353638332936382.com.

"stealing from the poor.

i found a tick on my leg this morning. i might have lyme disease. according to roommate, she's sure i've been infected, but she assured me that it's 'the least of my problems.' i've managed to stay away from all the diseases that kirtland girls get from various friction-intensive activities, but now i probably have one that's different, yet the same. i found the tick after i came back from existing in the woods today. it was attached to the back of my calf. it probably latched onto me when i was crunching through the leaves, or it found me when i was sitting at the base of that tree, or it crawled onto me when i was walking through the tall grass. i don't know if ticks can fly or jump or if they just walk, but somehow it found me. i imagine the reason that it was so easy to get the tick off of me was because it had tasted what it feels like to be me and just couldn't tolerate the poison. i have that effect on almost everything around me. i picked him off my leg, then, looking at the blood filled little black tick i said, 'this is why i never let them get close.'

I hope you understand."

My Takeaways:

One- Getting too close to anything will undoubtedly cause you inconvenience for the rest of your life.

Two- Every action has an unequal and unfair reaction.

I need my poor, mysterious, fragile, hip, insecure, desirable, blonde Kirtland University girl now more than ever.

People say everyone is here for a reason, and I think I now agree with them. If I had never met Joan, then I never would have had a steady relationship. If I lacked a steady past relationship, I'd have no idea what I needed from one. If I had never fallen in love with Joan, then I wouldn't know when I found the right person. I wouldn't be as sure about ~her~ as I am right now.

~

I arrive at Joan's funeral, alone. I'm holding some fresh flowers that Noni left at my door earlier in the morning. Never once did I think Noni was leaving the flowers to console me- she was leaving them for me so I could bring them to the service. The blank card that was held in the bouquet with a little plastic stilt was confirmation of this. I personalized the business-card-sized piece of thick paper with the message, "*Joan, Thank You.*"

My hair is combed back and I'm wearing a black Michael Lorrie suit that had taken up space in my closet, unworn, until this morning.

I view Joan's funeral as the trial run for the next funeral I'll have to attend. Experiencing all of this grief and tear-stained sadness in the context of it centering on Joan makes it easier to process.

No matter how hard Joan tried, she was not my mother, but she was close sometimes.

I accept the moment because there are no other options, and I kneel down, then begin to pray in front of the expensive box they put Joan in. I peer inside the coffin and Joan looks good for a smooshed person. If they really wanted to make her look beautiful, they should have dimmed the lights, brought in a movie projector, and played a copy of *The Blessed Nothing* on the wall behind her casket. I've decided that's how I'll remember Joan... in that moment at the Waldorf.

I stand up, then walk over to the condolence line which is not unlike the line at the end of a little league game where the winners hide their smiles as they shake hands with the losers.

Joan's father shakes my hand, then puts his other hand on my shoulder and quietly mentions something about how Joan thought she was being stalked. "Everyone says I'm crazy, but I think that has something to do with her death," he whispers to me.

I quickly assure him it did not.

After the service, as I exit the funeral home, I take one of their business cards.

The trial run is complete.

Today was difficult, but not impossible.

When Joan died, I got pieces of myself back, which gave me the strength to say goodbye. When my mother dies, I'll lose so many more pieces than those I've gained here today.

~

After someone who was consistently in your life makes a permanent exit, it takes some time to learn to exist as an island. I'm having trouble dealing with the fact that I have to make my own meals every night. I don't like that I have to clean my own apartment. It's much harder to go to sleep without someone going with me. I have to bring my phone to listen to music when I grocery shop. Watching comedies in my apartment, laughing alone, feels sad. The worst thought that has entered my mind in the aftermath of Joan's death is that if I got hit by a car today, I'd have no one at my bedside when I regained consciousness in the hospital.

Joan absolutely would've been there when I woke up, then she'd begin complaining about what my nurse said to her.

I no longer have someone that I can rely on to comfort me completely when something terrible happens, and this scares me because of what I'm counting down to.

~

The task of replacing Joan begins.

Finding my poor, mysterious, fragile, hip, insecure, desirable, blonde, Kirtland University girl isn't going to be easy, and until I seem to be close to achieving this massive goal, I need a stand-in. Until I find ~her~, I will accept a girl that I think looks like ~her~ to keep from closing off to the world. I got this idea from a YouTube video about stand-ins for high budget film projects. This particular seven minute clip focused on River White's stand-in. A baritone voice narrator explained that when a movie is being filmed, it takes a massive amount of time to light the scene before they can shoot. Making sure the lighting is right is a very tedious job, and actors of River White's caliber have become so accustomed to delegating their less-than-desirable responsibilities to minions, that the big star opts out of being present for the lighting process. To get the lighting perfect, while not bothering their A-list star, the filmmakers will find someone that's about River's height, with somewhat similar facial features, then they'll use this stand in for all of the lighting calculations that must be done.

I make my way across campus, actively casting my poor, mysterious, fragile, hip, insecure, desirable, blonde, Kirtland University girl's stand-in. Without a stand-in, everything could go wrong when, "Action," is yelled, and I'm aiming for perfection when the cameras begin rolling.

The stand-in must be blonde, so I begin pursuing blonde haired girls exclusively. Either I'll find ~her~ or I'll find the perfect stand-in.

Automatically, the fat girls are excluded. This eliminates much of Kirtland's female population, so much so that I find I have to abandon campus.

I walk into town and head to a casting hotspot. Once inside Starbucks, I start talking to the blonde girl who's behind me in line. "You don't usually come here, do you?" I ask.

"Why do you say that?" the blonde girl asks, looking somewhat annoyed that I started a conversation out of nowhere, but curious enough that she's willing to continue it. Her voice sounds like it should be coming out of a 50's pinup girl.

"I know you're not a regular because you don't have a laptop."

The blonde shoots me a sly smile, then says, "Actually I spilled a cup of organic shade grown Mexican on it last week."

I have a nice enough conversation with the blonde girl, we order our drinks, then we walk outside and her mom picks her up in a minivan.

~

I speak with a blonde girl in line at the grocery store. She takes out one of my earbuds, and asks, "What are you listening to?" Her voice sounds like she should be older than she is. If I had talked to her on the phone before meeting her, I would've had a completely different mental picture of this girl. She's a girl with the voice of a woman.

Even under the harsh fluorescents, she looks too pretty to be starting unprovoked conversations with someone like me.

I want to answer her question by saying, *It doesn't matter what I'm listening to because it's just a stand-in for a song that I'm still searching for,* but instead I choose to hand her an earbud, and she uses the sleeve of her hoodie to wipe it off, then she puts it in her ear, and we listen to a Voxtrot song called "The Start of Something."

At the end of the song, she hands me back my earbud, along with a piece of paper with her number pre-written on it.

"Text me when you have an extra bud again," she tells me.

The conversation ends, and I watch the blonde girl get a text, leave the line, then walk to the pharmacy part of the supermarket where she picks up about ten little white bags.

I put the paper she gave me inside a *People* magazine in a rack by the register.

~

I meet an in-uniform blonde cheerleader, and I help her look for her contact lens in the foyer of Kozinski. "I'm always blinded at inopportune times," she tells me. Her voice sounds like a dumb cheerleader's voice, and I appreciate this because it's so on-theme. She's more of a caricature of a cheerleader than an actual cheerleader. She's like a movie character cheerleader, and she must be playing a part because we don't have a football team, and I can't think of any other sport that is going on in mid-October. Basketball, maybe?

I doubt Kirtland has cheerleaders- it requires way too much positivity. It demands cheering for a common goal.

We don't find the contact, and the cheerleader tells me, "My name is Martha. If you see my contact, let me know."

She doesn't provide a cell number or an e-mail address. She must assume that I'll stalk her online. Maybe in a parallel universe.

~

I begin to introduce myself to another blonde girl on campus, immediately starting a conversation about music, but her ugly brunette twin sister comes over, and says, "Ew, don't talk to him," then pulls the blonde away by the elbow. The brunette's voice sounds like the blonde's voice.

The brunette is right. Pull them away. Pull all of them away. The crew isn't restless yet. They know that when the star arrives, every second of waiting will be paid back a thousand-fold with the joy of capturing and creating something beautiful.

~

I don't attend class for a significant stretch of the month of October. Everyone says they understand. They don't, but their supposed understanding has brought me freedom. Every day, I get e-mailed notes from a @kirtland.edu address that I don't recognize. I get extensions for papers that I never knew were assigned. Before I can get half of an excuse out of my mouth, people say, "Don't worry about it. Is there anything I can do to help?"

There's an urban legend that if your roommate dies, you get straight A's. What happens if your girlfriend dies? What happens if she gets squished by a sofa? I slowly find out, and feel surprised by how many people at Kirtland are aware of my existence, and who I was dating. They probably just recognize me from the funeral, or the picture that was on the front of the school paper.

My mind is only momentarily occupied with these thoughts before I start worrying, *If everyone is noticing me, what if ~she~ did as well, and what if ~she~ felt apathetic about me?*

Shut up, continue your investigation, I decide. Find things out. Collect facts. Think critically. Hope earnestly. Maybe even pray. When in doubt, 4353638332936382.com.

"*the first of forty.*
i wonder what the fine is for owning a cat here. i want one desperately. he would have to be small like me. he would have to have green eyes, unlike me. i would name it 'eek' even though no one would get the reference. since no boys ever sleep in my room, he can stay at the end of the bed and no one will kick him off because of their allergies. eek will be very nice to me, but he won't pay attention to roommate. i'll tell people, 'eek hates you,' then eek will look down from the bookcase with a sneer that confirms this fact. i'm sure i'll never get eek because i never break the rules. i need something alive in this dorm to remind me how beautiful two skittish creatures living together can be.
i hope you understand."

My Takeaways:
One- There was a time that she lived in a dorm on campus.
Two- She also seems to feel the same emptiness that's pinning me to the ground so brutally that I leave deep impressions when I walk.

My poor, mysterious, fragile, hip, insecure, desirable, feline, blonde, Kirtland University girl knows what it's like to yearn for the impossible.

~

You could follow my trail to the Rite Aid, just look for the annoyed blondes.

I grab deodorant, some hair products, and paper towels, then make my way to the checkout. There isn't much of a line so odds are there won't be any good eavesdropping opportunities or stand-in castings.

I sing, "...*Drink up until they're gone...*" and wait for the guy in front of me to pay for his plunger.

"Okay, I just have to say this. I want to let you know how sorry I am to hear about what happened. When I met you, I didn't know who you were, so I'm apologizing now. Maybe I can make it up to you, I know it must be killer. Not killer, ugh, but difficult," a 50's pinup girl rambles, to my back.

I turn around, and come face to face with a blonde haired girl. Not ~the~ blonde haired girl, but *a* blonde haired girl.

With only seconds to place who this girl is, I search my mind, and I come up with a fleeting image- this girl getting into a family van outside of Starbucks.

I raise my eyebrows in response to what I feel is a warm gesture made by a girl who could have easily stayed quiet, and I confirm what I think she wants to hear, "Yeah, it's been really tough." I look down, brood, and grind the toe of my shoe into the shiny buffed tile floor.

"If you want someone to talk to, I'm not doing anything after I buy this candy," she mentions, then shows me three chocolate bars. If I had *the money*, I would buy them for her. The notion that she's likely buying this candy with her mother's money unites us in a twisted way.

"That'd be nice. We can talk," I say, not breaking the unity.

Realizing that we both rely on our mothers for support, I begin to really study the blonde girl. I notice the light freckles on the bridge of her nose, and that her smooth skin ripples at the corner of her mouth as she smiles at me. This girl is a wonderful stand-in.

I pay for my items, then wait for the stand-in to check out.

She drops her candy bars on the counter, then asks, "Could I have a pack of Pall Malls?"

The stand-in takes out a twenty from her huge wallet, then slides out her ID without being asked. The cashier takes the ID, looks at it, looks at the stand-in, then looks back at the ID for what must be at least seven seconds. It's almost as though the register girl sees that the stand-in is the same height, the same weight, and she has similar features as the girl on the ID, but she doesn't believe this girl is who she claims to be.

The Pall Malls are placed in a bag.

We step outside, and simultaneously, the stand-in and I take out our cigarettes, light one, then exhale with pleasure.

"To be honest, I didn't think you were old enough to buy these," I admit, holding out my cigarette.

"I really am. I promise," she says, then takes her big wallet out of her purse and hands me her ID, "See, 19."

I've become the world's skinniest bouncer, and this makes me feel embarrassed. I'm now worried that the stand-in might be seeing me in the wrong light. "Sorry, I guess it was the whole minivan thing," I say, as I twirl her ID in my fingers.

"It's okay, I'm glad you asked."

"You are?"

"Yeah, my ID picture is my favorite picture of me," the stand-in admits.

I stop twirling the ID and stare at the stand-in's picture. Her hair is a little shorter, but the smile on her face, the look in her eyes; it's all electric. This is a very good picture of... I look at the name to the right of the picture, *Mia Malone*.

"That is a picture that proves exactly who you are..." I tell Mia, "...someone special."

The stand-in makes the most unlikely of transitions. A dream becomes a reality with a simple confirmation- a small admission- a new light.

"I'd let you keep it, but, ya know, it's my ID."

I take one last look at the perfect picture of Mia Malone, then hand her back her license.

~

My instincts are reaffirmed back at my apartment. Mia's juvenility was obvious from the beginning; I see through girls.

The moment I open the fridge door, Mia drops to her knees, then puts her mouth up to the spout of a box of red wine that sits on a shelf in my fridge.

Staring at the condiments, with Mia on her knees, I say, "The glasses are in the second cupboard to the right, in the kitchen."

Mia stands up, then wipes her mouth with the back of her hand. She smiles at me, I smile back. She gets the glasses, then we fill them too high.

Mia sits on the futon. I sit next to her. She puts on a movie about fathers, but I choose not to read into it.

I look away from the flat screen, and Mia wipes the bangs out of her eyes, then wipes the bangs out of my eyes. My right hand touches her hip bone, above her jeans, and when I feel the lace band of her underwear, I dip lower and glide my palm across her short pubic hair that feels almost sharp. She angles her hips toward me, helping my fingers reach her lips. As I rub my hand back and forth, I feel her drip onto me, and when she kisses me, my middle finger enters her. She keeps pushing into me, and when I open my eyes, Mia looks even better than she does on her ID.

~

I wake up next to Mia, naked, sore in my lower back. I wonder how I'm lucky enough to have sex with a girl who has such a good ID picture. My ID picture looks like everyone else's. My skin looks yellow, my hair looks matted, my eyes look stoned, my smile- cockeyed. I suppose it pays off to have a picture that screams *I'm not high, I just look like this,* but I was struck with genuine jealousy when I saw Mia's ID. I come to the definitive conclusion that my ID is something to be ashamed of. The next time I'm ID'd, I'll just quietly walk away with my head down.

With each girl I have sex with, I gain a new insecurity.

Before Mia leaves, she turns around with an innocent look on her face, then tells me, "I want you to know I didn't fuck you because your girlfriend is dead."

"I know," I say.

"I'd like to see you again."

"You will, I've memorized your address off your ID."

Mia laughs, then looks me in the eyes, and says, "Feel better."

I walk over to my desk, write Edie a letter about Joan, recopy it, then send it.

Walking back from the mailbox, I regret how personal the letter about Joan is.

I return to my apartment, heavy with a weird emptiness that I can't place. I again write to Edie- this time a letter about Mia. I recopy it, then send it.

I return to my apartment again. I look at my phone/ I have a glass of wine/ I read over some notes that were e-mailed to me/ I check the online blackboard/ I write a paper about fiscal policy and find a way to mention Joan in it.

~

With Joan gone, I miss my mother more. I have a nagging desire to go to the mall with my mother. I want to sit across from her as we eat out of styrofoam containers with white plastic sporks and watch as the trapped birds fly from decorative tree, to light fixture, to air conditioning grate, then back again. Birds flying in either panic or perfection. I want my mother to sit and pick at her sesame chicken and ask about school, and girls, and my friends; questions I refuse to answer. I want her to cringe at my purchases. I want her to scoff at price tags. I want to ride up the escalator while she takes the stairs due to a vague and bizarre safety concern. I'd accept her detour without questioning it. I'd wait for her to catch up with me.

~

The singing I belt out during the walk to campus escalates to the point that people notice me, expressing looks of genuine displeasure.

"...*we're compiling a file, we're taking a name...*"

A guy crosses the street to make sure I'm not following him.

I can't afford to take the chance that I pass ~her~ and ~she~ doesn't notice me. I need to stop ~her~ in ~her~ tracks with something more extreme- but safer- than a rain of furniture. Good impression or bad impression, the first step becomes making an impression- stepping out from the shadows and into the light.

In Socio-Mackerel-Somewhat-Comical class, I take down every word of the lecture because I've had multiple complete sets of diligent notes e-mailed to me, and my compulsion to create uniformity has surpassed my lethargy. Somehow, I've started collecting class notes. I might even have to borrow someone else's notebook in the class to make sure my notes are the definitive collection.

Rule~ I need all of the information. Every scrap, or nothing at all. Dinosaurs? I don't understand them, so I regard them as fantasy, like dragons. I look at their bones and tell myself, "This is the package that our gasoline is shipped in." Then there's a topic like celebrity divorces on which I could write a book. Once I learn about something, I need to learn more and more and more until I'm content, until I understand. There's no sense of accomplishment having an unfinished puzzle on my bedroom floor. The pieces will start to stick to my feet or get kicked under the sofa. The floor becomes off limits in the section where the puzzle is located. I rearrange my life around incomplete pictures until I can devote my complete attention to them.

~

I sit in the booth at Rubie's, alone. This is how I eat now that Joan isn't here to force me to meet her in the café or take her to dinner. Rubie's is one of the local diners where Joan outright refused to eat. She was convinced that the place was a mob-front. Rubie's is made up of two rows of six red felt booths, and has so few lunch and dinner offerings that the entire menu fits in this acrylic plastic table top holder- the type of thing usually reserved for a wine list. Rubie's doesn't have a liquor license, which is good because it keeps me sober for the hour it takes me to finish my meal.

I force myself to eat alone at Rubie's. I would love to invite Noni- my treat- but I never extend the invite because of how it would look if ~she~

walked in and saw me sitting across from a girl in a very date-ish type way. Noni and I would undoubtedly appear, to the uninformed, as a couple. In my head, when we're together, to other people, Noni and I are a *thing*.

I light up a cigarette because even despite all the legislation, Rubie's is so "whatever man" about even the concept of rules, that as long as I charge myself a convenience tax and up my tip, no one says anything. The diners who populate the other booths in Rubie's don't complain because they're all hiding from social interaction by eating here. We are a band of depressed introverts quietly boycotting any of the local restaurants where people make complaints about the lighting, and send food back to the kitchen, and bitch because sweet potato fries are on the menu, but the supplier's shipment is late so only regular french fries are available. There isn't a manager at Rubie's, and the one time that I overheard someone asking to speak to one, the waitress pointed to a Mr. T cutout taped to the door leading to the kitchen. The customer was given permission to air her grievances with Manager T until she was blue in the face. Ultimately, she chose to swallow her outrage. No one likes to be pitied or considered a fool.

I eat my slice of the pie-of-the-day, I drink my coffee, I read the back of one of the pseudo-sugar packets stacked on the table, and I wonder why Edie hasn't been writing me.

No one walks through the door of Rubie's, so I leave a twenty on the table and walk out.

~

In Brit-Lit, the old professor comes up to me before class and tells me that we're going to be discussing a book about "some chick who ends up dying, so if that type of stuff is still ruffling your feathers, you'll probably end up squirting some tears before the day is through."

I assure him that I'll be fine, and I find it oddly refreshing that he was able to put things to me so crudely. I would have respected him less if he had done it any other way.

Brit-Lit remains my favorite class.

~

I meet up with Gerard on the Green, and he immediately informs me that his current long-term goals are securing soft pretzels and pot. I fear this will send us to the mall, so I dismiss his dreams because stepping into the mall will remind me of my own dream. There's the desire to see my mother again, to become a kid again, to patch my wounds with the healing power of capitalism.

"To the mall we go," Gerard declares.

"Let's just go to Revere's," I suggest.

Gerard shakes his head, then says, "No, Revere doesn't have soft pretzels."

We stand in a stalemate, and I'm unable to offer an alternative to the mall trip.

"Can we take the bus?" I ask.

"As, like, a way to confront your fear of trusting other people after- you know- Joan..."

I nod at this, not sure what the answer is to Gerard's psychological assessment. It sounded like something that would come from ~her~ ex-roommate.

~

We wander the mall. I try on a pair of trendy, slightly shiny jeans and a small navy blue t-shirt. I stare at myself in the mirror and wonder what ~she~ would think. I decide ~she~ would like it so I buy the outfit. I'll find ~her~ tomorrow, looking brand new.

A fresh start.

An overpriced eighth and even more overpriced pretzel later, Gerard and I are sitting on the curb in front of Macy's.

"It's such bullshit that they don't put benches out here," Gerard informs me, sounding genuinely disgusted by this injustice, like the ghost of Joan had floated out of the shoe department and possessed him.

"It's because you can't buy anything outside of the mall," I tell him.

"Besides pot."

"Yeah... besides pot, but I'm sure the mall doesn't get a cut of that," I say.

"It keeps them in business though. Kids buy pot, get stoned, then go to the food court. That's every suburban boy's coming of age tale. This whole mall thrives because of drug use," Gerard declares, and in an effort to not appear as the Silent Bob to his Jay, I say, "That's categorically untrue."

"Your statement is the only untruth I've heard," Gerard says, then he hops up and starts pacing back and forth, his thin frame being dwarfed by the giant mall that looms behind him. I recognize this behavior. Gerard is going to go on one of his signature rants and there's nothing I can do to escape it.

"You think these kids- these junior employees- would work every day for shit pay if they weren't high or working to get money to buy drugs?" Gerard asks me, just as Press Parker walks out of the mall. Neither of us says anything as Press passes us. It's unclear if he even sees us because his Wayfarers are reflective and they were on long before he ever reached us.

Gerard and I both watch Press' perfectly ironed shirt flap gently in the breeze as he navigates through the parking lot. His shirt is so bright that Gerard squints while looking at it, and this sort of explains away the sunglasses being on before Press stepped outside.

"Press doesn't do drugs, and he lives for the mall," I say, watching him get into his car.

"The motherfucker's name is Press. I mean, he's the exception. His parents obviously did drugs before they named him."

"I bet if they had a spread of guys shooting up in *GQ*, Press would start buying bags of H in that sketchy park behind the tennis courts," I say.

"Press doesn't disprove my mall theory. He's addicted, just not to drugs," Gerard declares, "He works all day long at Michael Lorrie, and my friend Jenny works there too, and she says that he doesn't even get a check."

"Bullshit, that's illegal. They have to pay him," I assume.

"They do pay him... in store credit," Gerard reveals, "That's how he's come to own every piece of each collection Michael Lorrie has released for men in the past two years."

"You think he'd want to make some dough and move out of his parents' house."

"I pity Press, but I also wish I loved something like he loves Michael Lorrie. Each collection, every season, is different, and he learns to love it."

"Yeah, but imagine what happens to Press when a collection comes out that he doesn't like. His whole identity will shatter," I say.

The bus rounds the corner, then pulls up to the curb, and we get on.

I presume we're going home, but as the ride continues, we pass home.

I follow Gerard's lead- not standing up until he does- and two stops later, he yanks me off the bus by the sleeve.

We walk along the shoulder of the road, stepping over stiff abandoned clothes and beer bottles, until we reach a crappy townie-looking dive bar.

"Please, no," I request, but my request is denied, and Gerard continues to pull me by the shirt, leading me on a journey, without a shared plan.

Inside, we have to push through a mess of people to get to the bar, but these aren't hillbilly people, these are people-people.

"How'd you find out about this place?" I ask, looking at the giant painting of a cat in a jelly jar that's mounted to the wall across from the jukebox.

"The sign out front," Gerard says, being romanced by the atmosphere for what is at least the second time, and could possibly be the hundredth time. Without looking at me, without looking at anyone, Gerard puts his long arms on the bar, then hoists his legs up so he's standing four feet above us all, next to the beer taps. He doesn't look out at the crowd- his eyes are focused on a shelf on the wall. He leans over, eventually making contact with a bottle, and no one stops him as he pulls the label-less liquid off the shelf. The crowd is indifferent to Gerard; his conduct is met with casual acceptance, if not outright indifference.

Gerard hops off the bar with the bottle in his hands, then reaches into his back pocket and takes out a couple of bills. He hands the money to a bartender, then gives me the bottle and demands, "Escape until the nostalgia is unbearable."

~

I sip the green liquid from the bottle, and stare into the screen at 4353638332936382.com.

"to my best friend from fourth grade.

when your father died, i didn't know what to say. i was your best friend, and i knew it was my job to make things a little better. i didn't do that, and i bet i disappointed you. today, i found out that you're roommates with cindy metfessel at b.u. and i remembered that cindy was the one who got you through that time, while i stood by, frozen. i didn't know what to say to you. i might know now. i would have told you that just because someone made you, it doesn't mean they make you. i'm really sorry about your father, and i'm sorry i didn't go to the funeral. i didn't have a car, and i was afraid to call you for a ride. i figured you had so many other more important things to worry about that day. i didn't want to add to it all. i didn't like to see you sad. your father was a lot of things to a lot of people, but i was never sure what he was to you. i want you to know that i liked being your best friend, and i didn't like the way your father treated you, but maybe having a father like that was better than having no father at all. i'll never get a second chance to fix what happened or what didn't happen, and odds are, if i did get the chance, i wouldn't be able to find the confidence to tell you this anyway.

i hope you understand."

My poor, mysterious, fragile, shy, hip, insecure, desirable, feline, blonde, Kirtland University girl.

My Takeaways:

One- I can be her second chance.

Two- She would want to be there when *it* all happens.

I finish the bottle of green liquid, and my father appears in the door frame. I close my eyes and he disappears, yet still looms.

I would never hand ~her~ the poem, I would never allow things to remain in the shadows after reading how she carries this ambiguity and revisits it often.

~She~ won't have to help me with my father. I have complete closure on the situation. Nothing is left to talk out. There are no missed moments that haunt me. Sure, there were things that we didn't do together, but I don't regret these lapses. We never played catch. We never went to a professional football game. We didn't have stereotypical American male bonding moments, but I thank my father for that. He never made that once-a-season, feeble attempt to get us on a trip so we could finally connect. I think he recognized that it would take more than a basketball game or some duck hunting for us to meet eye to eye.

It wasn't for his own lack of trying that we didn't work well together. He tried to teach me how to ride a bike, but it simply didn't work. One day, he removed my training wheels, took me to a somewhat flat stretch of sidewalk, then ran alongside my bike, holding onto one of the handles, yelling, "Pedal! Pedal!" and I tried, but I fell, and I fell, and I fell. I became so bitterly frustrated that my father couldn't "teach" me better, and he became so visibly embarrassed that I was having so much trouble with such a simple task, that after only a few test runs we quickly walked the bike home and left it in the bike rack outside the complex. I had a bike lock, but didn't use it.

The most important part after making a mistake is that you learn from it. The second most important part after making a mistake is to never repeat it again.

My father had his world, and I had mine. He'd give me money, and in turn, I'd tell him where I was going, what I was doing, or who I was seeing. He knew things about me; the type of films I liked, the music I enjoyed, the people I sat with at lunch. He knew all of this because I told him; I told him because he paid me. This was a conversation that we could have that didn't involve sharing thoughts or butting heads. All we had to do was exchange words.

I respected him because he respected me enough to not force me to love him, and in the end, I love him for that.

~

I want to try to distance myself from ~her~, to dull the all-consuming obsession. I go on YouTube, and in a click spiral, I end up on an interview with Johnny Cash that looks like it was filmed in the 70's or 80's- after he was off most substances or at least told people he was. Deciding to commit to an extended viewing of this video, I carry my laptop into the kitchen, then begin a search for something to eat.

In the fridge- Mustard/ Ketchup/ Hot sauce/ Lemon juice/ A box of wine/ A Pepsi/ Five Busch beers.

I grab a beer, and drink it as I watch Johnny play a song in the middle of the interview, and they start splicing in shots of Cash's ranch as he sings. He sounds good, better than I've heard him sound on the MP3s I have on my phone.

Rule: Never opt for the remastered version. Even with ~the song~, I'd want the tape version that I fell in love with because of the campfire crackle, and those cricket-like noises that whoosh in and out. A polished version won't feel the same. I count on music to take me somewhere, and the sterile sound of the remaster always takes me to a super sanitary white room. Music lives in sound and to "clean it up" sullies what's so special about it.

Johnny's song ends, and I go back to the fridge.

He's been everywhere.

...Pickles/ Bacon/ A questionable block of cheese/ Baking soda.

He shot a man in Reno just to watch him die.

I shut the fridge door, then continue the search.

A single aluminum paperweight wrapped in a washed out label is all I find in the cabinet above the sink. Traditional split pea with ham. I hold the can in my hand and actually debate putting it back and making bacon, then sprinkling some discolored shreds of the cheese on top of it, but the Cash video has already been on for 21 minutes, and I fear that once the bacon is ready, Johnny will be finished,

Letting out a sigh, I pull up the tab on top of the soup can. I don't have a can opener so every can I buy has to have an easy open tab. As soon as the lid is pulled back, the vomitesque contents is exposed, and when I pour it in a white ceramic bowl, it looks even worse.

I glance at the laptop screen and see that Johnny Cash's home was filled with crystal and dishes.

I put the bowl in the microwave, then cover it with a plate. Three, three, zero, start. I open another one of the Busch's, then watch as the soup rotates inside the microwave until it burps and the plate rattles, and I flinch.

The microwave beeps. The video is over. I don't even bother taking the soup out of the microwave. I walk into the bedroom, and stare at the picture from the flea market.

~

I drink a six pack of beer behind the liquor store where I bought it. I burp and foam comes up. The taste makes me nostalgic for summer.

I look around for my poor, mysterious, fragile, shy, hip, insecure, desirable, feline, blonde, Kirtland University girl in the park.

I slip on some leaves and fall in a pond, or at least it feels like it was a trip and fall, but when I reach the other side of the pond and pull myself out, a girl with jet black hair tells me, "You should straighten your legs when you dive, otherwise you look like a frog." Her voice sounds like the way the yuletide log looks on TV. It gives off a fake warmth and I have to wonder if it's real or if it's been elaborately constructed on a computer.

"I'm cold," I tell the girl.

"I'm Alice," she tells me.

~

I'm in Alice's room in a sorority house whose letters I didn't catch. I click through her iTunes, and I think she let me choose the music because she knew I'd be restricted to her terrible MP3s.

"I really define myself by the music I listen to," she tells me, looking over my shoulder.

She owns a bunch of shitty pop records and some radio songs organized in playlists with names like "retarded mix" and "gangsta shit."

I take a Kirtland University baseball cap off her desk and I put it on. My hair is starting to dry and Alice doesn't have the right products to fix it. The sweats she gave me to wear while my clothes dry, say, "SILLY," on the ass and the shirt she threw me has long striped sleeves and a brash plunging neckline.

"I'm pretty sure you're the only person I know who doesn't own a t-shirt," I say, as I glance in the mirror and see an ugly he-bitch.

"T-shirts are for kids," she says.

"May I remind you, my t-shirt is outside drying?"

"May I remind you, that you jumped into a pond?"

"May I remind you, you're in a sorority and you girls make T-shirts for everything?"

"May I remind you, I met you while you were a swimmer wearing no swimming attire? The uniform isn't mandatory," Alice says, then moves toward me, clearly enjoying the tension.

I don't even know why I'm here. My poor, mysterious, fragile, shy, hip, insecure, desirable, feline, blonde, Kirtland University girl obviously doesn't live here, ~she~ lives in one of the dorms, so every moment I spend with Alice is a waste of time.

I can't leave until my clothes are dry, so I stay.

Alice chooses a playlist called "sexxxy mix" and the music sounds tinny coming out of her laptop, so she turns it up loud to compensate.

She starts to dance, and I join her, because the alternative- sitting on the edge of the bed listlessly- seems more pathetic. Before I know it, her right hand is up my low cut shirt, and her left hand is down my "SILLY" sweats, grabbing my ass. I get disoriented, and when I'm undressed to my damp boxers, I no longer feel any ties to Alice.

In my boxers, I simply walk out of the room, down the hall, down a flight of stairs, through a living room, then onto the porch.

I take off Alice's hat, throw on my musty smelling clothes, then walk out onto the street to continue my search.

~

Between classes, I walk to Rubie's, but the only person I see inside is the waitress, and I briefly consider asking if she's ever seen a blonde haired girl come in and eat alone, but the more I think about it, the vaguer the question becomes. If she asks for any details concerning this blonde girl's appearance, I can only give her non-visual attributes.

I decide to have lunch at Rubie's anyway. This way, if ~she~ comes in, ~she~ will be stalking me. Rubie's is *my* place, not hers. Since I'm the only one having lunch, she'll have to notice me. It's almost more awkward to sit in separate booths if there's only one other diner in the entire restaurant. It would be more uncomfortable for her to ignore me than to approach me.

I tip the waitress ahead of time so I can stay here and smoke.

I eat some baked mac and cheese.

I bite my fingernails down past the skin.

I use a stack of paper napkins to soak up all the blood.

Three little red-stained filters sit in a tea saucer turned ash tray.

I pay my bill and leave a second tip.

I don't ask about ~her~.

I walk back up to campus, possibly to attend a class, I'm not sure. When I get to the gate, the Grim Reaper comes around the corner, then starts walking toward me.

I pause, and between the bars, I stare at his tall sickle, and his skeletal face, and his dark robe, and his bony fingers. I consider running, but I can't be sure if that's what he's planning on me doing.

The gate swings open, and suddenly, we meet.

Only moments ago it seemed like he was so far away.

As he passes me, the top of the Grim Reaper's hood brushes against my hand. The little three foot tall harbinger of death passes me without a word. I watch him continue down the sidewalk, and I notice the residential houses, as well as the styrofoam graves among a carpet of orange leaves. I notice the cotton spider web, the red porch lights, the carved pumpkins, and a scarecrow at a killer slant under inflatable ghosts hanging from the tree branches.

Today is Halloween. The Grim Reaper was trick or treating in the café because he knows that the guy at Nathan's gives out full sized candy bars to kids, but only mustard packets to college students. I remember, as a child, how fast the word would spread when the big daddy candy bars had been located. My excitement for this holiday is missing Halloween becomes a distraction, a complication, a temptation. How am I supposed to find ~her~ when everyone is wearing masks and wigs?

~

Noni appears in my living room, in full zombie makeup. She's holding a severed arm in one hand, and a full bottle of Jack Daniels in the other.

Immediately trying to get me into the Halloween spirit, she plays Alice Cooper videos on my laptop, and makes me drink enough of the Jack that I feel warm.

I accept that I have to dress up for Halloween, not because I feel that it's a significant enough day to alter my appearance, but because I know that Noni will force me to go to a party tonight, and I don't want to appear there as "Regular Dan." Whatever frat house we find ourselves in the basement of tonight, surely Regular Dan will be present. Regular Dan comes to every Halloween party- he frantically rings your doorbell, he smirks at your Elvis costume, he thinks he's the first person to ever go as Regular Dan, and he is, universally, the worst. Regular Dan can barely wait for someone to ask, "Dan, you are aware that this is a costume party, right?" so he can sport a shit-eating grin, then say, "I *am* wearing a costume, I'm going as Regular Dan." The rest of the party will think, in unison, *Fuck your regular jeans, and your regular t-shirt, and your lack of regular sideburns, Dan.*

Noni and I search through my clothes to find something that can be used as the foundation for a costume, but most of the ideas I come up with are references only Noni and I would understand. Last year, I went as Ed Wood and everyone called me "Drag Queen Guy." They treated me as if I was wearing a low cut shirt and "SILLY" sweatpants; like I was going as Irregular Danielle.

After turning away from the closet, Noni's eyes go wide, and it looks like she has something close to an idea. Smiling, she asks, "Do you have any tape?"

"I think so," I say, then shrug.

"Do you think it's strong enough to support a severed limb? I don't want to carry this fucker around all night," Noni says, holding up her arm prop.

We walk out of my bedroom, and into the kitchen, then I pull out the drawer under the counter and find the roll of duct tape. We attach a big circle of tape to the middle finger of the severed hand. Noni puts on her new necklace, then deems it, "Perfect."

Before I can return to the bedroom, one of Noni's non-severed hands flies up and knocks me in the chest. My ass hits the edge of the counter, then Noni quickly grabs the tape and looks at me coyly.

"What? What?" I ask nervously.

"I have an idea," Noni purrs, and Halloween gets scary.

~

The first person I see at the party is Mindy Charleston, and she asks, "I don't get it?" which isn't really a question, but she says it looking for an answer. Her voice sounds like the whine of a rusty chain on a swing set.

I point to the word, "Regret," scrawled in black marker across the layers of duct tape wrapped around my torso. I show her the tape that's covering my forearms, and my biceps, and my lower legs, and my thighs and my stomach- everywhere, duct tape on skin. "At some point, it's not going to be Halloween anymore, and I'm going to have to take this costume off," I tell Mindy, and she winces, then laughs a good laugh, not a confused laugh or a pity laugh. Despite the immediate misidentification, this year's costume has already surpassed the response to my Ed Wood costume.

The party unfolds in snapshots.

Noni and I finish the bottle of Jack.

I dance with Snow White.

I help SpongeBob get unwedged in the stairwell.

Regan from *The Exorcist* takes a shot of watermelon vodka, then immediately vomits. She wins the costume contest moments later.

Skinny Elvis is very rude to me, then Fat Elvis apologizes on his behalf.

The party fills with a faux fog, and I locate its source, then slide behind the smoke machine, and with a wall of white surrounding me, I take out my phone.

4353638332936382.com.

"and you try, and you try, and you try.

and you end up talking to strangers again. you return to the hope that these new people will 'get it.' you tell yourself that this group seems different, then you find out that your judgment is still off. everything hangs with a perfect predictability. an oft-repeated saying claims that there's someone for everyone, but that's not true. there's someone for a piece of everyone. there's someone for 60% of me. sometimes 40% of a person is broken, and there's no one for 40% of some people. no one at all. not a single person can fathom how another human being could arrive at those 40% thoughts, carry out those 40% actions, say those 40% words. even the other people who might have the exact same defective 40% won't be able to accept it, because they fucking hate that awful 40% of themselves. the 40% of shared wrongness will be something that they can direct their anger and disappointment toward in the other person. sharing the same 40% as someone else can be deadly. and here i am. returning to this site, to start anew, only to instantly begin sharing my ugliness, advertising the 40% that no one will accept. the last time i attempted this sad chronicle, i deleted it, hating what i wrote, hating the person i saw reflected back at me, hating how trivial this terrible girl's life seemed. after i deleted the page, i felt more empty- i had a room with all the furniture removed and i was still finding items going missing. it seemed impossible to not funnel my filth somewhere.

i will build a tower of words, then knock it down again.

i hope you understand."

I stop scrolling, or rather, the page stops scrolling.

This is the end.

There's nothing left.

I push through the fog and the bodies, then sprint up the stairs.

I lock myself in a second floor bathroom.

The tub is filled with green liquid, and I'm not sure if it's a party prop or a plumbing problem because the light marijuana scent pervading the house masks everything.

I rip off all the tape on my body, screaming with each pull, then I get into the green bath.

~

Losing it; knowing there's nothing left. I go to Rubie's. Waiting for the call. I go to Rubie's. Cutting gum out of my hair. I go to Rubie's. Cutting the other side of my hair to even it out. I go to Rubie's. Sitting in an idling Lincoln outside of 614 Terrace View Ave, with Noni, watching and waiting. I go to Rubie's. Gerard kicking me out of a band that doesn't exist. I go to Rubie's. Napping, not sleeping. I go to Rubie's. Buying a carton of Pall Malls. I go to Rubie's. Finishing the carton. I go to Rubie's. Googling my mother. I go to Rubie's. Smashing some jars of pickles in the grocery store. I go to Rubie's. Writing a check. I go to Rubie's. Getting lost in my comforter. I go to Rubie's. Shaving off my pubic hair to feel like a kid again. I go to Rubie's. Playing Xbox for eleven hours with Revere. I go to Rubie's. I don't try the coke. I go to Rubie's. An empty mailbox. I go to Rubie's. I want to try the coke. I go to Rubie's. Don't try the coke. I go to Rubie's. Gerard tries the coke. I go to Rubie's. I don't try the coke. I go to Rubie's. Don't. I go to Rubie's. Do not. I go to Rubie's. Looking down from the bell tower for seven hours, scouring the campus. I go to Rubie's. Revere cuts me a line. I go to Rubie's. *When you have money, then you can do the coke.* I go to Rubie's. A bracelet on Noni's right wrist that's either from a hospital stay or a concert. I go to Rubie's. When you can buy a brick, try the coke. I go to Rubie's. Don't try the coke. I go to Rubie's. Not yet. I go to Rubie's. I try the coke. I go to Rubie's. I try the coke. I go to Rubie's. I try the coke. I go to

Rubie's. My belt digging into my hip bones so hard it creates a cut on either side of my body. I go to Rubie's. Getting complaints about hair in someone's mash potatoes because the waitress said I was the manager. Managing Rubie's. Masturbating in the back of an unlocked utility van before class because both the boys and girls restrooms are locked in the Arts building. I go to Rubie's. Still no call about my Mother. I go to Rubie's. A girl says, "Ugh," and walks away, and I miss Joan. I go to Rubie's. Sleeping at Rubie's. Waking up at Rubie's.

~

The huge foreheaded register boy's neglected coffee is undrinkable today. I greedily finish my cup, wincing at the last gulp. I slept for the first time in two days last night. I should feel refreshed, but I still want to sleep forever.

Stepping onto the Green, I light a cigarette. I'm heading toward a destination that I can no longer name. The head-rush I get from the cigarette is something I haven't felt since middle school. My vision turns into black dots, intermittently. Breathing becomes a conscious activity on this uncharacteristically sunny day. The dots in my vision are growing. I'm a pilot looking for a corn field to make an emergency landing in.

Through the spots, I see everyone on campus going about their day, singing ~the song~.

The boy with the backward hat sings:

> *"You laugh a subtle laugh*
> *And your face opens the door*
> *Then the ceiling slowly slides*
> *And your ear cups the floor"*

The girl in the see-through yoga pants sings:

> *"The words don't translate*
> *You lose your tongue*
> *Play your vocal cords*
> *And the melody's off"*

The groundskeeper picking up my cigarette butts sings:

> *"The room will spin for anyone*

It just takes the right conditions
And you've... met them"

The basketball player dribbling his ball sings:

"Let's make our introduction
Interested, we smile
The details won't be processed
No evidence for a trial"

The priest clutching his bible sings:

"We're stacking information
We're compiling a file
We're taking a name
Only to burn it"

The commuter without a home on campus sings:

"I knew lots of presidents
And I knew lots of freaks
All of these close friendships
Are not what they seem"

Then everyone stops what they are doing and pauses where they are going.
The campus takes a breath, together, then they turn and look at me.
It's my turn to sing.
I stumble over to a tree, putting my back to it, then I begin slowly sliding down, as little pieces of bark chip off and fall to the ground.
In my half-conscious state, I sing:

"They're shaking your hand
And the grip's a farce
The freak is approaching
And he hands you a poem.

"-he hands you a bone. The freak hands you a bone, not a poem," I'm told by a voice that sounds like Winona Ryder's, but there's no reason for Winona to be on campus, so I search for the source of this divine correction.

My vision is immediately clear as the track plays in my head, and I hear that she's right, it *is* "bone."

I feel what I imagine Joan may have felt the moment before she was smooshed, as I turn my head and see the source of the voice- a small blonde haired girl tying the yellow laces of her running shoes. Her blonde hair hangs down and cradles her pale white face, while her perfectly straight bangs cover her eyebrows, almost hiding her eyes. She looks like she could be Irish, possibly German. Her outfit ranges from tight to flowy. Layers are compounded like she couldn't decide what to wear and said, "Fuck compromise," and put it all on. I get the feeling that there's something this girl knows that she isn't telling the world, like there are a billion secrets locked up in her little frame.

Everything seems to be moving fast and slow at the same time; my thoughts are running into each other, and words cannot be forced. The questions don't get asked, and they bounce around inside me, jumbling into an indecipherable mess.

The girl finishes tying her shoe, then stands up straight, a frame of brightness around her, like her pale skin was radiating sunlight.

Still sitting with my back to the tree, unsure of my balance, I manage to say, "Kurt, my name, ya know, is Kurt Jones."

The tiny black spots are back, but I quickly blink them away.

"Okay, Kurt. Well, my name is Lindsey," she says, looking down at me with curiosity instead of concern. Maybe she didn't witness the mental and physical crash that I experienced moments ago? She probably didn't even realize I was there until I started mumbling those incorrect lyrics.

I need Lindsey to stay, so I say, "I... I bet he says poem."

"Okay. It's a bet," Lindsey decides, then she holds her hand out, and I take it.

Even after she's helped me up, I continue to hold onto Lindsey. Her eyes go wide, and I can see that she wants to escape this interaction.

I release her hand, afraid to lose her, and once I do this, she seems to regain the soft comfort that she previously hummed with. She knows that she has information that I need, and now we're bonded by a bet.

"What do I win if I'm right?" I ask.

Lindsey starts walking, and says, "We'll never have to cross that bridge."

I stand in place for a moment, waiting for her to look back at me, to invite me to follow her, but she never does. Instead, I'm pulled forward by fate, and I quickly return to her side.

"We're going to have to listen to the song in my dorm. I don't have it on my phone. I'm not kidnapping you," she explains.

"Kids generally don't run after their kidnapper," I point out.

"Are you a kid, Kurt Jones?" Lindsey asks me, and my brain buzzes when I hear my name on her tongue.

"I'm a junior," I say, then add, "Like... junior year."

"I'm only a sophomore," Lindsey says, then suggests, "Maybe that means that *you* are kidnapping *me*."

"I don't know where we're going," I admit, relinquishing power, asserting innocence.

At this point, I'd follow Lindsey anywhere. I almost hope we're headed toward a burning building. I'd grab her hand as we walked into the flames, just so I could spend eternal life fused to her. They'd add us to the collection of Kirtland memorials, and we would forever remain as a unified presence on this campus- a landmark among the etched bricks.

We make a right, then walk into the lobby of The Grove- a seven story dorm that, to my dismay, doesn't even smell like burnt popcorn.

Instead of taking the elevator, Lindsey leads me to the stairs. I don't ask her why we're avoiding the elevator, because I secretly hope we're headed to the roof. Lindsey's pure white glow in the late-fall sun remains burned behind my eyes as an image I could stare at forever.

When we reach the fifth floor, Lindsey pushes the fire door open, then we walk down a hallway that's painted a shade of purple that doesn't seem appropriate for on-campus housing. Kirtland's colors are blue and white. It's almost as if one of the residents took it upon himself to repaint the hallway, Abe Carrol-style.

When we reach the third door on our right, Lindsey keys into a room- *her* room.

The door opens, and I'm invited in.

I think to myself, *This is how it happens*- Not through a post or a blog/ Not through a hazy bar or loud party/ Not through a digital profile or a meddling mutual friend who thinks you'd be perfect for her down-on-her-luck roommate- a connection like this can only be born out of coincidence, destiny, and mystic synchronicity.

Lindsey found me. Maybe it was the energy I was putting out into the world, or maybe it was the energy the world was draining out of my body. Whatever it was, it worked, and it's authentic, and everything that would have otherwise separated us simply parted and allowed the moment to happen.

As I follow Lindsey into her room, I feel my body fill with a sensation that I haven't felt since I was a kid. I last experienced this pulsing excitement when I begged Cara Feldman to take off her bikini top, and she responded by reaching back for the clasp.

The room is dark, except for a few cracks of light peeking through the gaps between the blinds and the window.

There are two beds in the room, but one of them has no sheets on it. There are two desks in the room, but one of them is empty. A small TV plays an old, muted, black and white movie.

Lindsey drifts across her dorm room, then sits on the bed that has sheets.

Without being asked, I walk over and sit next to her.

We look at each other, and it's a pause that pops with importance- two fiercely introverted people at a loss as to why all of this has been so effortless. I feel that we both want to be here, together, and this shared time doesn't present itself as a responsibility, but instead, as a luxury.

Lindsey holds up the pointer finger on her right hand, gets off the bed, then reaches under the raised bed frame. She slides out a banker's box, and when she lifts its top, I see that inside the box are neat stacks of cassette tapes. She takes out five tapes, looks at their spines then puts them on the edge of the short dresser to her right. She takes out another five tapes, looks at their labels, then lines them up perfectly next to the first five tapes. She takes out six tapes, looks at their labels, then puts the stack down. She grabs the third tape from the top and puts it aside, then five by five, she places the unneeded tapes back into the banker's box.

Lindsey grabs the tape that she had set aside, then hops over the clothes on her floor so she can get to a massive stereo. She puts the tape in the bottom left deck, then presses play.

Adrenaline surges through me, and my anticipation causes my lip to twitch. A static washes over the room, then the first notes are plucked down on the piano. It's the start of ~the song~. Every follicle on my body stands on end, and for a moment, I smell my mother's perfume.

The baseline melts over the piano, then the high whine of an electric guitar's hanging notes joins the wall of sound. The moment arrives fully as the drum kicks begin, then the man begins to sing, and so many memories come rushing back, leaving me profoundly overwhelmed. My entire consciousness is consumed by the song, but Lindsey never fades into the background.

I'll always remember the last time I listened to this song with my mother- what she wore that day, what the weather was like, the way her hand felt wrapped around mine. Those memories stay with me. I keep them in pristine condition.

Giving myself to the music completely, I lie down on Lindsey's bed, and she lies next to me.

Impossible.

The song, all 7 minutes and 46 seconds, returns like a dream, and breaks like a fever. A song that I sang acapella for so long finally has its backing band again.

The singer's voice sometimes distorts due to the mic and sound system he's performing into, but this tape sounds fresher than my mother's copy did.

When the organ comes in, I experience a spiritual rush that connects me with someone who has chosen to keep her distance.

Lindsey and I listen to the song, the full song, without talking.

As the song trails into static, I wait for the next song, but it never arrives, and Lindsey gets up from the bed, then rewinds the tape.

We listen, again. She rewinds the tape again.

Already, we have a ritual.

We take turns getting up to rewind the tape. The fourth time we listen to the song, Lindsey moves her hand over to mine, and our fingers lock.

When the song ends once again, I sit up, but Lindsey doesn't. For a moment, I watch the silent black and white movie playing on the TV. No, this isn't a movie; it's a black and white episode of the *X-Files*. Mulder, in a white t-shirt instead of a suit, crouches down in the woods, above what looks like a feral woman. I don't remember a black and white *X-files* episode, but this entire moment feels so surreal that nothing is completely impossible.

I know that Lindsey is ~her~ but I also tell myself that she isn't, because the girl on that page would've never invited me here. Before I begin diagnosing Lindsey, like the last person she shared this room with, I allow myself to pay attention to every detail, just in case I'm asked to leave forever. Lindsey lies, eyes closed, and I watch her for what seems like a single moment, but probably creeps into unflinching minutes. I've always found myself fascinated by women at rest. It's sick really. I like to see women at their most vulnerable. I've convinced myself that maybe I'll be able to catch a glimpse of who they really are if I see them without the "extra," without the performance that may or may not be occurring.

When Lindsey sits up, the light from the TV reflects off her dark blue eyes. She blocks my view as she grinds her palm into her left eye, as if she was getting up from an extended nap.

For the first time, I dwell on the fact that the next step must be taken. Up to this point, I merely floated at her side.

I need a cigarette to level out, but I don't want to ruin things. What if she doesn't like guys who smoke? Maybe her mother died from lung cancer. Maybe she smokes? No, she doesn't smoke, I can tell by someone's room if they smoke. Instead of worrying, I decide I'll just ask. For the first time, I will start something with a girl that isn't just a layered game of hide and seek.

"Would it be alright if I smoked a cigarette?"

Lindsey looks up in the air, then points; "We have these smoke detectors, so you're going to have to smoke out the window."

I slide off the bed, and Lindsey apologizes, like the girl from the journal would, "Sorry that it's kinda like the Batcave in here. If I don't close these blinds, then the sun comes in and turns this place into an oven. It's either dark and comfortable or bright and hot. There's no happy medium."

I move the shade up a little, then slide the window from right to left. There's no screen in the frame, and I'm surprised that the university would allow this safety hazard, but it makes things easier for me. I light my cigarette, then hang it out the gap, and twist my body so that I'm facing Lindsey.

She walks over to the stereo and ejects the tape. Above her, stuck to the wall, are dozens of Polaroids. I lean forward, my arm totally pinned back, and I review the pictures. There are photographs of old bums, and old yuppies, and old looking dogs, and old houses, and young teenagers. From this fixed point, I don't see any pictures of Lindsey.

Making sure not to point with my cigarette, I ask, "Who are they?"

Lindsey puts the tape back in the box, in its rightful place, then glances at the pictures, and quietly says, "Acquaintances. Friends. Animals. Randoms." She walks over to the wall and unsticks one of the Polaroids. "This one. *This* is the one," she says, as she makes her way to me, then hands over a picture of a tanned girl with big eyes who's wearing short shorts and cowboy boots. Lindsey runs her finger across the picture like she's able to feel the doe-eyed girl.

"You're right. That's the one," I say, handing the picture back, then turning to puff my cigarette. After exhaling smoke out the window, I turn back at Lindsey, and ask, "But, where are you?" then point at the wall.

"I'm... here," Lindsey says, becoming the girl from the journals again. "I don't need a picture of myself. I have a mirror."

"But, pictures are all about capturing moments, keeping the seconds that are worth reliving."

"I'm always taking the pictures so I can't be in them. Besides, if I was in the pictures I think they would lose their feeling. I like them the way they are, without me. I mean, I do have pictures of myself, they just aren't on the wall. I have them in a book," Lindsey says.

"Can I see them?" I ask, and this sends Lindsey back to the wall to place the photograph in its rightful space, then she pauses. Maybe I'm wrong, but I get the feeling she's trying to decide if *she* wants to look at the photos- like she's afraid to see how she looks to everyone else. I drop the cigarette out the window, then push on the frame to seal us off from the outside world.

It's silent. We don't put on another tape and *The X-files* is still muted.

Lindsey continues making decisions, flipping through thoughts, as she walks over to a bookshelf, then grabs a book with a red spine. She holds the book, but doesn't open it. Her expression drops, and a near-smile becomes a near-frown. There's nothing I've done to cause this change because I've remained frozen.

"I have work," she says to the universe, then puts the book back in the bookshelf. A decision was silently made; my access to a portion of her life was denied. I want to know why she was afraid to show me who she was in the past. Reading my face, she asks, softly, "Walk with me?"

I don't steal the tape, because it's an excuse to come back.

I've found ~her~, and she played me ~the song~.

five.

I say, "What's up?" with hostility, to a kid standing in the door frame, blocking my entrance to the Great American Novel class. Not answering my question, the kid stares at me with confusion soaked wonderment, and says, "Whoa, I didn't know you were still in this class!"

"I took a little time off," I snarl.

His face changes into a mask of panic, as he quickly provides a string of apologies while getting out of the way. "You look refreshed," he tags on, as I make my way to an open desk.

I sit down next to some dorky looking black guy, and he says, "Sorry to hear about your girlfriend."

"Thanks. It's been hard, but I'm finally starting to feel better."

The black guy takes a good look at me, then says, "Well, you do look refreshed."

During the class, we talk about some semi-interesting topic, and I even attempt to participate.

After forty minutes of talking about The Beatles, I petition to be able to talk about Bob Dylan during the next class, but the professor says, "I don't think Bob Dylan is entirely relevant." I have to wonder what lesson she's teaching in which Bob Dylan isn't completely relevant.

The professor notes, "It's good to see you again, Mr. Jones. You seem well, the rest of the class on the other hand... if only we were all as refreshed as you."

I've been told I look "refreshed" by three different people, each conversation mutually exclusive of the other. The feeling I currently have is anything but refreshing. I feel disappointed. I'm disappointed that I didn't find Lindsey last year- that I didn't find her at 18- that I didn't find her at 15- that I didn't find her at 10. I've wasted so much of my life without Lindsey. This is not a refreshing thought. The thought that I need to keep her for the rest of my life becomes my new obsession, and I feel completely devoted to it. This is an obligation and a challenge; a privilege and a goal.

~

We sit at my usual table at Rubie's. I look at Lindsey, then look down at her plate. She has some mashed potatoes and one piece of chicken left. She motions with her knife to my plate. My mashed potatoes are untouched and I have three pieces of chicken left.

"You hate it here, don't you?" she asks, then bites her lip, "I'm sorry, really. I forget that people don't always like to eat where I like to eat, and now you don't like your dinner."

I smile at her, then she smiles back reflexively.

Sometimes an action can tell a story better than words can. I take out my cigarettes, then light one.

"I don't think you can smoke in here," Lindsey says, her voice coming out small and squeaky, as she clearly doesn't want to nag me, yet also fears the attention I'm conjuring.

"Don't worry," I tell her, "I have an agreement with the manager," then I nod in the direction of Mr. T.

Lindsey glances at the cutout, and our smiles dance again, "You don't hate it here," she realizes.

"I always come here," I say. I briefly consider telling her that I know she comes here because I've read every word of her journal, but I decide that I will keep one secret from her.

This is a girl who scares easily, and the way I found her is scary.

"Do you think we were ever here at the same time?" Lindsey asks me, willingly providing me with a way to explain how I first discovered her. I could say that I saw ~her~ here before, but was afraid to make the first move. I could bury the weirdness, but I don't.

"I would've noticed you," I say.

"You didn't notice me during your tailspin."

"How do you know that?"

"Because I noticed you first. I watched your crash."

"And you still spoke to me, after seeing all that?"

"You looked like you needed help."

"I do. Still," I say, and Lindsey looks away.

~

We're lying on Lindsey's bed, in the dark, listening to ~the song~. Now that she knows I'm a little off, and appears not to care, I can ask, "Who sings this song?" and I don't fear the impending conversation that could follow.

Lindsey looks up at the ceiling, and says, "Jackson Sharpe." She takes a breath, then adds, "He's dead."

This information soothes me. I had a latent awareness that this man had died; it's in his voice. It's that Cobain thing, that Joplin thing. The voice on the tape crackles like branches being shaken by the wind in a graveyard.

"How'd you find the tape?"

"At a church Trash-to-Treasure sale. I don't know how anyone could've thrown it out," Lindsey says.

"Even if you throw it out, once you hear the song, you can't escape it."

"Some kid was probably just going through his mother's stuff after she died and brought it to the church," Lindsey says, and to escape a negative reaction, I quickly add, "That, or the kid died and his mother brought his tape collection to the church."

"I doubt it." Lindsey snaps, then she rolls over and faces the wall, which is the exact reaction I wanted to have when she made the mother comment.

"So, this is the first song of the Jackson Sharpe album?" I ask, trying to pull her focus back to me.

"No such thing," she says.

"He died before he made the record?"

"Yup."

"What are the other songs on the tape if Jackson isn't on them?" I ask, realizing that we've always hit rewind the moment ~the song~ ends.

"I don't know. I sort of get stuck in the song. It makes me feel like I don't need any other songs," Lindsey says, turning back to me.

~

I walk to the window and light a cigarette, while Lindsey begins to change her clothes. The campus church bells ring, to let me know that I'm late for my 11 AM class. When I'm in the dorms, everything else melts away, so the bells, today, feel like a prompt that a hypnotist would use to bring his subject out of a trance.

When I'm sure that Lindsey is dressed, I drop my cigarette, then pull the window shut.

I look to Lindsey, and admire her in a fresh outfit. She's wearing dark jeans and an off-white shirt that looks almost Victorian, but it's more form fitting and modern. It suits her complexion and fits her personality. She goes back to the closet, takes out a blue vest, then quickly slides it on. Stylistically, this vest is the first fashion related error I've seen Lindsey commit. She puts a black denim jacket on over the vest so I just pretend like it's not there.

We leave the dorm, again taking the stairs, and when we step outside, Lindsey starts walking in the direction opposite from where I thought we were headed.

I stand in place, but she doesn't look back.

"Lindsey?" I say, and this prompts her to turn around.

I raise my eyebrows; she smiles.

"I have to go to work," she says, then points in a nonspecific direction.

"Oh, right... work," I say trying to mask my disappointment that she won't be walking with me to class or joining me in the café. I want everyone to see us together. I want the entire campus to acknowledge that I'm with Lindsey, because I feel like this connection is one of my finest accomplishments.

"Wait," Lindsey says, walking back toward me, "Did you think that I'm wearing this vest because I like the way it looks?"

"Sorta, yeah," I respond.

Lindsey shakes her head, getting closer, telling me, "That won't do, Mr. Jones. You obviously don't know me well enough yet. Where can I meet you after work so we can fix this?"

"What time do you get out of work?" I ask.

"6."

"Rubie's," I say.

Lindsey smiles, then pulls me close, wrapping her arms around me so tight that I can feel her heartbeat.

On my way to class, I stop at the admissions office, masturbate in their bathroom, wash my hands, then fix my hair. The admissions office bathroom is always the cleanest on campus since it's the bathroom that all the parents use when they finally arrive, fresh from a hundred mile drive. Even if I hear some nervous high school senior's dad walk in, I'm confident that he wouldn't look in the stall.

They should put a plaque in this supremely clean bathroom that says, "Feel free to touch yourself in this stall, in preparation for the fact that Kirtland University will be fucking you for the next four-plus years."

~

In Business Management class, everyone is being sectioned off into groups of five. I become concerned and mildly paranoid about this segregation. I can't tell if I'm being hyper-delusional or appropriately vigilant.

I pop my head into each group, searching for Gerard, but I'm met with near-identical looking strangers. Gerard knew better than to show up today. He must have been tipped off about this little scheme in advance, and this begs the question, *Why didn't he warn me?*

As the groups begin to exit the classroom- everyone carrying their books and laptops- a chill whispers through me, *Maybe they're leading us to the slaughter.*

I try to pretend like everything is fine as I follow my class across campus. We seem to be headed to the parking garage, and I realize that each group includes at least one commuter. These "leaders" must have been selected merely because they have some form of transportation to offer up today.

I'm accepted into a group by osmosis; I don't start a conversation, I don't ask if I can be in the group, I just walk alongside them, and when we approach a gray four door sedan, I wordlessly accept the middle seat in the back.

We leave campus, and no one in my group seems to be questioning what's happening here, which makes me think that the Business Management professor is truly gifted at his job. He was able to easily persuade his little worker bees to actively participate in a mission that is of no clear benefit to us.

I sit, shoulders crunched between two guys who may or may not be in my Business Management class, and I ask, "Where are you taking me?"

Everyone in the car laughs at this question, then someone starts talking about a TV show that seems to be about a colony of mummies who, when they remove their bandages, look like normal people. Each mummy has to find a live body, which they bandage and seal in a sarcophagus in their place.

The kid to my left says, "It's really miraculous that Arnold Darrante was able to make protagonists out of a group of mummies. If Ramses doesn't get his warmsuit by the end of this season, I will seriously cry."

I volley my line of sight between each person in the car as they all make a hateable statement about the TV show, almost as though they're attempting to one-up each other with the pointlessness of their observations. Everything is so depressing that I find myself unable to look at my group members, so I look past them. My eyes follow the landscape as we leave the town- as we head north.

Forty minutes later, a fleet of sensible cars adorned with Kirtland U bumper stickers come to a stop in a cul de sac, in front of a pinkish colored McMansion.

A guy wearing pleated khakis and a teal polo shirt with a vaguely menacing company logo on it walks out of the McMansion, then across his too-green-for-November lawn.

Before our professor can say anything, the polo shirt dude starts giving us a welcome speech, "Kirtland University's best and brightest. I see our future standing before me, and I am in awe." This introduction makes me close my eyes tightly.

As the guy in the polo continues giving what is obviously a pre-prepared speech that he practiced with his wife last night, I take out my phone and text Gerard the address of the house, then tap out, "If you don't see me later tonight, I'm at this address and I've been recruited into a pyramid scheme."

Gerard sends back a smiley face, and a message, "Enjoy Chip Garris' tales of inspiration."

The dude in the polo shirt finishes his speech with, "I'm about to give you a class at Garris University. You'll have to check with your professor to see if the credits transfer," then he either winks at us, or realizes how truly terrible the line is and momentarily feels physical pain over his own existence.

Chip Garris leads us inside the McMansion, and I immediately start formulating excuses as to why I can't invest in a timeshare.

We pause the house tour in the living room, and we watch giant flashes of glowing nothingness blast across a TV screen that's being controlled by a disc-shaped remote. "Aspect ratio," "Digital Comb Filter," "Screen Burn In," "Motion Adaptive Noise Reduction," and, "Fucking Sweet," are terms that come spilling out of Chip's mouth, while he toggles settings that seem to only marginally modify the brightness of the set. Right before he shows us each feature, he says, "...and check this out," then he presses a button and steps back so as not to obstruct our view of whatever pointless filter he's chosen.

I look at the Gen Xer, and I envy him. I don't envy him for his job. I don't envy him for his wife. I don't envy him for his car. I don't envy him for his big fucking TV. I envy him because he has complete and total confidence in his abilities, no matter how absent they may be. He believes that everything he does is a triumph. I find myself wondering what it would be like to not have looming self-doubt hit me in the face like a brick every time I make an irreversible decision. I can't fathom what it's like to say, "Yes," because I want to, not just because I need to provide some kind of answer. I sometimes link confidence to stupidity, but through his own unchecked stupidity, Chip has flourished. If I become blind to all of the repercussions stemming from the decisions I make, then maybe I won't be so hesitant to make them. Becoming dumb enough to actually believe everything works out in the end would put me in a place where I could say, "Yes," and mean, "Yes," and feel like, "Yes," is the right answer. But knowing that, "No," is also an option? Yes, it could drive a man insane.

Chip hands me the remote, then asks, "Wanna try it out, Kurt?" and I recoil when I hear him say my name.

I remind myself that, in the same vague way that he knows me, I know this guy. This is a man without a single unique flourish in his being. This lack of a true-self creates an identity that other men his age have been adopting for decades. Even without speaking with him, I know things about Chip. I know that he doesn't have normal fears. He doesn't face normal frustrations. He's not outraged by the price of a Heineken at a professional basketball game. In fact, he likes that it's expensive because when he's buying rounds for every person around him, it demonstrates how much money he has. Obviously, he can't bring his TV to the game. This guy may have had a dream as a kid, but it was mutilated beyond recognition when he ran it over with his Beemer, so now he has no choice but to cover its remains with deposit slips and quarterly dividends. He's the prototype of what our fathers expect us to become. He's a nickname using, fast talking, perfect tie tying, foreign car driving, homophobic, sports obsessed, receding hairlined, beer gutted, money making machine. All of his hobbies have "extreme" in front of their name just to make bowling and Scrabble jealous. This man cares what people think in some instances and remains blissfully ignorant in others.

I press a big blue virtual button on the top of the remote, and it changes the channel from sports to static.

"Oops," Chip chirps in a panic, then he quickly snatches the remote back, mashes a couple of buttons, and brings us back to a TV land populated with screaming ads.

Chip and his big dumb TV wall are supposed to inspire us. This is supposed to get us fired up about our major. I can sense the thoughts of some of the students behind me, *Is this what makes him happy, this giant glowing box? When does he even watch the thing? He works 15 hour days to avoid his family. Why would a Digital Interlace matter when he turns the TV on and immediately passes out on this horrible smelling leather sofa?*

We go from the living room to the second floor/ From the upstairs, back downstairs, then into the back yard/ From the backyard, back inside to Chip's home office.

As Chip launches into a multi-decade breakdown of his entire career, I have to fight to stay awake. I can't see outside, but somehow the room begins to feel different, and I know the sun is setting. We've been here for a while and will probably continue to be here for a while.

Chip's pathetic banter drones on, until some of the captives begin to talk with him about the football season.

Ten minutes into the football tangent, Chip keeps glancing at me, almost to acknowledge that he's aware that I'm drifting from the conversation. Chip is wrong though, I'm not drifting, I'm mentally sending him a message: *This needs to end, this needs to stop right now. It's 5 PM.*

"What do you think, Kurt?" Chip eventually asks.

"I don't watch football," is all I can think to say.

We leave the office so we can go look at Chip's cars, and as we walk into his garage, no less than four guys say, "Whoa." Chip's garage is so big that if his wife shut the doors and turned on one of his GenXmobiles to attempt suicide, the car would run out of gas before she felt anything more than a headache. The odds seem good that she's attempted this experiment before, and this plunges the garage into a darkness that my peers don't seem to see.

After ten minutes of Chip informing us of the time it takes his various luxury cars to reach 60 miles per hour, I make up an excuse for why we have to leave. I tell the driver of my group's car, "My mother is sick, and I need to give her a shot at 6 PM every night. We need to leave now to be back by 6." I announce this with complete sincerity, making it clear that this is an unavoidable responsibility.

I don't feel any guilt about using this excuse- my mother *is* sick. Having a sick mother has almost no perks, so I should be allowed to exploit the few there are.

My mother would want me to escape from this place, because, in a way, she did exactly that once before.

The members of my group thank Chip for his time, then we drive back to campus. To pass time on the drive, the kids discuss their different ideas for a startup so we can, "...actively position ourselves in exactly the way Chip suggested."

When we reach the parking garage, I hop out of one car and make my way to another.

Through a series of text messages, I had arranged for Lindsey to be waiting for me.

"I need to see you," I demanded/ "I have to tell you what I've just suffered through," I teased/"I can't wait another moment, I need you. Meet me in the garage by the baseball field," I begged.

She responded to every text in exactly the way I needed her to.

She assured me that I'd see her/She told me that she couldn't wait to hear about how terrible my day has been/She told me where she's parked, and sure enough, here she is.

Lindsey is sitting in the driver's seat of a gray Honda Civic with a cloth interior, and it's infinitely more desirable than any of the vehicles that will possibly kill Chip in a fiery wreck.

I get into the front seat of the Honda, and Lindsey tells me that we're driving to Rubie's, even though it's close enough that we could walk. She tells me about work. She tells me about the old customers that came in, and what their weird requests were. The drive feels good, and relaxed, until Lindsey's phone rings, and she glances down at the glowing screen.

Who's calling Lindsey? An ex? A kid in her Astronomy class she thinks is cute? Some long-lost high school crush? A new co-worker? Her boyfriend from another college?

Lindsey sends the call to voicemail, and I can't help but feel suspicious and jealous. When her phone beeps to tell her she has a new message, Lindsey presses the screen, enters her password, then hits the speaker button. It was almost as though she sensed my silent panic and wanted to prove to me that I have nothing to worry about.

"This will be my friend Belle, and she will be drunk," Lindsey tells me.

The message begins, and "Sup, bitch!" is the caller's shrieking introduction. Her voice sounds like that one random girl at a concert who yells an indistinguishable statement while the lead singer is intro-ing the next song. The message continues, "Lindsey, I never see youuu. Come drinking. I mean, I know you don't drink anymore, but come stand next to me while I drink! I need you here, now! I've been drunk since 1... not, like, age one. I didn't start drinking until a decade after that, and I think that is cause for celebration. Let's celebrate *your* current sobriety and *my* long gone ten years of very admirable sobriety." Belle laughs maniacally, then caps off the call with. "You can send me to voicemail, but you haven't seen the last of meee," and it should sound threatening, but her sing-song delivery makes it sound cute.

Lindsey deletes the voicemail as we pull into the parking lot of Rubie's, and I have to ask, "You don't drink?"

Lindsey looks over at me, then says, "I drink with you. I don't drink with Belle. So, if we're with Belle, even though I'm with you, I don't drink."

These are rules. I live by rules. Lindsey's mind seems to work precisely in the way that mine does and the comfort I feel regarding this is absolute.

Inside Rubie's, we sit across from each other in my usual booth. Lindsey keeps leaning toward me as we're talking, and I like it. Neither of us glances at the single page menu, and we're both able to order without asking the waitress any questions. Even after we get our food, Lindsey continues arching forward toward me, and I raise my eyebrows at her when she leans so far over that her butt isn't even touching the seat anymore.

"Let me see your hands," she demands.

"Wait. No. Why?" I ask.

"I think they're beautiful."

"My hands?"

"Well, hands in general. I need to check yours," Lindsey says, then reaches across the table and grabs my sleeves.

I push my arms forward and she moves her hands down to my knuckles.

"I would've fixed them up if I had known," I say.

"Guys can't fix up stuff like that; they just end up biting off their nails until their hands bleed."

I look down at my hands. How have my scabs healed so quickly? I specifically remember bleeding in this exact part of Rubie's not long ago. Is it possible to remember something that never happened?

After Lindsey deems my hands, "Cute. Acceptable. Not bloody," I finish off her root beer, while she finishes off her hamburger, then she asks if I want to see a movie. For some reason I tell her a story about going to see this Nic Cage movie and abandoning my friend halfway through the film's brief runtime. I realize how dumb it sounds to freely admit that the reason why I left a Nic Cage movie was because there were too many scenes with Nic Cage.

I pay for our meal, then ask, "Want to go to the Waldorf with me?" because I'm curious to see how Lindsey will look bathed in the light that made Joan so breathtaking.

Without hesitation, she responds, "Let's go," then slides out of the booth.

As we're walking to the car, she bets me, "You won't leave. You'll stay until the end credits."

Since this all started as a bet, with ~the song~, I instantly presume that whatever movie we're seeing tonight will change my life, and I will be forever different after I leave the theater.

During the drive to the Waldorf, Lindsey lets me go through her CDs and choose the music. The only reason we don't listen to ~the song~ is because the car doesn't have a tape player.

I'm excited to see a movie at the Waldorf and not even screen three can fuck that up.

~

We lie in Lindsey's bed, and I respond to her question with, "Gallo."

"Gallo?" she asks, not expecting this answer, and I'm excited to explain myself.

"Vincent Gallo would direct my life on that reverse stock film- the type of film that might not even come out when it's developed. Big ideas would have to be thrown away because they were too sensitive and didn't cooperate. The universe would have a cut of the workprint. The movie would be filled with those tight-yet-revealing shots, the type that remind you that actors are people too, not some perfect android beings. The flashbacks- the moment that fantasy melds into reality- that's how my life would have to be projected to be true."

Lindsey relaxes on my answer for a moment, digesting everything I've placed before her on an invisible platter. Eventually, she smiles, understanding, and the volley arrives in her court. She's already thought about her answer to this question, I can tell because her feet rub together under the comforter, and it's an excited movement that assures me I'll be receiving the information I desire, while I stiff arm sleep away. She admits, without the formality of being asked, "I'd pick Argento. The dark mood, the pulsing soundtrack, the loud noises, the ultraviolence, the look of terror on the supporting cast's face, the way the words don't match up perfectly with the characters' mouths. Did you know that the killer's hands in Argento's movies are his own, so he's killing the actors he carefully chose? My life would be presented with a colorful, beautiful, out of sync, foreign desperation."

It's funny that she used the word ultraviolence.

Argento is wrong. Kubrick is right. He starts films the same way people meet Lindsey. A long tracking shot, we see the scenery, we're getting closer and closer, drawn to this figure... it's a slow process, there's some sort of anticipation building up, but never a feeling of, "Get on with it already." It's a beautiful slow waltz until we finally focus on the subject. The volume is turned up on Lindsey; the extremes are something I expect. Every sentence that comes out of her mouth feels like it's the result of a hundred takes. I can imagine her rehearsing the day's scenes during breakfast to make sure that when all eyes are on her, the presentation is flawless. Her words are always sincere- always tied to her emotions- so it never seems like a performance, which is in such contrast to the embarrassing play that Chip performed in his yard.

I'm nodding in and out of sleep, and Lindsey repositions to wake me up fully.

"Kurt," she says in a little girl's voice.

"Yeah?"

"Aren't movies weird?"

"It depends on the movie."

"No, I mean about how you can go on a date to a movie. It doesn't make sense."

"It's a great way to share a common experience," I say, slowly, my eyes closing.

"I know, but if you're on a date with someone and you spend a two hour period not talking to them, for any reason, that would be awkward, yet somehow, when you go to the movies, you can do that without it being weird. It's not only an acceptable option, it's the only option."

"It's the whole dinner and a movie thing. You see the movie, then you talk about it over dinner. I guess we did it in reverse."

"Let's not do that again," Lindsey decides.

"Movie before dinner, got it," I say, drifting closer to sleep again.

"No. No movies ever," Lindsey makes a rule.

"What will replace them?" I ask.

"You'll see," she says, and the night ends on a cliffhanger.

~

We skip class, and Lindsey drives us to the one remaining bookstore on the planet.

"What are you picking up?" I ask her, as we make our way across the parking lot.

"I'm not sure."

"School or pleasure?"

"A movie replacement," Lindsey says.

"A book?" I ask, expecting that this idea won't work, but also willing to try it.

"You'll see."

Inside the bookstore, Lindsey buys me a coffee that costs as much as a book and we share it as we walk the store, passing it back and forth, in the way that Joan and I used to share cigarettes, except we aren't fighting.

"Here are the rules," Lindsey says, and I find this statement sexy because of its absoluteness. "The first thing we need to establish is that reading our agreed upon novel will be our version of going to the movies. A dinner and a movie date is special because you have to go somewhere for the experience. This means that we're going to have to find a book that there are two copies of here, and choose titles that won't disappear. The only time we can read the novel is in this bookstore, together. Second, a movie is special because there are food and drink options that cost a ridiculous amount of money so each time we come, we'll get coffees and maybe, like, an overpriced scone. We'll read the book for two hours, in complete silence, no talking, then when we're done, we'll go to Rubie's, and discuss."

I agree to the rules, and Lindsey smiles at my compliance.

Picking the book will be a delicate process. We walk around the bookstore, taking a survey of the aisles, judging the sections by their fanbase.

Fatty in "Self Help"/ Beardy in "History"/ Oldie in "Fiction"/ Teens in "Graphic Novels"/ Elderly in "Mystery"/ Preggo in "Romance"/ Brownie in "Travel"/ Dorky at the "New Release" table/ No one in "Poetry," but we disregard this section because it would be like seeing a series of short films, and people don't go to the theater to do that.

No one is in the "Horror" section, and this lack of interest attracts us. The entire aisle is eerily deserted, and I wouldn't be surprised if a menacing fog begins rolling in as we start to review the dusty spines. With all the customers cruising the other aisles, anyone could buy any book at any time, but in the "Horror" aisle there's no fear that the copies of our chosen book will be gone.

"Why do you suppose no one reads horror novels?" Lindsey asks, as we begin to review our options.

"It's just the nature of the written word. Think about anything that scares you- it's probably the uncertainty of what looms in the dark or the sound of someone jiggling the handle on your door when all your suitemates are home for the weekend. Sights and sounds just scare better. You know how hard it is to send a chill down someone's spine with a word?"

Lindsey thinks about it for a second, then says, "One time I was reading a true crime book about the Manson Family and it said that when they broke into that house where Sharon Tate was, one of them said, 'I'm the devil. I'm here to do the devil's business.' That's the only time I've really been scared of something I've read."

"Yeah, but if you were that scared reading it, imagine how scared you'd be hearing it."

Lindsey turns away from me, not willing to imagine the moment. She slides out a book with River White on the cover, but I use my palm to slam it back in line on the shelf.

"I guess we won't be reading that one." she says, sounding a little surprised.

"Sorry, it's just that I hate books that use movie stills from the adapted movie for a cover."

Rule~ Novels can't have a movie poster for a cover. It turns the source material into merchandise for a film, like a lunchbox or a happy meal toy. "Now a Major Motion Picture" books are a splashy admission that film is king. There's a cheapening of the source material. It's not right. There isn't a picture of a chicken on an egg's shell. This is why I like this date choice so much; it's a jostling of power.

Accepting that I've added a rule to our novel experience, Lindsey makes a seemingly random selection from the shelf.

We both look at the book's black and red cover. In a splatterpunk font, the title reads, *Limber*.

Behind the line of books, where they keep the extra copies, I see that at least three other *Limber*s sit, dusty and pathetic. I slide one of them out, and read the back. The novel is about a zombie apocalypse, and to rationalize the boring talky parts, the back of the book notes that it's a "biting satire."

We deem this our book, partly because of the large quantity the bookstore has on hand, and partly because *Limber* has to be the most un-scary, vaguely yoga-esque title of any book, ever. If someone was to walk into the Horror aisle to get a book, they would definitely buy something with "Dead" in the title, so our book should be safe.

"Do you think a girl will fuck a zombie?" Lindsey asks, giggling.

"I hope," I say, as we take our identical books to an unoccupied sofa that resembles dorm room furniture.

Lindsey takes out her phone, then puts it on the table and taps the screen. "At 1 PM, we'll stop reading," she announces.

I open the book and begin something new.

We don't pause to discuss the book, because we didn't pause to discuss the movie we saw in theaters.

When I'm on page 19, I hear Lindsey laugh, and suddenly my reading becomes focused on locating the statement that triggered this reaction.

The plot of the book is that some sort of circuitous chain of events has led to a very small number of Americans being infected with a virus that gives them an unrelenting and unrestricted hunger. The typical outside "tells" that a zombie has- the slow walking, the drooling, the rotting body- are not present in *Limber*. These zombies are just fat. They're fat slobs. They're fat slobs who cannot stop eating. This creates an obvious problem because so many Americans show signs of being infected, when in actuality, they're just fat and hungry. Yes, these zombies eat people. Yes, America's fat people are herded like cattle into camps, tested for mutations, then they're tagged for tracking. Yes, only the most fit and limber survive. Lindsey and I would both breeze through this apocalypse. Maybe, that's why we continue to read the book, sometimes smiling, sometimes exchanging glances, sometimes snarling at the cliché ridden prose.

When Lindsey's alarm goes off, we stand up, the credits rolling on our first day as novel-daters.

"Let's take the long way out, I'm afraid to pass the people in the Self Help section now," Lindsey tells me, and this is an inside joke we're allowed to share because of our dinner and a novel date.

On our way out of the bookstore, I see a display set up that wasn't there when we were searching for our book. There's a metal folding table that's completely covered with the same book from end to end. A lone twenty-something sits, holding vigil over the copies. Intrigued, I approach the display.

Frank Mitchell introduces himself to us. Today, Frank is doing an in-store signing for his short story collection, *UNTALENTED REVIEWER*. The big, bold, red letters stand out on the stubby white cover.

"What's with the title?" I ask.

Frank wipes a tuft of hair out of his eyes, then says, "I named my first collection, *The Swiftest Swimmer*, and it was the biggest mistake I've ever made."

"I think that's a fine title," Lindsey says.

"That's what I thought too, then people started reviewing the book. The reviews had awful titles, like, '*The Swiftest Swimmer* Sinks,' or, '*The Swiftest Swimmer* Drowns in Self-Righteousness,' or, '*The Swiftest Swimmer* Needs Water Wings.' Every fucking review was like that. They weren't all negative, but even the positive ones had something like, '*The Swiftest Swimmer* is a Shore Thing.' It was an irresponsible and reprehensible use of words. I wanted to make sure that I didn't make the same mistake with this book, so I named it *UNTALENTED REVIEWER*. This way, if they want to use the title of the book in their headline, they'll have to put, '*UNTALENTED REVIEWER* Not Worth Reviewing.' In order to be punny with a headline for their review, the reviewer would have to out their opinion as being useless."

"So, you aren't afraid that reviewers will give your book bad reviews just because of the title?" I ask.

"I think I'm more afraid of puns," Frank Mitchell admits.

I take out my wallet and buy a copy of the book.

Frank Mitchell has given me the contents of a letter that will be used to end the growing silence that has festered between myself and Edie.

~

When we get back to Lindsey's dorm, I put *UNTALENTED REVIEWER* on the bookshelf above her computer, then say, "Happy birthday."

"You're giving me your new book?"

"Well, I really want to read it, and now that it's yours, I'll have an excuse to come over."

"Okay, well, I guess I have to accept the gift, even if it isn't close to my birthday."

"It's an early present," I tell her.

"Or maybe late. My birthday was last month," Lindsey reveals.

"Shit, I didn't know you then, so you'll have to accept this book as a birthday present, now," I respond, but I'm forever curious about Lindsey, so I ask, "What's the exact day?"

"October 22nd," she says, then adds, "And it's okay if you forget it. I'm terrible with landmark days. Birthdays, holidays- even the big college kid ones- I mean, I can't even remember when St. Patrick's day is, and look at me, I could be its mascot."

"We need to buy you a calendar. That will be your second birthday gift."

"No, no," she says, with a bizarre urgency.

I watch her rush to her desk and pull open a drawer. She takes out a sketch pad and says, "You won't buy me a calendar. We'll make one."

"We don't know when the holidays are, though."

"Hence the calendar," Lindsey responds, then counts out thirteen pieces of paper from the sketchpad and carefully rips them out. It makes me feel good that it's a clean tear and the edges of the paper just need to be evened out a little with a pair of scissors.

We spread the pieces of paper out on the carpet, then I allow Lindsey to take the lead because I'm not sure about where any of the holidays belong besides Christmas.

I perch myself on the edge of the bed, while Lindsey sits on the floor.

Lindsey picks up a blue pen and starts writing out our future, my mind flashes back to the schedule on Joan's wall. A semester planned, but never finished. This makes me sour on the calendar idea, but as Lindsey boxes out the sheets of paper, I hear her mumbling, "It's thirty days has September, April, May, and November, all the rest have thirty one, except February."

I laugh, "Isn't that supposed to rhyme?"

"The 13th piece of paper is in case we mess up," Lindsey says, ignoring my question. She writes "january" at the very top of a piece of paper that sits midway between us, and I notice that her handwriting is in all lower case- just as it appeared on her website.

"Okay, Kurt. What holidays are in January?"

"New Year's."

Lindsey pens in New Year's on the 1st, then asks, "Okay what else?"

"That's about it. New Year's. Or do bank holidays count? I think Presidents' Day is the 17th?"

"Bank holidays don't count because we still have college and I still have work."

"On Valentine's Day we'll still have college and work, but I want to put that on the calendar," I say.

Lindsey smiles at this, and I selfishly assume it's because she realizes that she'll have a Valentine this year, but then I change my view when she says, "You're right. All the holidays need to be marked down." She adds "presidents' day" on the 17th, then asks, "Okay, what are you doing on the 21st?"

I cycle through the possible holidays that could fall on January 21st.

Lindsey helps me, "You know, Saint..."

"Saint..." I say struggling to remember what holiday she could possibly be referring to.

"Saint... Laurent's Day," she blurts out, half discovering the holiday for the first time herself.

"Oh, right," I say, "To celebrate Saint Laurent's Day last year, I wore exceedingly tight pants and accessorized with a neck scarf."

"Yeah, I've already started beading my tights. You can never start preparing too early for Saint Laurent's day."

"Maybe we should only add the real ones," I suggest, afraid of what Lindsey is capable of when she's put in charge of the world's rules.

"No Kurt, that's boring." I'm quickly dismissed, then she marks down "st. laurent's day." She takes "january" and hands it to me, "That's all for January, no sense in starting out the year in a frenzy."

Lindsey writes "febuary" on the top of a new sheet and slides it into the old spot where january used to be. This misspelling further cements her identity as the girl whose existence I discovered in the computer lab.

She hurriedly starts on the holidays, somewhat uncomfortably. "Okay, February. This is easy, the 14th is Valentine's Day," she says as she marks it down. "What else?"

"Let's see... on the 5th there is Take Your Cat to Work Day," I remind her.

Lindsey marks the day down, "Hooray, my hypothetical future-cat, Eek, is so excited. All those shelves for him to climb on."

"And don't forget about the 24th," I keep talking, and I need to think of something quick, so I say, "Dr. Lindeberg Day. Where everyone brushes for the full two minutes in honor of Dr. Lindeberg's great advances in the field of dentistry."

Lindsey marks it down, "It's a shame, I don't think I've ever actually celebrated Dr. Lindeberg's day."

"9 out of 10 dentists recommend celebrating," I tell her.

febuary is placed atop january, face down.

Another sheet, "march."

"Okay, well, we have St. Patrick's Day," Lindsey says, then her hand hovers around the center of the page, eventually plopping down on the 17th to scrawl, "st. patrick's day."

"Then on the 8th there's Native American History Day. If we didn't slaughter them before they could make more history, then they'd totally have a week," I say.

Lindsey marks down the holiday.

"March is such a crazy month for drinking, I mean with St. Patty's Day and Native American Day in the same month," I notice.

Lindsey moves her hand to March 18th, and writes, "bar day," further escalating things, providing us a chance to go on a bender not because of culture or genetics, but instead just because we're college students.

"We're going to have to avoid Belle for the entire month of March," I say.

Lindsey moves her hand up to the 13th and writes, "dollar day."

"What happens on Dollar Day?" I have to ask.

"Um, hello, it's where you give an old person sitting at the bus stop a dollar and tell them, 'It's all I can spare, I'm sorry,' then you hug them," she says.

I laugh.

"march" gets handed to me, and goes upside-down on "febuary."

"april" is next.

"Easter," I say.

"Okay... that's the... first Sunday of April?" Lindsey guesses, then "easter" is marked down.

"April Fools' Day, the first," I remind her, then add, "That's when we play harmless pranks on people which will somehow escalate into an unforeseen circumstance and create a communication breakdown that will last until long after we graduate."

"Tragic," Lindsey remarks, then brightens up, "At least Hat Day is the second Tuesday of April."

"hat day" is marked down. This takes me back to high school, when the concept of being able to wear a hat during class felt like some sort of wild freedom.

I reach down to grab "april" thinking that it's complete, but Lindsey pushes my hand away because she wants to enrich "april" more.

The 19th of April is marked as "run away from home day." I raise an accusatory eyebrow that Lindsey can't see, but must sense, because she explains, "The way it will work is that the first one to remember it's Run Away From Home Day will run away, and the other person gets a single clue on a post-it and has to go searching.

"What happens if I can't find you?" I ask.

"What happens if you're the one who runs away first?" Lindsey responds back.

"Never," I say.

We continue on as the 23rd of April is marked as "greeting card day," and as Lindsey writes this, she says, "Such a fucking Hallmark holiday."

"april" gets handed to me, then it goes upside-down on "march."

Lindsey slides the next piece of paper over, flattens it, and brands it "may."

"'Memorial Day, the 18th, when we remember those who fought for this country," I state.

"memorial day" gets marked down.

In rapid-fire succession, I say, "May Day, the 1st, when we run around a pole holding streamers. Steak on Face Day, the 2nd, when we put a frozen steak on our face to reduce the swelling caused by a bully's fist. Zoo Freedom Day, the 17th, when we give all the zoo animals the day off and release them back into the wild so they can go see their families."

"That about does it for May," Lindsey says, cutting me off before I fill every day of the month. She pens in "cinco de mayo" on the 5th, then "may" is handed to me, and gets put upside down on "april."

"june" is carefully printed on top of the next sheet of paper.

We both sit in silence.

I look down at Lindsey.

Lindsey looks up at me, sighs, then decides, "We're going to have to break up in June on the 15th, then get back together on the 16th."

Breakup? We're dating? I don't say anything, because I'm afraid my voice will crack.

"anniversary" gets marked down on the 16th.

"june" is picked up, and I try to take it with a steady hand.

"july" is marked on the top of the next sheet.

"Fourth of July, to celebrate the birthday of this great country," I say, because it's one of the best holidays for calendar making. The straightforwardness of the holiday makes it almost un-American. We no longer appreciate or exhibit this directness. Now, everything has to be packaged in a soft vaguery.

Trying to find the more difficult holidays in the month, I say, "Then the 17th is Trash Day, where we all go out and pick up trash on the highway like common criminals."

"No, Kurt," Lindsey cancels Trash Day, "That holiday is just stealing from Arbor Day."

"When's Arbor Day?" I ask.

"It can be on the 17th," she decides, making a compromise, then she extends her acceptance by saying, "And I'll give you the 11th for Trash Day, but the day will just consist of us buying each other outfits at Walmart."

"I look forward to owning my first piece of camouflage," I tell her.

"I will be stunning in overalls," she beams.

In a totally selfish moment, I say, "On the 29th of July, we celebrate the birthday of your great boyfriend." Since she suggested our breakup, I must be her boyfriend.

My birthday is marked down as, "bf's b-day."

I'm her boyfriend.

I'm handed my birthday month, then "august," begins.

We both pause again.

"How about Presidents' Day?" I suggest.

"A second Presidents' Day? We already celebrated in January."

"I'm using my power of executive order to get a Presidents Day in August," I declare.

Lindsey marks the 11th as "presidents' day pt 2."

"Columbus Day," I hazily recall being in August.

"Okay, but we have to space it away from President's Day because that's too many sociopaths being celebrated in too short of a timeframe."

"Before or after?" I ask.

"Bef- After. Yeah, after," Lindsey works it out in her mind.

"The 20th."

"columbus day" gets marked down.

"august" gets handed to me, then put upside down on "july."

"september."

"Labor Day, the 1st."

"labor day" is marked down.

"Um, my Mother's birthday is the 16th. It's a day we can listen to some Sharpe and stay in," I suggest sheepishly.

"kurt's mom's b-day" is marked down.

"september" is handed to me, then flipped upside down on top of "august." Lindsey gives my mom the rest of the month.

"october."

"The 15th, Sleep in Your Car Day, where we bring some blankets and pillows and book a night in our mobile motel room," Lindsey says.

"The 9th, New Day, where everything is new. You wear new, eat new, think new- become new. Anytime we hear someone say, 'It's a new day,' we'll be like, 'No. That's next week. Please update your calendar.'"

"new day" gets marked down.

"Halloween, the 31st," Lindsey mentions.

"Can we just celebrate it the whole month?" I ask.

"Only movie and novel wise."

"The movies better be at home."

"You want to add a 'home movie' holiday?" Lindsey asks, giggling.

"halloween" gets marked down.

"october" is handed to me, then gets turned upside-down.

"november" is written atop the next sheet.

"The 9th, Spa Day where you can swim in all indoor hotel pools across America and the employees won't be dicks and ask you which room you're staying in," Lindsey says, as she marks it on the calendar.

"The 24th? Thanksgiving, where you have turkey and give thanks."

Thanksgiving gets marked down.

"november" is handed to me, then goes upside-down on top of "october."

"december."

"The 25th, Christmas, when Santa comes, Jesus was born, and we release an album of holiday covers as a sign to our fans that we've truly given up," Lindsey says, marking it down.

"The 3rd, Doogie Howser Day when we try to get people to believe we're qualified to work jobs that we're obviously not."

"doogie howser day" is added.

"And finally, the 31st, New Year's Eve, a day of dissatisfaction and frostbite."

"new year's eve" is carefully placed on the 31st.

The last sheet of paper is abandoned on the carpet, and our year is set.

Lindsey stands up and takes the pile of days from me. We both go over to the empty bed near the window, and begin taping up the months next to a Modest Mouse poster showing a bunch of white arrows stuck into a striking green wall that, from the holes, drips pink blood.

These holidays arrive like rules, but part of me considers them pointless because, right now, Calendar Day is my favorite day of the year.

~

I'm waiting for Noni at the Village Trattoria. I don't order anything because I know if I eat now, I won't be hungry when she shows.

The powerlessness of waiting for someone is mental torture for the person on time, which is almost always me. I have no choice but to remain in my seat, or pace, or chain-smoke outside, or send a series of texts that contain fewer and fewer smiley faces each time, knowing all the while that there's no guarantee the late person will ever arrive.

Then comes *the* question, *When do I leave?*

If I've waited thirty minutes, what's another five? If I've already invested that much time into waiting, I might as well stick with it.

Noni eventually shows up, and her bangs are pinned back so I can see that she did her makeup in the style that made me first notice her. She knew I'd be okay with the delay if it led to the privilege of being able to sit across from her, looking precisely how I like her. As she walks toward the table, she smiles at me, and all of the animosity I've built up disappears when I'm faced with that busy grin. When she gets closer, I notice she has a white bandage where her upper arm meets her forearm. Maybe she injured her elbow, or no, maybe she gave blood, or no, maybe they took blood, or no, maybe she shed blood.

"Mr. Jonesss," she hisses, as she sits down.

"You look nice."

"Oh, I know, I haven't slept in ages."

"Still trying to find your brother, I take it?"

Noni doesn't look at me when she nods her head to confirm that she is.

"So, you haven't found him?"

Noni looks up at me and shakes her head in a somewhat no-ish manner.

"What if he doesn't want to be found?"

"I'm sure he wants to be, Kurt," Noni says, very directly, "I'm positive that he's waiting for someone to put in the effort to find him. It's just the type of person he is."

"Well, how close are you to finding him?"

"There's no bus line that goes near enough to the possible studio locations where he could be, and I haven't been able to borrow the Lincoln since that one night."

I don't know what night or which car she's alluding to and this makes me sad. I always used to know the backstory with Noni. To not dwell on my new ignorance, I push forward, "Have you checked the internet to see if he's even still working with the guy from Interview? Maybe he moved or something?"

"Kurt, you saw my room. I was filling notebooks, I was printing out every web page that mentioned him, even in passing."

"Did you find out much about him?"

"No, most of it was about the art scene here. People who probably know people who could possibly know my brother."

"Have you talked to any of them?"

"Of course, lots."

"And?"

"I've been to so many bad art shows," Noni says, then picks up a squat glass jar of parmesan cheese, and says, "Nothing is sadder than bad art, which makes all of this so much harder emotionally."

"Let me know when the next one is. I'll go with you."

"Actually, it's a poetry reading," Noni says,

"How does the poetry reading fit in?" I ask, wondering if she truly is searching for her brother, or if she's merely *searching*.

"One of the poets is the roommate of an artist's brother- an artist who might know my brother," Noni lays it out.

"You're really scraping the bottom here," I tell her- something she must already know.

"You have to start at the bottom."

"You've progressed very little."

An angry looking employee in a Jets jersey brings Noni the slice of pizza I bought for her when I arrived, and this surprise pulls her out of her funk. "Noni and Kurt are going to a poetry reading. What happened to us this year?" she asks.

I shrug.

"Let me see your hand," Noni demands, and I feel a weird déjà vu that raises my body temperature.

Noni waits for my hand, not changing the subject, not asking me what's wrong.

I put out my perfectly cut nails and finely maintained cuticles, and she pulls my hand further across the table.

Noni's hands are always cold, which I loved *that summer* when we walked along the boardwalk. I'd wrap her arm around me, and she'd leave her hand clutching the side of my stomach under my T-shirt. It's a feeling I left in the season, but still feel great nostalgia for.

Noni takes a gel pen out of her purse, then in my open palm, she writes an address that I can't make out because it's upside-down to me.

"We can have coffee. Maybe they'll even let you bring your cup. You know how these art house coffee shops are, too liberal to instate rules, too stuck up to wash dishes."

"I hope you find your brother," I say, looking at my palm.

Noni looks at her pizza, and says, "I know you do. You're the only one who knows exactly what it's like to look for someone who's willingly abstaining from being a part of your life."

~

The coffee table order is *Esquire/ Harper's Bazaar/ People/ Rolling Stone/ The New Yorker*.

The CD player is 3:53.

The light switch is ON.

The walls are peeling.

The dishes are breeding.

The milk is expired.

The TV is screaming.

The ceiling is thumping.

All these days, and no one came to check on me, no one complained about the blaring television. I could have rotted to dust here and no one would notice. Returning to my apartment, I feel like I did when I went in 5E. This place is set up exactly how my apartment was, but this is a stranger's home.

Trying to reclaim my home, I begin doing the dishes, but stop halfway through and write down the address to the poetry reading on a post-it before I wash away the location of plans I now regret making.

I finish the dishes, then leave my apartment. I take the elevator downstairs to check my box on the false hope I'll have a letter.

I flip through the contents of the box- A credit card statement/ Akkuta's magazines/ No letter from Edie. As I'm organizing the new issues in my hands, my cell rings, so I put my mail under my arm, then answer the call. Now that Joan is gone, I no longer feel the need to check who's calling me.

"Hello?"

"Kurt Jones," Lindsey purrs cutely, and I immediately ask her to come over. I tell her I'll walk her here/ I tell her I'll pay for a taxi/ I tell her I'll carry her here. She tells me that she'll be over in ten minutes. The emptiness of Edie's silence no longer feels so severe with the promise of Lindsey's presence.

I step in the elevator, and my finger hovers over the 4 as I try to decide if I should go see Noni. Ever since leaving the pizza place, I've been debating about how to handle Noni's quest, how to handle her dedication, how to handle her desperation. Should I tell her; should I let her know the things I had to learn all by myself? It doesn't feel right to kill a piece of Noni that's coming from such a pure place.

I press down on the 4 button, and the doors close. The same things I learned on my own will have to be independently discovered by Noni because she's not me, and this means that her quest has a better chance of success than mine did. She needs to learn that she can never give up, but she needs to stop trying so desperately- that's the only way to get through it. And as for winning... is this a battle that can even be won? Maybe, for her.

I get out of the elevator on my floor, arriving at the conclusion that Noni will be able to take care of herself tonight. The more pressing issue becomes the condition of my substandard apartment.

After I set down the mail on the coffee table and organize it properly, I begin fixing and hiding all of the most embarrassing flourishes I noticed when I returned here.

I make sure the pictures on the wall are straight/ I make sure my bed is made/ I make sure the light switch is ON/ I frown at the peeling walls and cracking ceiling.

Lindsey has already accepted the biggest imperfections I've presented to her- cracks that breach the foundation- so these surface imperfections seem insignificant.

~

Lindsey is standing in the hallway, posing. "Did someone order a pizza?" she asks, in her best porno voice, which isn't very good because she's doing a man's porno voice, not a woman's. She has the pizza box balanced on her right palm, while the pointer finger on her left hand twirls her straight hair.

This moment captures the too-good-to-be-true feeling of the pizza delivery pornos. A moment this good never happens, except when it does.

Before I can react, Lindsey is in my apartment, her eyes scanning everything, her curiosity so strong that she hands off the pizza to me.

"I'm going to repai-" I start to say, but she interrupts me, "-it's an old building, it adds to the charm." I had assumed she was complaining about the paint job in her head, because Joan always did it aloud.

Lindsey stops in front of the Harrington Street sign, then says, "We're going to have to get rid of this, you don't live in a frat house."

My Takeaways on what a girl will do once she views herself as your girlfriend:

One- Remove the items they view as an embarrassment.

Two- Erase any emotion you may have felt or still feel toward another female.

By verbally nixing the street sign, Lindsey was succeeding with both goals. I'm not going to resist the minor image tweaks that Lindsey will undoubtedly attempt with me. I've learned in the past that resistance to change is counterproductive. My entire life, I've carefully balanced my personal preferences with things that I think will attract girls. Somehow, along the way, these two distinctions have melted together and become my identity. The items acquired with a motive- the Burberry cologne, the overpriced sheets on my bed, the designer jeans- have just seamlessly melted into my own taste, and they're now part of Kurt Jones. Next time, when I'm out of cologne, I'll end up staying with the preferences of a girl who meant the world to me, then moved a world away. I'm pretty sure most girls are aware of this process, so they're obligated to demand these small changes to set the whole thing in motion again. They don't want you to put on your cologne in the morning and be reminded of the weekend you spent in bed with some other girl. They want to haunt you in new ways, so they set up the building blocks of nostalgia before they're gone.

For the second time in a matter of hours, I sit down to eat pizza with a brilliant, complicated girl, and I wonder how I've become this lucky.

I turn on the TV, and Lindsey winces at the reality show on the screen. I take a bite of the pizza and it tastes so much better than the slice I had earlier.

"It's sad... all of us letting our lives pass us by because we're watching other people's lives pass them by in exchange for a cash prize," Lindsey points out, snarling at the screen.

I swallow a bite of pizza, then say, "It's all about presentation, anyone's life could be affecting with the right editing. I guarantee you that somewhere out there is a person who would make your life a masterpiece."

"Can I?" Lindsey asks, pointing at the TV.

After I nod my approval, I watch Lindsey get up and walk across the living room. She starts pressing buttons on the side of the TV, calibrating everything to her liking, then she returns to the sofa.

The TV's picture has been drained of its color. Blacks and grays cover the wide canvas. From now on, we'll be watching this reality show like it's *Manhattan* and the news like it's *Night of the Living Dead*. This is why the TV in her room is always playing black and white *X-Files* episodes. It's her choice- a preference that I will now co-opt. I want to leave the TV like this because it's how everything has become in comparison to Lindsey's bright aura.

We eat pizza, and watch the reality show. The experience has been enriched, but the content is still dull, so I repeatedly look to my side, sneaking glances at Lindsey's shocked-blonde hair, perfectly clear complexion, and tiny little brown freckles. The colors missing from the TV screen seem to radiate from Lindsey.

I feel everything on the wall begin to fall off like the chipping paint. The Takeaways I had assembled so recently now seem too narrow. I'm not being forced to change, I'm being nudged to evolve. I stayed with Joan, not because it felt right, but because I was afraid to work on myself. I would actively delay my happiness, forever saying, "Once my mother dies..." but Lindsey has taught me to appreciate the moment. The holidays we planned aren't a delay of satisfaction, they're a promise.

~

The morning sun beams into the apartment and for a moment, I'm blind, but it doesn't matter. I can still smell her perfume- a mix of magnolia flowers, strawberry candy, and hairspray, so I know that she stayed the night.

Last night, armed with only a pizza, Lindsey arrived at my building, presumably scared, then walked down the hallway of my building- a hallway that makes sure every person between its walls dwells on the unquestionable fact that they have made a grave mistake in their life at some point that has led them here. That hallway is a hospital waiting room for the cuts and bruises of poor decisions. Lindsey should have turned around, and I honestly feel as though the girl in those journal entries would have fled, but she continued to the door. She entered my apartment, and she stayed.

My vision returns, and I watch as Lindsey squints her eyes, finding the sun to be an uncomfortable alarm clock. This is clearly an unfamiliar way for her to wake up. She reaches over and grabs her phone off the nightstand, then lets out a huff when she sees the time on the screen.

The moment she starts to get up, I let out a deep, long, "Nooo."

This doesn't stop her. She slides her legs off the bed, then walks over to her purse. I watch her as she takes out her vest, unrolls it, then puts it on. I realize that I have no idea where Lindsey works. I have no idea what she does. I have no idea where she's going, that causes her to look so miserable.

Lindsey sees me staring, and says, "I know, it's a very flattering vest, thank you for resisting the temptation to ravage me after seeing me in it."

"You don't have to put that on until you get to work, if you don't want to," I suggest.

"I know, but I like to ease into the misery, putting on a vest like this the exact moment that I begin a six hour session of indentured servitude is just too much. For my mental health, I find it's easier to slowly build to the soul-sucking climax so the shock doesn't hit me all at once when I get there."

"Where's 'there?'" I ask.

"The pharmacy next to the UPS place."

"You work at the drugstore?" I respond, angry with myself because all my trips to Rite Aid could've been made to Lindsey's store instead. So what if my snack shopping would've been limited to cough drops? I would've had Lindsey in my life earlier.

"Actually," Lindsey says, "We don't say drug store anymore, it makes our business sound like a crack-house."

"Well, what do you call it?"

"A pharmacy."

"When I imagine a pharmacy, there is always candy, but where you work, the most exciting item is a fully collapsible walker."

"That's the point, you know, to make people think about their old time mom and pop pharmacy and avoid the fact that we really only sell stuff you need if your mom or pop has a body that's giving out, or life has dealt you a bum hand," Lindsey says, sitting on the edge of the bed, fixing her hair.

"So this makes you a pharmacist?"

"No, it makes me a stock girl."

"I never understood the idea of the stock girl," I say.

"Yeah, it's a pretty complicated job," is Lindsey's mordant response.

"No, I mean, I understand what a stock girl does, but I don't understand why one needs to be there for six hours a day. How much stock are you guys going through that they need the shelves constantly replenished? Don't you just reach a point where the shelves are full?"

"Well, yeah, then I do stock management. Which entails-" Lindsey looks down at her phone, "-shit I need to run."

I raise an eyebrow.

Lindsey lingers in the room, and asks, "So, are you walking me to work?"

I get out of the bed, then in the light of day, Lindsey and I re-visit the path she took to visit me.

The winter hasn't fully descended yet, so we walk into town instead of going to the garage to get her car. It gives us time to talk, and Lindsey explains her job further, "What I do for stock management is I take all the aspirin bottles off the shelf and put them in one of those plastic hand baskets that you use when you need to buy more than a handful of stuff, but not enough for a cartful. Once they're off the shelf, I mix all the aspirins up. Next, I'll randomly pick out one of the bottles and look at the expiration date, and if it's close, then I put it in the close pile, or if it's a while away, it goes in the medium pile, or if it's brand new and the expiration isn't for a while, it goes in the long pile. Once everything is in its respective pile, I take the long pile and put it on the back of the shelf, then I take the medium pile and put it in front of the longies, then I take the closies and put them right on the front of the shelf. This has to be done because otherwise we'd always be putting the newest bottles in the front and the other shit would sit back there until the store closes or there's some horrible outbreak where expired medicine is the cure."

"You still sell the expired medication?"

"Most of the stuff has a two year expiration, so if it doesn't sell in two years I put it in the front of the shelf, hoping someone will grab it without checking the date."

"So you do sell expired drugs?"

"Pretty much, don't make it sound like we're shooting puppies, almost all medication is just as effective after its expiration date."

"Then why don't they just move the expiration date back?"

"Same reason I left your comfy bed to show up to rearrange aspirin. Money. A good deal of these drugs are being sold to old people. You know how much time an old person has to read labels? Their entire life in that wheelchair is like a constant trip to the bathroom and they're desperate to read anything they can reach. They see that their aspirin has expired and they don't fuck around, they go out and buy a new bottle because when you're that old, all it takes is one missed expiration date and you've met your own."

This entire system makes sense to me, and I don't question it- I relate to it.

Too often, I feel like a bottle of expired medication being repositioned by a beautiful girl in hopes that a sick woman will reach for me.

We arrive at the pharmacy, and after I say goodbye to Lindsey, I walk to the grocery store so that there will be food in my apartment the next time she visits. If she didn't arrive with pizza last night, I would've only been able to offer her a plate of mustard.

My cart thumps through the brightly lit grocery store as one of its four wheels protests its lot in life.

I glance down one of the aisles and see a shattered jar.

I think about Edie's silence. I thought I had come to terms with her apathy, but her memory seeps into my existence like ink on a page.

~

I get back to my apartment, and I start going through my mail. There's no response from Edie to my *UNTALENTED REVIEWER* letter so I go into my desk and take out the stack of old letters. I undo the twine string around the pile of loose leaf, then I grab from the middle, and start reading.

"Remember that crappy bar that Levi Banes' dad used to run- the one that had the giant wooden bear statue on the outside- where I would always tell people the place was haunted by a guy who was playing the KISS pinball machine and dropped one of his quarters under it, but when he crawled down to get the coin, he jostled the bad leg so it toppled over and crushed him- well, I snuck in there because I wanted to get in the heating duct and pretend to be the ghost of that dude, but while I was scoping the area, a guy named Eric walked up to me, and he was wearing a Southern Comfort T-shirt in a bar, so obviously he was proud bar trash, and I began talking to him, you know, small talk to find the entrance to the ducts- stuff like mentioning that it's awful hot, then asking where he thought the heat is coming from, and for some reason he started telling me about how he teaches second grade and that he hires people like me to be aides and assistants for the kids, and I asked him how he controls the kids, and he said 'Fine,' and when I asked where he when to school, he named at least three colleges, then said he was a piano major, and when I asked him what a piano major does when he graduates, he said, 'Teach

*second grade,' and I forced a laugh, which was a mistake, because then he
asked me to write down my number and he told me he left his cell phone
at home because he got ditched, then he asked me if I wanted to dance to
the cover band doing a rendition of a Third Eye Blind song, but I said,
'I'm not much of a dancer,' and he said that he is, then proceeded to take
his phone and his keys out of his pocket and asked me to watch them for
him, and he danced for a bit, then came back, and told me he loves music,
and I said, 'I do too,' and I asked him if that was his cell phone I was
watching, which forced him to admit, 'Yeah, I lied, I did bring it, but I'm
not answering it because I was at work and I gave a girl my number and
she's been calling me constantly,' and when I asked him what happens if
he gets caught or if her parents find out, he looked horrified, then he
clarified that it was a full grown woman- the school nurse- who gave him
her number, and this information made him less interesting, and I said
that my trust had been broken, and I asked if his name was really Eric,
and he said, 'It is,' so I asked, 'How do I know that when it could be Sean
or Mallory-' and he cut me off all psycho-like and asked me why I said
Mallory, to which I shrugged and said, 'I don't know,' but he was really
stuck on it, and he was all like, 'No seriously...' and I told him it was the
first name I thought of, then drumroll please, the big reveal, he goes,
'Mallory is the name of my daughter,' and I looked Eric in the eyes and
told him, 'I know. I have gym class with Mallory,' and he almost vomited,
but I cut him off on the way to the men's room, and once I was inside
there, I propped myself up in a stall and climbed into the heating duct and
when I started my ghost bit, people got so weirded out that they turned
off the music and before I got out of the vent I said, 'Your souls will be the
ultimate retribution for your sins... unless you give Kurt Jones free drinks
the next time he's in here,' so, now are you ready to come home?*
    xx Edie."

I am.

I'm ready to take Lindsey and bring her to my grandparents and
introduce her to Edie. My grandparents could take me to my mother, and
I'd say, "This is her, Mom," and she'd nod her head, and she'd see Lindsey
and realize that every bad thing people said about her as a mother behind
her back was merely conjecture.

~

I stir my coffee and reluctantly add a new type of crystallized sugar that the bookstore is now offering.

Lindsey follows my lead, then picks up her massive cup, takes a sip, and scrunches her nose.

The sugar crystals in this new stuff must not be as strong as the fine, sand-like grain of the normal sugar, and we choose to compensate for this by quickly downing half of our coffees while competing on who's been more negligent with their coursework recently.

With the caffeine and sugar surging through us, we open up our copies of *Limber* to where we left off, and it strikes me that the printed words on the page have the same monochrome palette that our TVs now display. In a way, we're watching a muted, black and white story, but instead of 24 frames per second, it's one frame per minute, yet within each frame is a short film.

We read our book for exactly an hour and twenty minutes.

Instead of immediately leaving when the time is up, Lindsey and I compare pages- she's on page 177, I'm on page 162.

"Do you think this book is good?" Lindsey asks, and she seems nervous about this question, but I can't pinpoint the source of her nerves.

My answer isn't a yes or no, but instead a yes-no-kinda-absolutely -sometimes-hardly- occasionally. Reading a novel for pleasure- knowing that there is no final test, there's no paper to write, there's no requirement on the work- feels confusing. I keep thinking about a statement that Gerard often makes, which goes something like, "No one ever leaves a concert whistling the pattern that the stage lights flashed in," and that's how I feel about this novel. With *Limber,* at some points, the flash is what I leave thinking about. The prose work is rarely lyrical, the verses aren't a set length, the melody isn't steady, but there are moments when all of these dueling elements collapse into each other and they hum.

"I think it's good," I tell Lindsey.

"I think it's good, too," she confirms.

"Say your favorite part, up to 162, on three," I demand, then I count up, "One. Two. Three."

"The fat dad scene," we both say, simultaneously, and I've never wanted to purchase a book more than I do right now, but the rules prevent this. In the "fat dad" scene, a fat guy has to explain to his daughter that he's not a monster, but she doesn't know if she can trust him. The beats of this little girl's confused heart were rendered brilliantly in the novel.

We throw out our coffees, put our *Limber*s back on the shelf, then leave.

While we're walking across the parking lot, Lindsey presses down on her key fob to unlock the car doors, and I whistle the pattern that the lights flash in.

Even after we leave the lot, the moment inside the bookstore courses through us and we share more of our favorite parts of the first 162 pages of our date-book, until there's a tiny lull in the conversation, and before it can be replaced by literary criticism, it's broken by Lindsey yelping, "Fuck."

I scan the road and see nothing in our way, so I relax in my seat, then ask, "Do we need to go back?" She doesn't say anything for a couple seconds, then finally exhales, "It's nothing."

No matter what anyone says, yelling "fuck" never stands on its own. A person can't yell out, "Fuck," then continue reading their Kindle on the subway without someone coming over, and asking, "Dude, are you okay?"

"I need to find a child psychology book, then read it, tonight," Lindsey reveals, as we hammer down the left lane, the car doing close to 80.

"Is this an elaborate way to tell me you're pregnant?" I ask with mock sincerity.

"No, I wish it was that simple. I have this stupid paper due tomorrow and I was going to pick up the child psych book when we were at the bookstore, but I got all hopped up on coffee and fat-shaming subplots, and I totally forgot. Do you think the library is still open?"

"Maybe," I say, because Lindsey's driving scares me, and I don't want her to make a U-turn.

"Oh... okay..." she says, easing off the gas. Her frantic panic dissipates, then she calmly remarks, "They should put a coffee shop in the library now that they're expanding the hours."

She's right, maybe she's already taken the Business Management class I'm in.

We reach campus safely and park in the garage, then immediately head to the library.

We pass through the book detector that they set up at the entrance to keep the volumes from walking away. These gates are the reason that I don't have an off-campus library in my apartment that Lindsey could peruse for her assignment.

With only fifteen minutes until the library closes, the carefully curated chaos, confusingly sectioned off, becomes an enemy. It was easy to search with Lindsey at the bookstore. We browsed the clearly marked sections, then we found our title in an alphabetical line. It's not that simple here. There are shelves upon shelves and rows upon rows and floors upon floors of books. As is the case with most things in life, if I don't know where I'm going, I almost immediately give up.

Time ticks off the clock, and the only option becomes to separate. I decide that I'll start on the top floor of the library and Lindsey says she'll start in the basement. We synchronize the clocks on our cell phones to give our mission some sense of importance and professionalism, then we agree to text each other if we find a book about children or psychology, and we agree to call each other if we find a child psychology book.

I take the elevator up to the top floor, then review the books on the wall. This casual lounge is filled with oversized volumes stacked in lines to the ceiling. Based on a cursory review of the books that I slide out and flip through, this is a photography collection that features, largely, shots of naked women. I can't figure out if these books are being hidden up here, or if they're up here to turn people on in close proximity to the long curving sofas. I'm skeptical that the student librarians would want this, until I consider that there most likely are cameras up here.

I take the stairs down to a level closer to Lindsey. I search for the book, not only to help her, but to merely see her again as soon as possible.

I traverse aisle after aisle of towering shelves filled with books whose spines have the titles scrawled in Wite-Out on them.

Finding nothing that mentions kids, and few titles even remotely related to psychology, I become discouraged and start to glance into the little isolation booths. If I was taking a virgin survey, it would be almost unanimous that everyone on this floor would be confused by the books upstairs. The two people I would not deem virgins here are the gay couple I heard fucking in one of the study rooms near the books about architecture.

Bored by the virgins, I go back to the books, scanning the titles for keywords, doing the world's slowest google search.

After every additional aisle, the mere thought of this library becomes more and more overwhelming. Thousands and thousands of books, each taking thousands and thousands of hours from some poor sap's life to write. As a freshman, I walked into this library feeling like I could be the next Hemingway, then I saw the lines upon lines and rows upon rows of high, high, high shelves, and I walked out thinking, *What's the point? I think we've reached our book quota.*

This library is a tomb of the desperate, screaming. Did all of these people worry that if they didn't write a book before they died, their entire existence would be meaningless?

Maybe my mother should write a book? When she passes, she'll only leave two things on this earth. I've never seen her write anything, other than grocery lists, and those were disposed of with the receipts- a temporary need fulfilled. Maybe she feels like what she's leaving is enough? Maybe she's focused all her time on the one thing that she believes will make a difference after she's gone? The writing would've provided an avenue for closeness that would make her prolonged distance meaningless. It would've stood in the way of what she wanted to leave. Maybe what she wanted to leave was permanent, not in the sense of a book or a film, but a memory that can be passed down in the same way?

My phone vibrates, and Lindsey's text reads, "Found it, now find me."

~

I lie in bed and listen to ~the song~, while Lindsey sits at her desk and reads from *Interacting with Children in Their Environment.*

I push the pillow down so I can look over at Lindsey, and when my eyes focus on the front cover, I ask, "What do you suppose that title means? Do kids have an environment separate from ours? Isn't their environment just life at a shorter vantage point?"

Lindsey hisses, "Shhh," without looking over at me, and I imagine this is also how the author of the book fields the question.

I've been left with nothing to do besides stare, and in this simplicity, I'm satisfied. The fluorescent desk light mounted under the shelf is the only light in the room. My thin lazy frame is draped in the shadows and it's almost like I'm not here. Lindsey is turned in her chair so that the left side of her face is in the shadows and the right side is bathed in light. Seeing her as a student briefly inspires a feeling of motivation in me, but this quickly passes when I remember how my previous attempts at studying have gone this year. There was a point in my life when I could sit up and read all night. There were so many nights in high school that consisted of tattered pages and reading lights because it was the first time that I had books containing information that I cared about. I wasn't studying for tests, I was studying for me- the tests on the material were secondary.

Now I'm someone who uses his dead girlfriend to get him out of class. I'm a college kid who's already accomplished the impossible task of finding someone to make my existence feel less pointless. I no longer stay up late at night ingesting knowledge- forced or otherwise. I now stay up late at night, ingesting Lindsey's being. I don't have to cultivate a skill that can make me money because that need will be satisfied by my mother's death.

four.

I promised myself that after Thanksgiving break, when the semester resumed, I would regularly attend every class I'm registered for.

Now, with December arriving, I begin to make good on that promise.

Taking my seat in the Sociopathic-Extremonical required class, I feel like a visitor. I find myself sitting inside a photo shoot for a new pamphlet that shows the true Kirtland University- the distracted and the defeated- the apathetic and angry- the segregated and sad.

To my right is a girl I met at the orientation Kirtland forces all students to attend before their freshman year begins. After this orientation, I was convinced that college was about locating buildings, and catching blindfolded people whenever they fell backward. This understanding was shattered when freshman year began, and everyone quickly learned where the buildings are located, then we stopped catching each other when we fell.

The orientation girl's name is Jenny- I remember this because we had to wear name tags during orientation, and one day, about two weeks into the semester, I saw her wearing the same black shirt she had worn at orientation, and she'd forgotten to take the name tag off. I didn't make a big deal about it, and figured at least she was already showing a mastery of the college laundry system, which is the only recycling done at Kirtland. At this point, none of the freshman class had gotten into the groove of doing the things that their parents had previously taken care of. Except me- I was used to it.

As long as I've known her, Jenny's been one of those people who's constantly recapping. When I met her, she recapped a story about a boy in our orientation group, who she had gone to high school with. I believe the exact quote she gave was, "Trev Westwood has gotten six girls preg since 8th grade. One of the girls told me it's because his penis is so long that the sperm doesn't have that far to swim, so conception is easier." Jenny's voice sounds like how a hand smells after it's touched an old piece of metal. I still don't understand the female anatomy enough to know if Jenny's medical assessment holds any merit.

When I saw Jenny after spring break that year, she recapped, "I was lying out at the resort when this guy who I used to live next door to came up to me and told me that he thought I was my sister, and I was like, 'Thanks a lot, my sister is ugly as fuck.'"

When I was sitting in the café one day, Jenny hunted me down so she wouldn't have to assimilate with the commuters, and she recapped, "I was walking with Gerard and his cell phone went off, but he ignored the call, and I looked at the screen and saw you were calling him."

As class ends, and I'm collecting my stuff, Jenny immediately breaks into a recap, "I just want you to know, I'm here for you. I know how it feels to have someone you care about get hurt. This one time, at The Brink, Tim pulled me toward the stage, and while we were sliding between people, a crowd surfer kicked Tim in the face. I was like, 'What just happened?' then I saw he was bleeding, and was like, 'Call 911,' and the DJ was like, 'Call 911,' but not in the helpful way, more in the let's-get-the-party-started way."

Every memory I have of spending time with Jenny is of me not making eye contact with her, as she recaps something that doesn't involve me in any way. I wonder how she has all these stories when she's constantly discussing the past. Maybe I'm the only one she does this with. I might be the way she purges out all this information that she's carefully collecting while we're apart, then when she's ready to re-up, she leaves me and goes back out into the world. She's one of the many girls on campus that does this- it's not uncommon. Maybe we're all writing letters to Edie.

I leave class, and despite my avoidance of the textbooks I purchased at exorbitant costs, I'm filled with the sensation as though I had made it all the way to chapter four, turned the page, and inexplicably, I've been presented with chapter two again. I'm wasting time with something I've already bled dry, meanwhile I'm squirming in my chair to find out how the story ends.

I'm stuck reliving dead time.

~

In Brit-Lit, we talk about a story that I had read in Noni's dorm room last year while she researched how to buy a domesticated bobcat as a pet.

My classmates rest their heads on their desks, and I take this opportunity to raise my hand and participate four times. I feel near-universal support from my peers because none of them have read the story, and the more Takeaways I provide, the smaller the chance is they'll be called on to give their own. The old professor seems pleased that I'm answering his questions, but he also seems aware of the terrified looks on the other students' faces.

After running his hand across his beard, the old professor says, "Mr. Jones, thank you for your Takeaways, but you really have an unfair advantage on the rest of the class."

"What's his advantage?" someone asks, possibly on my behalf, possibly because they fear they're missing an opportunity to be a victim.

"Well, Mr. Jones has had more than enough time to read the assigned stories because his schedule isn't bogged down with, say, attending class."

I nod in agreement, he's right.

The fact that I didn't read this story for Brit-Lit, but instead, for myself, makes my attempt at looking like a student feel transparent and insufficient.

I sit silently as the rest of the class stumbles through their own vague Takeaways. The look in the old professor's eyes is not of disappointment, but instead of expectation fulfilled.

~

I get back to my apartment and Lindsey is missing. I've already formed expectations regarding her perpetual presence, so as soon as these unreal conditions aren't met, I immediately become paranoid.

I take out my phone and check what day it is. It's Wednesday, a non-holiday, which means she's at work.

I do some studying because I feel like the old professor's tired eyes are watching over me ominously like the eyes of Eckleberg in an incorrectly assigned novel. I do enough of the reading for the next Brit-Lit class to form two solid Takeaways, and when I check my phone again, only an hour has passed. Lindsey will still be at work for two hours. Time slows while I'm waiting. Even in her absence, Lindsey consumes my thoughts. Caffeine can speed up time so I need coffee, good coffee, not campus coffee, and this sends me to Starbucks.

I sing to myself as I walk into town.

The sky goes dark as a cold rain begins, bringing with it a feeling that snow could appear tonight.

I resist the temptation to walk into the pharmacy where Lindsey must be, and instead choose to pass by with only a glance inside. Instead of seeing my girlfriend, I see my reflection in the storefront, which inspires me to stop and fix my damp hair in the next window. Continuing on, I proceed past a group of businessmen watching a flat screen TV through the glass picture window of a bank branch. On the TV are a thousand tickers, all scrolling information, and each man seems focused on a different ticker. This communal moment strikes me as antiquated when every shred of information these men are receiving could be accessed on the internet.

I cross the street to get to the Starbucks, and I notice Gerard out front, smoking a cigarette. His hair is tamed from the sprinkling rain, and he exhales smoke in long, seemingly endless ropes that, when exhaled, encircle his head.

As I approach him, I notice he's wearing two different shoes. One shoe is red and white. One shoe is black and gold. Both shoes are lefties. I make sure Gerard knows I'm not going to brush this off, and I focus on the shoes for a couple of seconds, then say, "Nice."

"The black or the white?" he asks looking down.

"I wasn't commenting on your shoes, I was commenting on your charisma. Somehow, you pull this look off."

Gerard smiles at his two left shoes, then says, "Thanks, dude. I briefly felt skeptical," then he licks his thumb and bends down to wipe a scuff off the already-wet white shoe. A guy with two different lefty shoes on is worried about a scuff. He stands back up, and I can see he's trying to find the right words to change the subject but he flounders, so we both stare out at the dark clouds and squint as the cold rain plunks our foreheads, while police sirens howl in the distance. "It wasn't intentional. It was born out of necessity," Gerard says, staying on the conversation just to say something, "I had to go to Accounting. I gave a presentation. It was either go barefoot or with two left shoes."

"What happened to the matches? The righties?"

"I was hoping you had them," Gerard admits.

We walk into the Starbucks, order our usuals, then sit down.

Gerard begins shifting in his seat, while reaching down his pants. I become convinced that he's going to take out his dick and create a public scene to punish me for neglecting our friendship. This is something that Gerard does with a somewhat predictable frequency.

When his hand reappears, to my relief, Gerard is only holding a smudge-covered phone. "Since you've been dealing with the smooshing of your old girlfriend by devoting every moment of your life to a mysterious and unseen Juliet, I've finished some songs," he says.

I'm surprised, not only by this revelation, but also by Gerard's ability to produce proof. Gerard is always thinking up names for bands, but nothing would ever materialize after the name was chosen. I want to hear his songs, and I want him to tell me how he recorded them. Maybe he just turned on his phone, hit record and started playing. Maybe the songs aren't on the phone and he's just using it for demonstration purposes. Maybe the phone is just a prop to get me to pay attention.

"Very cool, man. I'm proud of you," I tell him. Gerard needs all the encouragement he can get. His dad called him "retard" a lot.

"You know stuff about music so I sort of wanted to get your opinion," Gerard says, arching his back so he can dig into his pants again. Thankfully, his hand goes in his pocket this time.

"I'd love to listen to your songs. When's your next practice?"

"Actually, I sort of wanted to ask you a question," Gerard says, pulling out white earbuds, then putting them on the table.

"Shoot."

"What makes something good?" Gerard asks, with a childlike innocence that I haven't seen in him since back when we found his Mom's dirty playing cards that had pictures of guys wearing short shorts with their cocks snaking out the right leg hole. It worries me that I remember which side it was so I quickly answer Gerard's question with, "A backlash."

"So people hating it makes it good?"

"Some people hating it makes it good," I clarify.

"If everyone enjoys my music wouldn't it be considered good? If people like it, that seems like the best thing a song can have going for it, isn't it?"

Gerard clearly hasn't thought about this as long as I have.

"No," I say, then demand, "Put on a song."

"You're stalling," Gerard says, looking at me from under his eyebrows, his chin tilted toward his chest.

"And you're anxious to hear my reasoning," I say.

Gerard sighs, slaps the table, then takes his phone back and puts it in his pants. We remain stuck in another silence until he resumes our conversation, like we were a film crew who had to pause as a plane flew overhead. "So, if lots of people think something is good, then it isn't good?"

"Think about all the content in the world that people think is good. Think about all the books, all the movies, all the TV shows, all the styles of clothes, and all the different types of music. If this stuff is good and everyone thinks it's good, how much of an impact does it have?"

"A lot," Gerard says, then sips his coffee, and adds, "You see it everywhere. It becomes a part of... ya know, the culture."

"Name a well-liked CD," I request.

Gerard thinks about it for a moment, then says, "The English Prices' first album. And see, I like that album because it's good and even you yourself said it was good when I played it for you. Everyone I've played it for has liked it."

"How much of an impact did it have though?"

"A lot... to me."

"Yeah, but I'm saying in general. Did it go anywhere? Did it do anything? Everyone you played it for liked it, but everyone also likes about a million other CDs too. It's a good CD and that's its fault."

"So what you're trying to say is, there are a million good CDs out there and a lot of them go undiscovered because they're just good?"

"Because they don't evoke a response. They evoke, 'This is good.' You don't want to write a letter to their record label when you hear it. You don't want to call up a friend and complain about the release. You don't want to picket out in front of every Target in the nation to stop it from being sold. You don't want to tattoo the album's name on your ass cheek... you just want to put it in your rotation for a couple weeks."

"So I have to make something that provokes most people to feel anything besides good?"

"There are thousands of three and a half star reviews in the *Rolling Stone* archives," I tell him.

"So..."

"So, make an album that has a fifty percent chance of getting one star and a fifty percent chance of getting five, and work like hell to make sure it doesn't split the difference."

~

I get back to my apartment and start going through my phone. I don't have any new texts from Lindsey, and this sends me to my e-mail inbox. I don't have any e-mails from Lindsey- just a couple of sale announcements, an Amazon book recommendation, and a Kirtland U "Community Alert."

As I'm reading the campus safety alert, I get a call.

My heart beats faster than the tempo of my ringtone.

"Hello?" I answer the call, and I'm hit with a frantic Lindsey, "Holy shit, Kurt. Listen to this!" I love conversations that begin with this six word exclamation spit like an excited demand. I've rarely been disappointed with the information that follows a breathless, "Listen to this."

Lindsey takes a deep breath, then says, "Okay, there was some dude who lives in the Grove, and I guess his girlfriend dumped him last week, or whatever, so you know what he did? He shot her."

"The Grove? Like the dorm?"

"Yeah. Like where I live. They haven't caught him, but a couple of the girlfriend's sorority sisters saw him leaving campus. The girls didn't intervene because, ya know, the whole prospect of getting shot."

"Are you alright?" I ask, knowing the answer, but still needing to hear her confirm it.

"Yeah, it's not like *I* dumped him."

"What's his name?"

"Kevin Thomas."

"Okay, let me look him up."

"My two first name theory is totally right," Lindsey says, sounding victorious amid tragedy.

"Huh?" I ask, as I google the name.

"Oh, well, I've decided that everyone with two first names has some sort of identity crisis that will eventually drive them crazy."

"I can see that," I say, scrolling down Kevin Thomas' Facebook page, which is already being defaced with hateful comments. Kevin lists "learning Japanese" as one of his hobbies, and I realize that he's exactly what the commuters are looking for; a no-nonsense, Japanese speaking bad ass. If the authorities don't catch this Kevin guy, the commuters will find him, and hire him for his services, causing the niched ecosystem of the café to be disrupted.

"This sucksss," the caged bird sings.

"I'll walk over and get you."

"We're on lockdown," Lindsey sighs.

"Lockdown, like jail lockdown?"

"Yeah, they're almost positive he left, but with stuff like this, the guys always come back for their Xbox or whatever. No one can go in or out of the Grove. I bet my RA has pissed his jeans."

"So you can't leave?"

"Nope."

"And I can't visit?"

"No, sir."

"So, what do we do?" I ask, feeling genuine panic because I'm not sure I remember how to fall asleep without Lindsey next to me.

"I don't know, kill that Kevin asshole?" Lindsey says, then giggles.

"I'm sure the cops are already working on it."

There's a momentary silence on the phone, then Lindsey begs, "Don't hang up, okay?" and she finally lets her fear show. I appreciate this revealing moment. I've become necessary.

"I won't hang up. I promise. I was just thinking about how we could salvage the night."

"Okay, so the plan is?"

"The plan is..."

My eyes dart around my apartment, and I think aloud, "Shit like this will be so much easier once I get the money. We could escape like we were Kevin Thomas' accomplices. I'd sneak you out, then we'd get on a plane."

"Get the money, what money? Did you carry out a hit on Kevin's girlfriend, then frame him?" Lindsey asks, and the tiny crack in her casual facade is quickly patched.

I haven't told her. I've met a girl that I can tell anything to, and I haven't told her the single most important piece of information that exists about Kurt Jones. The more I think about it, the stranger it is that I haven't let her know this hugely significant story. My emotions get all fucked up and between missing Lindsey, and missing my mother, I almost curl up into a ball, but I recover before too much dead air peaks Lindsey's suspicion.

I want to keep her from things that might hurt her. I keep her on the line, while drifting somewhere else.

~

I key into my mailbox.

No letter from Edie. I need one right now. Nervous questions cascade as I take the elevator back upstairs- *Is she alright?/ Is she still alive?/ What if she got arrested?/ What if she broke up with her boyfriend and he shot her?/ What if she dropped a quarter and the KISS pinball machine crushed her?*

I get worried enough that I consider moving beyond letters, and making a call. All of my past phone conversations with Edie have been matters that a letter couldn't begin to address. This silence doesn't exceed the crisis thresholds required for a call to Edie. A phone call without a reason is the only thing worse than a letter without a story.

The next time I hear Edie's voice it will either be soaked with sobs or pitched in sunny celebration- I desperately hope it's the latter.

~

When she's gone- at class, or at the pharmacy, or during that short visit she made back home for Thanksgiving- time loses its uniqueness and I ritualized checking my phone for missed messages, and I think about the people that I haven't heard from, and ~the song~, yes, ~the song~. It returns full blast, clearer than ever.

I sing myself into finals week, as the campus mutates. Beyond Lindsey, Kirtland turns gray and dull. My peers are cramming all the work they should've been doing during the semester into a handful of caffeine-fueled days. I have to keep busy, otherwise I'll guilt myself into studying, and I've found most study spots on campus are now ugly traps filled with sleep-deprived zombies. Almost every girl has her hair up in a bun, and is wearing a university provided T-shirt that's two sizes too big so she can wear it without a bra. She'll usually also have on sweatpants that have the school's name in shaded block lettering down the outside of the legs. Many girls also have their glasses on, glasses from high school with dated touches- the rhinestone accents or purple semi-translucent frames revealing their age. The boys at Kirtland fare no better. They're all sporting flat hair, or baseball caps lined with wavy, salty sweat stains along the perimeter. Their T-shirts bear their frat letters or the name of a tongue-in-cheek intramural sports team they were on last year. It's unlikely that their shirt has been washed since the last party or scrimmage. Their ill-fitting jeans are frayed at the bottom of each pant leg and there's another salt wave near their heel. They're all wearing basketball shoes far past their day in court- the toes creased, the laces gray, the rubber worn away on the back of the heel. With each step, the shoes emit a smell that's both familiar and entirely unique.

The air feels unbreathable amidst the complete and total reprieve of hygiene standards, and I leave campus to escape it. Unfortunately, when I arrive at the bus stop, the situation is no better. The smell of a cigarillo hangs in the air, and mixes with a sweet smell that might be unwashed hair. Everyone is wearing puffy jackets, and scarves that are nearly blankets, and they periodically drop their shopping bags because their chunky mittens can't grip the slick plastic. The way everyone is dressed makes me realize that we're well into winter, and once again, I think about Lindsey's short story.

The bus mercifully arrives, and I climb aboard, then put my money in the fare collector. Grossed out by most of humanity, yet desperate for a story, I search the faces around me. Most of the people on the bus are sitting with someone, and the single riders don't look ready to spill their guts; they look ready for a head-on collision, or another loose cannon stepping onto the bus, only to turn it to ashes.

I start getting creeped out by my potential seat companions, so I decide to sit next to a guy that looks like he could be my uncle or your uncle- he's definitely someone's uncle.

The uncle doesn't say anything, he just sits in his seat and counts out a bunch of change. He mumbles some numbers, points to a nickel, and in a loud whisper he says, "Fuck," like this was the magic word that would turn it into a quarter.

When the nickel remains a nickel, I reach into my pocket, take out some change, then ask, "Need some help?"

My seatmate accepts my help, and in return, he helps me. I find out that the uncle I'm sitting next to is Alan Breck. Alan Breck appreciatively receives my change, and in exchange, he takes out a book from his backpack and tears out the blank first page, then hands it to me, at my request.

Fingering a quarter that was once mine, feeling our great ex-president's indent, Alan Breck tells me his story, and I transcribe a first draft, "*Remember...*" is what I start with, and I don't have time to reminisce because the story keeps arriving. I get right into it, knowing I'll fix the letter on the second draft,

"Right now, I'm on the bus, sitting next to Alan Breck. We made a trade, and I ended up getting the better end of the deal. Alan Breck is currently unemployed, but he wasn't always jobless. There was a time that Alan Breck worked at a local city college teaching English. There's always a poetry section in an Intro to English class, and last semester the poetry section 'fucked' Alan Breck, as he so poetically put it. Alan Breck assigned his class what was a pretty standard Intro to English task, 'Write a poem about something that you feel the need to express, but can't without being afraid. Fight your paranoia and work out your fear, in front of an audience.' Alan Breck tallies that, out of his thirty students, he received twenty three poems about general bland dissatisfaction channeled into nature metaphors, five students didn't turn in a poem, and one student handed in a plagiarized poem from Reader's Digest. That

leaves Brent Screnton. Brent Screnton handed in a poem, the best poem, a poem about something other than 'fall and some rich kid's depression.' Brent Screnton's poem was entitled 'The First Time I Killed A Foreigner.' As was the tradition in the class, Alan Breck read the best poem aloud. Cindy Spade's poem about her stress growing on her like moss was not read. Benny Dorcese's poem about his Italian roots being like the roots of a diseased tree was not read. Chris Nelson's poem about his premature balding being represented by the leaves of fall was not read. Brent Screnton's 'The First Time I Killed A Foreigner' was read aloud. The white girls balked and clucked as Alan Breck tried to do justice to the one poem that did what he asked, in the way he was hoping for. Guilt was immediately assigned. Brent Screnton didn't carry out the act he was detailing in his couplets, but he would be blamed for it. For Brent Screnton, this poem was about how he was programmed, growing up in America. It was about the propaganda he saw on TV. It was about the news he was reading on his laptop. It was about his own isolation. It was about how, every day, he was told who should be viewed as a hero and should be viewed as a villain, and often, both of those classifications of people were committing the same acts, just against different people. It was about how violence can be condemned, or celebrated, based on the target. The poem did end with a death, and the poet expressed pride in his actions. The poem was a reflection of a man asking if he's winning by committing an act that will only serve to escalate the hurt. Brent Screnton learned what it was like to become the villain. No one cared what the point of the poem was- by the time the title was read, Alan Breck was already unemployed. Desperate to keep his job, to salvage his reputation, to put all of this behind him, Alan Breck apologized and said that Brent Screnton didn't write the best poem. He said that the poem about Chris Nelson's thinning hair was the best poem. He said he would fix things and make amends, but none of this mattered because the only thing that the outraged students were interested in was revenge porn. Alan Breck told the school that's exactly what the poem was about. The school told him that he was a disgraceful bigot to say those words to his students, to disrespect our proud heroes, to demean the diverse student body. They asked him to pack his shit and leave immediately. Alan Breck told me, 'I'm sure once all of this blows over, I'll be a better person,' but I rolled my eyes and refused to accept his bullshit. I told him that he's a worse person now. I told him that now he's closer to the man in the poem than he is to the poet. Alan Breck admitted he read the poem because it embodied poetry to him. The arts are the only escape left for ugly emotions and confusing internal conflicts. Brent wasn't killing the equal opportunity scholarship foreigner in the class, but they didn't know that because no one reads into context anymore. 'I disagree' will always inevitably result in a heated discussion with demands for retribution. Somewhere along the way, we've found it acceptable to declare someone's opinion wrong. Alan Breck displayed the type of cowardice that he could only reveal in this verbal poem he performed for me as the bus made its way through the snowy streets.

The weird thing is, I feel jealous of Brent Screnton, because at least he got a reaction to his words.

Love, Kurt."

The bus sighs to a stop in front of the mall, and I say goodbye to Alan Breck. I wish him luck in his job search, and I let him know that if he ever sees me on the bus again, and he needs some change, he can ask me.

Instead of waiting for the bus that would bring me back home, I decide that I need to buy a notebook so I can add the intro, recopy my draft of this story, then immediately send the letter because I've been reminded of the power words have to destroy the man who crafted them.

Even if Edie doesn't have an opinion about the letter, it will arrive, and she will know that, whatever she's going through, no matter how ugly the topic, she can discuss it with me and she will not be punished.

~

Lindsey dusts snowflakes off my shoulder as we walk from campus to my apartment. Staring up at the ugly tower, she asks, "Why only move across the street? I mean, you made the decision to live off campus, might as well commit to it, and live off campus, not, like, next to campus."

"I couldn't stay in the dorms, I had to leave, I had no choice," I say, confirming that my unglamorous housing was exactly as it appeared- the final stop on a long string of mistakes. I decide to reveal small portions, not pull back the curtain, but at least lift it to provide a glimpse. "The thing is, freshman year, I had this roommate that the administration selected, and I didn't know him until we moved in. We stayed out of each other's way, and we didn't get into any drama because we had no mutual friends, so we decided to continue with the room arrangement for the next year as well. Midway through our sophomore year, the roommate breaks up with his girlfriend. His girlfriend kept him busy, and when she was in the picture, it worked out perfectly for me; I would pretty much get the room to myself every weekend because this chick he was dating lived hours away, and she fucking *hated* Kirtland. It was one of those long distance relationships that was terrible for him, but incredible for me. Since they were so far away, he'd have to call her every night, and after noticing how many times I smirked at his conversations, he started walking around campus while on the phone, talking for hours about the most mind numbing shit, using that voice that people use to speak to puppies with. He would talk about moving to Nebraska to start a family- shit like that. After the breakup, the kid went into some pseudo mid-life crisis, and ended up declaring himself a tortured musician. Now, this wasn't Conor Oberst, this was Conor *N*oberst. Every day, at all hours he didn't have class, he stayed in the room and learned the cords of the most generic songs. He took all that time he spent bullshitting with his girlfriend and put it into learning shitty covers of passionless songs. All the music that he could have pursued, he focused on cover songs. From then on, my second year of college was miserable. I would come home after getting in a huge fight with someone and I'd have to sit through an hour and a half of fumbled versions of Foo Fighters B-sides. By year's end, I vowed to never share a room with another guy as long as I lived."

We reach my building, and Lindsey says, "So, if I promise to refrain from bad rock covers, I can stay, right?" She's biting her lip, knowing I will give in.

"Yeah. You can stay," I say, withholding how ecstatic I am that, once again, this beautiful girl not only accepts where I live, but also requests to stay there.

I'm glad she asked; I need her close. I can't be alone in this apartment for another moment.

In the elevator, my mind echoes with words from a meeting I was forced to attend. I recall a bill that was covered by health insurance. I see flashes of a man behind a mahogany desk informing me that I have abandonment issues. I'm sure that if he found out about Lindsey becoming such an important part of my life with such immediacy, he would directly relate it to my "issues." He'd tell me that I wanted Lindsey to move in because she was young and supportive, and she doesn't remind me of how finite everything is. I wanted to spit in his face when he referred to my mother leaving as her "abandoning" me.

My mother did not abandon me.

I've never been bitter toward my mother because I understand her. I *am* her, for the most part. I have my father's eyes. I have my Mother's soul. I would have done the same thing in her situation.

I would have left myself.

The man behind a mahogany desk said that she didn't want to disappoint me, but in leaving me, she did. This was a simplistic observation regarding a complex issue. By leaving, she saved me. She shielded me from having my last memories of her as this frail, pathetic, diseased skeleton who could no longer take care of me- her condition forcing me to spend the best years of my life taking care of her.

The memory my mother left me with was of a beautiful, intelligent, strong, happy, healthy woman. I take the elevator up to the fourth floor with a girl that I would describe in the exact same way.

~

Lindsey comes back from her finals, and I ask her how they went. She says, "Mostly, they were like this, 'Explicate this angsty poem,' then I went, 'A moving piece examining the dichotomy of a woman's need for independence clashing with her financial reliance on her mate,' and my teacher will probably go, 'Excellent,' and the jocks in the class will go, 'Whaaa? I thought it was about fire,' and the poet will roll over so hard in her grave that the friction will start an underground fire, then, yes, the jocks will be right in the big picture scheme of things."

"Sounds like it went well," I say.

"Totally. I finished writing my essay without vomiting. How did your tests go? Didn't you have like three?"

"Yeah. They went well. Remember the game Battleship where you try to guess where the battleships are on an unseen board? It was kinda like that."

"Ohh! That sounds like fun, I love Battleship."

"Me too."

We make a pizza in the oven to celebrate the end of the semester, and when it's ready, we sit at the tall table by the window, and we watch the snow fall, while we eat. As a side meal, we share a bag of Red Vines that Lindsey brought home from Rite Aid- a consumable piece of evidence that she's cheating on her employer with the evil empire.

As the last Red Vine leaves the blue package, and nothing is holding me back, I ask, "Are you going home for winter break?"

Lindsey thinks about it for a moment, then says, "Christmas, yes. I'm going home for Christmas."

"And other than Christmas?" I ask.

"I'll be back here, I promise."

Staring out the window, the flurries whipping by, I pose a question, "What would we be doing right now, if it wasn't snowing?"

"We'd be riding bikes," Lindsey says.

"But you don't have one," I point out.

"There are so many garages left open at night in this neighborhood," Lindsey says, and her mischievous grin is reflected in the window.

"My father bought me a bike, but never really taught me how to properly ride it," I say.

This energizes Lindsey, and she squeaks, "I can teach you! This winter, you will learn."

"Does your technique involve more than just yelling, 'Pedal, pedal, pedal,' as I fail?"

Lindsey nods enthusiastically.

"I still think I'll pass," I say.

Lindsey pushes my shoulder, and yelps, "Do not take this away from me, Kurt Jones. This is a milestone. I'm excited about this. I get to teach you a skill that you'll never lose. That's a gift to me. No matter what happens, every time you get on a bike, I will haunt you," she says, good-naturedly, and I glance to the empty space on the wall where the Harrington Street sign was.

My eyes return to the white out blustering on the other side of the window, and I ask, "Is this really the time to learn?"

"Absolutely," Lindsey says without pause, "You can't just rule out winter completely. It's best to learn how to ride a bike in the snow, that way you won't have a six month gap in your biking. In life, if you're always counting down the days until you can do certain things, there's a decent chance you'll never do them at all."

Lindsey still isn't aware of the countdown that remains in the forefront of my mind, but she notices that a clock is ticking, and she's devoted herself to being here for the remaining moments.

~

Finals are over, the semester is over; I walk by the light switch, and it's ON. Shifting my focus to the next item on my To-Do list, I go downstairs, then sit in the chair by the elevator. There's no furniture on the first floor of the complex besides this one rickety wooden chair painted the exact same shade of green as the wall. Staying in this chair is the only chance I have of accidentally running into Noni. She's been missing, and not answering when I show up at her apartment, but I need to see her before she has three weeks with nothing to do besides focus on her brother.

I stare at the graffiti on the red door to the staircase- someone has tagged it with, "Big Gig, Holla At Me," in the type of font that graffiti artists always write in. I turn and look at the marble floor in front of the elevator and envision how a girl could break her jaw on it. I feel bored, until I direct my focus to the window that faces the courtyard's sidewalk, and I see Lindsey framed perfectly in the center of the clear glass. She's carrying four long, gift-wrapped tubes that she struggles to keep hold of. In the jostling, one tube slides out and falls behind her onto the damp concrete. She doubles back to pick it up, and when she grabs it, a different tube falls. This happens again, twice, then she just drops all of the tubes and stares at them on the ground.

I casually make my way outside, as though I hadn't been watching her.

"I'm lucky," I state, to the universe.

"Kurt! Don't look!" Lindsey shrieks.

I pick up two of the tubes, then tell her, "I think it's too late."

She smiles and picks up the other two tubes.

When we get up to the apartment, Lindsey hurries into my room, and I follow close behind.

The tubes that Lindsey was carrying are held out to me, and she says, "Here, for you."

I take the two tubes, so now I'm holding all four of them.

Smiling from ear to ear, Lindsey caws, "Open themmm!"

"Which one first?" I ask.

Lindsey grabs three of the tubes, looks at each one, then trades the chosen tube for the tube I'm holding in my hands.

I open this first tube, aware of the genesis of this moment. As we sat and watched the storm, Harrington Street's whitewashing became very obvious, and Lindsey must have begun plotting her restitution.

Each tube I unwrap and open contains a new vision for my apartment; A man sitting on a stool playing the harmonica in black and white/ A white magnolia against a black background/ A shadowy vintage fashion ad/ Coney Island in the 50's.

"Merry Christmas, Kurt," Lindsey says, beaming, and I finally receive a firsthand Christmas.

three.

Lindsey goes home to celebrate Christmas with her parents.

I wait for a letter from Edie that never comes.

I wait for a call from my mother on Christmas day that never comes.

The only knock at the door is Gerard, and when I see him, a ghost guide pushes me forward, and I hug my friend.

Once I finally let Gerard go, he says, "Yeah man, Merry Christmas."

Gerard's matching sneakers squeak as he walks over to the futon and flops down. He reaches into his coat pocket and removes a little baggy then drops it onto the coffee table dramatically.

"I got you some lift tickets for Christmas, let's go skiing," Gerard says, then grabs the *Rolling Stone* from the magazine line, and asks, "Can I borrow your credit card?"

I take out my wallet, then frisbee the card onto the coffee table, but I keep my distance from the coke.

I won't try the coke. A tiny piece of me begs, *Try the coke*, because there's this perverse thought pattern that, if I didn't try the coke at Revere's, I never would've had that exhausted sing-along delusional crash. Lindsey never would've had a chance to pull me from the wreckage if I didn't crash.

What stops me from doing the coke is Gerard, rolling a hundred dollar bill, asking, "So, dude, where the fuck have you been?"

Lindsey has remained my secret, and I still hesitate to reveal her to my friends. I hope that Gerard will intuitively understand my reasoning behind withholding her from our discussion topics. He's the same way with bands. If he truly loves their sound, he fears that mainstream exposure will cause them to stop working off their instincts and instead cater to the opinions of the audience, so he keeps his discoveries to himself.

Gerard does a line, squeezes his nose, shakes his head, then says, "Listen, either you do this coke, or I'm going to cut you out of the nativity play I'm working on."

I shake my head in a no-ish way.

Gerard scoffs, then says, "Looks like one of the wise men won't be smart enough to make it to Bethlehem. Good luck explaining skipping Jesus' birthday party when you show up at heaven's gates."

I walk over to the futon and sit down. Gerard hands me the rolled bill. I take it, then put it in my pocket.

"What the fuck, dude?" Gerard says.

"I'll pay you $100 if you stop asking me to do this coke," I say.

Gerard sighs, then agrees to my terms. I hand him back the bill, and he cuts another line with my credit card, while asking, "Is some bitch twisting your melon?"

"No. I've been helping Noni look for her brother," I lie.

"What's Noni's brother's name?" Gerard asks, and he does this with interest, like he wants to help this stranger that he knows means the world to me.

"Nathan Butler," I say, and Gerard immediately snaps his fingers, hyped, and says, "Well, shit. You should have mentioned that earlier. He and I buy from the same dude. You want his address?"

"You buy from Revere," I point out.

"No, dude, I'm talking about where I buy my Adderall. My guy has a ton of artists coming to him. I'm pretty sure that Noni's brother shows up there, and, like, you're wasting all your energy looking for him..." sniff, "...and it's been majorly cutting into our chill time."

"I don't want your other dealer's address," I tell Gerard.

"But... why? I trust you."

"Because, I'll use it," I say.

Gerard nods at this, then does another line. His head popping back up, he asks, "Are you both..." then he shakes away the thought.

"Are we what?"

"Are you and Noni trading pain?"

~

When we step into the garage, Ben slides out from under his car. This legitimately scares Gerard, who's wound too tight to handle such a horror movie style pop-out.

The fact that Ben was still in town, and not at home with his family, makes me feel a closeness to him, and a sadness for him.

Ben gets to his feet, then wipes both his grease covered hands down the middle of his shirt. The marks he leaves remind me of Edie. His shirt now looks like Tuesday in a "F/U/C/K" week.

"Dude, okay, listen," Gerard says, his breath making puffs in the cold. This is always how Gerard starts a conversation when he needs a favor, but has nothing to offer in return- which is the case all of the times I've ever seen him ask for a favor.

The fact that Gerard is so focused on helping Noni seems like a truly selfless Christmas miracle. It's possible that he thinks I'm dating Noni- that Noni is my secret.

Sensing why we're here, Ben shakes his head, and immediately tells us, "It's busted."

"I bet it'll start," Gerard says, as though he could will a car into working order with optimism alone.

Ben raises his eyebrows and shakes his head, as he asks Gerard, "Didn't you see me slide out from under there? You can't borrow a car that doesn't run."

I look through the windshield of Ben's car and try to count the parking passes littered around the spring loaded Jesus. Every pass Ben has ever received is on his dash. Since Ben can't see his parents' bank account, the parking passes are the only way he remembers how long he's been at Kirtland. They serve the same purpose as the etches marked in an inmate's cell during a life sentence.

Ben looks at both of us, then says, "Besides, the last thing I want is for everyone to see my car cruising around town, picking up whores and bar trash."

Gerard makes a, "Pff," noise, then provides far more information than is necessary, "I haven't fucked a bar girl since our Database Management Midterm."

"As in, *during* the midterm?" Ben asks, obviously annoyed that we've shown up to harass him about his car, his broken car, the car he has to spend dozens of hours fixing.

Gerard, forgetting the focus of this trip, rolls his eyes, then says, "Oh, I forgot. Ben is all Tolstoyan about sex."

"What the fuck does that mean?" Ben asks defensively. He wouldn't have to collect parking passes if he understood Gerard's reference.

Since Ben doesn't have a working car, there's no reason to be nice to him anymore, and since Gerard's still coked up, he begins to rant, "Don't worry, we're all aware that we're a bunch of vile little animals to you, Ben. It's okay, we know you're a better human being and you'd never miss an opportunity to remind us."

Ben sighs, "To be honest, Gerard, I totally wish my car was working so you could borrow it and leave my garage. I thought by being kind to you, you'd soften. I mean..." he runs his greasy fingers through his brown hair, "...the weird thing is, I actually thought that the whole Joan thing might have some sort of eye-opening impact on you guys, but you're still treating everyone the same. You've never been choirboys so I don't know why I was expecting anything vaguely refined from you two."

"Am I not pure enough for you, Ben?" Gerard asks, then laughs.

The fact that Ben brought up the Joan thing in front of me makes me like him more. People are always actively trying to avoid the topic that Ben aimed head-on for. They warn their friends not to make a joke or a reference that I could consider "triggering," and I know this because I hear them whisper about it. Ben used the event as a crutch in his argument- it was supposed to make us leave. He was okay with being the bad guy, as long as it also meant he wasn't the focus of one of Gerard's signature rants.

"It's not a question of purity. It's a question of respect, it's a question of etiquette," Ben says, and I feel like this is a pre-prepared speech that I've always managed to walk away from before it got ramped up in the past.

Gerard and Ben are now on an unstoppable collision course toward the aggressive college kid debate that never changes minds and always leads to long-standing animosity.

"You need to understand that attending a Catholic university is about more than just smoking pot on the Green and skipping class. That's what separates us from the other schools, but people like you keep Kirtland from looking like the brochure," Ben says.

Gerard gets close enough to Ben that he can probably smell the grease slicked U. "Know what, Ben?" Gerard growls, his teeth grinding, "I sat in those religion classes that I was forced to take and let me tell you this, I believe in God. Don't question my faith. Having sex with a girl doesn't make me Satan's minion. I don't even feel guilty about it. Does the fact that you don't fuck your girlfriend make you more fit for heaven than I am?"

"No, I-"

"-I sat alone in Kirtland's library, and I read the Bible. I'm not ignorant to what you believe- what we believe. Showing up on campus, surrounded by people like you, I had no choice but to read the Bible, and the undeniable, indisputable fact is that what I read was authored by human beings."

"Human beings with divine inspiration," Ben says.

The car is broken. I'm not sure why we're still here.

Gerard, in a coke-spiral, keeps getting closer to Ben, instead of lurking further away like I am. He rants, "Yes, with divine inspiration. These humans must have known what they were creating though. They knew the words that they put in that book would become law. Every author wants their work to be appreciated by as many people as possible. Writing a book and having no one read it is like throwing a party and having no one show up."

Ben is silent, and paying attention. He knows that Gerard, as a broken prototype navigating life with great difficulty, read this book as though it was a manual on how to be a normal human being. Ben had responsibilities, while Gerard was studying. Ben had a Spanish midterm on Monday. Ben had an English paper due Thursday. Ben's Database Management presentation had to be completed. Gerard half-assed all his classes while giving himself an education.

"If I'm so bad, why loan me your car?" Gerard asks.

"Because I feel bad for you," Ben admits, and I see some guilt lower onto his shoulders.

"Why, Ben? Because I don't follow every one of those little rules that you're being oppressed by?"

Ben turns away, mumbling, "This is insulting-"

"-hey, you started this conversation," Gerard says, and I can't remember if that's actually the case. Gerard continues, "Listen, do you want to hear the rationale behind your crazy life-rules? A Christian guy and a Jewish girl have sex. The Christian guy heads on his merry way, happy he got off. The Jewish girl is left pregnant and she has the child, meanwhile, the Christian guy is gone forever. When she raises that kid, she'll raise him Jewish. A Christian man made a Jewish baby. Or what happens when an atheist girl and a Christian guy get married? Their wedding night rolls around, and they consummate the marriage. The atheist girl gets pregnant and the couple has a child. The mother keeps her baby home while the father goes to church every week. One weekend, the atheist wife isn't going to be able to take care of their kid on a Sunday morning, so the Christian guy takes the kid to church. He takes the kid to church once, then twice, and before you know it, the kid is going to church every week with his coloring book and his plastic bag of Cheerios."

Ben is actually letting Gerard speak, almost like he's intrigued by this argument that I've become a silent partner in.

Gerard continues, "In both situations, the guy got to fuck, but let's take a look at the scoreboard. Situation one- we end up with one Christian, while situation two- two Christians; there's the Christian guy then his kid who will grow up Christian, so then think about the growth. Things will increase exponentially. With situation one, you only have one Christian and when he dies, you have none. In situation two, you have a perpetuation of the faith handed down from father to child."

Ben waits to make sure the rant is done, then he asks, "Gerard?"

"Yeah?"

"You been doing any coke today?"

"I'd be having this argument with you even if I hadn't done any," Gerard says, providing a confirmation without an outright admission.

"I know," Ben says, nodding his head in agreement.

"So hit me with the rebuttal," Gerard says, his shoulders bobbing back and forth.

"My position hasn't changed on this since the last time we had this argument."

"Oh, shit. It's really hard to keep track of who I've had this fight with because there are so many of you people."

"'You people' being Catholics?" Ben asks.

"Precisely," Gerard responds, then swallows deeply.

"You go to a Catholic university."

"That's what I'm talking about. The whole fucking system is poisoned from the inside," Gerard says, then his eyes go wide as he sees a chance to begin yammering about a conspiracy.

"You win, Gerard," Ben says, desperately staving off this new rant.

Gerard celebrates confidently, fists raised.

After looking at me to see if I have anything to add, Gerard turns to Ben, and says, "Well... Merry Christmas, dude."

"Merry Christmas, guys."

~

I lie alone in bed, and I keep thinking about the fight Gerard had with Ben. First it was over a car, then it ballooned into the beliefs and doubts of two men. Reliving the fight helps me frame Noni's search. She's devoting so much time to the act of locating someone who doesn't want to be located, while I'm devoting so much time trying not to think about someone who doesn't want to be located. These propensities, at their base, are a disagreement on faith and belief.

Noni believes that action is everything. Inactivity is complacency. The world has been created to be malleable and its manipulation is our privilege and responsibility. To quietly accept the natural order of things is to violate a right that has been uniquely gifted to humans. If we're all going to stay on the tracks- if we're all going to stay inside the vehicle at all times- why bother with any of this? The world becomes a computer program executing itself without lag. Noni is going to find the person she loves and she will demand that he explain the absence he's established. If nothing else, Noni will secure an answer. She will sleep better at night for this, while I toss and turn.

I recognize that employing Noni's philosophy could be healing for me, but it doesn't inspire me to change. I believe that, sometimes, inaction is the kindest gesture. Inactivity doesn't mean apathy. The world has become so connected that all of our actions have ripple effects. To quietly accept the natural order of things is to believe in God's plan. If we stay on the tracks, inside the vehicle, then those behind us won't have their experience ruined. The world is an amusement park, and when you choose to go behind the scenes of the attractions and learn how they work, a lot of the magic dissipates. I'm going to let the person I love live her final days exactly how she sees fit. I won't make demands on her because to create an unprovoked argument is violating. The senseless argument that Gerard sniffled through taught me a lesson.

I don't regret not doing the coke with Gerard. My real Christmas present will arrive tomorrow, in the form of Lindsey's return. When I receive the text that she's back on campus, I'll be both giddy and afraid. She's had a moment away. There was something hermetic about our existence last semester. After less than an hour of knowing each other, we were in her room, listening to ~the song~. In a way, we never stepped outside the room, until she went home to her parents' house quickly for Thanksgiving, then longer for Christmas. There were the texts and the phone calls; the e-mails and the Facebook messages. There was communication, but there wasn't that heat of closeness. The winter feels like it will stretch forever. I met Lindsey on a sunny day long ago.

~

A text wakes me up.

The garage is nearly empty, but the one car I'm searching for is parked in an anticipatory idle.

Even after establishing some distance, here ~she~ is, waiting for me, so she can leave again, but this time, I'll be by her side.

The driver's side front door of the lone car pops open.

Lindsey bounds out of the car, then hops into my arms.

We hug.

We kiss.

We get in the car.

We drive.

We park.

We hug again.

We walk.

We say nothing to each other.

Walk.

Look.

Observe.

Silence.

Content.

Better.

Relieved.

The crunch of the snow under our feet is music.

My phone beeps, and Lindsey stops walking.

"Let me see it," she says, holding out a gloved hand. I place the phone in her palm. On her third attempt, she successfully powers the phone off without having to remove a glove. "Fixed it," she says, handing the cell back to me.

"Are we trespassing?" I ask, wondering why she didn't just put the phone on silent.

"Look," Lindsey says, her arm jutting out to the right, and I watch as a squirrel runs by us, then scales a tree. "This is what I do," she whispers. I wait for her to elaborate, and when the squirrel climbs too high and blends in with the bark of the tree, Lindsey calmly tells me, "Most people spend a lot of time trying to get everyone to like them, but since I don't do that, I have all this extra time. That's pretty much why I started doing this- I needed hobbies to fill the day."

"This is a hobby? Squirrel watching?" I ask. "I'm sorry, but you can't call something a hobby if it doesn't have its own online community."

Lindsey starts walking again, and explains, "Well, the squirrels are just a perk. And yes, I consider it a hobby because it's something that fills up time, and makes me feel good."

"Anything that feels good and fills up time is a hobby?" I ask.

"Yes. And you were wrong about the internet subculture thing. Hobbies are like fetishes, no matter what you like doing, no matter how bizarre, odds are that there's a website with over a hundred thousand monthly hits devoted to it."

"And what's the online community called for this hobby?" I ask, as we continue to walk.

Lindsey thinks about it, and without an urgency, she says, "Existers."

"Don't we all... exist?" I ask, feeling dumb for asking this question.

"I'm not thrilled with the name," Lindsey admits, then adds, "But everything needs a name otherwise it doesn't exist." She snarls her upper lip after she scrutinizes her own choice of words.

"When I tell people about this do I say, 'Lindsey and I Existed?'"

Lindsey laughs, "Yes. Exactly. Here we are. Existing."

"But the past tense feels bad," I say.

"Sure does."

I have the need to talk about the mutual conclusion we just came to, so I ask, "Is this always where you Exist?"

"Yes, and there are other Existers, so you'll tell no one about this place, unless you want to take someone to Exist with us, then you can bring them here. Existing is something that you immerse yourself in. If you start telling people about this perfect spot, before you know it, these trees will be covered in Budweiser posters and we'll have to plan our trip a month in advance just to secure a spot out here. Corporations will plan company-wide Existing retreats to reduce stress levels in their employees. Existing will become something that's mandated by a well-intentioned but ultimately evil corporate consultant. I can't have that- Existing isn't something that should be financially backed and forcibly suggested in an impersonal e-mail about a team building exercise. You bring employees here on a retreat and everyone will have their cell phones on, to stay in contact, to stay at their customers' beck and call."

"It's our little secret," I confirm, and as I say this, Existing provides another reward. A break in the static of snow arrives, and a huge rock covered in moss appears like a lush oasis. The moss is shockingly thick and green, and there isn't so much as a dusting of snow on it. Slicing through the moss, like veins in an arm, are tree roots. Somehow, a tree was planted in the tiny amount of soil atop this rock, then it reached out for permeable ground, determined to live.

This little green island, with its tree canopy, is at the edge of a cliff face that looks out over an incredible stretch of protected land. Lindsey takes my hand and we carefully step onto the spongy turf.

We both sit down on the moss and focus on the sun as it bleeds over the snow covered trees.

Lindsey squints at the sunset, and says, "It's funny that this happens hundreds of times every year, but most days we're in class, or at work, or on our laptops, so we don't even notice it. It's like we're missing all the best parts of life because they don't fit into our schedule."

I nod, "This is the first thing we're supposed to see when we wake up and one of the last things we're supposed to see when we go to sleep..." I pause this observation, unsure of where it's coming from. Since when do I know God's plan? I don't speak like this normally, but it's hard not to when looking out at the dying day.

Lindsey picks up my statement, "Instead, we sleep through the sunrise and work through the sunset, so all we get is too bright or too dark."

We both Exist in a moment that's lit like our stand-ins had been here hours beforehand making sure things would be perfect when we arrived.

~

As I make a perimeter search of the café for an open table, I nearly collide with Ben. I apologize to him for Gerard's coke rant, and he shows me that he accepts the verbal recompense by buying me a slice of pizza and an ironic Coke.

We sit down at a circular table far from the Asians, and I'm introduced to Ben's campus ministry friends. They are able to secure a regular table and always seem to have open seats because sitting down with them would be like knocking on a Jehovah's Witness' door. For the first time, I actually take note of these campus ministry kids. Everyone at the table is so painfully average looking that they aren't even different enough to be ugly.

A bunch of three star reviews.

I check my phone to see if Lindsey is out of her first class of the new semester, but I have no unread messages.

I shift my attention and focus to a girl in a pink V-neck sweater who sits across from me. I catch the end of her statement, as she says, "...you wake up and you're an alcoholic who drinks in moderation."

A girl with okay boobs says, "Less hangovers."

An Italian looking guy says, "Less fun."

A black girl asks, "Is it just me or did winter break go by really fast?"

I can't tell if she's looking at me, so I nod yes, then watch the cash register at the buffet entrance, waiting for Lindsey to appear.

When people direct the conversation to me, I rattle off some generic statements that receive universal acceptance, but I barely pay attention to the conversation that travels around the table like a campus ministry version of spin the bottle where all the kissing is replaced by dorky laughing.

After finishing my slice, I'm ready to leave with my Takeaways:

One- Many of the table members visited Penn State once and (insert a story of something that most likely happened to one of their more adventurous friends).

Two- The party scene here sucks and they all miss their friends back home.

One of the people we're sitting with tells me, "You look like you've lost your puppy," and I laugh a nervous laugh, then tell her I'm allergic to dogs and she corrects me, "No, you're allergic to their hair and dander," and I swirl my straw in my cup, then say, "I'm not really into the hairless ones."

I have no clear physical out to escape this situation, so I take a mental out and start thinking about squirrels, and sunsets, and songs, and zombies, and how I miss someone so terribly. This is the train of thought of a 15 year old girl, besides the zombie stuff, or who knows, maybe that's what 15 year old girls are into now.

I veer back into the conversation when the girl with the okay boobs says, completely out of character, "She looks like the type of girl whose pussy stinks... *bad.*"

I find the statement amusing, and the thought repulsive.

I quietly wonder if this conversation started because I said I don't care for the hairless ones much.

~

Noni agrees to meet me, finally, and I invite Gerard because, at least when he's doing cocaine, he's really concerned about Noni's well-being.

After a cathartic walk, we arrive at Rube's and sit in a booth, where we wait for Gerard to show up.

Noni has her phone raised like she's taking a selfie, but I realize that she's doing this to get a visual on the couple currently engaged in a loud conversation behind us. Just over Noni's shoulder, an old guy with a salt and pepper beard talks to an even older woman who has very curly blonde hair.

I hear the man with the beard ask, "Why on earth did the girl do that to herself?"

It's hard to hear how the woman responds because her back is to me, but it sounds like she says, "I know, I know. It's horrible. It looks like she did it herself and you want to know the worst part? (Inaudible) was on the counter yesterday, and I glanced at it and the haircut cost $130! I just don't understand. If she wants to look that much like she's rejecting society then the least she could do is save some money and cut it herself."

The man with the beard laughs, "All she'd have to do is grab a piece of hair and cut wherever the scissors ended up. It's not like there is a science to looking messy."

"At least it's still black."

"Give her time. I'm sure the pink will be back."

"Someday it's going to hit her that she can't look like a..." then the lady with the curly hair hushes her tone so I can't hear what she says.

I flinch when a lanky figure in a white V-neck undershirt thumps down next to me in the booth.

"Oh no! Someone accidentally invited Gerard," Noni jokes, never missing a beat. It must take practice to be so engrossed in someone else's conversation yet also constantly aware of your surroundings. If Noni knew some foreign languages, she'd be the perfect spy- actually, then again, she still hasn't even located her brother.

I notice that there's a paper bag sitting in front of Gerard, and I know that whatever is inside the bag will complicate things. I'm a little worried that whatever 's in the bag is alive, but I'm even more worried that it's dead.

Gerard looks around to see if anyone is paying attention to us. When he's confident that we aren't being watched by anyone besides the Mr. T cutout, he says, "In this bag are bagels. And cream cheese. I have enough for everyone. Do you want to go eat them in the car?"

"You brought bagels... to the diner?" I ask, then shoot Noni a glance to make sure she's laughing. She is.

"Yeah," Gerard says, "Well, I want to eat them in the car, not the diner, it's just we said we would meet at the diner, and I had to bring them in because I was afraid you wouldn't believe I had bagels and without bagels how could I get you out to the car?"

I accept Gerard's plan, because I don't like being in Rubie's without Lindsey.

We don't say anything to the waitress as we leave, we just make our way out to the icy parking lot.

Gerard leads us to a car that isn't Ben's, but it's too cold to refuse to get in, so Noni and I slide in the back, while Gerard sits in the front passenger seat, leaving the driver's seat empty. We have the entire back seat to spread out, but Noni pushes close to me to conserve body heat.

Gerard hands us both a tinfoil wrapped, cream cheese slathered bagel, then flashes us a smile, and says, "Enjoy."

"Who are we waiting for?" I ask, fixated on the empty seat.

Gerard stares straight ahead, and says, "Okay, well, I have to tell you a story, but Rubie's is too small and somehow, someway, someone would've been listening, then they'd tell everyone what I was talking about, and my parents would find out. It always happens. Without fail." Gerard swallows a big piece of bagel, then begins his story, "So last night, I'm sitting on this bench in your courtyard, then a lady in a black dress shows up and sits next to me."

Immediately, I search for an easy way to end this conversation. "Good story, Gerard. Let's go in and eat a real meal," I plead in a totally nonchalant way. I start sweating, while staring forward at the open driver's seat.

"Fine, I'll fast forward to please your crippling ADD..." Gerard says dryly, then continues recapping an event that's a carbon copy of the night I spent in 5E. It becomes clear to me that the couple requires a non-contact viewer for their ritual to be complete. First it was me, then it was Gerard. Tomorrow, it could be Noni. I fear that Gerard will refer to the semi-bald guy as our mutual friend. I stare at Gerard's eyes in the rear view mirror while he explains the process, providing no new insight into the event. I'm petrified that he'll blurt out that I've been up there- that I've watched bruises form. I don't want Noni to view me as someone who gets off on the pain of others. Noni comes to me because she knows I'll help her, and I always do my best to view her crusades as noble. If she finds out that I'm a passive observer, I'll lose her forever. If I'm placed at the scene, Noni will assume the worst. I don't expect her to believe that I left before things got good. No one leaves in the last two minutes of a close game, and the game I had front row seats for was as close as it gets.

I sweat in the cold, over an event that never happens. Gerard doesn't mention me being there. He never hints that I may know the Sneaker Girl.

Reading my mind, Noni asks, "What's the point of this story?"

Gerard is silent for a moment, then turns to us, and says, "I was hoping that you'd be able to tell me."

~

Lindsey cracks the spine on her copy of *Limber* and I want to get her a new copy immediately.

Rule~ I never crack the spine. I only open my books just enough that I can see all of the words on both pages. It's not a full fanning of the book, and I have to hold my thumb in the crack of the spine for stability, but it keeps the book looking new.

I stare at Lindsey's book, then raise my eyebrows at her. With surprising speed, she reaches over and grabs the book out of my hand, then cracks the spine. When she gives it back to me, she says, "There's a good chance someone will buy this book if it looks new. Now that I've given it a distinctively secondhand appearance, no one is going to want to pay full price."

I sit with the cracked spine in my hand and I wonder how Lindsey arrived at this thought. Was this a parallel? Could she sense how desperately I needed her touch the moment she returned to Kirtland after Christmas break? When we got out of the car, to begin Existing, I hugged her so tightly that I almost cracked her spine. I don't want her to see me as a man so afraid that someone else may pick her up that I purposely try to make her look less desirable.

Limber is all about these broken fat people- the zombies- and their attacks against the people who have it together and look good enough to eat. I'm twenty pages behind Lindsey, but I don't do any skimming to try to catch up. I read every word, never glancing at the clock, occasionally smirking at the jokes, often gulping coffee, sometimes casually sneaking a hand onto Lindsey's thigh.

When I tighten my grip on her leg, she looks at me and flashes an uneasy smile. I pull my hand away, because I feel myself shaking. I had never seen this smile before- it wasn't Lindsey's true, somewhat awkward, wide smile, it was a tiny physical manifestation of annoyance. It was an expression that a well-meaning stranger would receive when burdening Lindsey with contact.

I dive back into the book, and I'm thankful that there are so many characters in *Limber* whose touch causes grimaces. I start to relate to the fat zombies. One day someone can love you, and the next day, your presence is poison. This is a horror novel. This is why the Horror section is always empty.

After an hour, we hide our cracked spine books, then begin the drive back to campus.

Eyes trained on the road, Lindsey asks, "So, would we get instantly eaten by the zombies or would we be the ultra-fit survivors in the apocalyptic world of *Limber*?"

"We'd be the people who got killed taking out the trash, oblivious to the fact that the rest of the world was battling zombies for the past week," I decide.

Lindsey laughs, "It would be like three weeks into the zombie crisis and we'd only notice when the internet connection dropped."

"Who are the real zombies in that scenario?" I ask.

Lindsey thinks about it, then says, "Sometimes it feels like we're trapped in a zombie novel, but no one gives a shit about brains."

~

Noni is watching a runway show on her laptop. All the models are wearing intricately patterned dresses that sit dully on their un-complex frames. She's not technically *watching* the show, she has her back to the laptop screen, and she's looking at the wall in her living room. She has pictures on the wall, just like Lindsey does in her dorm. There are no females on the wall. Tacked up everywhere are boys with long, long hair, wearing girl's pants and tight rec program t-shirts.

"Are you tracking a mafia incapable of strong-arming anyone?" I ask, staring at the wall.

Noni giggles, then says, "When this girl who had some information for me came over, she saw these pictures and told me that my friends are the 'prettiest girls around.'"

"Are these... prospective boyfriends? Is this... a new fetish of yours?"

Noni shakes her head, then says, "Skinny boys are fine, I mean, it's the whole sharing clothes part that I question."

"Not that I agree with their choice of wearing size zero jeans, but us skinny guys have it bad. It's pretty damn impossible to buy clothes that fit. There are always more XXLs than Smalls," I say.

"Oh, that reminds me..." Noni says, then goes to her bookcase, and picks up a folded pair of jeans, "The waist on these is way too tight on me. They shrank or I'm disgusting. Do you want them?"

"I refuse to wear women's jeans. I'm not one of your wall boys," I say.

Noni presses the jeans into my chest, then leans in and whispers, "You're wearing an old pair of my jeans right now."

I look down. She's right. I remember getting these from her over the summer. "Yeah, well, okay, I forgot these were yours. The pockets are so unisex that a girl would have no business wearing these."

"Well, the pair I just gave you is pretty unisexy too," she assures me.

I hold the jeans out in front of me, then say, "Look at the crotch, there's no room for my dick. Besides, I'm not sure how Lindsey would react to finding a pair of girl's pants that aren't hers in the apartment."

Noni's head whips in my direction, and she asks, "Who the fuck is Lindsey?"

"Who are these men on your wall?" I counter.

I stare into Noni's eyes as they turn thin and catlike.

Unable to keep it up, I flinch, and Noni feels as though she's won, so she walks over to the wall, then points to a boy with Brillo pad hair, and says, "This is who we will be seeing tonight."

"We?" I ask.

"Or... you can answer my question and we'll stay here," Noni offers an alternative.

"Where are we going?" I ask, positive and chipper due to the detour I've stumbled upon.

"A poetry reading at The Crisper."

"Again!" I bark out, my cheer all but gone when I learn my fate. "Damn it. Damn it!" I curse as I pace, then ask, "How many poetry readings can one college town have?"

Noni snaps, "Listen, you think I enjoy this? You think I *enjoy* hearing poetry? I mean, I feel like shit supporting poets, knowing that it's a world where the creators outnumber the interested, but it just so happens that the same type of narcissists that think two pages of their thoughts have worth, are also the same people that my brother is hanging out with right now."

"So, we won't be going for the poets-"

"-we'll be going for the crowd," she completes my statement.

I reluctantly agree to join Noni, then we agree to meet out front in ten minutes.

I take the elevator down to the fourth floor.

The moment I step inside the apartment, I know that Lindsey is at work. I can tell when she's here- it's warmer and brighter- it smells better and the old walls seem so alive that I expect them to begin healing at any moment.

I don't spend any time on my appearance because no one else at the reading will be reciprocating that courtesy.

I grab my olive green coat with the furry collar, and I text Noni, "Meet me in the courtyard."

In the elevator, I text Lindsey- "Getting coffee @the crisper. Stop by after work, if u want," but the text doesn't send until my Dr. Martens are crunching down the unshoveled stairs.

On time, Noni bursts out of the building, her smile payment enough for this waste of time we're about to embark on. I walk with her, swallowing my complaints, while she begs and she pleads for my support. Deep down, I *do* want her to find her brother, so I work to keep her hopeful.

When we're a block away from The Crisper, I get a text from Lindsey, "i'll meet you back at the apt. i hate the crisper, but not you." I smile at the text, feeling close to Lindsey, even when we're apart. I catch Noni glancing at me, and when I don't show her my screen to share what made me feel good, she frowns and starts walking faster. I want to tell her about Lindsey, but I keep flashing back to when she asked who Lindsey was, and it was my responsibility to describe her and what we have together. I didn't answer Noni because it would've required me to over-think what I have with Lindsey.

We walk into The Crisper and I immediately tell Noni I'll buy us coffees so we can stay awake during the poems, and so she'll stop being cold to me.

I'm reminded that tonight is not about me, as I watch Noni's eyes dart across the crowd, desperately searching for a familiar face.

While I stand in the coffee line, I initiate a short conversation worthy of a bus ride, then I leave with two cups of an African blend and enough material for a letter.

I locate the table that Noni snagged, and luckily, it's far enough away from the performance that our laughs might not drown out the poet.

I place our cups down on the tiny circular table, straddle my stool, then pull out three napkins from the aluminum dispenser. I stretch out one of the napkins until there's enough tension to start writing on it.

A kid with a long goatee and pulled back wispy hair gets up on a stage that's only raised a single stair above the floor the stools are on. He starts off his poem with, "*Blackouts bring left wing ideals streaming over the stocks, eroding away what used to be the last cliff in this part of town, but is now just the wettest rock,*" and Noni starts giggling like she's watching people slip on an icy sidewalk. I'm reminded of something that Lindsey said to me once while we were driving home from one of our *Limber* dates- *"After the zombie apocalypse, when the dust settles, a new genetically superior generation will begin the cleanup efforts, and they'll find all these notebooks with shitty poems and text files with pathetic think pieces and they'll call the zombie outbreak a 'cleansing.'"*

I start a first draft of my letter to Edie so I can capture everything while it's fresh.

Noni looks at the napkin, then leans over, and says, "If you are writing poetry to perform, I hope it doubles as a suicide note."

I smile at Noni, slightly shake my head no, then start writing my first draft, *"Remember..."* but, again, I realize that I'm running out of memories to rehash with Edie, so I get right to my story,

"Today I was in line at a coffee shop with Virgil Williams and he told me about breeding cats. Virgil Williams is a 62 year old black man with a tiny goatee and a huge chin. He was wearing a Buffalo football hat, a Baltimore football jacket, and bright orange Miami football socks in penny loafers. It appeared that Virgil Williams is just a fan of the game, and he's not taking sides. Virgil Williams breeds cats and keeps them in a barn on his property. He has a litter box the size of a sandbox in his barn. Virgil Williams said that the black kittens are his most popular seller. I mentioned that black cats are a sign of bad luck, and Virgil Williams said, 'Not for me. For me, they're my good luck charm.' He leaned toward me and said that he knows why the black cats are so popular, and it's because all his customers are white. He said a lot of minorities get cats from a shelter, but white people like to pay for their animals. When a white person buys a kitten from Virgil Williams, nine times out of ten, they go for the black kittens, because, he stated, 'Whites can't buy a black human anymore so they buy a black cat.' Virgil Williams imagines this is the reason why black olives outsell the green ones. Virgil Williams presumes this is why the road is black. I asked him why sidewalks are white, and he said they're white because the sidewalks lead up to houses and businesses. The sidewalks lead to jobs. The roads can only get so close before they are cut off. Virgil Williams said if you want to park in a driveway around here you have to get across the white sidewalk. I asked him how the white cats sell and he said, 'Horribly. White cats are bad luck.' I asked Virgil what time of year he sells the most black cats, and he said, 'The fall.' I asked him if this was because of Halloween- if he was just selling props

that would be discarded like marked down merchandise, or used in dark
arts rituals. Virgil looked at me as though this thought had never
occurred to him, then said, 'Well, damn, I guess those black motherfuckers
do bring bad luck.'"

I keep the napkin on the table, but I don't work on the beginning
because I realize that the story, with its racial and kitten overtones, is just
an inferior version of the average user experience on Facebook.

I glance across the table at Noni, and see that she's writing too. I crane
my neck to read the bubbly blocky letters on her page because I'm not the
respectful person that she is. Noni doesn't care if I'm writing about her,
while I have to be very sure that she isn't writing about me, or if she *is*
writing about me, that it's something good, noteworthy, or at least vaguely
complimentary.

"This sucks," Noni whispers, as she squeezes her paper, but she doesn't
crumple it up yet. I suspect she displayed this immediate lack of confidence
because she saw me reading what she was writing, and she didn't want me
silently judging her.

"What's it about?" I quietly ask, half knowing the answer.

"The three most life-changing experiences I've had. It's for one of my
classes, but every time I write something, I worry everyone will read it and
they'll be like 'So what?'" she whispers to me.

"So what?" I whisper back, meaning that *their* reaction is not the point
of the assignment, not echoing *them*.

"I want to matter," Noni says through her teeth, and it's so desperate I
have to look to the stage, to the poet's carefully planned emotion being
robotically displayed.

Noni hisses, "I know that I may not have lived the most impressive life,
but I feel like it's worth recording. Will you read this and tell me if it's
worth recording?"

"Get up there and perform it," I say, aware that Edie asks me to write
her letters because I know what deserves to be documented when it comes
to other people's lives. I'm a very good arbiter of what's "worth it" and that
scares me because what if Noni's milestones aren't worth a letter?

Noni finishes her coffee, then she sounds like Lindsey as she says,
"Three hundred years from now, someone will stumble across my three
most life-changing experiences- and even though I'm long dead, my words
will remain as a reminder that Noni Butler *did exist...* and not even three
impressive things happened to her during all her years on earth. It's like..."

Noni stops because the futility of it all sinks in, and we don't find her brother in the coffee shop, and she cries out on the street as I hold her head against my chest, and I desperately want to give Noni a life changing experience, but I'm not sure how to do it. This is how poetry becomes an important part of my life.

~

Lindsey presses herself against me, and asks "Where's your Mom?"

~

I'm sitting by the mailroom in the café, next to Ben, and I watch as an Indian girl opens an Amazon package. She runs a pen along the taped flaps on top of the box, then I experience another secondhand Christmas as she takes a blue Kirtland University sweatshirt out of the box. This same sweatshirt can be purchased in the university bookstore across from the library. Something about this circuitous purchase feels oddly appropriate because it shows the mindset and habits of the Kirtland student body. The convenience of living life behind a glowing monitor is evident/ The compulsive need to consume at any hour of the day is evident/ The need for something to look forward to, in an otherwise boilerplate existence is evident.

I glance at the Asian kids' table and watch them type for a while.

I don't glance at the conspiracy theory commuter table.

"Gerard says you're disappearing again," Ben tells me, snapping me out of my sociology study.

"You're on speaking terms with Gerard?" I ask, raising my eyebrows.

"Yeah, I mean, my car is fixed so he comes to borrow it occasionally."

Curious, I ask, "What did the problem end up being?"

"With the car or with Gerard?" Ben responds, and I laugh. He answers both questions, "With Gerard- based on his deep swallows and grinding teeth, the problem was coke, with the car- based on the fact that it wouldn't turn over, the alternator."

"Sounds accurate on both accounts."

"Now, the answer to my question..."

"You didn't ask a question," I say.

"I brought up a topic of conversation that could progress no further without an answer from you- an answer you dodged."

"I'm not disappearing. I'm just... going other places. Here and there... I'm into... poetry?"

"Poetry?" Ben asks, then runs his hands through his hair, "Kurt Jones... is into poetry?" he scoffs in disbelief, then he arrives at the only logical conclusion, "Who is she?"

I smile.

"Show me a picture," he says, wagging his fingers into his palm.

Then it strikes me -I don't have a picture of Lindsey. One of the first questions I ever asked her about was why she didn't have pictures of herself, and now that question will be asked of me. "I don't... have any pictures... right now," I say quietly, hoping Ben doesn't know the internet exists.

"You don't have a picture of your girlfriend, Kurt? Does this girl know that she's your girlfriend, Kurt?"

I look at the table and nod my head yes.

"Then why don't you have a picture of her?"

I flip this question in my mind.

It's hard to find a specific moment that makes me stop everything, just to take a picture of Lindsey. When I'm with her, I don't have to capture moments- she just gives them to me. Lindsey is more than a picture, more than a single frame. Her existence is an energy, and a feeling, and a scent, and a warmth. A 2D image can't capture the experience of *Lindsey*.

"What's her name?" Ben asks.

"Lindsey," I respond, realizing that I can't say her name without smiling.

"And she goes here, to Kirtland? How do I not know this girl?" Ben asks.

"There are over five thousand students here," I say, citing a statistic I've never believed.

"Are you not telling me more because of that thing with Gerard? The coke assault on my religion?" Ben asks.

I shake my head no, then I slide out of my chair, stand up, and put my backpack on.

Ben looks up at me, and says, "I'm not the person that he made me out to be. Gerard came that day to get into a fight, not to borrow my car."

"Did he change your mind?" I ask, lingering at the table.

"Did he change my mind?" Ben restates the question.

"He's not the person you made him out to be, either," I say, walking away from the table, toward the buffet side of the café. I need to escape the conversation about Lindsey, and I know Ben won't waste a swipe just to follow me.

I give my ID to the register lady, who swipes it and hands it back, then I grab a tray and perform two full circles around the entire buffet spread before deciding on some baked chicken and a salad. Indecision lingering, I get a fountain Pepsi, then pause before selecting a table. I want to call Lindsey, but I'd rather have her call me, and I want to distract myself from thinking too much, but I'd rather have someone distract me. Almost on cue, I'm ambushed by a distraction, in the form of Laura Mellin. She slides in front of me, and says, "You were so drunk when I saw you last night." Laura's voice sounds prettier than she is.

"Was I?" I ask her.

Was I? I ask myself.

"Yup, you were explaining to me why you never learned how to ride a bike."

I was drunk last night? I must have been very drunk if I told Laura that. I barely know her. The point of reference for our friendship was that she used to have a crush on my roommate. She no longer has the crush; I no longer have the roommate.

For some reason, I feel required to continue the conversation, so I say, "Well, did you have fun last night?"

"Of course I did. I drank with you... but maybe I overdid it. The drinks made me feel like shit because I probably have a stomach ulcer. My stomach hurts badly sometimes. Lately, I can barely sleep because of it."

I look at her tray, and so far her entire meal is a bowl of yogurt and a bowl of applesauce.

"You should go to health services," I suggest.

"I will. I want them to give me something," Laura's shoulders squirm as she admits this. "That's the only way to handle this. It's easier than hoping my wisdom teeth grow back so I can get those painkillers... hydrocodone, I think they gave me before," she says, then she tongues the back of her mouth.

I never know how to respond when someone tells me about their health issues, so I quickly fill the silence with the first thing I can think of, "I heard they give you morphine for stomach ulcers if it's bad enough."

"Oh, I hope you're right," she responds, as warmly as if I had assured her that her stomach ulcer would be gone soon. Laura pauses for a moment, then says, "I'm confident that, by the end of the semester, I'll have my morphine and you'll have your mother back."

I told Laura.
I told Laura about my mother?
I wonder how long it took before I mentioned this.
I wonder if I cried.
"I need to go meet my friend," Laura says, then she waves her little hand, brushing the conversation away.

~

Lindsey and I lie in my bed, as the tape crackles. She brought the cassette here. For me.

"She left," I say, interrupting Jackson. I had to bring up my mother because my conversation with Laura messed me up a little. I think it's making me feel guilty, like I'm hiding things from Lindsey- things that I'm not hiding from others.

"I can tell you miss her," Lindsey says, and she leaves it at that. She doesn't ask why my mother is gone, and I have to assume that she knows my father is dead. This gray area makes me clarify, "It's weird, I don't miss my dad in the same way. When he died, it just... ended, cleanly. Well, not cleanly but-"

"-the man you grew up with wasn't your father. Not biologically," Lindsey interrupts me.

My face goes slack. The song continues.

"That's your real Dad. Listen to him," Lindsey says.

I smile, "Sharpe is my father, huh?"

"Yup," Lindsey says simply.

My dad's voice crackles through the speakers. Maybe Jackson *is* my father?

Lindsey waits until Jackson completes the song, then gets up and rewinds the tape.

Click, zzzzzzzzz, pop, click.

After returning to the bed, Lindsey rolls near me so we're facing each other, and I can feel her warm breath.

As Jackson starts singing again, Lindsey tells me a story worthy of a letter. "Do you want to know how it happened?" she asks, and I nod. Looking in my eyes, she begins a story, "About two decades ago, one November day, your mother was driving to meet a friend who had moved away. She got a late start, and the days were so short that fall. All alone, with only a map, your mother drove down a series of questionable back roads that the confusing handwritten directions made her take. She drove in the darkness, looking for a street sign to give her a hint that she was on the right path, but there were no indications as to if she missed a turn, and no obvious places to make a turn. She could only continue on this straight path, and when the path got darker, it began feeling less 'right,' so she had to stop and ask for directions. That was when your mother saw it- a nightclub with a sign so neon she couldn't read what it said without squinting. The line outside the club must have been about from this bed, to the elevator. She asked the guy at the end of the line if he knew where Harrington Street was. That's where she was supposed to make a right, Harrington Street. The guy at the end of the line didn't know where the road was, and the guy ahead of him didn't know, and the girl clamped to that man's waist didn't know, and the old guy in front of him didn't know, and your mother kept asking and asking, and next thing she knew, she was at the door. The bouncer had never heard of Harrington Street and told her to ask the bartender, then he let her inside, and pointed her in the right direction. In the club, everything was so bright compared to the darkness of the street outside. The crowd sat at scattered tables, with their chairs angled toward a wooden stage. On stage, stood a well-dressed man with messy hair and the bluest eyes your mother had ever seen. He started singing and your mother couldn't take her eyes off him. She drifted instinctually to a chair, then sat down. As this man performed with his misfit band, your mother felt the best she had in months, and also terribly sad at the same time. Tears were in her eyes, but she worked to keep them from running down her cheeks. Her makeup stayed flawless. When the man was done with the song, he said, 'My name is Jackson Sharpe, and I'm glad we were able to spend time together tonight.' Your mother had never felt so connected with a stranger before, and she was glad to spend these moments with Jackson. She arrived at the club feeling like the world was too big and too confusing. She felt she was ill prepared to navigate through life without help. She didn't find directions in the club, but she found *direction* in the club. There were town regulations on how long local businesses could stay open, and before your mother knew it, the bar owner flipped on even more lights and shooed people out the door. After a few minutes, the crowd had left for home, but your mother remained seated in her chair, waiting for Jackson Sharpe to return to the stage. She knew that her friend was waiting, but she didn't make a call to cancel their plans. She refused to leave or break her focus, confident that Jackson would reappear, and this faith was rewarded, as Jackson, holding a half full highball glass in one hand, walked back out onto the stage, and he looked out at his audience of one, then winked. Sitting at the piano, Jackson sipped his drink with one hand and he played the piano with the other. Even though she was the only person in the club besides the owner, Sharpe didn't say anything to your mother, at first. After Jackson finished his second song on the piano, your mother moved closer to the stage. A song after that, when she saw Jackson put his empty highball glass on the piano bench, your mother approached him, and said, 'Hey,' but it was awkward and sounded like a yelp. Jackson looked down at her and smiled. Your mother saw her future flash before her eyes- The tour bus/ The cheap motels/ The smoky bars/ Sitting on a chair at the side of the stage/ Sipping a draft beer while Jackson played his guitar, or his harmonica, or his piano. Your mother never got to go on tour with Jackson, and she never got to her friend's house, but after that night, something amazing began and she wouldn't have been able to sit in those smoky bars anyway. The man you grew up calling 'Dad' never found out about this night, and Jackson never knew the extent of his actions, and maybe your mother didn't even believe it happened, but it did. Someday, she will tour with Jackson and every moment will be as exciting as the first time she heard this song."

~

I'm in the café, waiting for a short Asian girl to locate the extra dollar she needs in order to pay for her pita wrap. I dig in my pockets to see if I can donate a dollar to end her frantic search, and I pull out what I hope is a twenty, but upon closer inspection, reveals itself to be a piece of paper. I unfold the long rectangular paper and read the red writing on it, which says, "my void seems to be filling up nicely." It's written in Lindsey's cute, but scribbled, all lowercase handwriting.

How did she know that I'd wear these pants today?

Probably because I've been wearing them for a week straight.

Her void is filling up nicely.

Maybe that uneasy smile was just a mistake. Maybe it was the weird lighting in the bookstore. Maybe it was an accidental twitch of muscles. Maybe, I was imagining the whole thing, creating a fiction worthy of the volumes on the shelves that surrounded us.

She's happy. She must be. I'm happy and I need to stay happy, so she needs to be happy, but if she isn't happy then we're both fucked. Feeling at home in this negativity, I decide if I'm more positive then maybe Lindsey will be too. Maybe she thinks that she's boring me because we don't go out.

Maybe she thinks that she's being a burden because I have to buy the eggs and the milk since they don't sell stuff like that at her pharmacy.

If I show her how perfect I feel about ~us~, then maybe she won't doubt another moment.

I can't fuck this up; I need her to feel at home with me.

The register boy swipes his hand at me, wordlessly telling me to just take the coffee. I give him a nod as a thank you, and he manages to bob his giant head in reciprocation.

I take my coffee to the table near the mail room. I reach into my backpack, but before I can take out the magazine with the Winona Ryder article in it, someone sits down across from me.

I'm surprised to find that it's Brittany. She's brighter and less babydoll looking than the last time I saw her, but it's unmistakably her. I never really notice changes in a person if I see them every day, but with a little distance, they can look brand new with the slightest of modifications.

"I think I did good on my test," Brittany tells me.

"I don't," I say.

"That's mean. Just because you probably did good doesn't mean I flunked."

Choosing to be nice to Brittany, and feeling genuinely curious about where she's been, I lie, and say, "I worded that wrong. I meant to indicate that I didn't do well on the test I took today."

Brittany smiles a smile that's brighter than it was the last time I saw her, then she grabs my coffee and takes a sip. "That's not very good," she says, setting the cup back down.

Brittany displays displeasure, and I'm totally thrown off guard.

"Isn't it funny how people pop in and out of your life?" Brittany asks out of nowhere.

Do I have faith that the people I need will pop back into my life?

No. I don't.

"Why do you think that happens?" I ask.

"We would use each other up without a break," Brittany says.

I stare at a very unneutral Brittany. This Brittany now has opinions and insight. She's changed, for the better, and I can't help but selfishly wonder if I was a catalyst in her metamorphosis. It's a same-yet-different type of change she's exhibiting.

"I felt excited to see you, and I saw it in your eyes, you're excited to see me," the unneutral Brittany says.

"You don't know what you have until it's gone," I realize along with her.

"And if it comes back, you feel like the luckiest person in the world."

Both Brittany and I have changed. Maybe we've achieved a goal, maybe we've accepted a reality, maybe we can now look at each other, imperfect, and see someone who's been trekking on the same journey in the same direction, and this could make us feel less alone.

"I heard about your girlfriend," Brittany says, and I nod, acknowledging the situation, but Brittany stays with it, and I become curious why. "I know what it's like to get surprised by life," she tells me, and once she confirms I'm engaged with her train of thought, she continues, "My dad divorced my mom." It's like the words jumped out of her mouth, because the statement could only arrive as an ambush. "And now I like him," she adds, almost with guilt. "The man he's become, he... seems like the dad that I've needed my entire life. I didn't understand him when he lived with us, but it was because my mom wouldn't let him be himself," Brittany says, then sighs, "I don't know why I'm telling you this."

"Because I'm interested in what you have to say," I assure her, and unneutral Brittany's pearl white smile flashes wide again. She tells me, "When my dad lived with us, he had to hide his possessions and passions in drawers, and in the trunk of his car, and on shelves in the basement. Everything he owned in that house was covered up, or boxed up, or thrown out. It seemed like he never did anything around the house because he sat in the TV room all grumpy after work. Then he left, and I began to realize what he had been silently doing around the house; I could see that certain things simply weren't getting done anymore."

I nod at this, I understand exactly what she's trying to share. After Lindsey gave me a new father, I started thinking about my deceased dad. The money that I will receive was his. He gave me my future.

Everyone's dad does things for them, but sometimes these acts go unnoticed, because they're seamless. Mom's job was to go to the store to pick out those Jordans, but Dad was the one who paid for them. It's Dad who keeps the internet on. It's Dad who the family will rush to when a stranger is hammering his fist on the front door. There is a silent gift that fathers are perpetually giving, only to receive very little in return.

I remember when my father was alive, he would do things for me, and I wouldn't realize it. One night in my youth stands out as the paramount example of this. It was when my mother went to a musical with her friends, but my father stayed home, claiming that he'd love to go, but someone had to watch me, I couldn't be left alone. My mother and I both found this convenient. I was my father's excuse for missing the musical, yet I didn't see him once that entire night. Instead, I sat in the living room watching TV alone. This was a common area, I didn't lock myself in my room, he could have joined me at any time, but he didn't. I sat and watched bad sitcoms about cool cities like New York and Boston, and I enjoyed the wit of all these fictional characters as they tried to get out of a situation that would take exactly 22 minutes to solve. When the local news came on, I searched for another escape. I was flipping through the channels, finding nothing. Channel 75, 76, 77, then I came upon it. Channel 78. It wasn't blocked, nor was it scrambled. The cable porn channel, for the first time ever, was available in crystal clear perfection. It was like when a nearly blind person puts on a pair of glasses and they finally realize what everything truly looks like- *So this is what I've been missing for all these years.* I put a tape in the old VCR we had and taped over an old crappy made for TV cable movie that didn't contain a single nipple or shaved vagina. I taped in SP quality because I wanted these images to be duplicated as accurately as possible. My fear was that after this amazing two hours, I would rewind the tape and find the same message that served as a firewall to the goods. Much to my pleasure, the tape recorded perfectly, and after watching it so many times, I can still replay back its entire runtime in intimate detail merely by closing my eyes. It was the Jackson Sharpe of VHS tapes for me. That was the one night channel 78 was ever available- the night that my mother went out. The more I watched the tape, the more I wondered how it happened, then one day, the answer was clear- my father had ordered the porn channel that night.

Sometimes, it's not clear just how much a person has given you because good deeds are often transparent.

"Hellooo, Kurt?" Brittany says, waving her hand in front of my face.

"Sorry, what?" I ask, mentally stumbling back into the conversation.

"You'll listen to it, right?" she asks, a desperate hopefulness overcoming her.

I blink rapidly, until Brittany puts her long pink nail on the CD case sitting in front of me, then restates the question, "You'll listen to my demo, right?"

I pick the CD up and look at the cover. It's a painting. It's not Brittany in a bikini or a leather corset, it's a painting of a bathroom in a country house, with a woman's leg hanging out of the tub, the rest of her out of sight, soaking.

Gerard started a band, and his phone is purportedly filled with their music. Brittany saved up for a demo, and now I have her CD.

~

Accepting that I can no longer ride the wave of Joan related pity, I actually do some homework in the library. For the first time this semester, I read through my schedule and pay attention to the names of the classes. There's so little change in the course names- Micro to Macro- only the size of the playing field fluctuates. I stare at notes I made, on autopilot, throughout February; I barely recognize my own handwriting.

With a focus that I thought was only possible via assistance from Gerard's Adderall guy, I accomplish so much during my study session and spend so long doing work that when I start packing up, I glance out the window, and see that it's dark outside. The whole time that I was in this self-sentenced academic boot camp, I was researching, and typing papers, and making up homework assignments, and sending e-mails, and submitting portions of projects to groups of strangers. I systematically addressed my assignments by due date, putting the close due dates on the top of the pile, then making my way to the bottom. It took me until the third assignment before I noticed Lindsey's fingerprint on this technique.

I've caught up on being a college student, instead of embracing the easier route of ignoring the inevitable while hoping that the end comes before finals begin. Brittany reappearing did something to me. I had assumed that she had dropped out of college when I didn't see her on campus anymore. I'm well aware that the university won't keep someone around if they don't go to class/ If they don't turn in their assigned work/ If they don't remain a functional appendage of the student body.

I meet Gerard on the Green, and we wordlessly decide to leave campus.

The normally busy street that runs parallel to the gate is empty, and the perpetually alive frat houses aren't blaring rap music. The snow on the ground seems fake, and I can't help but feel like I'm on a movie set in a big warehouse that's spruced up to look like a quiet college town. The lack of wind, the untouched snow, the occasional flakes drifting down on my shoulder- all of it makes me look up, half expecting to see a guy with "Bob" sewn onto his shirt, climbing down a ladder with a half full box of white shavings because he hit his mark and needs to get ready for the next scene. I wait for the director to yell, "Cut," but he never does.

~

Lindsey is watching a movie where all the actors are dressed in 90's era grunge outfits. On the black and white screen, a girl just left a guy after issuing a firestorm of complaints. Her tear-filled exit is something that's always reserved for the end of the second act, and this intrigues me. I lie on the futon with Lindsey and watch the movie, with no knowledge of what caused the fight. I like not getting it. It now seems that the only things I find intriguing are engulfed in a shrouded mystery. I'll start movies in the middle just to play catch up in order to find out who is who and what's what. I've become addicted to assembling stories and motives. I can't watch most Hollywood blockbusters because there's nothing to untangle; there's no mess.

I try to untangle the person that sits next to me on the futon, but instead we become entangled.

~

Lindsey is sitting on the counter, eating frosted flakes for dinner. I watch as a flake of paint chips off the ceiling, then falls into her bowl. She picks the unfrosted flake out of the cereal bowl, flicks it into the sink, then continues eating. The eggshell white paint is chipping everywhere. My apartment looks like it has some sort of disease. I pray it's not a sign of things to come.

"We have a plan for tonight," Lindsey says.

My heart beats a little faster. Why is there a plan? We've never had a plan before. Why do we need a plan?

Lindsey reads me, and says, "I thought about going out last night, but we didn't, so I think that makes it a plan if I've been doing all that pre-thinking for almost a full day."

"What warrants this much pre-think?" I ask.

"Umm. It's sorta like..." she trails off, then wraps her blonde hair around her pointer finger.

"When does the plan go into effect?"

"It's already started," she says, putting her bowl down, then hopping off the counter.

"Are things going as planned?" I ask.

"So far? Yes."

"Do I need a jacket?" is the next question I have.

"Yes," she responds, and with that answer, we start getting ready.

"Does this have to do with poetry?" I ask.

"What?"

"Poetry. Will we have to hear or write poems?"

"Oh, no. No. I'd never betray your trust like that," Lindsey says, while putting her coat on.

I feel a profound relief and allow myself to get excited.

We leave the building, and begin making our way to campus. No longer do I need to fill these moments with ~the song~ because I can now speak to the girl that helped me with the lyrics. "Will we need codenames?" I ask, hoping we will.

Lindsey shakes her head no.

"Is..." I take out my wallet and count my bills, "...sixty-eight dollars enough for the plan?"

"Put your money away," Lindsey says.

"Will anyone get hurt?" I have to ask.

Lindsey slides her ID through the card reader, then I pull the gate open and hold it for her. She must see the concern creasing my face because she assures me, "No one will get hurt."

"Am I forgetting a holiday?" I ask, trying to think about the "febuary" calendar in Lindsey's room.

"No holiday today."

We make our way across campus, then leave through the far gate that people try not to use.

We begin to approach the part of town that college kids avoid, unless they're looking to purchase the types of drugs that Lindsey's pharmacy can't carry.

Lindsey takes my hand, and I can't figure out where we're going, or why we didn't take her car.

The town quickly melts into a city- not a city with skyscrapers and businessmen and martini bars- but a city where everything is in decay, and it becomes difficult to imagine this place ever feeling hopeful.

We watch the people buzzing around us, carrying black plastic bags, and massive laundry sacks, and children. Everyone looks so anxious to get where they're going. Either these people also feel the unease I begin to fill with, or maybe this is just how things are in the backstreets on the wrong side of the gate.

I make sure that we walk faster when we're between the street lights, and storefronts, and headlights, almost as though the weather in the patches of darkness is worse.

After a couple more minutes, when I get the feeling that Lindsey doesn't have a destination, I ask, "What do you say we head back?"

"Okay," Lindsey agrees simply, and we start walking away from the city, back to campus.

As we walk, I ask, "What were we looking for?" and I wait for an answer, but Lindsey remains tight-lipped and almost timid. She seems to be consciously avoiding looking up, so I scan the stretch of road she's averting her eyes from. A black guy in a black winter coat is crossing the street, walking directly toward us, with purpose.

Lindsey's grip tightens on my arm and I move her hand closer to my body.

I have no way to divert our path, without doubling back, and then we'd be moving further from campus with each step. With no choice, I move forward, and when we're about two feet away from the guy, he says, "Gimme your fucking wallet."

Lindsey lets out a sound that reminds me of a protesting kitten.

Holding on tight to my world, I try to keep walking, ignoring him, but he steps in our path, and says, "I won't ask you again," then adds, "I have a gun."

His hand is in his pocket- I don't see a gun- but when someone says they have one, it's best to err on the side of caution.

"Okay, calm down, the thing is, my money isn't in my wallet," I say quietly.

The conversation ends as the man lunges forward. Everything is a blur, and suddenly Lindsey is on her ass, next to me, because our arms are still locked. With my free hand, I dig into my pocket and take out my $68. The guy brings his hand out of his coat, and I say, "Fuck, please don't shoot me," then instantly restate it, "Shoot me, don't shoot her."

I hold out my money, my hand trembling. I feel like I'm on a movie set again.

The man snatches the money from me, then I watch him flee, in a rush, like everyone else around us.

I lie back on the concrete sidewalk slab and look over at Lindsey. We remain on the ground, locked together, as the cars roar by, and the lights in the buildings get turned out, and we just Exist. We Exist on our backs, listening to the city, looking up to the sky, with nothing to lose. This moment feels like it's worth so much more than $68.

~

Lindsey leaves for work, and I'm awake enough that my mind resumes racing about last night.

There was a very real possibility we could have been shot. If I was shot, my final act on this earth would've been weakly begging, "Fuck, don't shoot me." Famous last words. Think about all the people who went out with those words- All the soldiers/ All the gang members/ All the cops/ All the good looking girls on spring break in Latin America/ All the people who aren't me.

I search for the right thing to say at gunpoint, and I decide it's...

I love you.

BANG.

Of all the things to say, "I love you," is what I should have chosen. Those three words will be my parting farewell if I ever again find myself in an endgame situation. It would be how Lindsey would remember me- stating an absolute truth that she could believe completely, forever. It would be how my murderer would remember me, the beginning of a haunting. Every time someone mentioned those three words to him, he'd be reminded of his ugly and brutal act. Every time someone on this horrible planet wanted to express to my killer that he makes their world a little bit better and they care deeply for him, all of their good intentions would be not only eradicated, they'd be annulled. It's with these words that I would want him to envy my fate.

~

Sitting across from Lindsey in Rubie's, I bring up the subject of the robbery.

"Interesting night last night, huh?" I say, in a tone appropriate for the situation.

"I know, right."

I know, right, is the best she can do. Lindsey is so nonchalant about the whole thing that it's almost discouraging. She pops a french fry into her mouth, then goes back to watching the people behind us through the camera on her phone, just like Noni did.

I don't tell Lindsey about what I've decided to say if we were ever to get robbed again. Given where my apartment is, there's a pretty good chance of a similar scenario occurring- at the earliest- tonight. I don't mention that I would tell the man with the gun, *I love you.* This statement and the concept of love is something that I've noticed with such frequency lately. Casual moments now buzz with an extra layer of importance, and resonate on a higher frequency. I see love in new places. I now see love in the act of an owner and his dog jogging alongside each other in perfect rhythm. I see the love of a parent, even as they attempt to control their misbehaving child in the grocery store. The other day, I was looking at a desk phone at the bank, and on the keypad, there were little letters under each number. I mentally pressed the 4 three times, the 5 three times, the 6 three times, the 8 three times, the 3 two times, the 9 three times, the 6 three times, and the 8 two times, spelling out a message with my actions once again.

For a moment, the man behind Lindsey stops fighting with his girlfriend, and even in this break, I feel their love.

Lindsey, out of the blue, says, "We're leaving the apartment again tonight," and I feel love in her use of the word "we."

~

We park at the end of a long line of curbed cars in front of a big house in a suburb about ten minutes away from campus.

"Am I meeting your parents?" I ask.

"No, I mean, I wish these people were my parents, but they're my friend Belle's parents, so I guess she got first dibs on them."

This name sounds familiar, and after running through a rolodex of moments I've had in the car with Lindsey, I arrive on a call, a demand for Lindsey's presence, a nagging yet good-natured taunt. I remember Belle's voice, and I feel excited to meet her.

We get out of the car, and instead of using the long sidewalk that leads to the front door of the brick house, we take a well-trafficked path on the side yard, then move toward an in-ground cellar door out back. I don't question this possible B&E, because I trust Lindsey. The fact that she would again leave the comfort of the apartment, trusting me with her safety, keeps me from assuming I ruined things with my cowardice. I go along with the detour, and for a second I suspect we might be stealing someone's dog. Maybe that's where Edie went, she dyed her hair, changed her name, and enrolled at Kirtland.

As we enter the cellar, I hear the unmistakable noise of party chatter.

"You don't... think it's my birthday today... do you?" I ask, following Lindsey into Belle's basement.

Lindsey turns back to me, and says, "If I was throwing you a surprise party, no way could I get this many people to show up." I laugh, then she reminds me, "I still have the calendar pages in my dorm, and I took a picture of each month with my phone."

Lindsey is in control tonight, of this I am sure.

To my relief, and minor anxiety, the basement contains a party. Along the edge of the party, the walls are covered in stickers. Some of the stickers are labels from jars, some are band stickers, and some are the type of stickers that a third grade teacher would put on an aced spelling test. I scratch a purple smiley sticker, then lean in and sniff. It's lost its smell.

Lindsey forcibly pushes through a crowd so sparse that it doesn't require forcible pushing to get through, but I don't want to take away from Lindsey's hobbies so I allow it to continue and so does everyone else.

We shove our way through a maze of strangers, until we reach a blonde girl with bleached eyebrows who's holding a tabby cat. The cat is so calm that I have to watch its eyes closely to make sure it isn't stuffed. Next to the blonde girl is a man with tall hair who sits on an old wooden chair behind a piano. I realize that these two are the focal point of the night. There's a large space cleared behind them where the party does not extend.

The basement crowd begins to fall quiet before Lindsey can even say anything to this blonde girl, who I presume to be Belle.

Without so much as an acknowledgment of the people in front of him, the man with the tall hair starts playing his piano, and the blonde girl with the invisible eyebrows puts down the tabby, then picks an acoustic guitar up off the ground and slings it over her shoulder.

When the perfect moment strikes, the girl, Belle, begins to play the guitar and sing. This near-ambush of a performance sends a chill rocketing up my spine. It's like Belle and the boy were waiting for us, and once we arrived, the concert began. The fact that our presence triggered everything to fall into place bothers me in a way. Lindsey made sure that we were here for this tiny little show her best friend is putting on. My best friend makes music, but I didn't even reach over and take his headphones to listen to his songs on his greasy cell phone. Maybe Gerard is holding off on performing until I finally give him my attention? It becomes less about me wanting to listen to Gerard's music, and more about Gerard needing me to hear his work.

Song after song, we sway with the crowd, and I know that if Noni was here, she would force us to dance. I have no idea how Lindsey would react if confronted by Noni's perpetual ballet. The songs being played are slow and plodding, but I know that Noni would still find a way to move to them. If Gerard was here, he would get bored, because the music doesn't display the same frantic energy he demands. The lyrics are too personal; the audience is too respectful. Scored to a beautiful soundtrack, I build the realization that I've compartmentalized my life as a strategy to feel safe. I fear linking everyone together because if one link in a chain gets pulled, the rest must follow, but unchained, links can be removed without impacting the others.

I used to have the same need for fire in my music that Gerard harbors, but I've felt things change recently. I can appreciate how keyed-in Belle is to these songs. When I fell in love, my music taste took a vicious blow. Other than the Jackson Sharpe song, I've found the music that I'm attracted to now is warmer and happier, but also sometimes quiet and crooning. All the emotion-soaked, raw, real music is about the misery of a relationship crumbling, and for obvious reasons, those thoughts feel slimy to me now. I can tell by Belle's lyrics that she's in love with the man who sits at the piano- I wonder if he knows. In love, all of the amazing music I could be listening to has been replaced by the earnest music that I can relate to as lyrics that once felt kitschy now feel essential.

After the fourth song, Lindsey grabs my hand, then turns her back to Belle and we push through the crowd until we're at the far wall. The music is still playing, but Lindsey leans in and tells me, "I like the moments when it seems like she's possessed and the song controls her body. It becomes so furious and out-there that people stop moving because the tempo gets lost in this soundscape of confusing emotion. You can tell it's spontaneous. You can't plan it, what they're doing right now."

Lindsey is silent, just as Belle reaches a spiritual level of performance. Everyone is swaying to a different beat, but all together, and I'm so happy that I've found Lindsey because she catches things that would slip through most people's fingers.

~

I feel I'm being made fun of when Lindsey says, "These are cute," as she picks the scissors up off my desk. This particular pair has one white handle and one turquoise handle. When the scissors are closed, no metal shows, only a plastic body that comes to a nice semicircle tip.

Rule~ All scissors must be primarily plastic, extremely dull and tip-less. Think second grade arts and crafts. Think having to cut each sheet of construction paper separately because you can't get a clean slice through a stack of two or more sheets. Think of this because thinking of a real pair of scissors feels deadly.

Overall, I have only two destructive impulses that arrive as intrusive thoughts.

One- When I see a sharp, shiny, pair of scissors.

Two- When I see a long glass display case.

The sharp scissors give me an uneasy, irrational feeling that I might pick them up and drive them into my forehead, or for the sake of an easy penetration, my eye socket. I desperately don't want to drive a pair of scissors into my head, but there's this little repressed side of me- almost like an instinct- that begs me to do it. I'm worried that I'll have a momentary lapse in judgment and my hands will move quicker than my mind.

The display case impulse is a base urge that I cannot locate an evolutionary purpose for. I don't know why, but when I'm at a department store buying cologne, or at the thrift store eying the few items that have value, I'll get an incredible desire to run my elbow through the center of the glass pane in front of me. I want to grab the shoulders of the person on the other side of the case and drive their head through the glass. I want to find the biggest, heaviest object in close proximity, then heave it gloriously into the air, tracking it with my eyes, until it smashes down through the glass. I probably wouldn't even shield my eyes, the sight would be so beautiful.

Both of these scenarios seem to end up with me potentially having a razor sharp object driven through my skull, so I make sure to avoid such situations. I'll never be a jeweler, or man the register at any gift shop on the planet, but when I get my money, I won't have to worry about these jobs being off limits to me. I could open my own gift shop with wooden shelves instead of glass display cases.

I stare at Lindsey, as she chops the air with my kindergarten arts and crafts tool, and I explain, "They're safety scissors."

"You could still put an eye out with these," Lindsey says, then slowly brings them up to her right eye, and I wordlessly reach toward her, stopping an act she would never go through with. "There are so many things in this world- hell, even in this apartment- that you could pop your eye out with," she reminds me.

How is it possible that I've found someone with a more macabre view on life than me? It's moments like these that make me realize how much trouble Lindsey is in.

I strongly consider listing a series of warnings regarding the various dangers that the world holds, but stop myself when I acknowledge that Lindsey is acutely aware of the threats we're facing. I continue to watch her as she reaches down and takes off one of the neon socks she's wearing, then begins cutting off loose threads from the toe of the sock. When she's finished, with the sock in one hand and the scissors in the other, she moves toward me. I don't ask what she's doing as she climbs onto the bed. I'm on edge, and she must notice this because she starts rubbing my back. I stare at the *GQ* on the desk that has somehow strayed from its place.

Suddenly, my vision is taken from me, not with a scissor stab, but with a blindfold. My senses reduced, I hear the cackle of a laugh behind me. Lindsey has tightly tied her sock around my head. A large knot digs into the back of my skull. I hear feet hitting the hardwood floor, as I ask, "What is this?"

No response.

"...Lindsey?" I call out, uncomfortable in the silence.

I stand up and step on a CD case.

After I remove the blindfold, I walk out into the empty living room.

I can sense she's still here, so I quietly make my way over to the coat closet, then I slide the door open.

Lindsey is standing between the coats, hiding.

I reach out my hand, she takes it, then I pull her out of the tiny closet.

"It worked," she tells me.

"Was that a test?" I ask.

"I wanted to make sure that if I were to ever disappear, you'd be able to find me... That you'd come to find me," Lindsey says. A moment hangs between us, then she cups her hands together and shrugs. I've seen moments like this in movies, but it's odd how different it feels when someone I love does it, and says it, and means it. It's like the difference between black and white, and color.

I wonder why we play these games.

For the first time in a while, I'm passing tests without cheating.

~

I wake to music. I recognize the song. Earlier this week, Lindsey picked some CDs out of my collection and since then, she's listened to them on repeat. She made odd selections- bands that friends or relatives started. These bands recorded an album, then someone in the band fucked another band member's girlfriend and they never played together again.

"You can hear it in their music," Lindsey tells me when I sit up.

"Hear what?"

"The impending doom."

Lindsey's perspective is becoming increasingly eccentric, but with these bands, I can't really tell if she's right or not. The lead singers and drummers and bassists were all so close to me that I don't know how their music sounds from a distance.

As we listen to my cousin's band, The Luddites, Lindsey tells me, "I could never make music. I'd be afraid of what would come out. It's supposed to be so cathartic, but artists are always still so depressed- taking a shotgun to the face, or a needle to the vein, or a razor to the ear."

"Maybe they would have done that stuff even earlier without the music," I say, but I know firsthand that the music doesn't resolve an internal battle. I have the confidence to mentally declare this because I tried to make my own songs at around 12 or 13. My mother had bought me an acoustic guitar because she said it was better than playing video games all day.

I wrote a song about a dream I had where everyone's TV exploded and blinded the entire viewing audience/ I wrote a song about a lost love I met in Spain, even though I had never left the state/ I wrote a song about a week where the sun never set and everyone loved this change at the start of the week, but were exhausted by the end.

I don't know where the lyrics came from, and I had no idea if they were good, so I played a small set of my one-man-band songs for my mother.

After patiently listening to each track, she said, "Oh, Kurt. Let's go play some Mario."

And that's what we did.

I hadn't been playing the guitar long enough to require a name for my band, but I had filled a notebook page with possibilities. I had it narrowed down to a choice of five prospective names:

> Anorexia Dreamboat
> Trip Backwards
> Bravura
> Breed Quarantine
> Sinking Hardships

I've always been a fan of avoiding permanent decisions when at all possible, so quitting before picking a name wasn't that hard on me.

My mother never bullshitted me. She never made me think I was a perfect exquisite model of human excellence that demanded the utmost attention and respect. When I wanted to play soccer in elementary school, my mother bought me cleats and shin guards, and she would come to my games and watch me play. I would run up and down the field, following-yet never quite touching- the ball, and the cleats gave me the traction to fail, and the shin guards protected my shins, but not my self-respect.

After the game, on the way home, my mother didn't compliment me on my determination on the field, she didn't tell me how proud she was of me- all she did was call every thug we passed a "soccer player."

When we drove by a group of Hispanic guys harassing a girl in a sweatshirt bearing the name of a nearby college, my mother said, "Look at those friendly soccer players chatting with that girl."

I still remember the uncomfortable look on the girl's face.

A block later, a group of frat guys pulled up next to my mother and honked their horn to get her attention. I could see in the rear view mirror that my mother made a face like the college girl. She turned around, looked at me, and said, "Those soccer players must recognize you. They must know you're a soccer player too."

When we got home we watched the news and they reported on a man who got the death penalty for raping and killing his roommates- I'm not sure if that was the order, but either way, the end result was the same. My mother shook her head, then said, "Well, that soccer game certainly got out of hand."

I had no idea what I was doing on the soccer field, but I knew, with certainty, I didn't want to make girls uncomfortable. I didn't want to harass middle-aged women. I didn't want to kill people. From that day on, I didn't want to play soccer. I asked my mother if we could skip the next game, for our health, and she agreed. I never went back.

I thank my mother for this. Soccer is inconsequential in the scheme of American life, and she knew that exiling me from it would have no serious repercussions. I think I would've hated her if she had let me stay on the team. Imagine being lied to throughout your entire childhood- being told that you could do something, that, in reality, you had no business even attempting. Imagine how that changes you.

My unconditional support Takeaways:

One- Perpetual, unwavering support breeds an inflated ego and a self-confidence distanced from reality.

Two- Without being clearly redirected away from my failures, I'd never really know if I'm succeeding or if everyone's lying to me.

My mother misled me greatly, but she didn't lie to me about my abilities. The information she provided me wasn't true, but it came from a good place. It was very clear that she supported me in the areas that I was talented in, and she made sure I didn't waste time in any dead-end endeavors. Because of this, when she told me something nice, when she said, "I love you," I knew she meant it completely.

On that day, on the last day, when she whispered in my ear, "This is the hardest thing I've had to do in my entire life," I believed every fucking word.

~

Lindsey puts her coffee down, then I pick mine up and take a sip. Both cracked spine copies of *Limber* sit in front of us. They're the same copies that we picked up when we started this tradition. There's always the same number of *Limber*s on the shelves. I put my coffee down, then Lindsey picks up her copy of the novel, and says, "It must be so shitty to be the dude who wrote this. There's no interest in this book, except our interest, and our interest isn't expressed in a purchase, so he'll never know that his creation became completely important to us. He has no idea that we've made so many dates out of his unpopular book. We should write him a letter or something."

"No way," I say, "We'd have to start it out with a backhanded compliment like, 'We really enjoy reading your book, not enough to buy it, but enough to keep reading.' It would be the most depressing fan letter ever."

"I'm sure he'd be more than happy to get some mail."

"Maybe if we're convincing enough, we can get him to do a book signing here, and we can bring the store copy up for him to sign... then proceed to put it back on the shelf."

"I'd buy a copy if he came," Lindsey says.

"That's breaking the rules."

"It's okay to break the rules if you're saving someone's life," she responds, and I begin to disagree with this, but stop myself when I think about the possibility of Edie, at home, reading and re-reading my letters, briefly considering writing back just to let me know that I'm not irrelevant- that I'm not forgotten. I eventually disregard this idea, viewing it as foolish.

"You're right, we should write him a letter," I admit, as Lindsey's point sticks with me.

We read for an hour and a half, then I buy a notebook before we leave so I can start on the letter.

That's my plan for the rest of the night- work on two drafts of the letter with Lindsey- but that plan immediately is discarded when we pull out of the parking lot, and make a right, instead of the left that leads back to campus. There was no obstacle that caused this change of pattern, so the change becomes the obstacle.

Ignoring my attention, Lindsey feeds the CD player The Luddites, and my cousin is the only one who says anything for five minutes. That walk to nowhere that started with a wrong turn outside of the campus gate keeps replaying in my mind. I fear this is another challenge that Lindsey is organizing on a whim. Once I'm ready to remove the blindfold, I ask, "Where are we going?"

"You can start the letter," Lindsey tells me, then looks down at her gauges, and says, "Our destination is, I'd say, about fifty-miles from here."

I leave the notebook in the bag. The author can wait. I watch Lindsey rewrite the script we've been rehearsing for months. Various sets are wheeled away, possibilities are eliminated, extended scenes are drafted.

Mansions whip by/ Liquor stores whip by/ Fast food joints whip by/ Identical houses whip by/ The sun whips by.

One moment it was light, the next it's not. I lean across the seat and rest my head on Lindsey's shoulder. I don't look at the gauge to see how close we are to that fifty mile mark. From my slanted angle, I'm able to get a glimpse inside some of the houses on the strip of road we're driving down- People watching TV/ People eating dinner/ People folding laundry/ People playing with their kids.

I stop focusing on the outside when the song we're listening to loses its musicality and morphs into a repetition of dings. Things are going wrong, everything is coming to a halt. Instead of continuing down the road, the car coughs, knocks, and stops.

"We're here," Lindsey announces.

"Where's here?" I ask.

Lindsey leans forward, toward the dash, and she searches the stretch of road in front of us, then admits, "I'm. Not. Sure."

We get out of the car, which is now an expensive paperweight until we find a gas station.

As we stand, bookended by the headlights, Lindsey points down the street. I look in the opposite direction, almost by instinct, because I momentarily forget that Lindsey still has a dorm room so she doesn't live by the commuter code. Unsure of what's caught Lindsey's focus, all I can think is, *Please be pointing at the beautiful glowing lights of a gas station.*

"Let's go in there," Lindsey says, her finger divining our path.

I'm afraid to look where she's pointing, so I keep my head down and agree with her suggestion. When her hand lowers, I grab it, and we set off down the road, together. With our backs to the sparse and slow oncoming traffic, we make our way to where Lindsey wants to be. The street is quiet, and I experience none of the nerves I had on that day we left campus and explored a place beyond the college town.

I now understand that when Lindsey looked at her gauges- she wasn't looking at the mileage, she was looking to see how much fuel she had.

When we reach the door that Lindsey pointed to, I don't look at the sign that hangs above it- I merely try the knob, and the door opens. We're facing a wooden stairwell with framed pictures on the walls for the entire climb. I don't look at a single picture as we make our way upstairs.

At the top of the staircase, I stand with Lindsey in the door frame of what appears to be the historical society of whatever small town it is that we ran out of gas in. An old man, his gray hair combed straight back on a spotty scalp, welcomes us in a strangled voice. He seems to be in disbelief that new, young visitors picked his historical society for a date. I'm not sure if this man is a tour guide, and I don't force him into this role because he seems frail, and he also may trap us in here providing more history than either Lindsey or I care about. Most of all, I fear that this man is incredibly interesting and I'll have to write to Edie about him. I don't want to write to Edie until she gives me a sign that my letters are like *Limber* and they're appreciated, no matter how obtuse and undetectable her reading ritual is.

"Wanna look around?" Lindsey asks, and I nod my head, because I do.

I'm going to acquire the full history of this town before I've truly interacted with it, which is exactly the way I got to know Lindsey. Before I met her, I had her backstory. I wonder if she's aware of this. I wonder if she's waiting for me to finally admit that I was her stalker. I don't know if carrying this secret is helping us or hurting us, and until I'm sure, I won't change how I've been handling things.

The study of a place- a settlement- a barren wasteland given purpose- takes a backseat to my observation of Lindsey as she makes her way around the long rectangle of a museum. I watch as she picks up an old photograph of a parade- she studies the picture like she's looking for someone in the crowd.

"Did you grow up here?" I ask, searching for meaning in this moment.

Lindsey shakes her head no, then puts down the picture and moves toward an old wooden beer box that's sitting by the old man's feet.

The man notices Lindsey curiously peeking at his disorganized collection, and with a frail voice, he says, "Go ahead. You can go through the box. These are just some things I had... things my wife kept. She collected antiques like this, but I figure they'll get more use here than they did at our house when she was around. I suppose these trinkets and photographs mean something to someone."

Lindsey smiles at the man, and instead of going through the box, she backs away till she's flush against the far wall. I watch her chest deeply exhale as though she had been holding her breath. Seconds later, tears roll down both sides of her face. She wipes them away with the backs of her hands.

I'm frozen on the other side of the room, next to an old phonograph. The track lighting above us creates spotlights in which dusty air moves in slow motion, and I'm glad the phonograph isn't playing because the scene would become too surreal with a soundtrack.

I look to the man, to see if he's weeping as well- if his display of emotion provoked the extreme reaction in Lindsey. He's not crying, and he tilts his head in Lindsey's direction, wordlessly telling me to get as close as possible to the woman I love, while I still can.

I hold up my pointer finger to our guide, requesting that he give us a minute to work this out, and when I look back to the wall where Lindsey was, she's gone. I hear a sob, and this makes me kneel down. From this vantage point, I see a little ball of Lindsey hiding under a scale model of the town exactly as it was in 1955. As though I'm trying to capture a wild fox who had found its way into the museum, I cautiously crawl toward Lindsey, then put my back to the wall where she's balled up. I lean in close to her, and she whispers, "Why am I crying?" I put my arm around her, and with my free hand, I wipe her tears away.

"Don't give my stuff away to some museum when I die," she whispers.

If that unthinkable end was to ever arrive in my lifetime, I know that I'd create some sort of Lindsey shrine. Everything she touched would become a Harrington Street sign. The posters she bought and hung would forever stay on my walls, no matter where I moved. My home would become a museum to Lindsey, like my heart is currently.

~

I wake up, staring into the sun, and I get the horrible feeling that we're still in that sad little town, but when I look to my right, I see Lindsey sleeping next to me, wrapped tightly in my sheets.

I get up and take a shower, while trying to deconstruct the Sunday we had.

Was yesterday practice for the future?

Was it a test?

Was Lindsey seeing exactly how far we could make it on a fourth of a tank of gas, just in case we have to evacuate when the fatsos start zombifying? To escape these questions, I decide I'll attend class today. It's a fresh start to the week, and I want to find a test I can cheat on, instead of the tests I've been facing that require me to answer questions that I've been running from.

As I'm walking to campus, I reach into my pocket to get my cigarettes and when I remove the pack, I also take out a little sheet of paper, which says, in tiny lowercase letters, "this is a 'get out of lindsey's terrible idea free' card. when lindsey is leading you on an insane quest that will only end in tears, hand this to her."

I take the piece of paper- a piece of paper that makes me smile from ear to ear- and I crumple it up, then throw it in a trash can on the Green.

Lindsey's insane quests are an essential part of my life now. They're as important as Christmas, or Thanksgiving, or my birthday. There's a surprise element to it all, there is an intimacy to it all, there is an excitement to it all, and most importantly these less-than-normal days keep me moving when it would be crippling to stop and dwell on the fact that I'm going nowhere.

I'll never hand Lindsey that slip of paper; I'll forever hand her my hand and we will confront the unknown, together.

These small missions Lindsey has sent me on make me think that Noni would love her.

I wonder where Noni is.

I wonder if she's okay.

I wonder if she's found her brother. I hope she has. I hope she's found something. I hope she's found a valid excuse for not speaking with me. A damn good, undeniable excuse.

The old, *Is it something I said?* bounces inside my soul, as I sit down for a class I have no interest in.

I try to remember the last conversation I had with Noni.

I can't.

I hope that I wasn't too supportive/ Or negative/ Or fatherly/ Or wordy/ Or wishy-washy/ Or distant/ Or fake. All of those things piss Noni off.

How bizarre that, as Noni searched for her brother who disappeared, she disappeared.

~

I wait in line for cigarettes and the girl in front of me is on the phone, freaking out on- most likely- her boyfriend. She's screaming things like, "Pay attention to me!" Her voice sounds like the noise a shoe makes when the rubber catches on the gym floor. Everyone in the store obliges her request, tuning in to half of a soap opera as they clutch their eight packs of bar soap.

"What's wrong with my outfit? This seriously looks slutty to you?" she asks, even though the person on the other end of the phone can't see her, and we can. She's wearing a tiny jean skirt that won't be remotely weather appropriate for months. She must have had a lot of clothes to premiere before the trends switch if she's continuing her skirt-wearing this far into March. As the girl yells, I can't help but notice that the outfit she's wearing would go great with a pair of blue pumps.

I can only imagine how her boyfriend is attempting to dig himself out of this situation that probably resulted from a single casual comment. For all I know, the boyfriend has been forced to wait in the car and he's sitting in the parking lot right now.

The girl on the phone squeezes the tube of lipstick she's holding so hard that the clear plastic top cracks, and she says, "Ugh," then leaves the damaged lipstick on a rack of candy.

The old checkout lady is moving the line forward with an awareness that we all want to get out of here as fast as possible. Escaping is as easy as a completed transaction, then we never have to see this angry girl in the jean skirt ever again. Her boyfriend, however, cannot escape her. The only way the boyfriend can escape this angry girl, is if he orders a new sofa- a sofa so big that it can't fit up the stairwell.

~

Lindsey is in bed, listening to The Luddites, cradling a bowl of oatmeal. I sit down next to her and slide off my boots. I see my notebooks have been removed from their home under the bed, and I try not to react.

Noticing my conflicted glance, Lindsey licks the oatmeal off her spoon, then asks, "Are those journals?"

I don't know what to call the notebooks. An archive maybe? Their contents is worth more to me than anything else I have in this world besides Lindsey, besides my mother.

Part of me is very flattered that Lindsey searched for my words, like I searched for hers, so I explain, "They're mostly filled with... drafts of letters... little... memories..."

"So they're journals. You can admit it. I once had a-"

No. Don't tell me about the site, I mentally beg.

"-notebook that I used as a journal, too. You don't have to be embarrassed," she finishes her thought.

I feel overwhelming relief, and I lie down on the bed. Part of me likes the idea that Lindsey found my journals, just like I found hers. Being the stronger of the two of us, she did what I couldn't do, and made the journals a topic of conversation.

Lindsey looks over at me, and says, "I don't know how you stick with it. I'll never write in one of those things again."

"Tell me about your notebook," I request, choosing my words carefully-not changing the topic, but redirecting it to a past that must have predated her site.

Lindsey moves close to me on the bed, then in an airy voice, she says, "One day, I was sitting in this park I used to go to, you know, to visit some ducks, and I was writing in my notebook. Between pages, I looked up and saw Kerry Palmer, a girl I went to high school with, and she was cutting through the park on her way home. Kerry had borrowed a pair of shoes from me for some play set in the 50's that she was doing, so I chased her down with the intention of re-establishing our friendship merely to regain my heels. As I walked with her, she told me how the play went over because I never saw a performance, even though she begged me to, multiple times. It wasn't until we reached her house that I realized I had left my journal on the table in the park, but I really wanted my shoes, so I followed Kerry up to her room. She started showing me things- clothes she had bought recently, pictures of a boy she had met on her summer vacation, a magazine her sister had brought back from France- and by the time I was able to extricate myself from this seemingly endless show-and-tell, it was dark outside. I rushed back to the park, my reclaimed shoes in a plastic bag, and when I got to the table where I had been sitting, I saw that my notebook was gone. I checked all the trash cans, and I checked the ground, and I went into a pavilion that had picnic tables inside, thinking maybe someone left the notebook in there so it wouldn't get rained on, but the notebook was gone. I couldn't believe how scary it felt losing those thoughts. It was like a piece of my brain had been removed- a tiny bit that wasn't essential, but did serve a purpose. Writing in that notebook was a ritual, and once it went missing, my ritual was going back to the park every day, searching the same place, and hoping for a different outcome. It felt kinda shitty that someone stole my innermost thoughts from me. A week and a half later, when my dad was bringing in the mail, he was like, 'Linds, I think I have something for you,' then he handed me the notebook curled in a C shape, but completely intact. I flattened it on the table and saw that someone had put a couple of stamps on the front cover and cut my address out from the first page and pasted it in the upper right corner so the mail-lady knew where it should be delivered. At that moment, staring down at my journal, I felt shittier than when I had lost it. I started crying and my dad left the room because he didn't want to get involved in whatever was happening with his insane daughter. I looked at the postmark on the cover of the notebook and it was hard to make out because it was smudged from the glossy finish, but it appeared that the person who found it put the notebook in the mail about six days after I lost it. I can only assume that during the time they had the notebook, they read what I wrote. I romanticized the thought that my notebook was filled with priceless prose, but come to find out, it wasn't even worth keeping. My thoughts were so inconsequential that the mystery reader actually shelled out two dollars and change to get rid of the seventy sheets of drivel."

"They were probably just being considerate. You know, a good Samaritan," I say. I can't imagine returning a journal to Lindsey. If I found Lindsey's handwritten journal, I would buy one of those cases they keep the constitution in, and I would treat the journal like it was a son, like it was a daughter, no, I would treat it even better because this would be something that could never disappoint me.

"You don't get it," Lindsey says, with mild frustration, "Like... have you ever found a book in the park or on a bench or sitting out on the curb in a cardboard box with someone's trash?" she asks, all in one breath.

"Yeah."

"Did you take it?"

"Well, I picked it up and started reading-"

"-so you read some of it."

"Yeah."

"Did you send it back?"

"Well, no."

"Did you keep it?"

I nod my head to confirm I did, then point to my bookshelf.

"See."

"It's different. A book is different from a journal."

"It's the same thing. You didn't send the book back because you liked it. In fact, I bet you liked it more than the books you had on your shelf because you found it, instead of buying it online. It had someone's name in it, didn't it? You liked owning this piece of someone else. You loved that the bookmark in the book was a postcard from the real owner's old friend, or lover, or child. It had an inscription in it. Someone received the book as a present and now it was yours. It was like getting a present from a stranger."

I want to tell Lindsey how I discovered her words, and they changed my life, but before I can, she says, "I was obsessed over this whole ego crushing incident, so about two months after I got my journal back, I purposely left my Poli-Sci notebook in the same place, on the same wire table in the park. The notebook was filled with class notes except the last ten pages, where I copied a short story I wrote when I was, like, 16. I went to the park, and sat at the same table, and wasted a half hour doodling in the notebook until the exact time in the afternoon when I chased after Kerry. I left the notebook there, just like the last one, address on the first page."

"Did someone take it?"

"Yeah."

"Did they send it back?" I ask, with massive reluctance.

"I checked my mail every day. No notebook. Kurt, they kept it. Sixty pages of Poli-Sci notes and a shitty story about sitting at a bus stop was judged in the court of public opinion as superior to my darkest secrets."

I listen to all of this, trying to formulate a comment that will stop her before she mentions how she started the website. I want to yell at her that the notebook had to be returned because it forced her to find something more permanent, to create something that everyone could keep. I want to scream at her that I'm glad someone sent that notebook back because without her journal we could have drifted in a tight radius around campus, never crossing each other's paths. It scares me to think of this alternate reality where Lindsey and I are two planets never summoned by the universe to collide.

~

My eyes flutter open as Lindsey pulls my arm, physically demanding that I get out of bed. She's fully dressed, her hair is straightened to a shine, and her makeup is done.

"Come onnnn, lazy," Lindsey moans, as she drags my body toward the edge of the bed.

"Alright, alright," I say, slowly leaving the covers and comfort of bed. Lindsey needing me this severely feels good.

I fix my hair, throw on a coat, then we leave the apartment. The entire walk, Lindsey is smiling her wide smile, satisfied with whatever she's planned. The sensitive and concerned girl from yesterday is replaced by a determined beauty who shines brighter than the pure white snow around us.

We make our way into town, shivering in the cold/ We pass Starbucks and Lindsey wrangles me in when I try to detour our trip/ We pass a black guy in a black winter coat and Lindsey squeezes my hand for the rest of the block/ We pass a bus that's stopped at a red light, then Lindsey starts running. Our hands are locked together so I'm dragged along, a couple steps behind, unable to let go, like an owner being pulled on the leash by his puppy.

Lindsey is dashing down the street, while I'm stumbling across sidewalk slabs behind her. We run, and we run, and we run, and we stop.

"What the fuck was-"

"-here," Lindsey interrupts me mid-sentence, giving me a dollar from her pocket, then keeping a dollar for herself.

Lindsey turns around and faces an elderly couple sitting in the enclosed bus stop.

She gives the elderly woman her dollar, and says, "It's all I can spare. I'm sorry," then she crouches down and hugs the sitting woman. I look at the woman's husband and give him the dollar, "I wish I had more to offer. I hope this helps," I say. The man responds in German and when I hold out a hand, he doesn't shake it.

As we walk away from the couple, I ask, "It's the 13th isn't it?"

"Happy Dollar Day!" Lindsey celebrates, then kisses me on the cheek.

This holiday arrives at the perfect time. I was getting worried about Lindsey. I thought she was becoming depressed... more depressed. Now, she's all made up, smiling, running, approaching strangers- all of this outside of the apartment.

While this by no means should be seen as Lindsey being happy about life, it *was* proof she's happy with ~us~.

The cold carries us back to the apartment complex, and as the guard buzzes us inside the courtyard, Lindsey's phone starts ringing.

I lag back a step behind her in the courtyard, so she can take the call, but she doesn't acknowledge the ringing in any way.

Before we walk into the building, I ask, "Aren't you going to get that?"

"No, it's day-drunk Belle, calling to gossip about people we went to high school with. I can't be moved to care about those people anymore. The whole scene is just so... lame."

I need Lindsey to start answering calls like this because when I get my mother's money, overzealous and gossipy calls from interesting people will start pouring in. The money will change the places I take Lindsey, and it will change the people we hang out with. All of our friends will be as equally hip as we are, and even if sometimes they're annoying, we'll still keep them around so we don't become the focus of the negative gossip. We'll walk into a party and Greg will come up and kiss both of us on the cheek and we'll be okay with that because we know that's one of Greg's things- it's been mentioned in articles in some of the magazines on the coffee table. Greg is always wearing jeans, but pristine jeans, because Greg's great-grandfather invented denim. I'll slide by Betty, whose great-grandfather invented Press on Nails, and Betty will be making sure she doesn't scratch Donald, whose great-grandfather invented AIDS. I'll make my way to Ronnie, a man who inherited his money from a father like mine, and we'll hug, then we'll converse about how great our lives are: mine- with all the money from my tragic genius father, and his- with all the money from his ancestors thousands of years ago discovering fire.

"Belle seems nice," I state, making sure Lindsey doesn't alienate herself further. I don't want her life with me to ever make her feel like my mother did with my father.

Lindsey counters by validating her isolation, "It's dollar day, not dollar draft day. I don't want to celebrate with Belle."

"Don't ignore her call," I say.

Lindsey groans at me.

Another ring.

Again, Belle's call goes unanswered.

Another person writing letters to Edie.

I take comfort in the solid fact that I'm the only call in the world Lindsey wouldn't ignore. This knowledge will soothe me when I'm at my most distant, and comfort me when I'm alone, hurting the hardest.

We walk inside, having been gone for less than an hour, and as we wait for the elevator, Lindsey quietly says, "You know, I almost called you twenty-six days ago." This is told to me as an admission, not an off-hand comment.

"Why didn't you?" I ask, feeling a dormant concern flare up again. I want to walk her back out to the winter sunlight. There are shadows inside the building.

"Well, uh," she says, staring at the piece of wall between the two elevator bays. "I was driving to get my oil changed, and you know that curvy part of the road that climbs the hill outside of town? I was driving there, and it was snowing these huge wet flakes, and a driver on the other side of the road, when he was about fifty yards from me, he suddenly slammed on his brakes, and it looked like something broke and flew out of the front of his car, but it was, uh, actually, a deer getting launched forward from the impact of getting hit mid-stride. I stopped when it happened, then... I watched to see if he was okay... if the deer was okay..."

I turn to Lindsey giving her my full attention, no longer caring about the numbers that tick away on the digital display. I listen as she describes this scene in a groggy way, "I stayed in my car, but the man- he didn't stay in his. And, uh, when he tried to get out of his car, at first he couldn't open his door, because of the impact, ya know, it crumpled the frame a bit. I was going to go help him, but he eventually forced the door open, and walked out into the road. It kept snowing, and through the flurries, I watched as he grabbed the deer by its left front and back legs. The deer... it was making these noises."

The elevator door opens.

"The noise the deer made sounded like... a creaking door. A creaking door that, no matter how long it creaked, it never opened all the way. The door was perpetually being cracked open, wider. Not for an entrance, but for an exit."

The elevator door closes.

Lindsey's eyes glaze over as she continues, "The man dragged the injured deer to the side of the road. Then... uh, then... he walked back over and kicked a piece of his headlight at the deer. When the light hit the deer, she made that creaky noise, but louder. Then the man squatted down, so that I couldn't see him, but when he stood back up, he was focused on the injured deer. Without even looking around to see if anyone was watching he stalked forward, with a piece of glass in his hand, then stood behind the deer and ran... the glass... across the deer's throat. It was..." Lindsey trails off, huffs, then continues, "Then, uh, the guy walked back to his crumpled car, and he stood there, and watched the deer bleed out. I would catch glimpses of this scene when there was a gap in traffic. Kurt, it wasn't a mercy kill- the deer continued to cry after he did it. And I continued to watch. The police came. A tow truck came. The deer died. It bled out onto the road. I tried to continue with my day, but the whole time I was getting my oil changed, I wondered what would happen to the deer. I wondered if there's someone that takes care of the bodies of the animals that get hit on the side of the road. They don't have owners to take them to the vet or a woodland health insurance plan, so I just kept thinking over and over, what was going to happen to her? When I was driving back from the shop, it was dark, but I could see that she was still there on the side of the road. I didn't stop, but anytime I got in my car, alone, I would always go back, and she was there the next day, and the next day, and the next day, and after about a week I could see other people hit her. After about two weeks, she got covered in snow. When it melted away, I noticed she was beginning to get skinnier and flatter. After about three weeks, she had this weird gray dust all over her, and yesterday, I drove by, and she was gone. The deer had disappeared and I wasn't sure what happened to her, but I can't imagine someone picked her up to bury her. Maybe it was another animal or maybe the highway department came after someone complained about the smell- I'm not exactly sure who or what took her, but I know that it took twenty six days for anyone to give a shit, no matter what their intentions were. Everyone kept driving by, just like I did. So... So... So! I want to know... I want... to... know..."

I lift my hand and touch Lindsey's face, and ask, "What do you want to know?"

"Whose job is it to clean something like that up?" Lindsey asks, and I can't answer her question.

~

My mother bought me a dog named Trixie after my father died. It was an oldish looking poodle dog.

I resented that dog. I was sure what its purpose was. It was a reminder of so much. When I was a little kid, I wanted a dog, but my father was allergic to pets with fur. After he passed, my mother brought Trixie home to take my father's place. At first, this substitution seemed pretty even. I was troubled that the relationship I had with my father was perfectly mirrored whenever I talked to this animal that didn't understand what I was saying, and merely reacted based on the tone of my voice. I didn't want to think about my father congratulating me for a report card merely because I came in with a smile on my face and joy in my voice; I didn't want to acknowledge that every interaction with him was based off a social cue.

I tolerated Trixie because I also looked at her arrival as my mother saying, "Now that he can't stop us, let the fun begin, let's do all the things we never could while he was alive."

My mother couldn't verbalize this at risk of sounding insensitive and Trixie couldn't say it because she was just a dumb dog, but together Trixie and my mother could send the message.

One day, my mother and I were taking Trixie for a walk, and when we were about fifty yards away from the door to our building, my mother looked down at the pup, and said, "It doesn't do very much, does it?"

Trixie sat on the sidewalk and watched the cars in the road whizzing by.

I was surprised how I felt nothing for the dog.

Without asking my mother, I bent down and unattached Trixie's leash, then removed her collar. The dog didn't immediately dash away- she kept dully glancing between me and the lot across the road. Finally, when the traffic cleared, without another look at us, Trixie took off across the street. We watched her dart through the abandoned lot- every now and then our view was obstructed by a passing car. We both stood there, wondering if, when the dog got tired, when she got hungry, she would run back to us. Trixie kept running, and eventually she disappeared from sight. She was off to her new home, or maybe her old home, wherever my mother got her from. I imagine Trixie died like Lindsey's deer did, but at least they both ended up meaning something to someone before they ate shit and kicked the bucket. That's more than a lot of dead bodies on the road can claim.

~

I'm staring at a jock-looking kid with a short mohawk that doesn't say *punk rock*, but it does say, *I often wrestle my friends and all the furniture in my dorm is broken.* The mohawked boy has convinced a semi-drunk mailroom student-employee to use her keys to get a package for him, despite the fact it's 11 PM and the mailroom has been closed for a very long time.

The stubby mohawked boy immediately disregards the girl after she performs the favor, and he begins opening the deeply longed-for package on the table to my right. After removing the brown packing paper, he takes out a blue football jersey. He holds it up, and on the back, in all capital letters, is the name, "ERLING."

I don't know who the stubby mohawked jock is, but I'm certain that he's not Barry Erling or Tyrone Erling or Mike Erling- he's probably Mike Nelson. Pathetic Mike Nelson has to wear an article of clothing with someone else's last name on the back of it to craft an identity.

What a depressing secondhand Christmas this has turned out to be.

"Look at this! You went from off your ass wasted last night, to sitting in the café reading a book tonight," a girl says to me. I look up. It's just Laura Mellin.

"Yeah, I guess I'm not in the mood for excitement tonight," I say, a little confused.

"The mood? Okay," Laura says, then shrugs.

I feel like she wants to continue the conversation, so I ask, "And what are you doing tonight?"

"Um, like, I have a stomach ulcer..."

"I recall."

"Oh, right, we went over this. Well, since I have the ulcer, I'm gonna go to my friend Brad's apartment and smoke a couple bowls. It makes me feel better- the smoking. I'm being honest, I'm not just doing it to be a stoner."

I shake my head in an up and downwardly manner, while she continues, "Then, I'm going to this magazine launch. Something that has to do with men's health or technology. It's like, good going guys, finally tackling the under-analyzed and super interesting world of gadgets that give you testicular cancer. I mean, why the fuck would anyone make a magazine about technology? That's like writing a book about the best way to burn a book. I don't know if people even read magazines anymore."

"I guess they must if they're still launching them," I say, considering bringing up Akkuta Afar.

"A magazine doesn't need readers to launch. Honestly, it's just a way for a group of guys and one lesbian to get girls to think they have a cool job. By the time they have to actually make the magazine, the one night stand will be over."

Another lull in the conversation.

"So, you really think they'll give me methadone?" Laura asks, hugging herself, even though it's not cold in the café.

"Maybe. Kurt Cobain had an ul-"

"-that's great, your medical advice is coming from a man who blew his face off to alleviate the pain."

"I don't think the shotgun blast to the face was a side effect of his stomach ulcer treatment."

"Not directly," Laura says.

I nod at this, then explain, "What I read was, he had a stomach problem and I guess they gave him methadone in some sort of pill. He blamed getting hooked on heroin because of it."

"That's not good," Laura says, bored.

I shake my head in a somewhat no-ish manner.

"I need to go meet my friend," Laura says.

"Bye."

"Bye."

As I'm left with my own thoughts, I begin to analyze them. I decide that I can't be right. They can't give you methadone for a stomach ache. It doesn't make sense. It feels like an excuse.

Everyone has lied to me, even my dead heroes.

~

The sunlight squeezes through the gaps in the blinds and sits on the living room floor. Lindsey is quickly filling her messenger bag with a stack of textbooks that previously sat untouched. When her bag is half full, she stops rushing, then looks at the ceiling where a small piece of paint just fell from above like it's starting to snow inside.

"What do you have today?" I ask, and Lindsey's shoulders jump when I pose this question, as if she didn't know she was being watched.

"Shakespeare class," she says in a tiny voice. This is the first time I've been given any insight into her spring semester schedule. I wonder if a list of each class she's taking is posted on the wall in her dorm next to the holiday calendars. I don't know if this is the reality because all I remember are the Polaroids and it's been so long since I've entered her dorm. I'm still infinitely curious about Lindsey, but I don't go through her things. The space I give Lindsey is bizarre because I'm obsessed with her, yet don't invade her privacy, while I had minimal curiosity about Joan, and I was always breaking into her dorm and messing with her possessions.

Since Lindsey is going to class, I decide I'll go too. Sadly, I have to go to a different class than Lindsey does. I still hold out hope that I'm forgetting that today is one of those special holidays in March where Lindsey will surprise me by celebrating a day called, "Drop/Add Day" or "Aggressively Audit Classes Day." I want a holiday where Lindsey walks into my classroom, and forces the Indian boy next to me to change seats. All of these unexpected, unexplained trips she's been taking me on have a once reclusive man hungry for the world, but only when I'm by her side. I'm the lucky one who gets a director's cut of life through the camera of Lindsey's eyes. With this perspective, everything is playing out on a TV screen that hasn't been correctly desaturated, and I begin to look at my first class as the set of my late night talk show.

By the time I make it to my desk, it's clear the professor is going to be late, so I assemble my props. I have my well-sharpened pencil that I'm flicking back and forth/ I have my notebook where I can write up some cards that contain speaking points/ I have my audience, seated and ready.

I sip from my coffee cup, then flip my pencil, catching it by the sharp tip.

After a quick survey of my peers, I decide that Cash Anderson, who sits in the smaller U in front of me, is my bandleader. He has a cool bandleaderesque name. His band could be called Cash Anderson and The Moneymakers.

To start the banter portion of this midday talk show, I break the silence by asking, "Cash, you ever been to the Poconos?"

Completely unaware of what's going on, Cash turns toward me, then asks "Um, what? No. Is that near Key West?"

I'm immediately energized, and my smile tells him, *Perfect Cash! This is going along swimmingly. This type of banter is what talk shows are made of.*

"How about Christmas, Cash? Did you go home for Christmas?" I ask, and since the professor isn't here, people start paying attention to me, looking up from their laptops.

Cash seems confused, like he's wondering what he did to subject himself to this line of questioning. "I'm a commuter, I live at home," he tells me.

"Good, good. You strike me as a family man, Cash. Is your lady friend going to be joining you for your next family dinner?"

"I-uh, I-uh, don't-" Cash stammers out.

I point with my pencil to Juliette Harris, a bottle blonde who's sitting next to Cash.

"She's not my girlfriend, I don't even know who she is," Cash says.

Juliette looks discouraged by Cash's statement.

"What better time to get to know each other than at family dinner, am I right? Don't you all think that he should invite Juliette to family dinner?" I prod the class.

A few kids provide the most confused sounding smattering of applause that I've ever experienced.

"So, what do you say, Juliette?" I ask.

She looks at me, then looks away, then looks at me, then looks away, mumbling "I'm, um, a vegan." Her voice doesn't sound like a vegan's because she meekly said this, instead of proclaiming it at the top of her lungs, with rich pride, as a challenge to everyone around her.

"Don't tell me. Tell Cash," I say, pointing my pencil to the confused young man next to her.

When the professor walks in the classroom, I mentally cut to commercial, knowing that the viewers will be left in suspense regarding the story of Cash and Juliette.

When I get my money, I can get my own online talk show.

I need to practice before this happens so that when I get the funds transferred, I can start immediately. Possibly Cash can come along for the ride. I'll tell him to leave his schedule open as he may have to quit school at any time. I mean, Cash's parents probably expect him to do that anyway. I'll have to find out if he can play an instrument or at least lead a band. When I get my online talk show, I'll invite a bunch of cool famous people and they'll come on because they'll know that I am rich and therefore they won't feel like they're doing an interview with a younger version of Kurt Loder. They'll be doing an interview with a young Kurt Jones, someone who matters. It will be simple getting everything together because I won't have another job, so my day will consist of fielding calls from the connections I make by going to parties.

Interrupting this fantasy, the professor picks up immediately where she left off last class- I assume, but can't be sure because people no longer send me the notes. My girlfriend died *last semester*. People have moved on; other guy's girlfriends have died more recently. My current girlfriend is alive.

I try to take notes, essentially starting a book in the middle, aware that I will never search for the beginning.

The next class I suffer through is nowhere near as entertaining as the last. We go over Excel spreadsheets full of statistics because that's the name of the class. There are no potential bandleaders in this Statistics class, and my coffee cup is empty. I start looking through the syllabus I got in the beginning of the semester and realize that there's no final project for this Statistics class and immediately I want to drop it because all I do, all day long, is collect information, then desperately try to sift through it for meaning.

~

I walk out onto the Green and look around at all the faces I don't recognize. I wonder where Gerard is, and I wonder where Noni is, and I consider that maybe the brochure wasn't a lie and there really are five thousand undergrads here.

I need Lindsey.

I don't know where she is or what she's doing, but I feel I need to talk to her. I call her cell, but it's off, so I get her voicemail, "You probably have the wrong number, but leave one anyway." I don't leave a message.

Cold and confused, I start following a girl who's wearing a hat that looks like a muffin and I eavesdrop on her cell phone call. She says, "Don't worry about her, she wouldn't hurt a fly- well unless the fly fucked her boyfriend... so yeah, actually, maybe you should worry." Her voice sounds like the way a CGI muffin in a Pixar movie about the virtues of accepting every body type would sound. The girl quickly turns around, and I slide past her and find myself behind a guy with a beard so bushy I can see it even when his back is to me. He turns to his friend, and says, "I can only imagine she's behind a Sunoco, huffing gasoline out of a paper bag because her life can't get any shittier," then he lets out these little stutter spurts of annoying laughter. Suddenly the guy looks back at me, and I realize that he's holding the café door for me, and I thank him, then walk inside the little glassed-in area where the ATM machine is. I smoke a cigarette in this little room, and watch kids take out money from the fee-free ATM that Bank of America provides to the campus so we'll be conditioned to go to Bank of America for the rest of our lives when we want to get drunk or high and are out of cash.

When there's no one at the ATM, I walk up to it, then take out my card. The machine accepts the card, then the Bank of America logo moves around the screen in a pattern that was likely constructed to hack my subconscious, further brainwashing me. Once the options come up, I click "Check Balance" and when I see that the amount is mostly the same as the last time I checked it, I know that my mother is still alive, and I feel relief when the machine tells me how poor I am.

~

I walk inside the apartment and check the light switch to be sure the little letters read "ON," then I move toward the TV, because it's the only light source in an otherwise dark space. In the glow, I see Lindsey's messenger bag sitting on the futon, so I look around for her, thinking that maybe she's concealed by the dark. I take out my phone and use the light to make sure she isn't hiding. I don't know why I remain silent, but something stops me from interrupting the calm with my neurosis.

As I make my way down the hall, I see a line of light silhouetting the bathroom door. I walk toward the light, pleased with the way it slices the dark, then meets at perfect ninety degree angles in all four corners. I put my ear up to the door, as close as I can be, and I listen. I hear a rustling- no, maybe those are breaths? Is she crying? No. Maybe. She's probably just putting on makeup and getting angry at herself every time she widens what's supposed to look like an effortless swift swoop. I tell myself, *These are the sounds of a frustrated girl, not a sad girl.* I'm not panicked by a frustrated girl- I can lend a hand and ease the frustration, but with a sad girl- all I can do is blindly search for some light.

I move away from the door, snatching up my backpack. I take out my laptop, and it seems to take forever to boot, but as soon as it does, I type in 4353638332936382.com, then face a familiar page. No new entries. Maybe she created a new website because she realized I had been watching the old one? Maybe the universe prompted her to make this page so that she could find me, and once we were united, the site had served its purpose? Now, she writes her posts in the stories she tells me, in the jokes she tells me, in the secrets she tells me.

I start to hear the noises again, and I know that for them to reach across the apartment, they must be getting more intense.

Uncontrollably, I begin doubting everything. I don't doubt that Lindsey remains committed to our connection, but I do doubt that it's an infinite bond, written in the stars, tattooed in the ether, unbreakable, forever.

I don't intrude on Lindsey's moment. I wait for her, filling the time by using my open laptop for light and sketching the closed door in my notebook. When I finish the basic drawing, I start on the shading. When I finish the shading, I start adding the grain of the wood trim.

Finally, the door opens, and Lindsey comes out. She's backlit so I can't see her face.

"Hi," I say.

"Hi," she responds.

I don't get up; she sits down next to me.

With the light pouring out from the bathroom, I can see that she's looking at me through eyes so puffy they can barely open, and she tells me, "I feel this weight today."

"What's the matter?" I ask, quietly.

"I'm... sick? There's this... siege in me. Remember the deer I told you about? Whatever she felt the moment that her peripheral vision caught sight of the car as it barreled toward her, that's what I feel like all the time. It's like I'm a moment away from impact, perpetually."

Time freezes and I have to fight the urge to reenact Lindsey's sniffling in the bathroom. I feel like the man behind the wheel. His post-crash actions don't make sense to me, but his guilt pulses in the vein that runs down the left side of my forehead.

Most of the time, soulmates remain apart. The universe made them so perfect for each other that matter would implode on itself if they stayed together. It seems that soulmates are always Romeo and Juliet. Are Lindsey and I being crushed by some strange force destined to draw us apart? Is this our polarized blood separating our bodies?

~

Lindsey shivers in front of the science building. The furry hood of her green jacket is pulled up, and it's peppered with thick snowflakes, making her look like a child. She's staring at her phone, and one of her gloves is off so she can type. I sneak up on her, but I don't quickly grab her, because it will be a prophecy fulfilled- a fragile creature inundated by adrenaline the moment before an inevitable jarring impact.

"Beautiful day, isn't it?" I ask, as I hold my arms out and the snow flutters down onto my jacket sleeves.

Lindsey looks up at me, hides a smile, then looks back down at her phone.

"Let's go somewhere warm," I suggest.

"Like the dorm where all the Indian kids live?" she asks, confused.

Making it up as I go along, I say, "No. Like... a vacation." I want her to be able to escape the pressures of her sophomore year.

Lindsey shakes her furry hood in disagreement.

"No?" I ask, crouching so I can make eye contact with her.

"No vacations," Lindsey says.

"I'll pay. We can leave Kirtland and we can go on vacation wherever you want," I promise, as I try to build a future.

Lindsey bobs up and down like a buoy in the water to warm herself up. Eventually, she puts her phone in her pocket, wipes her nose, then stops bobbing, and says, "When I was in high school I went on a vacation overseas and I vowed to never go again."

"Well, where did you go?" I ask.

"Italy, France, Spain. It was horrible. Want to know what I remember? France- my mom's purse was stolen. Italy- my dad got drunk at dinner and couldn't remember where the hotel was, so we followed him around and when my mom tried to correct my dad, he flipped out so we all just silently walked around Italy for hours. Spain- some five foot three Spaniard came up to me and acted out what he'd like to do to me by using a salt and pepper shaker- I assume he was the pepper shaker. Moral of the story, my mom got her purse stolen, my dad got drunk, creepy Spanish guys were always trying to flirt with me and that was our trip. Still want to hop a flight with me?"

She's right, vacations aren't about seeing paintings, or old churches, or walking at half pace on some guided tour- all those things are *excuses* to go on vacation. It's socially awkward to say you're taking time off but not going anywhere, so you need to come up with reasons why you can't show up at work.

Lindsey immediately reads my mind, and says, "The worst part is you need an excuse to leave. When you take a break from whatever you do and go on vacation, you'll be asked by everyone, 'Where are you going?' and you'll say some far away location like Paris, then the next logical question is, 'Ohh! What are you going to do there?' and you can't say, 'I'll relax, because I'm finally away from all you fucking morons,' so you have to create something of significance to do. You have to make up something like, 'I'm going to see the Eiffel Tower.' Which means, once you actually get to Paris, and you're looking for a place to have a drink, if you accidentally stumble upon the Eiffel Tower, you feel some sort of obligation to go up in the thing just so when you get back you can tell a location specific story. People will want to know details so they can verify that you actually went to Paris and didn't just say you were going to Paris when in actuality you just sat on your couch and googled what the stars of various 90's sitcoms look like now. Vacations have never been about sightseeing, they've always been about forgetting who you are for a week."

Maybe Lindsey is my vacation. The only time I would ever leave the country is to follow her.

"I guess I just want you to know that if you feel like things are getting to be too much here, we can find somewhere to level out," I tell Lindsey, staring her directly in the eyes. She blinks quickly, her eyelids brushing her bangs, then the moment is interrupted by Lindsey's coat vibrating.

"How has she already started drinking?" Lindsey asks, pulling her phone out of her pocket.

"Don't send it to voicemail," I say, and Lindsey sighs, then bites the finger of one of her gloves, pulling it off so that she can accept the call and put it on speaker.

The moment the call is answered, Belle's distinct voice sings, "You can't hide from meee."

"Stop stalking me, you creeper," Lindsey jokes.

"I have to stalk you because you've been hiding," Belle continues her sing-songy delivery.

"I've been busy."

"Lies," Belle declares, then says, "But you'll be real life busy this Friday, with me."

Lindsey looks up in the sky, then tries to think of a response, "Friday... is the day... I am..."

"Excellent, you're coming to my house," Belle says, clearly pleased that Lindsey's excuse factory seems to be on lunch break. "A lot of people we graduated with are coming over for another show, and we can talk shit about them, and laugh, and it will be like we're back in school, and you're coming. No excuses," Belle says quickly, verbally pinning down Lindsey.

"Okay, Friday," Lindsey says, and the fact that she agrees to this social event fills me with hope.

"Friday," Belle again repeats the day, well aware of Lindsey's uncanny ability to get out of plans. "It'll be fun, I'll have tons of mixers there so you can drink those, and my parents will be out of town and they always leave me with that emergency money so we can get beef and broc for delivery. If they complain that I spent all the cash, I'll just say that you went into a seizure because your MSG levels were low."

Lindsey giggles at this, and I want to grab her phone and thank Belle for putting a band-aid on a moment and giving Lindsey a tiny vacation.

~

I walk into Corporate Management, and for the first time I realize that this professor in front of me is a totally different person than the Business Management professor I had last semester. If Kirtland is going to have a nearly identical class, with a nearly identical professor teaching it, it seems like bad business to keep two men on the payroll. At least with only one old guy professor teaching both courses there would be some consistency. For a concept like management, there are a million different strategies to be implemented, and each of them contradicts the next. Some old white CEO retires amid a corporate greed scandal, receives a golden parachute, divorces his wife, loses half the cash, makes some bad investments, then, with all his free time, writes a book about his management style, and hundreds of thousands of young professionals with no soul read the book, then reference it during various dinners that are paid for on corporate cards. There's always a different tactic for managerial success- money incentives, or promotional opportunities, or hookers- everyone has a theory and unless you have one person teaching these management classes, no one is going to manage better than a 3.0 if we have to play Russian roulette with empty rhetoric topics.

The ambiguous professor talks the entire period about his various conquests and the entire class is dotted with eyes that wander or flutter to stay open. The professor bangs his fist on his desk for emphasis and half of the slouching heads pop up. As I scan the class, I notice that one student is paying genuine attention. Press Parker sits across from me in the outer U- his eye contact with the professor is intense, his posture is rigid. He's soaking up every morsel of bullshit the old man can crank out. That poor bastard Press isn't even a store manager at Michael Lorrie. He's probably had wet dreams about signing up for this class, then taking over the reins at the inconsequential, perennially empty store that his life revolves around. I bet if Press Parker had a choice between a million dollars, tax-free, or being the manager at Michael Lorrie, he would push through the stack of money to get to that managerial position. This is probably one of the few reasons that I envy Press Parker- he's driven toward an achievable goal and no one has to get die for him to get what he wants.

~

Lindsey is sitting on the living room floor reading Akkuta Afar's *GQ* when I get home.

"Learning how to be a gentleman?" I ask, setting my backpack down.

"I'm attempting to get joy from the bad so I'll start to only see good," she tells me, then points down at the article she's reading about a male socialite who proclaims, in a pull quote, "Everyone writes about me, but I don't mind, I'm a writer too."

Confronting the complicated and ugly has somehow evolved into Lindsey's coping mechanism, or, at its most basic, a distraction she can use to pause her tumbling mind.

"Do you hate that guy?" I ask.

"No," she instantly responds.

"Do you like him?" I ask.

"No," she instantly responds.

"Do you want me to leave you alone?" I ask.

"No," Lindsey responds, then stands up, and starts getting ready to go outside.

I keep my jacket and gloves on.

The next thing I know, we're in the courtyard, walking single file, because the snow from last night hasn't been shoveled.

My focus becomes not a destination, but *statistics*. If I was to make a spreadsheet, it would have the title, "What Does Lindsey Hate, And Why?" I need to study these things so I can loosen her binds, ease her discomfort, help her cope with the fear of the ever looming impact.

Making our way down the street, I begin the list, asking, "Do you like this town?"

"No. There's nowhere in walking distance to Exist. Every slice of this place is spoken for."

As we walk by the pharmacy, I ask, "Do you like working here?"

"No. The people who come in are always broken in some way. It's so sad."

Swinging all the way to the other side- thinking about Paz working at the vet- I ask, "Do you like Vicodin?"

She stops walking, looks in the picture window, a window she set up, then she says, "I hate Vicodin. It makes me puke."

We keep walking, past the dry cleaner, and I ask, "Fresh out of the dryer clothes?"

She stops and stares into the dry cleaner's window, at an old Korean man behind the counter, then says, "I hate doing laundry, and fresh out of the dryer clothes are a feeling I can only experience after I've forced myself to do something I hate. Plus, there's the subsequent work of sitting and folding for a half hour."

We keep walking. Lindsey reaches into her pocket and takes out some change. She gives me two dimes and four quarters. As we feed nearly expired meters, I ask, "Gumballs?"

Lindsey walks over to an expired meter with a Beemer parked in the corresponding spot, stops, looks at the car, passes the meter, then puts a quarter in a meter in front of an old VW Golf, and says, "I hate gumballs. The flavor is sucked out within the first minute."

Lindsey walks along a crack in the sidewalk, while I pause and light a cigarette. Once I start following her again, I ask, "Donuts?"

"Hate. I don't want to have to buy new jeans."

Our faces are red from the cold, and all I want is to go to campus, or to my apartment, and get in bed. I want to slide under a blanket, and I want to press my cold hands on Lindsey's warm body. I want her to laugh out demands for me to stop, while she play-fights me. I want to warm up fast.

We quickly reverse our walk, retracing our steps at twice the speed.

As we watch fat children run eagerly to a sub shop, I ask, "The fair?"

"Hate. Clowns."

"Soda," I say, realizing I've never seen her drink it, even at Rubie's.

"I like 7-11 slurpees better," Lindsey says.

"Ha. You love slurpees," I say, finally finding data for the "love" column.

"No, I said I like them better. Preference doesn't equate to love. I'd like getting eaten by a lion better than getting eaten by a shark, but would I *love* getting eaten by a lion? Maybe if during the foreplay, he let me pet his mane, but after that, nope, nope, nope."

Walking up to the campus gate, I ask the only question I *need* to know the answer to, "Me?"

"Asks too many questions," Lindsey says, then laughs and reaches for me.

The way I see it, she can hate Vicodin and fresh out of the dryer clothes, and gumballs, and donuts, and the fair, and she can even hate Diet Coke, as long as she always answers that last question in the same nonchalant yet playful way. Now, with that answer, she turns back into the Lindsey that corrected me when I was crashing.

I burn with warmth because there's a distinction between myself and everything else. Gumballs lose their flavor. I remain -with Lindsey by my side.

~

Lindsey is on the floor, and her furry collared coat is balled up under her head as she reads a big textbook by the light of the TV.

"Everyone dies at the end," I say.

Lindsey's eyes glance up at me, then she sighs, "These Advanced Child Development books always end the same."

The delivery of the line makes me laugh the type of laugh that springs from my core. To regain control, I put my bag down, then turn to see if the light switch is ON- it is. I reach over and open the fridge door, then I take out the box of wine and pour myself a glass.

As I begin to finally relax, I look at Lindsey and she's sitting in a ball on the futon, crying, her moods sloshing like waves. Moments like this make me question time- How long was I laughing?/ How long did it take me to get this drink?/ How long has Lindsey been holding this breakdown inside her soft frame?

I sit next to her, and she looks at me with her mascara smeared eyes glinting from the light of the TV, and says, "Instead of a vacation, we need something more permanent. Let's find a farmhouse and move away from everyone."

Since I have no idea where this is coming from I say, "We hate farms."

Lindsey remains set on a decision that she seemingly made between my offhand comment about the book, and her collapse on the futon. "Maybe we just hate the smell, ya know? Maybe we're farm people and we just don't realize it yet. I want to go somewhere, a place where we know no one and just forget everything, forget everyone we knew."

"So you're saying you want to move into a retirement home?"

"No, but it would have the same permanency as moving to an old folks home would. We'd stay forever and it would just be me and you in a farmhouse and it would be perfect. We'd... we'd... find your Mom."

"I came here to wait for my mother. I'm not seeking her out," I say, too loud, and I want to stop myself, but the same imbalance Lindsey is filled with, has infected me. "I'm not leaving- I'm not being forcibly moved. I don't think you get it. Lots of things happened- before I got here- lots of things and sometimes I'm okay with them and other times I can't- I can't move past them. But what's important is that there are some places I'll never go back to."

Lindsey wipes her eyes on the sleeve of my white T-shirt, and I look down to see my lily-white shirt is covered in black, smudged tears.

I think about the Love/Hate list we assembled, and I know that it's impossible to hate so much without having a deep-seated knowledge of the world around you and how your decisions can have a ripple-effect. Possibly part of Lindsey's unhappiness is knowing the repercussions of her actions before she takes them.

I wish there was a way to treat depression like there's a way to treat having fucked up teeth. If only someone would create an ugly contraption you could put on your head when you're a kid, then later on in life, you wouldn't have to deal with depression. It would become so common that to not have one on your child's head would seem negligent. Everyone would choose to be miserable as a child in exchange for a future filled with balance. I was unhappy as a kid, then things got progressively worse, until I met Lindsey. Before that miraculous crash, it felt like the braces of my childhood had separated my teeth further instead of fixing them and I was doing everything I could to keep the gaps from widening even further.

~

I'm being held hostage in Corporate Management by our guest speaker, Clarissa McGinty. Clarissa's purpose is to explain the importance of women CEOs. She owns her own flower delivery business. She hasn't mentioned whether her company is publicly traded, which I believe to be a requirement for being a CEO. I've taken this same class so many times and I'm still unclear on the specifics. I suppose it doesn't matter anymore. Anyone can start a company now by merely giving whatever hobby they have a business title.

I watch Clarissa write down statistics on the dry erase board, and I sense this class isn't close to being over. So far, the keenest observation I've made watching Clarissa's presentation is that her roots are coming in and she's really overdue for a touch-up. When a woman's roots come in, she looks infinitely older.

I take a sip of my watery coffee, then my focus returns to the front of the room and see percentages and dollar amounts and multiplication, and *Noni*.

With a mischievous grin, Noni glides into the classroom, then taps Clarissa on the shoulder.

Jolted by the unexpected touch, Clarissa turns to Noni, with a dry erase marker raised like a weapon.

"My friend Kurt is in this class, and he's really sick. I need to give him his shot now, do you mind if he's excused?" Noni asks.

Clarissa is unsympathetic to the whole matter, and she's still focused on her presentation so she looks at Noni, then at me, then says, "Do you know you'll only make a portion of what he makes for the same amount of work?"

"He's not getting a job," Noni says, looking at the lady like she's out of her league trying to incite this gender anger, "So, I guess you're wrong. I could work pretty much anywhere and make more than him. It's like trying to take a percent of zero. You're dealing with the abstract."

Clarissa begins shaking her head in disappointed disbelief, while Noni looks at the class, and announces, "History is made. I did it, ladies. I broke the glass ceiling. I make almost ten dollars an hour and Kurt makes nothing, so technically now there's a ceiling on him. The ceiling is comprised of the garbage that accumulates in his own lazy wake, but it's no longer our job to clean that up, gals!"

Noni controls the class, she demands our attention, she excites our idea that, yes, things can happen. This is a girl who doesn't fucking care, and that alone makes her far more powerful than the CEO with the exposed roots.

Noni is looking at me, wordlessly prodding me to keep the gag going, and this is too good to just throw to a bandleader, so I whine, "It's so unfair. I feel slighted," then I frown.

"Well, if he was getting a job and he got the same job as you, you'd make nine dollars, but he would make eleven dollars," Clarissa says to Noni, swallowing twice during the statement, trying to regain the class.

"That sounds about right. He'd probably be about one to two dollars better at the job than I would be."

Clarissa is frustrated, and I can see that she desperately wants to find comfort in another line graph, so she lets me go.

Noni takes my hand and we walk out of the class as everyone looks at us with one part jealousy because we got out of the lecture, and one part appreciation because Noni managed to stall Clarissa's presentation.

"What inspired you to do that?" I ask Noni, and she walks silently next to me for a full ten count before she says, "I needed to know if I could extricate someone I love from a bad situation, in the most public way possible."

I crack a smile, and tell her, "You were magnificent in there."

"Don't go back," Noni requests of me.

"You have me for the rest of the day," I assure her.

"I don't need you for the rest of the day," she tells me.

As we walk out of Kozinski and down the steps towards the Green, I think about what Clarissa said, and she's right. When I get my mother's inheritance, I'll be making millions, but when Noni's mother dies, she'll be lucky to get a couple thousand dollars- at best she'll get her childhood home.

Clarissa is right, Noni will only receive a fraction of what I will for the same amount of soul-crushing work and it doesn't seem fair.

~

In Business Writing, we watch some movie that everyone's really psyched about, except for one girl. Despite the fact that there's barely enough light to read in the classroom, this contrary girl is studying the textbook the professor forced us to buy. I find this girl far more interesting than the movie we are watching, and I study her like she's an open book.

The anti-movie girl has big glasses- the kind they wore in the 90's when glasses were tools to see better and not a fashion statement. She's wearing a shirt with some Disney character on it that could be perceived as cute and ironic, but is most likely something she's had since her trip to Disney World when she was 14.

I know this girl.

She's one of the students at Kirtland with no financial aid, and a tuition loan.

The Loanees don't look forward to movie days in class. They realize they're paying something like $170 for each hour and fifteen minute session they attend, and they don't want to spend it watching a movie that they could've seen on YouTube, for free.

I feel very bad for this girl and wonder what it's like to have to put yourself through college. I imagine it would remove a lot of the fantastic guilty pleasures that have been available to me while in college- The procrastination I embrace so I can go out drinking/ The procrastination I commit so I can go to some girls room at 2 AM to have sex/ The procrastination I indulge in so I can play Xbox at Revere's for 12 hours straight and not feel guilty.

The Loanees know they need a college education to get a good job, and they also know that once they get that good job, a large chunk of the money they make will go back to paying for their schooling. They know that after graduation they'll have to work two or three days at some depressing job, just to pay for today's movie.

But this is the system. Sorry your dad is a truck driver.

I'm distracted because of the Loanee, but there's also something more that's looming over me, something that I can't put my finger on, until I check my phone and I see that it's Friday.

~

I sit in the tub and watch Lindsey put on cover up, and eyeshadow, and mascara- she even paints her fingernails- a brown color- but because she goes over them twice, they look black.

When Lindsey leaves the bathroom, I get out of the bath, then follow her into our bedroom. I sit on the bed, naked, dripping into the sheets, and watch her go into the closet and try on three different shirts before she decides on one. She picks out a long black flowy skirt to go with a white blouse, and I very matter-of-factly say, "You're getting all dressed up for tonight, huh?" It's a stupid, super obvious observation, but it does the job, and she turns, then stamps her foot and says, "Damn it, Kurt. I'm not looking nice for boys, I'm looking nice for me."

I believe her, but there's also a piece of me that has dissected every moment of the conversation she had with Belle, and I specifically remember the part about everyone from their high school showing up. I think about all those stupid movies and sitcom episodes about high school reunions and how everyone is always trying so damn hard to impress that one person who never showed them any attention in 5th period Bio. I become one of those TV cops when my overprotective Spidey sense goes off. I start collecting evidence any way I can. I interview possible witnesses. I make excuses to gain entry to the suspected crime scene. Anything that will help me put my case together, I'll seek out.

So what happens once I have all the evidence? What happens after I find the smoking gun and my case has been built? What do I gain? I know what I lose.

Lindsey walks over and kisses me, over and over, to let me know there's nothing to worry about. Like a kiss could stop a freight train- I suppose if anyone's kiss could, it would be hers.

I get a kiss, then Lindsey leaves, her nerves and excitement both obvious.

I get dressed, with nowhere to go.

I maintain the position that I need to remain busy.

I sit at my desk and take a bunch of textbooks out of my bag and tell myself that if I do my work, I'll forget she's even gone.

Everything is carefully laid out on the desk, like the textbooks were magazines.

Here I am, hard at work.

Or something like work.

Here I am, hard at work's bastard stepchild.

Here I am, hard at activity.

This plan lasts for only a moment, then I lace up my boots, and walk out of the apartment.

As I stumble through the snow, I sing, "*The words don't translate, you lose your tongue,*" and I think about Lindsey. I feel the worry for her that I have felt for Noni. I take out my phone, but I see that my battery is at 6% and I want to conserve it. Everything feels partial and depleting. I have my cigarettes, but no lighter. I wander onto campus, looking for someone who's smoking, or lighting off firecrackers, or starting a fire on the Green in protest of the poor trash service the dorms have experienced recently.

I see zombies everywhere. I haven't read *Limber* in so long. Maybe this is how it ends. I wonder if I'm a zombie- the boy who shuffles his feet, searching aimlessly for purpose.

I walk to the freshman dorm and sit outside on the steps, waiting for someone to walk by and give me a light. When they do, I take my phone out to find the two best songs I can savor during the length it takes for the cigarette to disappear into my lungs. This is what my 6% will be spent on. Suddenly, I'm rating my music collection. What's going to be the song for tonight?

I settle on two songs from a frail-voiced boy who plays an acoustic guitar during a radio appearance that someone ripped and encoded into MP3's, which I somehow found, or Lindsey somehow found, or Gerard somehow found.

Where's Gerard? Is Noni all alone? Who is ~she~ standing next to at the party right now?

The paranoia is eating my face and my expressions don't do my feelings justice anymore.

~

Lindsey pounces on the bed moments after the light comes on.

"Hi!" she says, looming over me.

"Whyyy is the light on?" I whine.

"I wanted to let you know I'm back," Lindsey says in a little voice.

"A tap on the shoulder would've sufficed."

"No, I want to talk with you. I haven't seen you all night."

I grab her hand and kiss it. I do this so I can smell her fingers. They don't smell like latex, so I glance at my phone, then say, "It's two in the morning, I just want to sleep."

"Kurt! Stay up and talk," she demands.

"It's not that serious, we can talk over coffee tomorrow," I tell her.

She's back from Belle's now and it's pretty apparent that she didn't have sex with anyone tonight, and now I've become impartial to everything. I spent an hour tonight in bed, tossing and turning, worrying about what she was doing, hoping that I would hear the keys rattle in the front door. Now that she's back, I've realized how foolish I was to assume she was with another guy.

There's no cause to fight, and I want to sleep.

"No, it *is* serious. I think it is," Lindsey tells me.

I'm instantly awake. There might be something to fight.

"There is nothing serious to talk about, it's the act of talking that is serious," Lindsey says, lessening the stakes. She climbs onto me, then lies on my chest and in a little girl's voice, she tells me, "When one of us comes home, and jumps on the bed, the other needs to pop up and listen."

"Okay," I tell her, and I can feel her breathing begin to slow as she gets more comfortable. "I'm sorry I didn't pop up and listen," I say, and it's quiet for a long moment, but the moment is calm.

"I just had this vision, of back home," Lindsey says, fighting sleep. She coos, "My parents, when they watch movies, they sit on separate pieces of furniture. My mom sits in a chair and my dad sits on the couch. It's just those two... on two different pieces of furniture. It makes me... so sad. I thought about it and there must have been one day when my mom got off the couch... and went and sat in the chair... then she did it another night and another night... then before she knew it... it was routine. They never lie on the couch together. As disgusting as people find it that their parents are two people that love each other... I've accepted that fact and it depresses me that two people who love each other can reach a point where they don't share the couch."

I'll make sure that I never cause a big enough push that an unspoken, accepted distance becomes the norm between myself and Lindsey.

~

Since my texts have gone unanswered, I call Noni, but I'm immediately sent to her voicemail. "Hey, this is Noni, and I'm weathering a really brutal storm right now so if you have bad news, I'm gonna ask that you write it on a piece of paper and send it to me, so at least I have something to set on fire when I find out what else is collapsing around me."

Beep.

"Hey, Noni, it's Kurt. I'm between classes right now, but I want you to know that during my morning class today, I stared at the door the entire time, waiting to see your face. I want you to show up unexpectedly again. I hope you will."

I end the message, and I begin to wonder why I can call Noni, but I can't call Edie. To avoid fixating on this, I default to searching for Lindsey. I require someone to distract me from me, and when I'm next to Lindsey, her mere presence can ease my neurosis. I can ask myself a question, and immediately feel complete contentment- *How could things be going wrong if ~she~ is still next to you?*

I don't know where Lindsey is or what she's doing, but I feel like I need to talk to her. I try to call her cell, but I get her voicemail immediately. I decide to send her a text so when she does charge her phone, she knows I'm thinking of her.

I don't understand my panic. There are times that I feel extremely lonely, there are other times when I want nothing else but to be left alone. In the interest of my own balance, this is a problem.

As I'm typing out my text to Lindsey, I look across the Green, and see a girl that usually stops me. Today, I'll stop her.

~

I accept an invitation, and I accept a drink. I accept a seat, and I accept her company. I accept another drink, and I accept the calm. I accept the pauses, and I accept the lulls. I accept another drink, and I accept her attempts at humor. I accept her recollection of nights that I wasn't completely present for, then I accept another drink to forget them for a second time. I accept her touch, but I reject her kiss. I accept her pain, and I accept the bill. I accept the blame, and I walk out of the bar accepting that I have nowhere as a destination.

I almost turn around and go back- maybe to apologize, maybe to accept the kiss, but instead, I make my way back to the apartment. No one's in the art gallery, and everyone's in the liquor store, and no one's in the bagel shop, and everyone's in the Starbucks, and no one's in the dry cleaners, and everyone's in the other liquor store. I look in all the windows and see people pointing out what they want on their food through the glass, and I see people mull over which dress they want to buy through the glass, and I see people pick out which type of sprinkles they want on their ice cream through the glass.

I balance on the side of the curb as cars roar past me. A couple of drivers slam on their brakes thinking I might fall into the road, but most just continue on their commute home, not even noticing me. I hop from crack to crack on the curb, but just as I'm about to take off toward another crack I remember that children's rhyme, *Step on a crack and...* I fall forward, without grace, onto my outstretched hands.

~

Lindsey is in the kitchen making a sandwich, and she drops the knife in the sink when she sees me. "What happened?" she asks, and I wonder where this reaction came from, how she knew I was hurt. The answer is obvious when I look down at my white shirt and see two streaking, bloody handprints on either side of my ribs, spreading out toward my back.

"Oh," I hold up both my hands like I'm surrendering and show her the scrapes, "I tripped. It was my fault."

Lindsey pulls me by my wrist to the sink, and she starts running the water. I watch the peanut butter that was on the knife get washed down the drain. I hold my hands out, palms up and she looks carefully at them.

"What's my fortune?" I ask.

"I don't believe in that," Lindsey says, as she takes a washcloth and squirts some hand soap on it. She dabs the cloth on my wounds, and tells me, "It's like, if your future is imprinted on your palm, and you go to the palm reader and you find out that you'll live a long, safe, happy life, then you could just go out and cause chaos. If people find out that their future is gonna be pretty secure, then they'll treat people crummy, and as long as things don't end with a lopped off hand, they can always look at the map in their palm and know they'll be okay." Lindsey runs the washcloth under the water, and the thin blood touches the edge of the knife before disappearing in the drain. "I'm a big believer in free will; otherwise, what's the point?" she tells me, as she dabs my hands with a damp part of the washcloth.

I lean in to kiss her, and she accepts the kiss.

When Lindsey goes back to what she was doing before I arrived, I notice two plates holding half-made sandwiches, sitting on the counter. I was a consideration of hers, even in my absence. In my mind, there are always three plates set on the counter. Recently, a couple more have appeared. Sometimes they're needed. Sometimes they're not. There is always a spare plate. I still set that plate in my mind. I believe that I always will.

Lindsey hands me my plate, then asks for payment with honesty, "Where did you go tonight?"

I walk to the futon, and I don't have an answer because I feel I went nowhere, but if I say nowhere I'll sound suspicious, so I say, "I went looking for cigarettes."

Lindsey sits down next to me, and says, "I found a pack in the black pants you were wearing yesterday."

I know why Lindsey was going through my pockets. She places notes in every pair of my pants that are clean enough to be worn again. I want to stand up and check to see what today's note is, desperate to know if we're missing a holiday, but I don't move. I merely sit and eat my sandwich, and I know that she can smell the alcohol on me.

~

I feel complete again with Lindsey by my side, even if neither one of us is doing well. We are two fractured people that are chipped in the right places so we fit together perfectly when pressure is applied. Every jagged piece of Lindsey fills a gap in me.

Despite this unity, trouble bubbles. Unless we go to Rubie's, Lindsey now only eats one meal a day, usually chips and salsa or whatever takeout is left over in the fridge. I still see her look happy, though. A big smile opens across her face when she tells me about how much weight she's losing. The 15 pounds that Lindsey has lost is now glaringly obvious.

I still feel okay about us because of the conversations we have after we turn the lights off. She'll lie with her head on my chest and tell me, in cooing detail, whatever she's thinking about that particular day. It calms me down because I always think back to the boy in front of the glowing screen, and how much he appreciated every one of her words. When she's finished talking, I'll tell her that I understand, because I always do, and I want to be sure that, night after night, whatever memory she's sorting out, I'm involved in the process, even if it only requires me to listen.

As her head rises and falls with my breaths, she will tell me how she's been working, for years, to repair the damage she's inflicted on herself. She's slowly restoring herself like she's a classic car, and when she's done, she'll finally be *Lindsey*. She believes that if she can become a new, purer Lindsey, then she won't have any ties or obligations to her past selves. At night, we do the heavy lifting to get the old stuff out of the way, so there's room for the *new*.

She seems to remember everything, and maybe, by telling me these things at night, she hopes I will take possession of these fragments. It's possible that when she found my journals, she read some of my letters to Edie- stories of people's pain that I dined on. She may know that these are the scraps left on the table that I feast upon with unrivaled pleasure.

I'm given so much in these quiet times. Stories from when she was lost in a department store when she was eight years old, to washing her hands so much in middle school that they became so chapped that her skin would crack at the knuckle. One night she told me about how she buzzed her hair off when she was 14 and she hated how it looked so much, she bought a wig because she felt that looking like an attention seeker was better than looking like Lindsey with no hair. She didn't want a wig the same color as her own hair because she wanted people to know what she did to herself. She wanted it to be obvious that she had no idea what she was doing.

I don't remember the specific night I was told each respective story, but I vividly remember them all. It's almost like they were downloaded into my mind, or maybe I had created a legend about Lindsey before I even met her and possibly these stories aren't even Lindsey's. Maybe they were written by me, maybe they were mine.

I stare at the ceiling and listen to a new story- a story about when she was 15, a story about when she was ignored, a story about what she did to no longer feel ignored, a story that she wishes everyone would just ignore, but they still won't. It was mentioned at Belle's party, and now it will be even fresher in people's minds. She's worried about the story's freshness yet retells it to me, and I slowly begin to wonder if she places trust in me because I've respected my mother's wishes, despite the hurt it's caused me.

After she finishes letting me know about how she's busy erasing yet another memory from her mind tonight, I say, "This is good, it seems like you're really sorting things out, and soon you'll be *Lindsey*."

I feel her head lift, and she looks into my eyes. Even though it's dark I can tell she's staring directly at me, the back of my brain burning with an intensity that feels white hot.

"What if I'm not getting better?" she asks in a voice so quiet I'm not sure it wasn't sent by vibrating waves of tension.

I can't lie, so I put my right hand on the side of her face, then admit, "I don't know."

~

I stand at the top of the clock tower and no one seems to notice me looking down at them. It's not the end of the semester yet, I'm not an over-pressured Asian commuter, I'm not them, so I mean nothing to these little dots with their tails wagging- an arm elevated as they talk on their phone. It's a sea of people who have been constantly told how intelligent and unique they are by every adult they come in contact with, so those around them only exist to further their lives. It's a sea of people dumb enough to believe what they are told.

I can hear their raised voices, shouting into their cell phones, but they might as well be shouting to the heavens.

A girl wearing a pink hoodie says, "...and then I'm like, 'bullshit,' and you know what he said to me, 'You *are* bullshit.' ...Yeah. Yeah, it's a good line, but it's also a shitty thing to say to someone."

A girl with a blue backpack says, "Josh is the type of person whose wardrobe contains an orange hunting hat, and you're looking at him and you're thinking, 'Is it supposed to be ironic?'"

A punk rock girl yells into her phone, "You're pretty lucky if you think about it, but, you don't, so you continually feel like your life is shit," then she looks up after she says this, and I duck down because, in many ways, I feel like her statement was meant for me.

With my back to the cold wall of the clock tower, I light a cigarette. With every darkening of my lungs, I begin to believe that things are better, or at least are reaching some sort of conclusion.

When the final column of ash falls from my cigarette, I follow it down and lie on the cold floor, wrapping myself tightly in my coat.

I close my eyes, and a dream visits me. I'm standing in a parking lot- the type that department stores always have- and the sun is making my shadow grow next to me. I watch the shadow stretch until it separates from my feet, but before I can step forward to reclaim it, the shadow begins to run across the lot. Suddenly, my perspective changes and I'm eye level with the tire of a Lexus. I feel as though my organs are rotting in my body, but I still get myself back on my feet and start to run. I run so fast I taste blood in the back of my mouth and I just swallow it. I close the gap between myself and my shadow, until we're unified again, then my cell goes off, and suddenly I'm back.

I stand up, then dig my phone out of my pocket and answer the call with a groggy, "Hello?"

"Kurt," the girl on the other end of the line says. This girl's voice sounds like Edie.

I immediately have to sit back down again. I feel my eyes welling with tears. To be sure of my caller's identity, I say her name, and I hear hurt in her voice when she asks, "Could you tell me the airport story?"

I bury my head under my coat, then wipe my eyes on my sleeve, "Yeah, why? Are you alright, is everything okay?" I ask.

"Kurt, coul- could you start saying the story?" Edie begs, her voice trembling, "Please."

"Absolutely," I say, then I begin, "Remember... a couple years ago, I was waiting for you to come back from Florida, at the airport. Your parents asked my grandparents to pick you up, but I said I would instead, because I missed you. I waited in this little seating area because I couldn't go to the gate. At some point, I looked to my right and next to me was a pretty woman with short black hair. I noticed her because she had a distinctive smell. It wasn't a sweat smell, it was different. I'm positive even she could smell it, but she was okay with it, which somehow made me okay with it. Her comfort with the situation was like... the old person smell your grandparents' house has, but it didn't smell like that- it just seemed like that- expected, accepted. There was this little girl who was holding a giraffe stuffed animal by the neck that came up to us and asked the woman with short black hair, 'Is he your husband?' The girl's voice sounded brave. The woman with the short black hair scrunched up her nose, smiled at the little girl, then before she could answer, something possessed me to say, 'Yes, I'm her husband.' So, for a moment, the woman and I were married. The girl looked at the woman with short black hair, and asked her, 'Do you love him?' The woman looked at me, smiled, then said, 'Yes, very much.' The woman's voice sounded like she was telling the truth. It was at this point that the mother realized her daughter had wandered away, and she rushed over and collected the little girl, while offering us an apology we didn't want. There was this moment of silence between the woman and me, and the aroma sat between us, like our love did when the little girl was standing in front of us. I looked at the woman, and she tried to push her hair behind her ear, but it was too short, and she told me, 'You don't want me as a wife.' And... I wasn't sure why she said this, but when she did, she seemed very sad. She seemed like she was angry with herself that she couldn't continue this marriage because it wasn't safe to love someone like her. It sounded like she was telling the truth, and she was almost apologetic. I could have let it end there, but I didn't. I asked the woman with short black hair, 'Why?' and she looked at her fingernails, which were chewed to the skin, and she told me, 'Because of how I live.' I didn't ask anything about how she lived because I couldn't think of how to ask the question in a way that didn't seem like I was quizzing her about her continued biological existence, and the woman said, without muffling her voice, 'You're not waiting for *me* here.' It was supposed to be a reminder. I couldn't ask the woman what she does, and I couldn't ask why I wasn't allowed to love her, but I was able to ask, 'Do you feel like you've been taken advantage of?' Our eyes met, then she met my question with one of her own, 'Do you feel like that after you have sex?' I had to answer her question, so I said, 'It's different for a guy,' and she was still staring into my eyes even though I was desperate to look away. She asked, 'Why is it different, Kurt?' and I got scared, until I glanced down at the luggage tag on my backpack with 'Kurt Jones' written in blue pen on the white piece of paper. Before I could answer, an alarm went off on her phone and I knew she had set it to stay on time for her flight. She gripped onto the strap of her carry-on and stood up, then paused, like she was waiting for me. I looked up at her, and asked, 'Where are you going?' She looked down at me, then said, 'I'm leaving something good, for something not so good.' I knew I only had a moment, and I begged her, 'Don't go.' She had been walking, but she turned and smiled, then raised her hand and showed me a wedding band. It was that gesture that ended things, as I thought to myself, *That's our wedding ring, and she left still wearing it.*"

The story ends, and the line crackles with a long silence.

I finally hear a sniff on the other end of the phone, then I ask, "Why that one, Edie? Why always that one?"

Without pause, she answers me, "Because when you told it to me, I knew the woman you wanted me to grow into, and I also knew that you'd accept me as the woman I was quickly becoming, as I fell ridiculously short of that ideal."

"So which woman am I talking to this afternoon?" I ask.

"That's what I've been trying to figure out," Edie says quietly.

There's a pause that fills the line.

"Write me a letter," Edie pleads desperately, the words- a hammering gasp.

"I've been writing to you," I say, my contempt slipping through.

In a whispery panic, Edie tells me, "I hold my breath when I go to the mailbox, and I hold my tongue when I try to respond, so hold on the line, and hold off on guilting me for being gone."

Edie accidentally writes a song for me, and the cell connection crackles like a tape.

~

I get on the bus, knowing that I have class in two hours, but with the renewed knowledge that Edie still needs my words.

Luckily, I sit next to Mary Williams, and the ride instantly becomes a success.

Mary Williams is a black woman who's probably in her early 30's, and she has a buzz cut that gives her an air of coolness that usually fizzles out for women by age 26, or when they become a mother. She wears dangly earrings that hold blood red jewels in a golden casing.

I ask Mary Williams if this is the bus to the mall, and she tells me it is. I ask Mary Williams if she's going to the mall, and she tells me she is. I ask Mary Williams what she's going to buy at the mall and she tells me that she's been saving up for a gift for her mother. I listen to what Mary Williams has to say. I write the first draft of my letter to Edie in my Corporate Management notebook. I tell Mary Williams I'm sketching her. I kind of am.

I write,

"Remember...

...when you got a pair of AT&T walkie talkies for Christmas, and for some reason they could intercept the cordless phone calls that were happening over your landline, and you heard your babysitter have phone sex with a guy who said, 'I take out my floppy cock and slap you across both your cheeks with it,' and was serious? Well, if there was a redeeming message in his statement, it's that sometimes it's nice when people just come out and say what they mean, no matter how ridiculous it sounds. Directness is an asset. It's more torturous to get your toes cut off one by one then getting the whole foot lopped off at once. I always try to practice the floppy cock method when giving someone bad or uncomfortable news now, so, in a way, your babysitter's phone sex partner's floppy cock changed my life. I met Mary Williams today while she was on the way to see her mother for the first time in three years. She wasn't headed directly to this meet up though- first, she wanted to buy a gift. Mary Williams has had a complicated relationship with her mother ever since she found out her parents were getting divorced months before they told her. It was actually on Christmas day that she first noticed the possibility of this dissolution. That Christmas, Mary Williams got a board game that had something to do with a flying vulture. She was so happy that she told her parents they had to play the game with her. It was completely necessary to play the vulture game at that moment, but her father told her that first her mother had to open a 'special present.' As her mom tore off the Santa covered wrapping paper, Mary Williams saw that her father had bought her mother a $500 purse she had previously pointed out. One day at the mall, on the way to the food court, Mary Williams' mom pointed at the purse, then said, 'Teri Evans' husband buys her shit like that.' Mary Williams knew how this comment made her dad feel- she saw it on his face. This moment stuck with Mary Williams, but the ugly scar healed when she saw that her mom loved the present, and her dad understood that, for once, he got it right. Just as quickly as the moment came together, it unraveled. When it was Mary Williams' dad's turn to open his gift, he tore off the wrapping paper, and laid eyes on his Christmas

present... boxer shorts. All Mary Williams' dad could say was 'Oh, there are... six pairs.' Everything that was achieved with the purse gift was negated by the shame of the boxers. Ten months and six days after that Christmas, Mary Williams' parents sat her down and told her they were getting a divorce. Mary Williams said to me that she resented both her parents for dragging everything out for ten months. Those months could have been so much easier for Mary Williams if she just got hit with a floppy cock.

Love, Kurt."

I finish the letter as we arrive at the mall.

Mary and I get off the bus together, and before we go on our separate ways, I ask her, "What are you going to buy your mom?"

She stops to think about it, and I don't look at the ground because I'm afraid I'll see my shadow running away.

Mary finally says, "I'm going to buy her the board game with the vulture, and maybe when it's unwrapped, I'll remember how good I felt that morning, before the other gifts were opened."

~

The Honda comes to a stop in front of Belle's house, and before I can ask why we're here, Lindsey gets out of the car. My eyes never leave her as she opens the back driver's side door and takes out her backpack, then looks over at me and says, "Come on."

I follow Lindsey along Belle's side yard, the snow falling lightly, defying late March. Fatigued by a seemingly unrelenting winter, the neighborhood is silent with inactivity, and I check my phone to see how much time we have before kids return from school and parents return from work.

In the exact path that we took the night of Belle's performance, I follow Lindsey down into the basement, and I'm met with a once-full space, now empty; a perpetually music-filled space, now silent.

I use the light from my phone to illuminate Lindsey's path as she walks to the center of the concrete floor, then sets down her backpack and unzips it.

Still wearing her gloves, she takes out a blanket and spreads it on the floor. On the blanket, she places a candle in a glass jar. I walk over and use my lighter to light the candle. The wick ignites, and the flame flickers like it's about to go out, but it doesn't.

In the dancing candlelight, I look around the basement at the stickers on the wall which adhere to the old paint job like Band-Aids. I notice that the way the paint chips in this basement is exactly as it does in my apartment. Everything corrodes the same.

I redirect my attention as Lindsey walks to the edge of the candlelight, to the piano that Belle's bandmate was playing, then she eases down onto the frail wooden chair he sat in. Her posture perfect, she removes her gloves, then rests her fingers on the keys.

A song begins, and a talent is revealed. Lindsey's blonde hair bobs slightly when she presses down on the keys, but it seems like the sounds filling the basement are too powerful to be coming from her delicate touch. The notes meander slowly and the music makes me imagine that it's snowing in the basement. Lindsey isn't playing ~the song~, it's a different song. Not a replacement song- it's a companion song.

I consume it all, the pleasure never bitter, always sweet.

Ideally, this moment could be bottled- the piano notes and Lindsey sitting on the old wooden chair, the candle flicker, and the crisp winter air creeping into the basement would all get folded neatly and slid into the bottle. We could bury the bottle in Belle's yard, then a hundred years later someone would find it and open the bottle and relive this moment. They would understand that we weren't a bunch of perpetually angry, sex obsessed, war-mongering, racially hyper-conscious fools. Maybe they would understand that we were them, only earlier.

My phone vibrates, and this mechanical rumble momentarily disrupts the ethereal moment. Reality strikes me like a winter's wind, and I ask, "Aren't you afraid someone will see your car parked out front?"

"I have bigger fears," Lindsey responds, as she continues to play.

"What if someone's upstairs?"

"No one's upstairs."

"What if someone saw us sneak back here?"

"No one saw us sneak back here," she assures me.

"Okay, but I'm afraid of what will happen if they did. Why aren't you?" I ask, because if we *were* seen, if a breaking and entering *was* reported, then my grandparents would be called, and I can't have that happen.

Lindsey stops playing the piano, the song sighing to an end, and I allow the silence to hang, hang, hang, until Lindsey asks, "If you really want to know my biggest fear... I'll tell you, okay? My biggest fear right now is that you end up falling in the big massive void I've created. I thought it was filling up, but then I realized I'm just pulling you down with me. My fear is that we're lying at the bottom of this hole, putting all our muscle into burrowing further, and before you know it, we won't be able to go anywhere- it will be too far to go up, and too hard to go down, and no matter how far left or right we go we'll still be on the same desolate level. It's all a big countdown, and neither of us has the motivation to stop what's happening."

"What does that mean?" I ask, harsher than I should.

"It means that there's something wrong with me."

"There isn't," I assure her.

"If you think that, there's something *really* wrong with you."

Finally, we truly know each other.

Lindsey gets up from the bench, then walks over and lies down next to me on the blanket. I look at her and she's even more perfect than I imagined she would be when I was on my search. The whole time I was looking for Lindsey, I had an image in my head and while it wasn't that far off, it didn't come close to the reality.

I want to capture Lindsey in this moment. I want to add her image to my photographs- a collection that I haven't displayed as freely as she does with the pictures on her wall. Since she shared her pictures with me the day we met, I decide that it's time to return the favor, and I say, "There are these 24 pictures I developed from an old roll of film that my mother left for me, which I keep in an album." After I say this, Lindsey doesn't ask me a question, she doesn't beg for details, she just listens, and I continue sharing this secret, "In that stack of notebooks under the bed, I have them stuck in an album, in chronological order, and I know they're in the right order because I can see myself growing up, my father getting balder. The- uh- first picture, when you open the album, is me, and my mother, and my father in our TV room. We were all dancing to Bruce Springsteen. It's impossible to capture a song in a picture, but anytime I look at that picture, I can hear the song. I have more pictures than just that. I have the picture of my mother kissing my father, and the picture of me dancing on the coffee table, and the picture of my father lifting me up onto his shoulders, and the picture of all three of us on a ratty blue couch. That's a weird one. I don't remember that picture being taken, and I'm not sure who took it. Looking at the picture, I can never remember which song was playing, or what we were watching on the TV. The sensation I get when I look at that picture... it's like... I see myself as one of the kids I watched on TV with their perfect families that would always find happy endings after twenty-two minutes of trouble. The other pictures don't give me the same feeling because they aren't bright like a TV show. The flash didn't work on the camera we used to take the pictures, so everything turned out dark. I think we were so wrapped up in the moment that we didn't notice. Maybe we all just chose not to focus on the fact that the flash never went off. It was important to stay in the moment with my father. When I got the pictures back, we were these objects amid the dark. The backgrounds were black and the only other colors in the photos were the yellow tint of our skin and the blinding whiteness illuminating from a floor lamp." I look at Lindsey through the flickering light, and I tell her, "How everything looks now- how you look now- it's exactly how things were in those pictures."

Lindsey lifts her phone, and before I can process what she's doing, she takes my picture. The flash doesn't go off. She hands the phone to me, not to review her captured moment, but so I can take a picture of her. The left side of her face is illuminated by the candlelight, and the right side is hidden in the darkness. I pause a moment to appreciate how everything looks, then I capture the moment.

I now have a picture of Lindsey. She will enter the album, and she'll look like she belongs, completely.

~

Since Gerard isn't responding to my texts, I show up at Revere's on a mission. The apartment is full, and everyone is on something. A guy with a skinny headband around his long hair says, "If I was a Native American I would wear a cowboy hat everywhere I went. Think about it," and a British guy in a leather jacket responds to the kid's comment by saying, "Americans scare me."

"How Bowie of you," I respond, picking up a half full bottle of beer off the counter and claiming it as my own.

"How am I like a buoy?" the British guy asks, leaning toward me, and I want to spit beer at him, but I don't, because I think that British youth were the originators of the hostile beer spit, and I want to remain distinctly American to sustain my intimidating edge.

Eventually, I find Revere in his unusually spacious bathroom, and he's standing around with a bunch of other kids, passing a joint.

The kid with the joint says, "Tim, Tim settle this."

A kid, apparently Tim- Mexican, overweight, looking like he's not here for the joint, but instead the toilet- asks, "What?"

The kid continues, "What are your thoughts on *Armageddon*?"

Tim ponders this for a second, then asks, "Wait, dude... the movie or the event?"

The kid starts laughing giddily from the weed he just took a hit off of, and I ask Revere if he's seen Gerard, and he mumbles, "Not that I'm aware of," then turns to the Mexican, and says, "So, answer the question."

Tim shrugs, then says, "Awful, but not the end of the world."

~

I stare down at the scar on Lindsey's leg from when she cut it on the edge of the coffee table in our dark living room. I realize how many scars she's acquired since meeting me. The scar on her left palm is from when she was cutting an avocado she was holding and the knife went too deep. The scar on her right pointer finger knuckle is from when she was cooking me grilled cheese and nudged the side of the skillet; I run my fingers along the raised edges of these marks. Lindsey doesn't move- she wouldn't even if she was awake. She now goes to bed earlier than I do, and wakes later. This is a new silence, demanded by her body. These are the days that the silence is unbearable. Her spaced, calm breaths used to comfort me in this bed, but now they scare me. It reminds me of a horror movie, when the female lead is so freaked out that she tries to scream, but nothing comes out. That's the feeling in this bed. This girl is bursting with a scream that can only be silenced with sleep.

I continue to marvel at the sight of Lindsey at rest, yet I yearn for her body in the throes of adrenaline. I consider provoking her. I want her to throw dishes, or to beat her fists on my chest, or to yell at the top of her lungs that she's tired of my unflinching neurosis. She could easily throw a dish at me because they're piled on the floor, and on my desk, and on each shelf of the bookcase. A sea of glassware fills the room like fragile coral. It looks like we have a million little leaks in our ceiling and we're too lazy to patch them.

~

The tiny pause. The text, "I'm going to crash in my dorm tonight, I'm exhausted," prevented me from sleeping last night. Instead of pulsing with energy, or succumbing to my fatigue, there's a universality to the dullness I find myself in today. The color is fading from everything. I'm surrounded by cracking and tarnishing and decay. Bright colors fade, then disappear. I can remember how things were with the vivid shades from years past, and I miss it. Everything, someday, will be gray.

I look around the apartment, knowing I should clean, but I only have the energy to remain static. I run a bath, then get inside and read the textbook for one of my classes to distract myself. I try to remember which one of my business classes the book is for, but I'm unable to ascertain if the book is even for a class I'm taking this semester or if it's for last semester.

I walk out of the bathroom, soaking wet and naked. I drip onto the hardwoods, eventually finding that my towel had been used to cover some pasta that was spilled on the floor two days ago. I don't pick it up, and as I'm walking away, I catch my image in the long mirror on the wall. I confront my reflection.

I see a thin man, thinner. My beard is coming in patchy and my hair is so matted that the thought of running a comb through it makes me squint my left eye tight. I can't help but wonder where all my rules went.

Once I've dripped enough onto the floor, I put on a pair of olive colored pants that may or may not be mine, then I put on a yellowing undershirt and a brown cardigan that looks like it could have come out of my grandpa's closet.

My phone vibrates on the desk, and I turn the screen on, then click the notification. A red banner runs across the top of an e-mail that reads, "I got your message and you're probably right, it seems like some wires got crossed at a certain point."

My message to Noni has been received, heard, processed, and now, responded to.

I get ready by shaving, and combing my hair, but I don't bother to change into something nicer. I want Noni to view me as someone who can help, but not someone who's free from the mental battles we're all fighting as the semester lurches to an end.

Before I leave, I look at the coffee table- the magazines are precisely in place/ I look at the posters on the wall- they're at a perfect ninety degrees/ I look to the light switch- the little letters read ON. Everything is right in my apartment, so I head to Noni's, aware that, for her to e-mail me, everything is not right in her apartment.

In the elevator, I try to think of a way to explain why I miss her, and why I need her, and how I can help her.

I don't pirouette as I enter Noni's apartment. I visually take in a space that I suddenly feel desperate to spend time in. The paint seems to stay on her walls, but I'm sure that it's because she repainted everything the moment she moved in, while I left the blank canvas provided by the landlord. Noni's blood red walls remain uncracked. She once told me she painted the walls red because she wanted to feel like she was back in the womb. As previous reports show, Noni may be insane, but she's endearingly insane, and I sometimes believe she's capable of conjuring the impossible.

Appearing out of nowhere, Noni is suddenly in front of me, and she looks exactly as she did that moment in class when she aggressively re-entered my life, only to disappear just as fast. She takes my hand and we go into her room.

Everything is pushed up close against the walls and the center of the room is wide open. I feel under-dressed; I had no idea I was supposed to wear running shoes.

Trying to read the excitement on Noni's face, I ask, "Did you find your brother?" and the momentary flicker of her smile- the tiny drop of her curved glossed lips- tells me everything I need to know. I already feel as though I've fucked things up and removed the progress we made by reuniting.

"Listen to this," Noni says, her original excitement returning, and I choose to believe her facade as she reassembles into the girl I need her to be. I watch as she runs over to her stereo, then presses play. Electro-pop music blares out of the speakers, and Noni stands in the center of her room with her mouth open, looking up at the ceiling. When a synth strikes the song, Noni starts dancing. She moves her entire body. Arms, legs, neck, hair- her entire being sways and swings and twirls and kicks.

The way she's dancing is a release, not a celebration. Noni hasn't found her brother, so she found a song. I have to wonder, *Did she learn this coping mechanism from me?*

A girl's voice joins with the synthy madness. Her voice sounds like it's coming from a party girl, propped up in the studio, a vomit bucket by her side, as she's prodded to moan out enough slurred sounds so the engineer has the pieces to assemble three verses and a chorus. I listen to the lyrics, but they provoke nothing in me, besides mild frustration. Noni, meanwhile, takes in the song completely, releasing herself to it, dancing as the woozy girl on the track sings, what sounds like:

> *"Let's see one pogo your mouth*
> *Don't to run, those eyes, avail*
> *And mood or killer color mark*

Done fermented lover mother mars
Lowly grr
Dun up a wall again
Lowly grr
Alley, the murder fund
Lowly grr
Gone up a wall again
Lowly grr
Chafing beds..."

This song sounds like it was penned by the guy who wrote the book I leafed through in this same apartment so long ago.

Suddenly, the tempo changes, and Noni matches it, moving closer to me, her sliding groove conjuring a tunnel vision atmosphere, but after a few, "*Lowly grr, gone up a wall again,*" refrains, the tempo switches back to the way it was when the song started, and so does Noni's dancing, but this time she's slower and more spacey, even though the music isn't.

Maybe her dancing hasn't changed. Maybe my perspective has.

"Come on," Noni screams over the blaring soundtrack, and it's this shouted demand for participation that reminds me of where I am. I look around the room, at the furniture pressed against the walls, once again existing in the familiar configuration, and this time, I decide to join in/ This time, there's no reason to feel guilty/ This time, the girl isn't getting knocked down.

We dance together, following, leading, shadowing each other, and to the person who lives under Noni, I bet this sounds exactly like how the Sneaker Girl and the semi-bald guy sound on my ceiling.

The tempo becomes like the waves of the ocean, and I dance with a girl who was able to clear away the clutter so we could arrive at this moment.

In mid spin, Noni comes within an inch of my face and puts her pointer finger up to her lips, to silence my thoughts, then she grabs my hand and makes me move more freely, so that we're using every inch of the room. I immerse myself in the song with Noni, and as long as the music plays, nothing else exists. Every time the song stops, we both look at each other, pausing, then the CD clicks and the song begins again. I realize that I'm happy that I don't know any of the lyrics. My mother's song is ~the song~ I sing, Noni's song is ~the song~ I dance to. As time passes in my life, I find myself building a mixtape that will grant me a complete escape.

~

I'm sandwiched between Lindsey and the back of the futon.

I ask, "Do you have any homework?" and she says nothing.

I say, "I can't remember the last time either of us went to class," and she says nothing.

I ask, "Are you hungry?" and she says nothing.

I ask, "Do you have work today?" and she says nothing.

I say, "I bet if you pick up more hours, they'll start letting you work behind the counter." The only reason I say this is because the counter can be another barrier against guys striking up a conversation and getting close enough to create tension with her. I have no proof that this happens while she's at work, and I have no idea why a guy under 45 would be in the pharmacy she works at, but I know how Lindsey makes me feel- still, now more than ever- and it seems impossible to imagine that anyone- young or old, man or woman- could walk by this stunning stock girl, and not think, "She's the only medicine I need."

I say, "I'm going to go for a walk," and Lindsey says nothing.

She used to ask to go with me, or at least ask where I'm going, but now she just stares at the blank TV screen.

Before I leave, I turn the TV on so that she's not in the dark. I want her path illuminated, should she choose to follow me.

I slowly put on my coat and boots, then I take one last look at Lindsey before I step into the hallway. I don't lock the door behind me.

When I get into the elevator, I hold the door open until a small, annoying, alarm sounds. The alarm repeats, repeats, repeats. The doors try to close and eventually I allow them to glide on their path and further separate me from Lindsey.

I walk out of the building and pass the kids euphorically enjoying an unexpectedly warm spring night that stands for more than just a reprieve from the endless winter- it's a reminder of how open the world is- the possibility of it all- that life can bring a welcome surprise, if you muster the strength to get out of bed.

I like that I can walk, without rushing, without worrying about ice, without balling my fists together to make sure my fingers don't get frostbitten. It's so nice out, that ten minutes into my walk, I take off my jacket.

My ultimate destination becomes obvious to me, as my subconscious slowly loses its ability to shield its plan.

I accept that I'm headed to Ben's garage. Maybe I want to borrow his car. Maybe I just want to find someone that I know will listen as I go off on an overly aggressive rant. Maybe I just want advice from someone who must have been in this spot before, because he's lived here seemingly forever.

As I turn onto Ben's street, I see that he's in his front yard, looking up at the moon like he's savoring the feeling that we survived winter, while also welcoming another season, another downslide into finals week.

I make my way down the street, and I find myself searching the sky for what has transfixed my friend.

Never taking his eyes off the bright moon, Ben says to me, "Looks like you could use some coffee."

This ability to intuit other's needs is something that most students at Kirtland lack. Ben doesn't rely on sight as his primary sense, and this allows him to be more open to the world. He predicted my needs- a cup of coffee, and someone to sit across from- *that* is what I came looking for.

I think about Lindsey's blog, as I step inside Ben's house for the first time. She complained that there was nowhere to get coffee in town at night, and until now, I never realized that, yes, there are places to get coffee at night- you just need to visit one of your friends.

This is an expansion of my interaction with Ben, which began with a car, then sprawled to the café, and now leads us inside his home.

We walk through a living room filled with a diverse array of electronics in various states of assembly. Whatever is going on here seems habitual. Once the items are made whole again, I wonder if Ben will stop to soak up the feeling of pride in his completed work, or if he'll simply move on to the next task.

We walk into the kitchen, and I see that the coffee is already on. Ben is jittery, and I wonder if he's still on his first pot of the day. He pours me a cup, then hands it to me, and I thank him with a nod.

We sit down at a small wooden table at the far edge of the kitchen, and I take a sip of the black coffee, its bitterness instantly grabbing the sides of my tongue.

Ben waits for me to start the conversation, and I know this pause is purposeful because the last time we had a conversation, he told me I had to change, and if I didn't, things would never get easier. Ben seems curious about the ending we've arrived at, if this even *is* an ending. I don't want to tell him that he was right- or at least that I think he's right- but I am willing to admit that Ben is observant enough to have a perspective that shouldn't be discounted. I'm ready to listen to him now, I just hope he can sit through yet another argument where a boy makes it all about himself.

"I'm sorry about what happened last time we were here," I start off, clearing the air, giving us a fresh start.

"Pizza fixed it," Ben says.

"Gerard didn't though."

"That's Gerard, not you. He showed up for that fight, you showed up for the car," Ben says, his jitters somehow subsiding as he taps into the careful way he handled the situation. He sips his coffee, then says, "Lately, I've had to remind myself that just being a human is tough business. We all have the same breaking points and that fact both unites us and allows us to exploit each other."

This is information gained by experience. Ben is the forever-undergrad. He's practically a statue on the Green because he's been at Kirtland so long, and he's collected more than just parking passes during his tenure here. I figure he must have met a girl or two during these years, so I ask, albeit vaguely, "Instead of putting pressure on those breaking points, what do you do when you feel a distance begin to open up? You have your faith... which is an enduring asset, but the distance... that's got to fuck with you."

Ben seems unwilling to answer my question directly. We dance a different dance than the one Noni and I performed, and there are flashes of similarities between this dance and the dance that the semi-bald man and the sneaker girl meet for, but the entire interaction also couldn't be more different. It's clear to me that Ben understands what it is he's being asked, even if he doesn't understand why I'm asking it. He takes another sip of his coffee, puts down the cup, then he tells me, "I've fallen out of love, twice."

It seems like Ben's offering an open door and usually I work to kick doors in, so I don't even ask if it's alright to ask, I just ask, "How'd it happen- the fall? Did you know it was happening before it was too late?" I have to stop myself from wincing after I ask this because Ben is direct with me- he didn't dodge the Joan subject at a time when it was the largest taboo on campus.

"It feels..." he takes a breath in like he's taking a puff off a cigarette, then lets it out, "...like an orgasm."

"An orgasm," I say, then I lean back in my chair, looking through the open door, regretting my curiosity.

"It's not a good orgasm and there's no cleanup, but that's the closest feeling I can compare it to. You know how it feels when a relationship works... it feels... like you're moving, perfectly, together- the best designed machine operating exactly as intended- then there's this explosion- followed by a brand new perspective. Everything shifts, and the person you were becomes a stranger."

Lindsey and I are two machines in the same abandoned warehouse, and the only thing that slows our deterioration is the fact that we are together.

"Falling out of love is the one orgasm you never want to experience with your partner," Ben says. I can't help but wonder if this same metaphor would've been selected if Ben had never gotten into that argument with Gerard.

"You can feel it building," Ben says. "It's repetitive motion, the same actions, but with different effects. This time, that repetition, instead of being silky smooth, it's like... a chaffing leading to an end that is inevitable unless both of you stop and take a breather. If you stop and she doesn't, if she stops and you don't, someone will get hurt."

Ben doesn't tell me about the specific times he fell out of love, instead he says, "Some university did a study and found people can actually die from a broken heart," then he squints his eyes, maybe in ponderance, maybe from phantom pain. "I guess emotional stress can cause some sort of heart muscle weakening that mimics a traditional heart attack. This stress hormone gets released, too much of the hormone. What a way to go out. Your last moments, as your face contorts in pain, are spent thinking, "I'm unlovable.""

I didn't know this fact, but I also don't question its accuracy. The knowledge of what can happen doesn't stop relationships from happening, but I suppose many of my relationships end up collapsing not because of what *did* happen, but from the potential of what *could* happen. The hypothetical becomes as hard to deal with as the reality, and I get the need to change the real to eradicate the possible, no matter the shrapnel.

~

My cell rings, and Lindsey is sleeping on me, so I silence the call. I don't want to interrupt her peace. She's become my Lindsey-cat, forever napping, curling up on me anytime I become stationary in the apartment.

My poor, mysterious, fragile, shy, hip, insecure, desirable, feline, blonde, Kirtland University girl remains undisturbed- the call didn't wake her. Even if it did, whoever's on the line wouldn't be as interesting as my awake girlfriend, so in the attention hierarchy, Lindsey always wins my undivided focus. If she did wake up now, I wouldn't return the call- I'd begin asking Lindsey questions, requesting that she tell me a story, exactly as Edie did when she finally called me. As I think about that afternoon in the clock tower, I decide to check the screen of the phone to make sure that I didn't deny a desperate request from a girl I miss dearly.

I see that I have a new voicemail, and instead of letting it sit in my box until someone texts me that they received a "This mailbox is full" message, I go in and make some room by listening to messages originating months ago, from angry people wondering, "Where the fuck are you?" I turn the volume down on my phone, then listen to three of those types of messages before a voice comes on the line, and I close my eyes and press my palm into my nose, while I listen.

"Hello? Hello? Kurt? Can you hear me while I'm recording this? If you can hear this while it's being recorded, please pick up. This isn't a check-in, this, uh, is about a check-in. It's about... This sounds stupid, but I want to talk to you. It's not stupid that I want to talk to you, it's stupid that... I need to talk to you. I, uh. I, uh. Don't lose sight of the fact that your mother is my daughter. We not only share certain genetics, we also share a distanced love for your mother. There will never be anyone else closer to this situation than you and I, and I almost couldn't call you. I almost didn't call you because you are so close to *being me,* and if you didn't pick up, I would see myself not picking up. That would be... I don't know... I don't know where I'm going with this. This is me, pleading. Your mother is dying. My daughter, your mom, is dying... and I don't know what to do right now. She... she shares genetics with me too, and you too, and... why am I still here? What sense does that make? Why are you and I..." he pauses, collects himself, then says, "When you get this, will you call me? Will you even listen to this? Kurt... I don't know what to do. I don't... please call me."

I have to control my sobs because Lindsey is on my chest. I take the hurt and terror I'm feeling and try to replace it with a rational calm to keep my chest from heaving.

I think about the positives I've found at Kirtland. I think about Noni, Gerard, and Lindsey. I decide to devote the remainder of my time at Kirtland to expressing and dedicating my love to these three people, because, soon, after I make a single call, they will be all I have.

two.

I begin to put things in perspective. It's college. We all don't get enough sleep, and have broken hearts, and question our future, and don't eat enough, and drink too much, and use fake IDs, and hook up with our best friend's crush, and sleep in the back of class, and cheat, and waste our parents' money, and suspend disbelief, and hate our roommate, and live on the internet, and miss home, and study in frantic bursts, and sneak a cigarette on the far side of campus even though we told everyone we quit. All of our education comes in massive chunks that our still-developing brains attempt to make sense of, amidst the chemicals we pump into our bodies.

Five years ago, freshmen used cups of coffee to stay up and work on their papers. Four years ago, freshmen used cups of coffee and cans of Coke to stay up late so they could finish their papers. Three years ago, freshmen used cups of coffee and cans of Coke, and four packs of energy drinks to stay up and finish their papers. Two years ago, freshmen used cups of coffee and cans of Coke, and four packs of energy drinks, and lines of Addy to stay awake and do their papers. Last year, freshmen used cups of coffee, and cans of Coke, and four packs of energy drinks, and lines of Addy, and an online tutor to do their papers for them. Now, this year, I find that we're all zombies thanks to this repeated abuse that has been self-inflicted upon our bodies. We sit, staring blankly at our laptop screens, and we press down keys and hope what we assemble is something that makes sense. And if it's not long enough, we fuck with the spacing and margins until it is.

"Enjoy it while it lasts, it's the best time of your life," they say to us.

It's almost as though the brain, after surviving four years of relentless abuse, develops a hunger for extremes and will never again be satisfied as perfectly as it is in the safe mayhem of college.

~

Long after I decide to stay in bed and skip class. Long after the sun rises to a point in the sky where it's directly above the building. Long after the day has reached its halfway point, Lindsey wakes up. She smiles at me, and I say, "It's time."

"Time?" she asks.

I get off the bed, then walk over to the dresser and open the top drawer. I take out a black bra and throw it to her. She takes off my Ramones T-shirt that she slept in, then puts on the bra. I toss her a pair of black jeans and she slides them on. I toss her a chunky black JPG sweater, and she puts it on.

"Usually this robber getup works better at night," she says, looking at my black pants and black Blondie t-shirt. The moment makes me wonder how much of this clothing selection was unconscious and how much, like Joan's wake, is preparation.

"There will be no robbing today. Trust me," I say.

Lindsey gets out from under the covers, then waits for me as I pause, making sure, once and for all, that I want to do this.

"Do I need my purse?" she asks.

"Just your car keys," I say.

I haven't driven a car in years. I haven't visited where we're going in years. The last time I went there, I was with my mother. Since then, I've felt that I wasn't prepared to return, but with Lindsey, I believe I can make the trip. I had the benefit of Lindsey's journals to get inside her head, but there was no study guide that came along with her meeting me. I hope today helps her out.

We take the elevator downstairs, and the moment that Lindsey steps outside the building into the courtyard, she coos, "It's spring." To arrive at this observation so deep into the season makes it seem like Lindsey's been locked in my apartment, like the "Skank Wife" that my Brit-Lit professor was so misguidedly fixated on last semester.

While I walk to the parking garage with Lindsey, I'm desperate for Noni, or Gerard, or Brittany, or Ben, or even Revere to appear. I want to make the introductions that I've been putting off. I'm still in awe of how fresh Lindsey looks in the sunlight- her radiant blonde hair is so bright that when the clouds clear, I have to put my Wayfarers on.

When we get to her car, Lindsey watches me walk to the driver's side, then without questioning what's about to happen, she tosses me the keys.

I get behind the wheel, adjust the seat, then make the decision to proceed.

We leave campus.

Lindsey doesn't ask where we're going.

Each of us has pre-signed mental permission slips that allow the other to initiate an unannounced field trip. Never once have these trips gone wrong, to the point of regret- even the day we were robbed- and this is the source of my confidence about the day.

I speed through the college town, then beyond. The hours tick by, as the sleepy girl once again drifts off.

I don't put on music, and I don't sing. I focus on the road, and my eyes scan the lush, green trees that have returned anew for spring. I expected it to rain today, but the expanse of blue sky above us remains bright and cloudless.

I wake Lindsey when we reach the gate.

She rubs her eyes with her palms, then squints out the windshield.

"Come on," I say, then we get out of the car and approach the stone angels that bookend a stretch of wrought iron fence and ornate carvings.

Lindsey moves to the right, and runs her hand along a scene from the Bible carved in stone. Well, I think it's from the Bible- Jesus is there.

I take her free hand, then we walk under an ornate iron archway, into the cemetery. Returning here, I instantly feel a rush of memories, as though the ghosts of days past play on the tombstones like imperfect movie screens. The rolling hills, scattered with graves, should create a needle in the haystack feeling, but my mother would often bring me here to rest flowers where *he* would remain for the foreseeable future. As much as she wanted to escape him, she'd still come here, and I have to wonder if she did this to remind herself that she was free of him. Maybe seeing the stone was confirmation that he couldn't hold her back anymore.

I notice that there are more stones than the last time I was here. Eventually, they'll run out of land. Knowing there will not be room for me here, I wonder where I'll be buried when the time comes. Thinking about the scope of it all, it's eerie to realize that this country will become a cemetery plot, and the decomposed bodies of those long gone will be assigned newer, closer roommates out of necessity. Even the right to rest in peace has an expiration date here.

"His name was Mark," I tell Lindsey, and I don't even reach for my wallet. Without the poem, all of the words that used to come pouring out of me are now missing, jumbled, heavy.

I look to my right and notice that Lindsey is choosing to Exist as we make our way between tombstones. I decide to join her. We Exist, together in the graveyard, and even though the sun is still bright, I take off my Wayfarers and hook them to the collar of my shirt.

We get closer.

An angel to my right, black marble to my left.

A mausoleum to my right, the small worn away stones flat in the ground to my left.

An oak tree to my right, the familiar plot to my left.

Then I see it, the gravestone for Mark Jones.

Lindsey is still Existing. She doesn't ask me if I want a moment alone. She doesn't ask if I want her to go buy flowers from the man near the gate. She holds my hand and she Exists, and it's exactly what I need her to do.

We stare down at the name etched in the gravestone/ The dates etched in the gravestone/ The perfect ninety degree angles on the top corners of the gravestone/ The lack of personalization on the gravestone.

My mother couldn't decide on a quote to etch under my father's name because she was unable to find a single sentence to describe the complicated man that we both only sort of knew. The empty rhetoric he lived by wouldn't be fitting for a tombstone. He probably would've wanted something like, "Not a loser," as his memorial, but his method of exit made this statement an untruth.

We walk to the other side of my father's headstone, to the second plot, then Lindsey sees the name, and she sees a date. A single date. A space awaiting. A promise that we both want to be a lie.

"I got a call from my grandfather," I say.

Lindsey's hand tightens around my own.

~

Lindsey is looking straight down at her plate and I see the gears grinding in her head. Her fork drops from her frozen hand, then in a louder-than-normal speaking voice, but not quite a yell, she says, "We need a table away from this window." She scoots her chair back, then stands up, and waits for me to do the same.

I chose this table for its view of the lake, but it becomes clear that the view is the reason we're moving.

I put my napkin on my plate, then collect my silverware. I grab Lindsey's table setting as well, then we walk slowly to the center of the room, where Lindsey re-seats us at a round table too big for only two people.

When I sit down, I can no longer see the big glass picture window we fled from.

Lindsey wasn't lying when she said that she collects insecurities.

~

In the courtyard of my building, I sit down next to Gerard on the bench where I met the sneaker girl. Before I say anything, I pull out two cigarettes, then pass one to him. He's wearing ripped black and red plaid pants, and an earth tone mohair sweater. He's the same, completely, and this allows me to ease into the moment.

"Is... stuff... okay?" Gerard asks, staring at the unlit cigarette between his fingers.

I light my cigarette, then pass Gerard the green lighter.

The quiet calm I hum with in this moment is not shared by Gerard. I begin to wonder if I look the same to him.

"Stuff is. You know. The same," I say.

I feel Gerard tap me on the arm, and I see that in the hand not holding the cigarette, he's got a CD case.

Hearing my question before it's asked, he says, "This is where I've been."

The cover of the CD says NIGHT WHITE in a long, skinny font. The album art has Gerard wrapped in an animal fur pelt, and he's standing atop a pile of naked zombie looking models playing dead. There are dead Asian models, and dead Black models, and dead Indian models, and dead Hispanic models.

The title of the CD is *One or Five*.

This is usually when my lightning bolt of envy strikes- the moment I'm presented with a friend's accomplishment- but as I'm handed the CD, no jealousy follows.

I open up the plastic case, and I notice that there's a ticket inside. Night White has booked a show at The Brink. They're on the underbill, but they're there.

"I need you to be there tonight," Gerard tells me, and before I can ask him for a second ticket, he gets up and leaves me with a chance to do what I promised I would after I listened to that voicemail.

~

Night White isn't on for another two bands, so I stand in a handicapped stall in the corner of the men's restroom, and transcribe the lyrics to my mother's song onto the wall in Sharpie.

I hear a thud behind me, then recognize the two mismatched shoes which have appeared at the door of the stall.

"Let me in," Gerard says, with force, not caring how bizarre this all looks. I have to wonder how he knows I'm in here. Maybe Gerard's dad really does own this place and he has access to check the security cameras on his phone.

I rotate the little circular lock and the door pops open a crack. I see Gerard's fingers wrap around the edge of the door, then he violently forces himself into the stall. "What the fuck are you doing?" he asks, wearing the same bug-eyed expression that I was also about to sport.

"I'm... waiting for you to go on, just... chillin', having a good time," I say, with a faux casualness.

"Your little isolationist logic is flawed at best," Gerard says, backing to the wall, like he finds me to be the most disgusting part of The Brink's depressing bathroom.

"Ha. Isolationist. Isolationist? Gerard, we're at a concert right now," I say.

"We're in a handicapped stall in the men's room," Gerard yells, then bangs on the door.

"Sooo?" I exhale.

"So, it means that even in a situation where the occasion not only permits, but almost demands social interaction, you respond, predictably, by fleeing."

"I'm not fleeing, I'm still here."

"You're in a men's restroom. The men's restroom at concerts, train stations, ball games, or fast food places, is, by far, the least social gathering of human beings ever. No one seeks out a conversation in a men's restroom."

I look around the stall.

"Yes, Kurt, you fucking smart-ass, I do realize we're having a conversation in here, and that's my point. I had to show up in this stall like it's your fucking office just to have this conversation."

"Your point is?" I ask.

This type of aggressive intervention by Gerard is something I've watched unfold a thousand times, but I've never been the one he's directly addressing

We both stand silent and for a moment I believe that Gerard is about to fight me. I'm relieved when he doesn't make the jump to the physical, and he limits his assault merely to very intense eye contact. "My point is that you need to rejoin the human race. Do something! Don't just sit around campaigning for the bummer of the year award."

"Or what? Or I'll never be the most popular kid on campus?" I ask, taking out a Pall Mall, then lighting it.

Gerard shakes his head quickly, then says, "You don't need to be the most popular kid on campus- you just need to be a kid that people recognize on campus. You just need to be *a* kid, on campus."

"I may be a collector, but I never really got into the whole friend collecting thing. It's not finite enough," I say.

"People are not albums!" Gerard gasps out a yell, "They're people. No, you don't have to become friends with everyone at Kirtland, but a time will come when you're going to want to be friends with *someone*."

"So, that makes us?" I ask.

"We're friends, Kurt, but you're not present. You can't just hang out with people when it's convenient, when they have an extra ticket, when you're out of booze. You need to be there for them too. You need to make it clear to people that you care."

"I do care."

"Then show us!" he wheezes, and he looks at me, his eyebrows almost meeting in the center of his forehead at a point.

I force myself to accept that I am a man who establishes a perimeter.

Reminded of the vow I made when I received my grandfather's call, I break the perimeter and hug Gerard.

"You insincere fuck," he hisses in my ear, his right hand gripping my hair.

When he pushes me out of the embrace, I say, "I meant it."

"So did I," Gerard says, then knocks the door open with his palm, and walks out of the stall.

I'm left alone. I'm left to deal with the fact that Lindsey didn't come with me tonight. I try to understand her refusal. The noise? A history with Gerard? A bad experience at The Brink? I fear that Lindsey is home, alone, sleeping. Please let her be at a show in Belle's basement because that way both of us will be dancing to our friend's music. I choose this to be my reality. I push the stall door open, then wash my hands. There's no mirror to check my hair in, so I use my phone.

I look okay.

I feel okay.

I take baby steps into the crowd.

I swallow the claustrophobia I'm suffering from, then go even deeper into the mash of anxious bodies. I want to make sure that Gerard can see me when he comes out.

The stage is dark, but the drummer must be out there because someone is slamming out anthemic thuds on the kit.

A single light from the ceiling blasts onto the stage, illuminating Gerard's thin frame.

When the applause dies down, Gerard says, "For this first song, I want you to pick that man up. Bring him to me."

Gerard is pointing at me.

The band begins to play, and the crowd closes in around me like zombies.

~

We Exist in the woods, and I barely recognize this place without its fluffy white coat. As we walk, Lindsey's eyes dart up to the lush, thriving trees. So far we haven't seen any squirrels, but maybe it wasn't the act of seeing them that made Existing so therapeutic.

We get far enough into the woods that Lindsey can't easily run back and lock herself in the car to avoid the impending conversation we both know needs to happen. It's sickly me and sickly her standing amongst the thriving green trees.

"Lindsey," I say. She looks back at me while biting her bottom lip, but her tricks won't work today. "You need to tell me what's wrong," I demand, then I wait.

Lindsey chews her lip hard and her left eye closes. A tiny horizontal red slice appears when she opens her mouth. As the blood trickles out, so do the words, "I'm a mess. I-I-I find myself spending the entire week thinking about how I can't wait until it's the weekend and I won't have to go to class. When you're not with me, I don't even enjoy the present because I'm always looking forward to the future, but I'm also so worried about the future that my thoughts become poison. I get so ahead of myself that I never live in the moment. I romance a future that will undoubtedly turn out to be identical to the present."

The tears slide down Lindsey's face and her voice becomes strained, as she finally explains, "I want it to be summer when it's winter, and fall when it's spring, and winter when it's summer, and fall when it's fall because fall just sounds right. I mean, I'm so worried that I'm going to spend my life waiting for the good to start, then it will all be over. When I was a kid, my thought pattern was, 'Once I can drive, then I'll get out of my house, and I'll be free, and my life will start.' Then, I turned 17, I got my license and drove to the bank a couple of times, and after that, I said, 'I can't wait until I'm a senior in high school. I see how fun it is for them- all they ever do is drink and fuck off and read complicated novels.' Then I became a senior, and I had a beer, and I skipped some classes, and I read some Joyce, and I said, 'I can't wait till I'm in college so everyone will be as serious about life as I am.' I was convinced that college would weed out all the townies, and stoners, and jocks that were adding nothing to my life. And now, here we are in college, surrounded by different townies, and stoners, and jocks, and we're saying, 'I can't wait for your mother to die,' which even saying that makes me sick to my stomach, and I don't even know your mother. It's just... I just... is this how it's going to be, Kurt? Us waiting for something terrible to happen, yet running from it at the same time? It will end up with me saying, 'I can't wait to die, things will be so much better than suffering this pain,' and there's nothing after that? We would've wasted everything, waiting."

Tears run down Lindsey's face, and I'm holding her elbows, trying to stare her in the eyes.

"Even me? I don't even help?" I ask, indulging in a stupid, selfish question.

"You do, Kurt. You are the only thing I'm sure about. It's just everything else... I'm not even close to understanding or appreciating the *now*. Look at me, I can't even Exist anymore. I'm fully blaming myself, trust me, I know that I make myself feel this way. It's all my fault. I've considered leaving to save you from my suffering, but I have this persistent feeling that I'm going to cause you even more hurt by doing it."

"What happened, Lindsey? Something changed."

"You don't get it, Kurt. Nothing happened! Nothing has to. Just because I haven't had some monumental tragedy in my life, doesn't mean I'm revoked the right to be sad. You never hit me, my parents are still together, my credit card is paid off, I'm physically healthy. Sorry that I don't have the credentials to be depressed."

"It's not that."

"But it is! If Belle had been murdered in some alley, I could walk up to any doctor in this country and I'd have a reason to be this fucked up. I'd need to sit with a shrink for all of five minutes before he could find the cause of my damage and we could work on it. It would be something to treat. I went to Health Services and told them that I'm always sick, and always tired, and my moods are fucking out of control, and I hurt everyone around me, and they told me to change my diet and sleep more. They wanted me to rest more and become more social, and the fact that they don't see how that's a completely contradictory remedy doesn't even scratch the surface of how wrong they all are."

"Lindsey, I'm sorry."

"Why? Why are you sorry, Kurt? I should be the one who's sorry. I'm sorry I put you through this. I'm sorry that my mom and dad love me. I'm sorry I have a boyfriend that treats me well. I'm sorry that I continue to hurt all these people by being so unreliable, and I can't control it. There's something wrong inside of me."

Lindsey wraps her arms around me and grabs tight to the back of my shirt, then says, "I apologize for putting you through this. It's not fair."

The sad tragedy of my life is that the people who really need my help, I can't fix, and the people who are fine without me are always living by my advice.

Lindsey lets go of me, then walks deeper into the woods. She takes a couple of steps then changes direction. A couple of steps, then changes direction. She looks up into the sky, like there's something to see. It begins to occur to me that maybe she's looking up because it keeps the tears in. Everyone seems so impressed when an actor can cry on command, but to impress me, a person would have to be able to stop crying on cue. Lindsey does exactly that, then turns back to me, and says, "As obsessed with the future as I am, I also keep on saying to myself that I want to go back to when things were good and I was happy, but then I try to remember when that was, and I can't. The way I feel now, I've felt my entire life. 20 years. The one thing that kept me going was the thought that once I found someone that really cared about me, I wouldn't feel like shit anymore. And when I found you- I felt wanted, needed, comfortable- loved. But... I still. Feel. Like... I've found the one person whose love could save me, and I remain wrong. I know it's selfish, but I just can't feel like this anymore. I'm well aware you're standing here, blaming yourself for not helping me or whatever, and the fact is you've done so so much, but no one can give me as much help as I need. I've always believed that people can help each other get better, but now I understand that would make the entire world a mental hospital."

Lindsey looks at me in the way that no one else looks at me and knowing that someone can look at me like this will prevent me from ever going back to accepting glares, glances, stares, winks, and all the other obtuse ways that people see me.

A final tear rolls down her pale cheek, and Lindsey says, "I hope you understand."

~

Gerard's response to my text arrives almost instantly. In the body of the text, he provides the address I requested, and he's attached is a .jpeg of a smiling husky dog, that I didn't request. I had sent Gerard a simple question, "Could you ask your Addy guy if the Nathan Butler he knows is a sculptor? If he says yes, could you get me Nathan's address?"

I've chosen to become present and active with helping the people I love. Logic wanes; feeling reigns. I have the power to change things, and I've squandered it for far too long. Instead of counting down, I've learned to busy my mind with tasks that count up. I can look at the numbers and realize- *It's been over a hundred days that Noni has been searching*- which gives this information an immediacy. Every second is precious, and with this value placed upon time, it seems to click by faster.

Since I want to be able to give this information to Noni as the gift I view it to be, I write the address on a hot pink index card. On the flipside of the card, written in Lindsey's lowercase handwriting, is a quickly summarized teaching concept. I carefully cross out the concept so that Noni doesn't think I'm suggesting that she implement Constructivism in her life to achieve greater efficiency and establish clearer objectives with others.

I'm excited to give this card to Noni. I finally have something that can help her, like she's helped me.

I put on my black hoodie, then text Lindsey, "BRB. BNW XFILES 2NITE?"

Not waiting for an answer, I make my way out into the hallway, holding the index card between my fingers, then I wait for the elevator. When the doors open, I want them to reveal Noni, standing there, rubbing her tired eyes. I burn for a sign from the universe that going on this hunt will not destroy anything or anyone. Instead, I find myself staring at an empty elevator. I step inside, then select Noni's floor. At any time I can just drop this card in the gap between the elevator and the next floor. After all, I'm taking directions from Gerard's dealer, to find a man who seems to be hiding, but may also be merely too apathetic to show up for family holidays.

When the doors open, I walk out of the elevator, still holding the card.

I make my way down the hall, and I listen for the *Lowly grrr* that could loosen me up enough to go on this mission with Noni.

I knock on the door and I don't know why I do it, I don't know why I can't walk inside her apartment like I always do.

Moments later, the door flies open, and Noni appears. She's wearing jean shorts and a tank top- tempting summer to arrive before the semester ends.

I want to say something, but instead I just hold up the card.

Noni looks at the address, then snatches the card from my hand. I watch her big eyes fill with tears, and she's shaking her head in disbelief- maybe because Kurt Jones finally did something for someone else, or maybe because her brother is so close to Kirtland- only a bus ride away.

Noni looks back to me. She reaches up and wipes the hair out of my eyes. She stares at me, her lips curling into a smile, and they soundlessly mouth, "Thank you." I don't break eye contact with her, or respond, as a count-up, flips to a countdown.

"Will you?" the words finally find a way out of Noni's mouth.

I nod.

"What if I'm afraid?" she asks me, and I feel the countdown pause, like a wire was cut.

I press the wires back together, twist them, then say, "Where we're going is just an address on a card; we're going to a place that's a bus ride away, to look for a man you know well. That's not scary."

"How sure are you that this is the address?"

"It was provided to me by a lunatic," I admit.

"Then, it has to be the right place," Noni says, now completely sold on her brother's whereabouts. She gives me back the card, then turns and walks to where her purse is sitting on the floor. I feared for a second that she was giving up, but she's just getting ready. She changes out of her summer outfit into a spring outfit, and I don't like the feeling of reversal this gives me, but I say nothing.

On the elevator ride down, I check my phone, just in case Lindsey has already responded to my text, and when I see she hasn't, bizarrely, I'm relieved.

We walk in silence to the bus stop as Noni studies her phone to see which bus will take us nearest to the address on the card. This concentration belies Noni's essence. She scuffs her feet instead of pirouetting and she seems powerless.

"Okay, got it," she finally says, but her demeanor doesn't change with this assertion.

We arrive at an empty bus stop, and as we wait, I flash back to the story I read on 4353638332936382.com. There was a girl, Sarah, thinking about someone she missed, someone who didn't take things very seriously, which was in stark contrast to how she felt. I recall that the friend in the story, Beth, wasn't really there for Sarah, and I make sure that I am very careful in my attention with Noni, because I've been told how much it matters. Lindsey's only fictional piece of writing seems to hold just as much, if not more, truth than her personal journal entries. I understand why that person kept her Poli-Sci notebook. Lindsey's short piece of fiction endures with significance in my life.

"Can I have a cigarette?" Noni asks.

I take out my Pall Malls and hand her one, then light it for her. She takes a short drag, and I notice her hand is shaking. I don't take out a cigarette for myself; I'm content to sit and watch Noni.

"Would you look for me if I was gone?" she asks.

"Absolutely."

Noni takes another tiny puff from the cigarette, then exhales the question, "Why hasn't he?"

"I bet he has," I say, not sure if I believe this, but sure that it's what "Sarah" would need to hear, so it's what I maintain.

"You're the only..." Noni starts to say, then pauses, exhaling hard, even though she didn't take a puff from her cigarette. The statement is never completed. Noni looks away from me, then pretends she's looking down the road for the bus.

I'm left to fill in the words, and I find myself assembling two different statements- *You're the only one who would look for me,* or *You're the only one who understands that, sometimes, you can hunt down love.*

I see the bus approaching in the distance, and Noni hands me the cigarette to finish. I put my lips around the filter, and when I taste her, we become one.

The bus hisses at us, and I drop the cigarette, then dash in front of Noni.

After I pay both our bus fares, I look back and ask, "Do you want to sit next to each other or across from each other?"

Noni freezes at the beginning of the aisle, as the bus starts moving, then she decides, "Across."

In the front of the bus, the seats face each other, instead of being in split rows, so Noni sits on the left side of the bus, and I sit on the right side.

I smile at Noni, and she smiles at me.

Noni reaches into the pocket of her coat and takes out her phone. Her fingers move fast as she types something, then my phone vibrates.

I smile at Noni, and she looks up from her phone and smiles at me.

I take my phone out of my pocket and look at the screen.

"I'm sitting across from this total weirdo on the bus right now," reads the text.

I smile again and look at Noni.

She smiles again, then looks at my phone and opens her eyes wide, prompting me to text back.

"I'm on the bus too and I'm sitting across from a very successful looking girl. I bet she has the world in her hands," I send.

I look up from my phone, and Noni looks down at her phone, then smiles.

She starts tapping out a text, and I don't look at my phone until it vibrates again.

"Tell the successful girl that it'll be okay," I read off my phone.

"It'll all be okay," I say aloud, across the aisle to Noni, who gets up, and seems focused on closing the gap between us. She sits down next to me, and puts her head on my shoulder. She reaches into her purse and takes out a pair of white earbuds, then hands me one of the buds, and I put it in my ear. She takes the other bud and puts it in her ear, then hits play. The "*lowly grr*" song begins playing, and instantly, I want to dance, but Noni doesn't move. She listens to the song, and I listen to the song, as we get further from Kirtland and closer to Noni's brother. It's possible that this song, like the Jackson Sharpe song my mother and I have, is the anthem that Noni had been playing while she imagined what it would be like to see her brother again. It makes me happy that I can share this song with her. How bizarre that I can't figure out a single word from Noni's song, and Lindsey was able to correct the words to the Jackson Sharpe song for me. I can't correct the lyrics for Noni, but I don't think it matters- she hears what she wants to anyway, or maybe not understanding the words is part of the song's charm for her. Maybe she finds comfort in the fact that, just as she doesn't understand why her brother has abandoned her family, she also can't figure out what this girl is accomplishing with her song. The pointlessness of the journey can be frustrating, or boring, unless a rabid devotion amplifies the situation.

When the bus sighs at our stop, Noni and I both get up, earbuds still in, and we walk shoulder to shoulder, at the exact same pace, off the bus, and into the street of this strange, but not-too-distant place.

I can't play Noni my song, so we listen to her song, over and over.

As we walk, I feel Noni drift closer to me, as if keeping this intimate proximity could shield her from the hurt that could be on the horizon. I choose to do my best to drag Noni's reunion fantasy into reality.

When we've arrived at our destination, I look at a long, single level, brick building. There's no signage on the building, but it doesn't seem like a home. With so few windows, this must be a warehouse or a massive garage.

Noni curiously makes her way around the building's perimeter, until we're confronted with a green door. She looks back at me, so I step forward, then hammer my fist on the door.

The wait begins- Noni bites her lip; I try to prepare myself to step in and hold Noni if her brother chooses not to.

The green door opens, and a man with longish sandy blonde hair appears- his thin cotton shirt is loose and stained, his pants are made of a brown cloth that's rolled halfway up his shins. His opening line, setting the tone, is, "Yeah?"

"Nathan," Noni says in an airy voice.

"Yeah?"

"I found you."

Nathan furrows his brow, then needlessly confirms, "Yup."

"Where have you been?"

"Uh, ya know. Here."

"Why haven't you come home?"

Nathan looks up to the top of the door frame, and leaving his eyebrows raised, looks down at Noni.

"Mom's house," she clarifies, annoyed. "Why don't we see you at Christmas and Thanksgiving?"

"I have work then."

"What do you do?"

Nathan holds up his plaster-speckled hands.

"I can put down some plastic at home," Noni says, attempting a joke, her neck getting tight like it tried to stop the words from coming out, but reacted too late.

Nathan shakes his head in a no-ish manner.

"Mom would like it."

"Mom would like... plastic... on the floor?"

"You! Home! She'd like you home!" Noni yells, her teeth gritted, as she begins to lose it.

"I visited, like, uh..." Nathan scratches his head, "...a couple weeks ago."

"You did?

"Yeah"

"You did?"

"Yup," he says, popping the "p."

"She didn't tell me."

"When is the last time you've spoken with her?"

"Like... well, like..." Noni stumbles.

"Maybe *I* should be the one putting plastic down for *you*?"

"Nathan..."

"Yeah?"

"How about we get together for a holiday... like the Fourth of July?"

"I have work."

"You can take some time off to fix this family!" Noni yells, stamping her foot, her emotions like waves.

"No one has that much time," Nathan says, and he doesn't look away, he watches as the hope drains out of his sister.

This is a conclusion that Noni must've known was inevitable. She had to be aware of the way the universe would react- the count-up, the countdown, the predictable explosion that claims Noni's dreams of having a united family.

"I like your sculptures. I saw them online. You're very talented," Noni says, desperate to find any angle that could help make this search a success.

Nathan bows his head slightly to acknowledge the compliment.

"Okay, well," Noni says, realizing that this is the end of the conversation; she will not be let inside.

"Do you need a ride home?" Nathan asks.

Noni shakes her head no, then turns around and puts a hand up to her nose. Without pause, she begins her walk back to the bus stop.

A look of quiet shame flickers across Nathan's face as we make eye contact for a moment, but I don't give him the speech that's expected of me. I don't tell him that he's making a huge mistake. I don't let him in on the fact that his sister has been searching for him for her entire junior year. I look at him with pity, and it registers on his face that my sentiment has connected. Then, I turn and leave. It's my job to listen, and to shield Noni.

It's partly my fault this happened, but with the semester coming to a close, I can't think of a better time for Noni to gain her freedom.

The moment I catch up to the fleeing girl, she sobs, "He acted like I was crazy."

"You're not crazy, Noni. Let's just stop walking for a second and deal with what happened," I beg, afraid that, at any moment, she'll walk off the sidewalk, across the tiny strip of grass, and into oncoming traffic. She's a girl without a goal. She's a sister without a brother.

"All this time, he had no idea I was looking for him. All that work I did was pointless. I didn't even find him- you found him- and he wasn't waiting for someone to seek him out; he didn't even know he was hiding."

Noni still cares so much, and because of this, she's moving away from her brother with total urgency, yet no grace. This is when the supermodel breaks the mirror- a rare moment of deep betrayal, an infrequent occurrence, which makes the dramatic action all the more profound. The layers peel away and I look at the ugly core of this moment.

My Takeaways from watching Noni beg her brother to show his humanity:

One- I was able to see how things could have ended up if I refused to respect a selfish wish.

Two- The time-factor is the only difference between the situation I face, and the situation Noni must continue to wrestle with. She'll be forced to fight for days and months and years, with no relief possible, unless her brother changes, or the universe steps in with a permanent detour. This will be painful, but it's also more hopeful than what I'm doomed with- Noni and her brother will have decades to fix something that's broken, while my fractured relationship is about to resolve itself at any moment. I might not end up with closure, but the stalemate will soon end, and I will be free from one prison, then placed in another.

I have to wonder which situation is worse- knowing that the person I miss will be gone soon, or the constant prodding pain that Noni will now feel as the person she misses is a couple of towns away, not missing her back.

I hold Noni, and I pay attention to her. She's experiencing a death of sorts, and I'm tempted to use this afternoon as another trial run. I pause, and I consider that maybe I don't have to make this about me; maybe I'm already an expert in dealing with what happened here? I don't know what it's like to bring a life into this world, but I've become a veteran in knowing, feeling, and accepting the pain of watching a life slowly depart. I also know what it's like to experience a life quickly depart, and Noni won't have to deal with this, unless she totally closes off. I want to stop that from happening so I say to her, "You have time to fix this."

"What will time change?"

"So much."

"I'm giving up. I'm not going to chase someone who doesn't even realize he's running."

"You'll regret that."

"You have no idea what you're talking about," Noni barks at me.

"To understand why I'm telling you this, you have to hear about something that happened to me," I say, then I wait for her to break away from me, to cross the street, to establish a distance out of embarrassment.

"Tell me," she says in a tiny voice, staying close to me.

"I want you to keep your life open to your brother, because I lost my father, and it's permanent."

"The poem," Noni acknowledges quietly.

"I can turn the poem into a short story," I offer, and Noni, with the first hint of a smile since her brother turned her away, says, "Anything is better than a poem."

My arm around her, I walk next to Noni and I tell her a story that I've owed her for a while, "My mother and father married when they were both 25. I was conceived when they were 27. We were very rich. My father worked long hours. He'd hole up in his office in our apartment for days and days. He was into currency trading. Buying dollars, selling euros, buying yen, selling... whatever another type of money is. I didn't get into it. He would show me this program he used, but I never cared, and that created a distance between us. One day, after school, when I got back to our apartment building, there were cops and ambulances around everywhere. I saw my mother crying. I promised myself I would never swear like my father, but when my mother ran up to me, I said, 'Oh shit... he actually did it.' Seventeen floors, from his office window, bam, right onto a Honda Civic, complete with an 18 year old girl in the passenger seat. They took her away in a bag too. The biggest question I had about the situation was, 'I wonder if he aimed for the car?' because I knew, in a way, why he did it."

"Why- uh- did he?" Noni asks, and I sense her confusion at the male mind.

"Later, the full story came out. They told me that the day he took flight, my father had been involved in a highly speculative trade, and the world, as it does, did not cooperate, and a war, as they do, broke out and changed the entire landscape of the areas my father had invested in. He lost a significant sum of money, but it was a tiny fraction of the fortune he had amassed due to his savant-like ability to play a game that consisted of putting in quarters and receiving back yen. His broken glass flight was never about the amount, it was about the loss- it was about the genius being blindsided and never regaining his balance. I wasn't very surprised he did it, when he did it, how he did it- there were days when I thought he would jump over a thousand dollars, but I wasn't prepared for the situation I found myself in after he did it. My mother, in many ways, saw me as a remnant of my father- his ghost possessing the body of her innocent little boy. My obsessive traits were inherited, so she saw him in my actions, and every afternoon when I came home from school, I expected to see an exorcist sitting at the dinner table with my mother, ready to perform a ritual to cast out my father's posthumous presence."

"Do you think you're like him?" Noni asks, and it seems like the question is based in the fact that she's afraid to lose me.

"In certain regards," I admit, "One of the compulsions he had, that I don't, was that he couldn't lose. Anything- bets, arguments, or money. When I was old enough, and perceptive enough, to know that something was not normal with my father, I somehow got the confidence to ask him why he couldn't deal with something as neutral as an even-split tie. He told me, 'You don't want to be seen as a loser, Kurt. You're a Jones and we aren't losers.' My mother later told me that he made this point because, being a Jones, I actually *was* from a long line of losers- deadbeat dads, spousal abusers, compulsive gamblers, and drunks. My father was the first Jones to find success in America, so he was trying to rewrite the Jones history book. I was supposed to be the next chapter. It turns out I'll be the last chapter, because everyone else has died in some pathetic way."

"So, the money you talk about..." Noni edges toward the lingering subject.

"After my father died, my mother inherited everything. The money didn't change much- it was always there. We got a dog, then the dog ran away. The dog didn't fix things, and my mother's plastic surgery didn't fix things, so we left the complex and moved into a two bedroom house. Not exactly the home you purchase after you hit the macabre lottery, but it was hard to find an extravagant single level house near my grandparents. That was the requirement- every house we looked at had to be ranch-style. My mother planted bushes under every window, so if I was to use one as an exit I wouldn't fall- I'd be suspended by the branches of the bushes. With the money from my father, I was set for life, and since my mother never had a job, we spent a lot of time together in that house. I went to school only because I'm pretty sure it would've been illegal to stay home. It was just us two, and when I showed flashes of my father, my mother would turn bitter and angry, resentful and accusatory. We were just like every other middle-class family in America, except for the number of zeros that showed up on the invoices from the bank. I asked my mother why she never spent my father's money beyond the essentials, and she told me, 'The last thing we should be doing is letting it control us like it controlled him.' The way she said this made me understand, until she left my life. She left me. She, uh, got cancer, I think, based on the information I've been able to learn, that's what she has. And she's still alive. When she got sick, she sent me to my grandparents. I lived in the house she grew up in, and slept in the same room she did as a teenager. It was almost as though she sent me to her parents as an apology for how she turned out- like she wanted them to have a second chance at familial warmth. I haven't seen her since she dropped me off at my grandparents' house that one day. I didn't truly understand what was happening. I thought maybe she was fixing her face again. I would always ask my grandfather when my mother was coming back, and he would tell me she was sick, and when she wasn't sick anymore, I could see her again. I assumed this meant that she got more than her face fixed this time, and she needed to be left to recover, so I started waiting. In high school, my grandmother was essentially my mom, and my grandfather was my dad. My grandmother didn't understand me like my mother did, and my grandfather understood me better than my father did, but that was not a difficult feat. In her absence, I kept lots of happy memories of my mother. I put them in notebooks to make sure that they wouldn't be forgotten. For a period of time, I was convinced that she had died. Then, I didn't believe there was a sickness for a while. I thought the 'sickness' was a way to avoid telling me that she didn't want to see me. Not until I left for my sophomore year of college did my grandparents tell me they knew where my mother was and that they'd been in contact with her the entire time she was missing from my life. After that, I broke off contact with my grandparents. It wasn't that dramatic, I always felt isolated, and I always felt a sense of independent responsibility. The summer after my sophomore year, I stayed in our building instead of going home."

"I'm so glad you stayed. I needed you an elevator ride away. I still do," Noni tells me, arriving at a new appreciation for past decisions after her visit with her brother.

"I hadn't heard from my grandparents until August of this year, when they visited me, and said my mother was very sick. I said, 'No shit,' and they said that soon- it could be weeks, it could be months- I would be getting everything from the estate when my mother passed. I don't know exactly how much everything adds up to, but I know it's a lot. I'll pick it up one day, any day now. Millions, in a single day. I'm sure people think that's too much money for someone as young as I am, but I've been acting like an adult for years now. I can tell you though, above all else, every day that I don't have that money, part of me is overjoyed because it means I still have a chance to see my mother again. *That* is what keeps me going. If she doesn't ask to see me, before..."

I can't finish the statement, and Noni hugs me tight, then wipes a tear off her nose with her free hand. This understanding silence forces me to reflect on my recounting of how it all happened. It doesn't seem ugly at all to me, I'm not bitter about what she did. I need Noni to have this same clarity so I say, "Noni, I want you to know that the one thing you have on your side in your quest to put your family back together, is time. You might not reconnect with your brother tomorrow, or a week from now, or a month from now, or a year from now, but I'm positive that something, sometime, will bring you all back together. Even if it's only for a goodbye, you will get that moment you've spent your year fixated on."

I'm here for Noni today, because I know that she'll be there for me when ~it~ happens.

I miss my mother, and I miss being in a family.

I have to wonder if the sacrifices my family, and Noni's family, have made are worth it.

If the hurt of letting go is negated even in the tiniest fraction by the pleasure of creating a life, then, for the first time, I want a family of my own. The possession. A family of *my own*. I can never have a family of my own. I can have a family that I share, but control is an illusion, permanency is a lie. The stability, even when established, is resting on thin ice. Knowing that someone bonded by blood can simply walk away makes the notion of creating another individual unattractive. Why take that risk? Do we bring someone into this world to continue a legacy? To improve what we offered the earth? To fix the wrongs we've committed throughout our lives? Or, is procreation nature's cleanup crew- a beta version of an improved being that can be more careful and caring? Do we create with the hope that our creation will be mature and caring enough to not fuck things up with their family like we did?

~

If the *Limber* zombies were ever to attack, the economy would implode, and money would become worthless. I'd find that I spent a significant portion of the best years of my life waiting for my mother to die, only to gain an inheritance that had no practical value. I'd be forced to travel through this new nightmare, searching to find my zombified mother- the same woman I casually allowed to slip away on a slow slide of delayed happiness. With my inheritance out of the picture, I would sift through the garbage blowing in the nuclear wind of the depleted skyline, desperate for signs of my mother.

I stare at my phone and pray that it never goes off again. I don't want to get that call. I hope she outlives me. I don't want the money. What a horrible reminder. The fact that I might see her someday is worth more than the multi-figure inheritance that would appear on a statement in my name once she's gone forever.

I'm so often headed in the wrong direction, and I fear that everyone can instantly pick up on this failure when they meet me. I can sense it when I see myself in shop windows, and in the bathroom mirror, and in the camera on my phone, and in the blurred reflection on the polished steel elevator door.

My shell is going toxic.

In every zombie scenario, there's always that initial carrier that dooms everyone they come in contact with. In this case, I'm patient zero for a virus that's spreading like a rumor, and destroying like a weapon. I'm killing my mother, slowly. I'm killing Lindsey, slowly. I'm teaming up with the coke and killing Gerard, maybe not so slowly.

I walk into my building and the elevator doors open, expecting me. I walk inside, and press the "4," but when the doors begin to close, I reach out a hand and stop them, then flee the claustrophobic box.

I hang a right and find the staircase, then begin stomping up the stairs.

At the top of the staircase, in front of the door I'm searching for, there she is.

Lindsey sits on the highest stair, next to a ball of chartreuse colored string. I take the stairs two at a time, anxious to join her, relieved that the need to get out of the elevator was caused by a valuable sightless sensing of Lindsey's presence on the stairs. Maybe, I've been misinterpreting strings of destiny as pangs of panic? Maybe, Lindsey makes me feel emotions so strong that I experience them as fear because that's the only emotion I've conditioned myself to feel completely?

When I sit down next to her, Lindsey takes my hand, but instead of holding it, she moves it down to the ball of string. She presses my pointer finger on the yarn's little tail, then she tosses the ball forward, down the stairs. Lindsey and I sit and watch this big ball of sickly-green yarn unravel, and when it strikes the wall, it takes a left, then disappears out of sight, but I'm sure that the descent continues because I can feel the string move under my finger.

Lindsey either puts her head on my shoulder, or can't hold it up anymore so she rests on me. We stay like this for an undefinable amount of time- two slack jawed, chunky veined, puffy eyed, bloody fingered, crooked postured, used up props.

When Lindsey raises her head, she looks at me, then projects her gaze down the little green line.

I realize that she wants me to return things to their previous state; she wants me to clean up the mess. I stand up and begin curling the end of the line around my finger, to roll up the string, stair by stair. It would be easier to leave Lindsey and go get the ball, but I'm smarter than that. This isn't about completing a task as quickly as possible via the easy way, it's about continuing a repetitive motion, a seemingly pointless task with no reward- This is about witnessing the unraveling, then devoting myself to the manual re-raveling.

After restoring the past, then tying off the end, I hold the ball of string in both of my hands and I turn to show Lindsey, but she isn't there.

I leave the stairwell and when I peek my head out to locate her in the hallway, I'm met with an empty stretch of peeling paint on the wall and scuffed tiles on the floor.

I walk down the hall- 1 on my left... 2 on my right... 3 on my left... 4 on my right... I reach our apartment, but when I push the door open and call out Lindsey's name, I'm met with only silence.

I dash through the living room, past the kitchen, into the bedroom, and my eyes scan the rumpled covers of the bed, the laundry on the floor, the dishes collecting dozens of invisible leaks, and the desk with the notebook opened to a fresh page.

I walk to the desk, and delay my search.

I wait for Lindsey.

I remain in our bedroom, and I stare at my phone.

Eventually, I relent, making a call that goes unanswered.

I send a text that says, "I'm in our room," which pinpoints my exact location, but makes no demands on her if she wants to be alone.

I place my phone face up on the desk, and I consider that she left this notebook out for me.

I turn around and write to Edie about Kurt Jones, as a distraction.

"Remember... Kurt Jones, the boy you grew up next door to? I saw Kurt Jones today. He has de-matured into a pathetic, pink skeleton so brittle that his fingernails crack when he tries to carry a bag of groceries up the stairs. Kurt Jones has the abs of a Victoria's Secret model and it's for the same reason, but different. They've both experienced acute pain to get those abs and both don't have a choice but to sport them. When I asked Kurt Jones what he does- where he works, what he studies- he told me that he's spent a lot of time recently on the floor of his bathroom, curled into a ball so tight that his spine would resemble one of the mountain ranges you'd find on a 3D topographical map. Kurt Jones labors under the belief that his brain is being handicapped by a mist that hangs over it. He imagines that the inside of his head looks like the water in a mop bucket, and he imagines his brain floating in that scum. He fantasizes about being able to wipe away the filth, but he knows it's impossible. According to Kurt Jones, everything is falling away. Kurt Jones had a mother and lost her, but she is still somewhere. Kurt Jones had a soulmate, but his soul left and it turns out that his mate loved his soul more than him so she followed. He now awaits her return by wasting time writing letters. Kurt Jones thought that he could enter college and use it as his amusement park, then a weird thing happened and he stopped seeing everyone around him as a tourist. He realized that, yes, some people want to stay the night. Not everyone is trying to beat the traffic home. Kurt Jones learned that he might not see every person who's important to him every day of his life, and that's okay. To equate absence to distance is foolish. Kurt Jones was close to these people and they were there for him- when he needed a car, or when he needed to learn the right lyrics, or when he needed to dance, or when he needed to Exist, or when he needed to be yelled at, or when he needed to be carried- these people that Kurt Jones viewed as tourists, somehow seem to appear again, and again, and again, and again. When the visitors at the amusement park gained an importance, and fun was acknowledged as a moment, not a state of being, it took a call from management to remind Kurt Jones that in an amusement park, it's not all roller coasters, and cotton candy, and

*parking passes. Everything requires upkeep, and there's a fast
approaching date of obsolescence on even the most amusing parts of life.*

*Kurt Jones will never stop writing to you, and the miles this letter
travels are not a measure of distance between you both. You are with
Kurt Jones, always. Every time Kurt Jones meets a stranger, he thinks of
you, and he listens to them, like you listen to him.*

*Do you remember the day Kurt Jones left for Kirtland and he was
standing in his yard and you said that Kirtland was going to be where
Kurt Jones found himself? You were right.*

Love, Kurt."

I recopy the ballad of Kurt Jones, then slide it into a pre-addressed
envelope. I put the letter in my hoodie pocket, then I leave, searching for a
ball of string that had once again become unraveled.

I'm hoping that Lindsey will be where I last saw her, so I pass the
elevator, then open the door to the stairwell.

I've found her before- she's trained me for this moment.

I descend the stairs to the first floor, never encountering Lindsey, so I
traverse the empty hallway to the other side of the building, then open the
door to the other stairwell, revealing another climb. As I make my way up
the stairs, my head forever raised, I look for that bright girl like she was the
sun.

When I get to the top floor and the stairs go no higher, I leave the
stairwell, then walk halfway down the hallway of the top floor.

Beyond the bars on the window, the view stretches for almost a mile.
Looking out at this expanse, I feel a vertigo that has nothing to do with
falling.

I want to take out my phone and call ~her~ again, but I don't. ~She~
was in that stairwell, and something led me to ~her~. ~She~ was waiting
for me, expecting my arrival. I have to find ~her~ again, and I will.

I was able to stop my search and write a letter, because the universe told
me to. It didn't make sense, but I know better than to ignore the call. Today
is all about repetition and doing things the hard way. I know this, and it
gives me confidence that I will find ~her~ at any moment.

I continue down the hall, then take the stairs back down to the first
floor, passing no one.

I make my way out of the building and through the courtyard with the
letter to Edie still in my hoodie pocket.

I have no car. I have no choice. I have to walk. I have to find Lindsey. The three most logical locations where she could be hiding out are campus, Rubie's, and the pharmacy.

After I drop my letter in the mailbox, I keep walking, then slide my ID at the gate and step onto campus.

I pass my Management professor, one of them, and he averts his gaze.

I pass the clock tower and it seems to stretch into the clouds.

I pass the graffiti-less walls, and the perfectly measured parking spots, and the carefully pruned shrubs, and the new buildings paid for by old students with new money and tired morals, which bring in more money and more buildings and more students.

I walk by the church.

I turn around.

I wonder what it looks like inside.

This place, like the stairwell, exists only in case of emergency.

I'm not sure if this is an emergency, but I feel the universe pull me inside.

I pass through an empty vestibule, then stop in the door frame at a marble dish of holy water. I'm afraid to dip my fingers in it, so I walk forward, feeling small as the ceiling peaks seventy-five feet above me. Along the walls are little sculptures of different scenes leading up to Christ's crucifixion. I drift down the right aisle of the church and glance at two of the scenes in the story. I stop and notice the expressions on the sculpted faces; the way they look at a beaten, skinny Christ carrying the cross he will soon be crucified on. I shut my eyes tight because, in the next sculpture, there's a group of women all looking at Christ, all of them except for a woman wearing a blue cloak who averts her eyes completely from this man with his crown of thorns.

I redirect my gaze and stare straight ahead at the front of the church and wonder how much all of this cost. I think about all the churches, in all the towns and cities, in all the countries, across the entire world, and all that money left by all those departed believers with the hope that they would find a new home with this one-time mortgage payment. The church relies on these massive drops of cash. In a way, the faithful are waiting on their brothers and sisters to die to survive.

I stop walking when I reach the front of the church, just before the step up to an exclusive VIP area. Only those who are certain to arrive at this place every Sunday, without fail, are allowed to take this step up.

I exhale for what seems like a minute, and in my periphery, I notice the presence of someone else. I instantly know it's not Lindsey because my body doesn't buzz in this person's presence.

I turn to face this stranger, desperate for him to not be my grandfather.

The man's collar reminds me that *I* am the stranger here, and I want to rush up to this man and hold him by the shoulders, and demand that he pray for my mother.

Sensing my unbalanced yearning, the man in the clerical collar says, in a heavy German accent, "Overwhelming, isn't it?" His voice sounds like he's telling me a secret, while also whispering a warning. His face is tired and worn, like he's been cooking in the hellfire of his entire congregations' sins. I bet he was born in 1942 or some equally distant sounding year.

I nod my head in a somewhat yes-ish manner to answer the hanging question I've been asked.

"Father Niklas Schaefer," he says, extending a hand, introducing himself.

I move toward him, and shake his hand, then offer my name.

"Would you like to sit?" he asks, slowly and carefully, his German accent drawing out certain syllables.

Again, I nod my head in a somewhat yes-ish manner. I check my phone, and I have no missed calls, no missed texts, and four bars of service.

Father Niklas Schaefer and I sit in the front left pew, and we both stare straight ahead. I notice that the only time people sit face to face in the church is when the priest sits down in his presider's chair. For now, he has abandoned this throne, knowing that I need him to be on the same level as I am.

I wonder how Father Niklas Schaefer ended up as a Catholic/ How he ended up in America/ How he ended up as a priest/ How he ended up coming to Kirtland from Germany? I don't know what they worship in Germany- I only know they created Santa and it seems like they wouldn't have given Santa the 25th if they had known about Christ. I imagine a German version of me and a German version of Lindsey trying to plan when Santa shows up on a pure white calendar. Who knows, they probably made Santa to undermine Christ. That seems very German.

"I haven't seen you here before," Father Schaefer says to me.

"I haven't been here before," I confess.

"What's kept you away?"

I pause for a moment, then say, "The other people who come here, how they interpret things. I feel like they're really fixated on words, and totally uninterested in context. It's like... well, alright, it's like, when I moved into the apartment I currently live in, I inherited magazine subscriptions from the previous tenant, and in the magazines they always have an interview printed in small text, but then in big text, in the center of the page, they'll print something like, 'You learn that it's just comfortable to not have to wear underwear.' Out of all the things that the celebrity said, there is a pull quote of one sentence, and the lack of context creates a new meaning- the meaning that we want it to have, never mind the intention. Some poor little 23 year old actress is talking about how she had to jump around in a harness for some scenes in an action movie and found it uncomfortable while wearing underwear, but the massive pull quote causes most people to interpret that one sentence as her being a slut."

"I don't necessarily agree with your word choice, but I agree with your point," Father Schaefer concedes.

"So what's the answer?" I ask him, "Why are so many people in this building only interested in the pull quotes?"

Father Schaefer looks up at the ceiling or maybe he's looking through the ceiling, "We are far too quick to point out the splinter in another's eye while a beam is about to smack us in the forehead," then he hits himself on the head with the palm of his hand for emphasis. "It's important to reflect on ourselves first. We need to tend to ourselves before we can tend to others; we seem to have developed this fallacy that to do that would be selfish. It's only when we distance ourselves too far from our creator that no longer can we be repaired. Staying close to the one who created us allows us the luxury of being able to get nicked and dirtied, then with Him we can be made new. I've never lamented the period in my life when I was broken, it was then He took me in his hands. He dried my blood after offering up his own. I don't have any big quotes for you, only little quotes that I hope will appease your thirst when it cannot be quenched."

"Okay, well, there's this story you guys always tell... the story about the two brothers..." I start to say, trying to access a parable I've repeated in my mind occasionally, searching for its true meaning. "The prodigal son tale," I say, remembering the name it's often given.

"Ah, yes. We do always tell that one, don't we?" Father Schaefer says, letting me ease into my question.

"It's unfair to the son who was responsible," I say. I can't figure out which son I am, but I haven't asked for my inheritance, I've waited for it to be given to me, and I feel that, somewhere else, there's a version of me who found my mother, demanded the money, and is living a gifted life, earlier. I want that alternate version of me to be punished because it will allow me to feel less envious of his brave actions.

"That is not a story about sons. It's a story about the father," Father Schaefer tells me. "Near or far, at a distance or by his side, the father always regarded his sons with love. *That* is the message. It's not about reward and punishment, nor is it about the judgment of conduct. To me, that story is about a love that endures. If we model our love so that it is immune to distance and selfishness and revenge, then we are given a gift that will always be there, even when those we love are absent."

My vision blurs, and my throat tightens.

"I am glad young people such as yourself return to this home when they need help," Father Schaefer says, "Many among us have a hard time understanding that we don't have to be physically together to be close to one another. With the love we know, you can always return. It's *never* too late."

~

I try to make my way through a group of people who are staring through the bank window, watching a TV that's glowing with a clip of some sort of bus explosion. When I find myself in the middle of the pack, I join them in their gawking. It's clear what we're seeing, even when the giant screen stretches it all to a muddy pixelation. I watch as the loop begins again, and I follow the bus with my eyes, until the moment it enters a tunnel, then disintegrates. The amount of shrapnel- both from the bus, and organic- is astounding. There's a massive tremor that, despite the distance- both in place and time- makes my heart hop in my chest each time the event is repeated to the same end. I watch the footage as it loops yet again, but this time I focus on the cars following behind the bus. Each driver lays on the brakes in a momentum-freezing halt, and this quick reaction saves their lives- lives that are now damaged in a way that will remain branded to their being like a scar, even if they avoided physical injury.

We can't hear what's being said about the event; all we can do is watch as the doomed bus enters that tunnel, then exits just as quickly, in pieces. The drivers don't attempt to pull to the side of the road to make way for the emergency vehicles; they stop instantly, their windshields cracked with debris and painted with remains.

I take a break from the looping tragedy and I scan the faces of the captivated group around me. One woman puts a hand up to her lips, and keeps it there. A skinny man starts ranting about Muslims, his face red.

Finally, the first departure from the crowd happens. A woman leaves, fumbling with her phone. Maybe she knows someone who was taking the bus into the city? Maybe she knows someone who's a soldier and she wants to make plans to see him before he has to leave to avenge this act? Maybe she knows someone who's capable of destroying a bus, and sealing a metropolitan tunnel in order to make a dramatic statement, and she's going to call in a tip?

I look back to the TV, as the broadcast cuts to a newscaster- an ethnically ambiguous woman of indeterminate age- but they still play the bus footage in a small box above her shoulder. It's reasonable to believe that this event will hang over many shoulders, and remain in the back of innumerable minds, for days, months, years.

These are the building blocks of the collective American fear machine. We will use this event to establish prejudice, to confirm bias, to isolate, to attack without guilt, to perform this exact same event, somewhere far away, with the rationale that, "They started it."

I've grown fatigued by these tragedies that float even after the traffic clears and the disaster scene is cleaned up. The specter of this blast will linger, as though the souls of those lost today have been tattooed onto the walls of the tunnel and the entire stretch of dark travel will now be filled with so many silent screams and heavy hearts.

Tomorrow, the buses will run, but the drivers will wear a small pin on their uniform as a sign of solidarity with the driver and passengers that were lost. Tomorrow, the commuters will get on the bus, and they will look at each other with harsher judgment and a more dissecting gaze. Tomorrow, parents will walk into a room that contains the fragmented remains of a child who was stolen from them. Today, we all watch and pretend that our pleasure receptor isn't buzzing as we see just how bad things can get, from behind a pane of nearly unbreakable glass.

I move away from the storefront, resuming my search for Lindsey. The next obvious hideout is Starbucks.

As I cross the street, I find myself feeling paranoid about the traffic around me. Every person in proximity to a road must be asking themselves, *Are they done with just one bus?*

I don't gaze through the front window of the Starbucks as I approach it. The parallel would be too ugly. The moment I step inside, I know ~she's~ not here. I don't feel the buzz of her presence. I get a cup of coffee and sit next to the picture window. As the group in front of the bank disperses and walks by outside, they look at me with none of the interest they had when they were facing that TV. They don't recognize that everything inside me is speeding to a tragic end. Only I possess the knowledge that one day, I'll be passing through life, and in between my everyday tasks there will be an explosion that goes off, changing everything, permanently.

Maybe this new paranoia will bring us all closer? Will we look at the man sitting by himself, and search for the reason he's alone, or ask if he's waiting for someone? Will we make an effort to convert strangers to friends, or will we immediately deem them enemies because it's easier?

Everyone in Starbucks is talking about the bus bombing. Future tragedies cannot compete with today's blast because for something to have an impact we require there to be footage that we can share on our timelines- both digital and mental.

I finish my coffee, then begin my walk back to the apartment. I make sure to take the back alleys so I don't walk by the group of gawkers in front of the bank again.

Like so many times before, I look for ~her~ instead of singing ~the song~.

When I reach my apartment complex, I avoid the elevator, and head toward the stairs. I don't see Lindsey on my climb, and the fourth floor is empty. I enter my apartment, and find it exactly how I left it.

As I take my phone out of my pocket to end the game, a small piece of paper falls onto the floor.

An answer. Another game.

I bend down and pick up the paper, then I read the lowercase message in scrawled red pen, "we have your girlfriend and if you ever want to see her again, go to the vicinity of 33rd and sixth. bring soft pretzels and a 7-11 slurpee. i love you."

Today is Run Away From Home Day.

To get to 33rd and sixth, I would have to take public transportation, since Lindsey took her car. Lindsey would never take the bus, while I always take the bus. There would be no reason for her to take the bus... unless she wanted me to use the car.

I turn to the door, and I see that the capital letters on the light switch read ON, and around the raised finger of the switch are Lindsey's car keys, hanging from the key loop.

No.

Impossible.

The odds of this happening would be like...

...a sofa falling from the sky and crushing my girlfriend.

~

Everything is moving quickly- like that Madonna video, like that scene in the River White movie. The clouds are speeding past me, and I can't catch up.

The end is never glamorous.

When I arrive at the parking garage, I look into the windows of Lindsey's Honda, and see that the car is empty. She left the keys because she wants me to race to see her, in her car, so that's exactly what I do.

As I drive, I alternate my hands on the wheel so I can wipe my tears away.

When I get close to the tunnel, I hit the gridlock, so I park Lindsey's car and begin walking. The road has been closed off, but I stomp through all obstructions. Passing by the graveyard of cars that have been abandoned until security is confirmed, I look inside the vehicles and see the tools of men, the purses of women, the toys of children- all left behind.

There's a bizarre calm hanging in the air with the smoke, despite the sirens that become louder as I approach the scene. Why are the sirens still blaring? I hope it's because people are still being pulled out of the rubble, alive.1

The skyline and the treeline melt together and flow like the waves in the ocean, stretching and contracting, the two different planes quivering, loosely wrapped, dense meeting empty, intertwining in their unfair beauty. Holding on at the edge of the universe. Holding on to each other. Red and blue splotches peek through a maze of cars. As I get closer, there's more red than blue.

A crowd remains, and a tiny memorial is already being assembled. Glass crunches under the tread of my boot, but I'm still a hundred feet from the tunnel. Where is all of this glass from? I thought windshield glass was tempered and breaks in a sheet? Maybe it's glass from the headlights? I think about the story Lindsey told me about the deer. ~Her~ question, *"Whose job is it to clean something like that up?"*

I'm running to the tragedy.

I'm running from the tragedy.

The crowd in front of me parts, and that's when I see it, a dust-covered couple, embracing each other.

~

In my bag are two well-worn copies of *Limber*.

Despite my compulsion to finish the book- to find out how it ends- I'm revolted at the idea of reading it in my apartment, alone.

I'll keep the books, but I'll never open them again. This is not a museum I'm building; this is a library, with books that will live under glass. I don't need to find out the resolution when it comes to *Limber*. As far as I'm concerned, I know how it ends.

I know how every book in the bookstore ends.

~

When you fall in love, you don't really feel many new feelings. Love is great, not for the feelings it brings, but for those it takes away. When your precious love is gone, those emotions come rushing back, and they demand to be reckoned with immediately. I enter this tunnel of emotions and I try to keep it together.

My love for Lindsey still exists, but it has nowhere to go. Once again, I'm a boy who can only get as close to ~her~ as the words on a screen let me. This is the ultimate distance. I can't mute the warm burn that the words give me, even now. I'm careful to not mistake the feeling the words give me with the feeling Lindsey gave me. My problem is that the feelings I still harbor, to anyone else, would seem invalid.

To be in love with a specter.

To be in love with an idea.

To be in love with a person whose voice sends chills up your spine and tears down your face, but you never cry because you can only find her voice in an echo.

They say I'm crying wolf.

The professor looks at the lost boy with a skeptical eye, and says, "The deadline is firm."

The commuters take the Asian's café table in protest for the bus explosion that they claim was planned on those ever-present laptops that went unchecked.

The white girls are out in full force, scolding random people on the Green for their presumed silent blaming of Muslims for the attack, while loudly providing parallels to the crimes of white school shooters.

The congregation is missing- the vigil is over. The church is empty when I walk inside it. I look at the woman in blue and I understand how she feels.

The need for a friend drops away as Gerard laughs, then asks, "Who the fuck is Lindsey?"

The voicemail plays, and my grandfather warns me, "I will drag you out of that college by the scruff of your neck."

The laptop autoplays a video for the song that I danced to with Noni, and unneutral Brittany is on the screen, clawing at her flesh, growling, "*Lowly grr.*"

The boy cried wolf, while the wolves were eating his girlfriend, then it happened again and he realized that the wolves were the only ones that could hear him, and he was the only boy left.

I take out my phone, and call Edie. She picks up after one ring, and I say to her, "I want to tell you about this amazing girl I met and loved. Her name was Lindsey."

~

I know who did it, there's no mystery to solve. The bus bombing was an act carried out by an angry man. Or an angry woman. Or a group of angry men. Or a group of angry women. Angry people have brought about almost all of the changes that have created the present day world as we know it. All of our favorite things were birthed by angry people. Happy people don't have the fire to shake and shatter. Happy people watch and smile. Happy people often rely on angry people to make progress in our society. Anger is the fuel a plan demands. That anger lets hours feel like minutes. That anger makes weeks feel like days. That anger wakes people up, and that anger keeps them up. That anger consumes all. That anger, often, destroys people. Even then, in the rubble, what's left is a legacy. Angry people leave bullet holes, and blast zones. Angry people leave cures to the diseases that killed their parents. Angry people leave an impact, and they will probably leave earlier than the rest of us. The happy people will eulogize the angry people. The happy people might be turned into angry people after the angry people leave in a way that seems unfair.

I am an angry boy who desperately wants to be a happy man.

~

I wake up at noon.
Roughly fifteen hours of sleep.
The feeling is still there. It's weighing me down.
I fall asleep for another hour.

I snap awake to the thumping bass from a car parked outside my building.

The feeling is still there.

I eat a bowl of Crunch Berries dusted with paint chips from above.

The feeling is still there.

I turn on my laptop.

4353638332936382.com.

The site is still up. I still have ~her~ words. Another museum I promised not to build.

This is when the coping mechanisms kick in.

This is when I will look at the page and try to trick myself into believing that this isn't Lindsey's blog.

This is how I convince myself that my real poor, mysterious, fragile, hip, insecure, desirable, feline, blonde, Kirtland University girl is still walking around on campus.

It wasn't Lindsey writing these words that connect to my core. It was a coincidence. Coincidences happen all the time.

Sofas fall from the sky, buses blow up, and mothers die.

This all happened for a reason... or it was all random.

This all happened to guide me somewhere... or this all happened because I walked past the Grim Reaper, evading him, and now he's taking people around me to make up for his mistake. Everyone I love is dying. I am patient zero, and I harbor an immunity to the disease I spread.

A suggestion is made. I could stop the further spread of this disease by eliminating myself. The sins of the father. I'm a Jones. Jones' never take the easy way out- that was the legacy my father wanted to leave- but the *way* he left negated it.

I move through my apartment like a guest. I see her possessions everywhere, her fingerprints everywhere, her lipstick on a glass. I know that I'll keep all these items, but for now, I need to escape them.

I drag myself into the bathroom, but before I can climb into the tub, I take out my phone, and I stare at the screen. No one has called to say that they're sorry about what happened, or that they're thinking about me, or that they can't imagine what I'm going through right now. There are no texts from Lindsey, wondering where I am. There are no texts from Lindsey saying that she's giving up on this cruel joke.

I look up from my phone, and see my reflection in the medicine cabinet, and I hate what I see.

I throw my phone as hard as I can at the mirror, and since my bathroom is so small, I'm hit with debris from the impact.

I open my eyes.

The mirror is still intact except for a single long slanted crack.

My cell phone is in pieces on the tiled floor, shattered.

I leave the bathroom and walk into the kitchen. I get a can of soup. The label says, "20% more free," which means that it will be 20% more effective at shattering my mirror.

I return to the bathroom, then press my back against the wall.

I watch as my reflection throws the can at me, then falls to pieces. The shards of mirror dance on the floor. I drop to my knees, and look for a large piece of glass- a piece big enough to cut the important stuff- and I find the perfect jagged reflective slice next to the top half of my phone. I can't hold back the tears as I sit in the pile of broken mirror that pokes through my jeans and into my legs.

Maybe my mother knew I would do this. She managed to plant bushes under the windows to keep anyone from falling out, but what if I slit my wrists in the bathroom with this piece of mirror? Will she throw out all her mirrors? Will she plaster over the door to the bathroom so this could never happen again? I don't want to do that to her. I should've used the glass from my window instead of the mirror. I want her to be able to go to the bathroom. I want her to be able to look in the mirror and do her hair... if she still has any.

I'd throw myself out of the fucking window, following my father, but I'm too weak to open it.

Next to me, on the tile, I find some pills that were in the medicine cabinet. Lindsey's name is on the orange bottle. I pop the child safe cap and look inside. These are pills that ~she~ didn't take- pills ~she~ refused to take. Each pill brings with it a question- *What do these pills treat/ What will they do to me/ Will they take me to see her/ Did ~she~ leave them for me?*

We spent our days in this apartment, unmedicated beyond the beer and wine, drinking tap water, and eating mustard and cheese sandwiches, while the kids with addictions and dependencies were better off than we were because they had a way to deal with the shit, and all we had was each other, and now I don't even have that.

When a roof is being held up by two crumbling pillars, a collapse is inevitable.

I pour out five pills from the bottle into my palm, to become like the medicated masses on the campus. I take the pills without hesitation.

Nausea.

A couple more to ease the nausea.

Not right.

A few more.

Sweating.

A fist full.

Ab pain.

I take one more.

Confusion.

It's like I'm playing hide and seek. Lindsey is hiding, and I have to find her. I count, and the numbers climb, each pill that goes down feels drier than the last.

I grab for one of the many quarter-filled glasses of water on the floor of the living room. I need a couple sips of the stale liquid so that the pills will settle. Whatever the liquid is in the cup, it tastes horrible, but I refuse to let myself vomit. My body knows how flawed my mind is, and it's attempting to force me to gag up the pills. After resisting the gagging, I start singing ~the song~.

Pacing/ Singing/ Shaking.

I get my coat because it's freezing in the apartment.

Walk/ Sing/ Shake/ Freak. My heart is dancing inside my chest. I open both my hands wide and flex my fingers. My blood starts pumping too quickly, and I feel the music in my chest. I'm freezing. I'm sweating. It's cold. It's not freezer cold, or arctic cold, or cold like leaving the window open all night in the fall. I shake like I'm freezing to death, but I can't be. I can't feel warmer by drinking hot chocolate, or putting on an extra pair of gloves, or burying myself in a blanket. A fireplace won't do any good. If I try wrapping my arms around my legs, maybe the comforting action will help?

I stumble back into the bedroom and step on the right side of my headphones. The plastic cracks under my feeble weight. I deflate to the floor like a jacket that's fallen off its hook. I zone out. I come back. I don't die. I don't pass out. I just sit with my blood flying through my veins. I can feel it coursing through me, flowing backward.

I crawl through the living room, to the door...

...and flick the light switch OFF.

my

light

goes

out.

In the end, all I'm left with are endings.

~

one.

I wake up and I'm in a car. My grandfather is driving, and my grandmother is sitting in the front seat. She's wearing large black sunglasses and I'm not sure if it's because she's been crying, or because she wasn't able to do her makeup after spending too many days and nights in the hospital with my mother.

I glance in the passenger side mirror, and instead of a reflection, I see Kirtland behind me, getting smaller, disappearing out of sight.

"When you see her, she'll be in and out of consciousness," my grandmother warns me, and I feel as though I'm living a parallel life with my mother. The last time I had this feeling of two independent souls existing as one, I was reading Lindsey's journal.

"You can't expect the same person you remember," my grandfather says.

"Who can I expect, then?" I ask.

The Lincoln growls as it speeds up the hill. I stare out the window as we ascend, and part of me wants to suggest that we go somewhere and Exist together. I couldn't go to Lindsey's funeral. I couldn't tolerate the idea that she wouldn't be able to Exist far away from the commotion and the steady foot traffic, and that fucking billboard that looms at the edge of the cemetery, and that noisy, ugly, trash-laden highway just beyond the chain link fence. The plot her parents would pick out is not where Lindsey belongs. She belongs somewhere peaceful.

The trees blur by, and the Lincoln weaves toward a hazy destination.

"I thought she didn't want me to see her like this?" I ask.

"She didn't," my grandmother says.

"Then why are you bringing me to her?"

"Because she won't stop asking where you are," my grandmother says.

"What changed?"

"The timeline. The timeline changed and it dragged her along with it," my grandfather says tiredly.

"How do you feel?" I ask him.

"Betrayed. By time," he sighs.

~

I've counted down to this moment that is supposed to mark my freedom, and christen my rebirth. My fractured days have formed a stairwell that's led to this hospital visit.

I stand in the hallway, and wait for my grandmother to come out of the room, to tell me it's okay for me to step inside.

When I close my eyes, I keep seeing Nathan opening that green door and looking put-upon, bothered, found. I keep seeing Joan and Lindsey's faces, then they quickly fade when I reach toward them.

I hear the jostle of the doorknob, and I open my eyes.

My grandmother peeks her head out of the room, looks at my grandfather, then nods.

I stand up and my grandfather puts his right wrist on my left shoulder, and we walk together into the hospital room.

And there she is.

It ends the same way it began for me, in a hospital room with this exhausted woman. I don't remember the first time this happened, but the second time will live in vivid detail in my mind for the rest of my life, of this, I am absolutely sure.

My frozen search ends in the precise place that I knew it would. She lets me see her. She relinquishes the need to curate the final image I will retain of her. My eyes dart everywhere.

My mother is hooked up to so many machines and a seafoam green blanket lays across her lap. For a moment, in my blurred vision, she becomes the tree that I stood under with Lindsey. The cords run like roots, and the blanket covers her like moss.

I don't say anything.

She doesn't say anything.

I approach her bedside, then reach out a hand, and she lightly puts her fingertips in my palm.

This last visit isn't so we can catch up with each other. This reunion isn't so we can settle our scores. This closeness isn't so we can learn about each other, or see how we've both changed during our time apart. This meeting of the prodigal son and the prodigal mother is to confirm, to each other, that distance does not make love invalid or weak. Love, like a song, can be shared, and bought, and covered, and remixed, and reinterpreted; and it always expands. Love is a disease that, left to exist, spreads. A disease is about to kill my mother, and a disease will make her immortal.

The silence melts into a crackle, then the first few piano keys play and everyone in the room gasps. This is not the tape playing, this is Jackson breaking through, this is the universe's jukebox powered on. The drums crash and the organ strikes, and I lose my breath, as my mother begins to sing:

> *"You laugh a subtle laugh*
> *And your face opens the door*
> *Then the ceiling slowly slides*
> *And your ear cups the floor*
> *The words don't translate*
> *You lose your tongue*
> *Play your vocal cords*
> *And the melody's off*

My father didn't give me this moment before he died; my mother did. This moment is lit by a single lamp, not the twirling lights of a cop car. The music in the room is how our difficult slide into goodbye needs to happen. My mother is leaving, permanently, not by her choice, but by the universe's call. I've learned not to mistake a message from the universe as a reason to panic. With a frail voice, I join my mother. We sing:

> *"The room will spin for anyone*
> *It just takes the right conditions*
> *And you've... met them*
>
> *Let's make our introduction*
> *Interested, we smile*
> *The details won't be processed*
> *No evidence for a trial*
> *We're stacking information*
> *We're compiling a file*
> *We're taking a name*
> *Only to burn it*

My mother looks so old, yet she also looks the same. I hope that how I look doesn't hurt her more. All those times we fought about the shaved head haircuts, or the bleach, or the size of my jeans. I hope that she didn't hide herself from me, fearing how she looked, because, for so long, I defied her with how I looked. There are certain aspects of my mother's current face that I recognize from the past, aspects she removed that one day she arrived home in bandages. Despite her best efforts, these features have returned. Her face has thinned, but her smile has remained. Her hair has thinned, but her warmth has stayed. I'm so glad that she let me see her because, without this warmth, I most certainly would've grown cold. I didn't get this moment with Lindsey. I'm angrier with the universe for taking Lindsey away than I am with my mother for removing herself from my life for all those years. Jackson Sharpe has given me a gift. Listening to this song was the first thing I ever did with Lindsey, and it will be the last thing I ever do with my mother. We sing:

> *"I knew lots of presidents*
> *And I knew lots of freaks*
> *All of these close friendships*
> *Are not what they seem*
> *They're shaking your hand*
> *And the grip's a farce*
> *The freak is approaching*
> *And he hands you a bone*
>
> *The room will spin for anyone*
> *It just takes the right conditions*
> *And you've... met them*

During my junior year at Kirtland, I received an education. In September, everyone seemed invincible, and I kept people in my life only to prod them toward escaping. It was strange when Joan didn't leave me- she departed. The way I felt when it happened- the shock, the confusion, the bright aftermath- it helped me get to this moment, to understand this moment, to respect this moment for what it is.

On that day I saw the Grim Reaper move toward me, I realized it was Halloween and I found an escape. That same feeling of relief coursed through me when Joan disappeared and Lindsey appeared. When Lindsey left, I was shattered. I tried to coax that hooded figure back, but even with that little orange jar sitting empty on the floor, he didn't return; he was busy, elsewhere. No longer is there relief in the departure. No longer will a permanent change have a temporary influence on my life.

Before the next pang of eternal nostalgia hits, we sing:

> *"Focused on big nothings*
> *The questions in a row*
> *Recycled halfway through*
> *There's little we don't know*
> *The room has lost its bearing*
> *We've traveled through some time*
> *It's Tuesday or it's Sunday*
> *It's your pick*

I fight to sing, as my chest vibrates like a sick dog's. The image of my dog being let off the leash, dashing past traffic, then never looking back, reappears in my mind. I was okay with that moment before, because I was next to my mother. I remain okay about this moment now, because I am next to my mother. We sing:

> *"Right to brag about bragging rights*
> *Feeling glassy in the fog*
> *These times they are neurons*
> *Drink up until they're gone*
> *You're beating on your chest and*
> *You're losing your will*
> *Just like those keys*
> *They're both missing*

I sing with my mother. She can't dance, not in this fragile shell, but I felt her essence as she worked through Noni, and now I will forever return to that womb of an apartment, to turn up the music, to hold her hand, to spin her around, to move exactly in time with her. This is the last song I will sing with my mother, but there are a million songs left to dance with her, through Noni. Unneutral Brittany's pop music becomes essential. I've learned that people don't exist in a single shell, they exist in many moments. I immerse myself in this moment as we sing:

> *"The room will spin for anyone*
> *It just takes the right conditions*
> *And you've... met them*

They say death comes in threes.

It's times like these, I wish I did things differently.

Somehow, I understand my father now- even if I have so much, too much, I will focus on what I've lost.

All the love that I've acquired while waiting for the moment I was convinced would make me genuinely happy has turned out to be more important than the anticipated moment itself. In the end, when a person dies, their whole existence- their entire legacy- is a box of stuff- a cassette tape, or a book, or a building, or a company, or an electronic number signifying an exact worth. People have left these items behind for me. Other precious possessions, proof of other people's existence, are often so insignificant that landlords will keep the security deposit because they have to rent a dumpster to get rid of it all. Most of what the dead leave proves worthless to everyone left living. The inheritance that's really sought after, my mother and Joan and Lindsey were unable to leave me. They had it, but they couldn't leave it. They had it, and I hope their souls wrap around it as they make their next journey.

I'm going to end up with a bunch of stuff and no one to share it with. All I have now is God, and my mother, and Lindsey, and I can't call any of them even if I had a cell phone to call them on. My significant no one.

I feel the blood in my veins stop flowing, then switch directions, and we sing:

> *"Judging for this motion*
> *Is partially impartial*
> *If we forgot what to say*
> *The nice man will hear you*
> *This is what it feels like*
> *To know we know nothing*
> *No art in falling over*
> *It's all in getting up*

And after all the letters I wrote to Edie, and after all the posts I read from Lindsey, and after all the arguments I backed Gerard up on, and after all the girls I tried to plug the void with, and after all the days I helped Noni on her quests, and after all the times I heard Brittany and didn't recognize her voice, and after all those classes that I thought were useless but taught me so much, and after all those days at Rubie's when I narrowly missed ~her~, and after all those times I spelled I love you, only to realize that I

was typing it in every time I visited ~her~ words, and after all those coffees
at the bookstore, and after all the bus trips with those strangers, and after
all the color was sucked out of the fiction and the black and white was still
too lush to follow, and after all the pills I took, and after all the times I
wondered where my mother is, I am here, with her, and we sing:

> *"The bleach in your eye*
> *Dyes your mustache*
> *When you see again*
> *You say who is that*
> *He could be a brother*
> *He could be a brat*
> *Or maybe a son*
> *Or maybe it's God*
>
> *The room will spin for anyone*
> *It just takes the right conditions*
> *And you've... met them*

My mother is a song I cannot forget.
My mother is a song I will not forget.
You cannot be abandoned by a song.
You cannot forget a song.
When you hear a song more than once, it etches into your soul. Even if
you don't like the song, it becomes a part of you.
People go to concerts and want to hear the songs they recognize.
I went to Gerard's show and I listened to everything he was saying, and
it changed me.
I danced with Noni to a song I didn't recognize, and when I heard it
again, I *did* recognize the song, and who sings it.
A song's presence can't be seen, but it can be felt. That heart hopping
bass. That note that vibrates my vocal cords. That glass of water with its
perfectly replicating ripples. We sing:

> *The kitchen's shining bare*
> *But you have all you need*
> *Except for that everlasting pair"*

My mother is a song, and I feel blessed that we were able to sing
together before she left me.

acknowledgements.

God – Thank you for providing me with the talent to write this book. Without you, none of this would have been possible.

Mom & Dad – Your continued support and guidance has been more than I could ever ask for. Also, thanks for paying my tuition.

The Blonde Haired Love Of My Life – For being so understanding about my stalking.

My Editor – Thank you for helping me shape, clarify, detoxify, and solidify this novel.

Ashley Kamerling – Thank you for putting up with me as I worked on this book in my dorm and in our apartment. This novel received a lot of the attention I should have been paying to you.

Jess Burns - For assuring me that my first novel was good that day in the dog park.

Tom Nemecek - For being the best college roommate a guy could ask for.

I'd also like to thank: Seton Hall University, Woody Allen, Rev. Donald Blumenfeld, Ph.D, Vincent Gallo, Winona Ryder, Paul Thomas Anderson, Bob Dylan, Edie Sedgwick, Johnny Cash, Conor Oberst, Zach Braff, Lush, The Aislers Set, The Luddites, Crystal Vega-Huerta, Bret Easton Ellis, F. Scott Fitzgerald, Jay McInerney, Cory Kennedy, Vincent Gallo, Aimee Mann, Mike Isgar, Zeta Psi International.

boring legal shit.

Before you sue me about something in this book, e-mail me. I'll fix any legal issues related to this novel. Don't sue me. I live in Newark. I'm broke. What are you gonna win from me in court? My Fitzgerald novels?

Feel free to post excerpts of this book on your blog, Tumblr, Twitter, Facebook, or apartment walls. Please don't get any of this tattooed on your body. I once wanted a Thug Life tattoo. Imagine if I got my way.

If you downloaded this novel illegally... I honestly don't blame you. Paying zero dollars for a thing is way better than paying four dollars for a thing. I get it.

If you're an agent and you want to represent my unpublished novels, email me at: tjamesreagan@outlook.com

about the author.

Lovetrust was written at Seton Hall University and Seton Grove Apartments, between 2005 and 2007.

T/James Reagan currently lives in Newark, New Jersey.

He is the author of *Famous For Nothing, Empire Waste, Beach House Burning, Southland Tales: The Complete Saga,* and *Leeds House.*

He has fourteen unpublished manuscripts available for query.